ORDINARY PEOPLE

Part XII

PHIL BOAST

Order this book online at www.trafford.com
or email orders@trafford.com

Most Trafford titles are also available at major online book retailers.

Print information available on the last page.

ISBN: 978-1-4907-9406-8 (sc)
ISBN: 978-1-4907-9407-5 (hc)
ISBN: 978-1-4907-9409-9 (e)

Library of Congress Control Number: 2019936418

Trafford rev. 03/05/2019

Trafford PUBLISHING www.trafford.com
North America & international
toll-free: 1 888 232 4444 (USA & Canada)
fax: 812 355 4082

Table of Contents

Chapter 1

DREAMS AND MEMORIES

People, it seems, in one important regard at least, never really lose one another. Once an emotional connection is made, however tenuous, subconscious or subliminal the connection may be, it is never thereafter entirely broken. A person may not see, hear of or even think of another person for years, or perhaps decades, and then this person may appear as if from nowhere in a dream, or come suddenly and unbidden into conscious thought for no reason which is apparent, if indeed there is any reason. The unfathomably complex thing which is the human brain may have performed its' function well enough in the interim, and time, and a myriad of new emotions and experiences may come to separate two such people, but they will not be entirely lost to one another. Each may make new friends, fall in love, marry, have children, and become successful or otherwise in the business of life, but regardless of all of this, they will not entirely forget one another. Memories will fade, details and small, shared experiences will be lost to consciousness, but an image will remain; a ghost of something which once was, and once there it will always be so, and will haunt the deepest parts of a persons' soul forever. And not everything in any case will be lost. Conversations, moments of humour or intimacy; a smile or a place, these things may sometimes be remembered, like precious remnants of something which was once much bigger, and was at the time important, for all such things are important, in their own way. However a person may begin, that which they will become is after all nothing more or less than the sum – total of that which they will thereafter experience, and all experiences have influence, however small or unconscious that influence may be.

It may also be true that the older a person becomes, the more they begin to reflect upon that which has been, and the people who by happenstance they have met throughout their lives. In the busy course of youth and middle years, when there is often less time for reflection or retrospection, they may not dwell much upon long past experience or apparently forgotten people, but in later, quieter years, a persons' past may begin to catch them up, and they may even try to make some sense of it all, and to wonder how their lives came to be as they are, and perhaps how different it all could have been. In any case the next person to re - enter our story is a person perhaps more given than most to the consideration of such things, and they are someone of whom we have not much heard during recent pages of our tale, but of whom we will now once again hear.

Peter Shortbody, early – retired accountant and father to two daughters, had by now reached the fifty ninth year of his life. During his fifty sixth year, at a time when a man may begin to realize that a certain part of his being is nearing its' end, this realization had found expression in feelings towards a certain Alice Turner, who lived at number thirteen, and who was his junior by somewhat more than a decade. Here was a lady also approaching the end of her sexually reproductive years, and together in this regard they could be said to have made their swan – song together, and though neither in truth had for a single moment expected or intended it, the result had been the conception and subsequent birth of twin daughters, whom they named Bronwyn and Elizabeth, and who at this stage of our story are in the third year of their lives. Bronwyn, the firstborn by a matter of but a few moments, was named by her mother, who had thus given expression to her Welsh heritage and ancestry, and Bronwyn, rather in common with her mother, was a chatterbox. She took easily to the matter of communication with those around her, and was not backward in the matter of expressing her infantile approval or otherwise of the things which she saw or experienced. Elizabeth on the other hand, who had been named by her father, rather took after him in regard to her character and vocalization, being somewhat quiet and introspective. She would study people and things around her with seemingly intense and enwrapped interest, before diverting her attention elsewhere without making statement or comment upon that which she had seen. The young lady would stand for several minutes at a time studying the carpet, or a particular patch of grass on the village Green, but would not give forth as to that which had taken her interest, or anything which she may have learned or gained by so doing. She was so quiet, indeed, that it was even whispered by some that there might be something not quite right about her, a sentiment not in the least bit shared by Peter Shortbody; he knew what she was doing, and understood his younger and in truth his favourite daughter perfectly. His absolute faith and confidence in her intellectual development was confirmed beyond any doubt on one particular day, when she stood looking across the empty village Green; she pointed in the general direction ahead of her, and exclaimed *'Look, daddy, no people.'* Peter Shortbody could not but wipe a tear from his eye; his beautiful Elizabeth had begun to understand, and perhaps to see the world in the same way as did he; like father like youngest daughter, it seemed, and it was a moment which he would never forget.

Alice Turner and Peter Shortbody had only made love the one and most significant time, if indeed it could be said to have been making love, since they could scarce be said to be I love at the time of the act, and they had not since had sexual union. Indeed it was true to say that they had barely since touched one another or had any form of significant physical intimacy. They continued to live apart, she at number thirteen, The Green and he at number eight, and though they would quite often take their evening meal together, one or other of them would almost always walk the short distance home at some time during the evening. This somewhat eccentric way of living suited both parties quite well, particularly since in truth neither would have been the easiest of people to live with, and Bronwyn and Elizabeth seemed well enough adapted to having two homes, which was after all the only domestic circumstance that they had ever known. Alice, having in a sense and by some degree the less quiet spirit of the two parents, would travel abroad quite frequently. About once in a year she would go to Wales to have time with her extensive family, many of whom had not left the small valley in which Alice had lived during part of her young life, and she did not always take the children. She had twice since taking the twins to Borneo gone back there alone, returning each time with an increasing sense of loss and anger at the incessant destruction of her beloved rainforests, and the effect which this inevitably had upon the Iban people with whom she had once for a while lived so contentedly. She had travelled elsewhere abroad as time and money had allowed, and her work as a freelance writer and journalist quite often meant her travelling to other parts of England or mainland Europe, and at all such times Peter Shortbody took sole charge and care of the twins, and was happy to do so for such irregular and quite short periods of time. In truth Peter Shortbody, in contrast with his children's mother, did not care or consider overmuch where he was, so long as he was somewhere, and even this was something about which he was at times at pains to convince himself. When both parents were in residence the girls would for the most part live with their mother, but scarce a day went by when they did not also see their father, who, as their young legs grew stronger, would take them for increasingly long walks through the local wood and heath – land, or to the lake to see the ducks, and else or as well he would read to them from books which they could not yet begin to understand, until they fell into contented sleep of any given evening. Thus it was that if Alice was in large part the emotional and practical rock upon which their lives were founded, it was Peter Shortbody who for the most part saw to their physical, spiritual and intellectual growth, and the girls wanted for nothing in any regard, unusual though their lives may seem to be from the perspective of objective observation. Both of the girls had been born with fair skin, and fair, somewhat curly hair, and grey – blue eyes, their hair having darkened or straightened hardly at all during their youngest years. Time and life had not yet seen to any significant difference in their physical appearance, diverse though their characters apparently were, and they were regarded by all who met them as being quite beautiful children, though none but their parents and those who knew them well could yet easily tell them apart.

In any case so it was that the life of Peter Shortbody went on in a contented enough way. Tizer, his cat, took up nocturnal residence at the foot of his bed as he had almost always done, but otherwise he slept alone. He had cordial enough relations with others in the village, and was regarded by all who regarded him as being a somewhat withdrawn, self – contained individual, not particularly seeking or needing the company of others, and this impression was close enough to the truth of it. And then, one night, Peter Shortbody had a dream.

The end of the long, cold English winter and the coming of the warmer, early spring days affected all of the residents of the village of Middlewapping to a greater or lesser degree. One person who felt the coming of spring more keenly than most, however, was a certain Miss Emily Cleves, owner and primary manager of a piece of former estate land, upon which her main focus was the production of fine goats' cheese. Will Tucker, her beau and life – partner, had seen to the construction of the majority of the infrastructure pertaining to the keeping of livestock, but it was Emily who saw to the day to day running of the smallholding, and the milking and general care of goats was a far more pleasant or at least less arduous task in a warmer environment. Emily went about her daily rounds with that which was for the most part a positive attitude. She had done well enough at school to go on to further education had she chosen so to do, but she was not at heart an academic, and was glad now that she had turned her energies to something more practical and in her view rewarding. She had no husbandry or farming experience in her family, her father being a butcher, and thus being used to animals being already dead on arrival in his no doubt capable hands, which saw to the sawing, slicing and general preparation of raw flesh and internal organs for retail sale. Emily had thus had to learn everything regarding animals which were still very much alive by first – hand experience, and by making her own quite understandable and perhaps inevitable mistakes. By now, however, most of her mistakes had been made, and allowing for the still experimental nature of some of the cheeses that she produced, the great majority of her produce reached its' end in saleable condition. Her need to be in daily attendance upon her livestock and product meant that she sacrificed certain of the pleasures enjoyed by her peers. She did not take foreign holidays, or weekends away attending parties or other social functions, and in truth her social network was limited to a few the people whom she knew from the village and a few close friends from her school days. Emily did not really mind this. If she felt the need for the company of others she could at any time walk to the village to see Meadow, or Daphne, or Percival, but in truth she rarely felt such a need. So long as she had her Will she was content, and perhaps in a year or so she might be able to delegate some responsibilities to a willing and able assistant, but for now she was still learning the whys and wherefores of cheese production herself, so that was not something for now. In any case her days were now made more pleasant and companionable by the presence of Monty, the young German Shepherd dog, who was her constant companion in everything that she did, and the goats had quickly become used to his presence.

Emily's day was usually at its' busiest in the morning, when the milking was done, and the latest batch of cheese turned out of its' molds. In the afternoons she had more time to see how Blossom was faring with her eight piglets, to eat her light lunch, which was her first meal of the day, and to begin preparation of the evening repast, which Will would oft times see to the finishing of when he returned home from work. On this afternoon, however, her normal routines would be brought to an abrupt halt, for on this day Emily would have two visitors.

William Tucker had spent his first days of employment at Orchard House chipping old plaster off much older walls, and transporting the resultant debris to the waste container. The work would eventually become more diverse and interesting, but for now he had plenty of time to contemplate events in his own recent life, and in the life of his beloved Emily, which were in a sense one and the same thing, since everything in each of their lives affected the other. Perhaps inevitably, one such preoccupation was the matter of Sandra Fox, who had for almost as long as he could remember and certainly since their school days had designs upon him of a perhaps romantic and in any case certainly sexual nature. In all such regards his conscience was clear, since he had done nothing at least consciously to encourage her in her endeavors, and had at all times resisted her undoubted charms, although in the last regard he had to admit that it had on occasion been a close call. There had been the time, for example, when she had asked for his assistance with homework in her bedroom, when she had been dressed in a manner quite unnecessary for the doing of scholarly activities, and her agenda had he was sure been quite otherwise. Then at the party at Dawn's house when she had proposed that he spend the night with her and her very short dress, which would he assumed have been without the dress, and beneath which she had indicated that she was wearing nothing. In such circumstances a young man must at times call upon his last reserves of common sense and self - control, which are at any given time and circumstance a finite resource. Beyond the bounds of instant sexual gratification, of course, there lay a realm into which he had no wish to trespass. To enter into a relationship with the vixen would be to navigate unchartered waters, where no man had thus far been, and where the weather would doubtless be unpredictable. In any case in any and all of the deeper parts of himself he loved Emily, to the exclusion of all others, so there really was nothing to consider. But then the vixen had apparently tried to kill herself, and had very nearly succeeded, and nobody had seen that coming. That he was certain had in no part anything to do with him. That was to say that even in the hypothesis that they had in fact been together she might not have so acted, but their not being in said relationship had not been the cause of it, he was sure of that, or almost sure. But still, she had on this occasion at least survived herself, so perhaps her life would get better from now on, and it was none of his business in any case, except in respect of her still being his friend, so he would do what he could, as would Emily, although whether she was deserving of any help from that quarter was so far as he was concerned a moot point.

In all other regards, however, Will considered that his life was going along in a good way. Emily's business was growing by small but significant degrees, and he was quite content working with Keith and Damien, at the behest of Michael Tillington, and

Orchard House would in time become an interesting project, from which he would learn much of the ways of building. Two things of note had in this regard occurred during Michael Tillington's last visit, which had been yesterday. The first had been his unexpected announcement that he would in fact live in Orchard House after the completion of the renovation work. This would make little or no practical difference to the work in hand, but Keith expected that the specification of materials, kitchen and bathroom fittings and so on would now be upgraded, which would be no bad thing. He also asked, somewhat mysteriously, that this piece of intelligence be kept amongst themselves, at least for the time being, and that he did not wish the matter to be generally known. Thereafter during the lunch – break and after Michael's departure, the conversation between the three men revolved around whether a certain lady of Nordic extraction would also be taking up residence; this was after all more accommodation than would be required for a single male, a son and a nanny. Damien here accused Keith and Will of *'gossiping like a couple of bloody fish – wives'*, until it was pointed out to him by Keith that men did not gossip, they rather speculated upon possibilities, which was a quite different thing, and in any case this brought an end to the conversation. The second announcement had been that Michael now intended to employ a landscape architect to redesign the grounds of the old house, which was of more relevance to Damien than to Keith, since this was where his primary expertise lay. The relationship between a landscape architect and those building any given garden was not always a happy one, and Damien, who had experience in such matters from a contractors' viewpoint, speculated that he would no doubt be '*Some pretentious ponce who would charge a fortune and understand nothing about construction.*' and that he would have done a better job of it for half the price. In the event the pretentious ponce would turn out to be female, and to be nothing of either of the above, but this fact was yet to be revealed.

And so in any event did the day of William Tucker go along, and if his ears burned during the latter part of it then it would not have been surprising, for by now Emily was deep in conversation with another person, who was her second visitor, and in part they were talking about him. For now, however, he chipped away at old plaster with hammer and bolster, and hoped that his beloved Emily would have prepared supper by the time he had got home, and showered off the dust of the working day.

The first person to visit Jacob's Field on this day was Daphne, who arrived just as Emily was eating her light afternoon repast of bread and cheese; one of the cheeses had not made quite properly, and these she would eat, and give the remainder to Will for his lunchbox the next day. This was not the first time that Daphne had visited of late, and although she appeared to come without agenda, Emily thought that her friend seemed nowadays to be more thoughtful and distracted than was usual, as if there was something in her thoughts which she could not quite talk about. Daphne had been quite and perhaps even dangerously ill lately, and Emily wondered whether this may have something to do with it, but otherwise she thought little of the matter. In any case, on this day Daphne stood at the open door of the cottage, where she was first greeted by a small dog, who jumped up and pawned enthusiastically at her skirt.

'Monty, stop that....! Hello Mrs P; sorry, I must stop him doing that...'

'It's quite alright my dear, what are a few muddy little pawmarks between friends, eh, little scamp?'

'Come in, anyway...Tea?'

'Thank you dear, if I'm not interrupting anything important?'

'Not at all, I was just taking a break anyway.'

'Yes, I thought you'd be less busy by now.'

'Would you like some bread and cheese?'

'No, thank you my dear, I have not long since eaten my luncheon, tempting though your cheese always is.'

Daphne sat at the kitchen table whilst Emily made tea. These two had an easy and relaxed relationship, and this had been particularly true since the time that Emily had quite spontaneously turned to Daphne for support after the killing of the man from London; support which had been willingly and effectively proffered.

'I expect you're glad of the warmer weather, my dear.'

'God, I should say so; better than freezing my whatsits off every morning, I can tell you. And your garden must be starting to grow by now.'

'Indeed it is, and very glad I am of it. It gives me something more to do, you know?'

'Sure…'

And so began an easy conversation, which carried on for perhaps an hour, and only towards its' end did it apparently gain any significance, as Daphne was about to make her departure.

'Well, I suppose I should let you get on; I hope you don't mind my coming here my dear, it's such a pleasant and short enough walk, quite aside from the pleasure of your company. I can't walk so far as I used to these days, at least not yet.'

'No, of course I don't mind; come whenever you like.'

'Thank you…Anyway I promised myself an hour in the garden later today…'

'Right you are, then…'

'One must make the best of the good weather. I do so love the spring, and one is never certain how many more one will see.'

'Oh come on Mrs P…Not ill again are you?'

'No…Well, not really.'

'I thought the doctors gave you the all – clear.'

'Yes, they did, but I'm due some tests this week, and one only hopes that nothing untoward is revealed.'

'I'm sure it will all be fine.'

'Yes, well I'm sure you're right, but I have re – written my will in any case, just to err on the side of caution, as it were.'

'Don't go all morbid on me, it's too nice a day for that.'

'Well, one can never be too careful, especially when one gets to my age. Of course I have no surviving family to leave anything to anymore, so one must in any case begin to consider what will happen after one is gone.'

'Well don't consider it too much, will you?'

'The thing is, Emily my dear, I have always valued our friendship. I know it sounds silly but you have in a way become as a daughter to me.'

'It's not silly, and it's very sweet of you to say so, but let's have no more talk of dying, shall we?'

Daphne smiled.

'Very well; you're right, of course, I'm sure all will be well, and now I really must let you get on.'

But Emily did not get on, and nor did she then have any time to contemplate Daphne's rather enigmatic words, for just then another form appeared at the door; someone much younger, and perhaps fortunate to still be in the prime of her life.

'Hi Em…Sorry, I didn't think you'd have company. Hello Daphne.'

'Hello Sandra, dear, it's quite alright, I was just leaving. How are you now, quite recovered from your, ummm, illness I hope?'

'Yes, I'm much better thanks.'

'I'm very glad to hear it.'

It was still the case that only a few people knew the nature or cause of Sandra's illness, and why it should have required an ambulance and paramedics to ensure her survival, and Daphne was not among them, although Daphne had her suspicions. Nobody would talk about it, which meant that there must be something to talk about, and even Meadow did not appear to know, which probably meant that she knew full well. Daphne took her leave, and Sandra took her place at the upstairs dining table.

'Sorry, did I interrupt something?'

'No, it's okay, she really was leaving. Coffee..?'

'Thanks...Look, I'm sorry to call 'round like this.'

'I'm very popular today, it seems. Friends are a bit like buses, I don't see anyone for ages and then everyone arrives at the same time.'

'Well I won't stay long, but I wanted to see you on your own, you know?'

'Well here I am.'

Emily was not yet entirely sure how to talk to someone who had apparently recently tried to kill themselves, not even and perhaps particularly when that somebody was probably her best friend. She poured coffee and sat down in the opposite chair.

'So; what's happening then?'

'Well, in general what's happening is that I'm starting work again on Monday, that is to say I'm going back to the laboratory.'

'Well that's good then, so you're okay now?'

Which was something of an inadequate question under the circumstances, and Emily realized its' inadequacy, but she couldn't think of another way of putting it, and in any case the question was ignored.

'The thing is, Em, I just wanted to say how sorry I am for everything. Me to you, you know?'

'You mean like trying to kill yourself?'

'I mean for everything...'

'I think this sounds like a conversation which needs alcohol, doing deep and meaningful isn't easy in the afternoon.'

'You're never alone in the evenings.'

'True, but it's only Will, you know?'

'That's mostly what I'm sorry about.'

'Oh, that...Well I'll let you off, just don't do it again.'

'That much at least I can promise...'

'Not even when you're drunk, or stoned or whatever..?'

'Not even then; I know what a cow I've been, Em, and I want us to make the peace, you know, once and for all. When you've been through something like this, well, you begin to realize what's important. I mean not that Will isn't important, that isn't what I'm saying, but both of you have been better friends to me than I deserve.'

'Christ, someone give me a drink....But Will wasn't the reason, was he, why you, you know...'

'No, he wasn't the reason. It's hard to explain, since I can't even explain it to myself. I think life just got bigger than me, you know, although that's not right either, in fact in a way it's the opposite. I mean I'm doing everything I'm supposed to do, academically and whatever, and I'm set fair to have a shining career, and so on, but sometimes it all seems so insignificant and pointless, you know?'

'Yes, well I suppose everything's pointless when it comes down to it, said she downing her third virtual Blood Mary. I mean making cheese may be the pinnacle of my career, you know, so where do you go from there? I mean I get that you've been depressed, Sands, but everyone gets pissed off sometimes, you just have to get on with it, and I know that's crap advice but it's the best I can do sober....'

'At least you've got Will to get on with it with.'

'Yes, well lucky me, and that's it, really isn't it? You just haven't found your Will yet, apart from, you know, my Will, and we've agreed that you're not having him, but anyway plenty of people have happy and fulfilled lives without a significant other. Not that I'm saying you won't find anyone, or someone, but you can't force these things, Sands. Some of the best things in life happen by accident, so maybe you just have to do life and wait for it to happen.'

'As I recall you didn't exactly wait for Will, you went out and got him, which was a good move.'

'One of my best, I think, not that he resisted very much...'

'Yes, well anyway, I suppose I just haven't had my accident yet...I mean, here I am, well you know how old we are, and I'm still a bloody virgin, for Christ's sake.'

'Well there's no excuse for that, if that's what you want. I mean you're every young mans' dream, so if that's the problem then go and get laid or something.'

'I think I have to be in love first, and that's the bit you can't force, isn't it. Anyway, look, I didn't come here to talk about my fucked – up life.'

'Or un fucked - up life...Sorry, that slipped out, but anyway here we are, and I've got nothing better to do, and I suppose if you don't talk about it, you know?'

'I might end up trying to kill myself again....?'

'Don't even talk about doing that again.'

'I thought I was supposed to be talking about things.'

'Yes, but not that thing; better to talk about ways of avoiding it, don't you think? Are you still taking the happy pills?'

'Yes, I'm still on medication, although it's not very strong, like before. I just get...I just get these really black moods which come over me, which I can't explain or describe to anyone who's never experienced something like it, but I'm trying really hard to do life without pills, you know?'

'Yes, well that would be a good start...'

'Followed by emotional and sexual fulfillment, preferably, which are things I've read about, you know?'

'Trust me, it can happen.'

'Yes, we're looking at this from different sides of the spectrum, aren't we?'

'If you mean do I love Will then of course I do, and I don't exactly have to try very hard in the sex department, and actually

I don't think I could handle much more fulfillment, but that's me, and us, you know, and everyone's different.'

'Are they...? Well if you say so.'

'Just try to be, I don't know, a bit more natural, you know? Let things happen, Sands, and stop trying to be a control – monster all the time.'

'I thought women were supposed to be in control of their lives.'

'Yes, but you have to have something to control before you can control it. Being in control of nothing is still nothing, isn't it? Anyway some things can't or shouldn't be controlled, and if it's love you want then it's the kind of thing that the harder you look for it the less likely you are to find it, so I've heard anyway.'

'I know that, or at least I've heard that too, but...I don't know. I think that's the trouble with being a scientist, it's all about chemistry and hormones, and I can't help analyzing everything, including myself, you know, and my reaction to everything, and everybody, and yet I've got this ridiculously romantic notion of being a virgin on my wedding night.'

'Yes, well you don't seem to have been that analytical or virginal when it comes to Will, and if you carry on thinking like that you'll disappear up your own fanny one of these days. There are plenty of nice guys out there, in amongst all the assholes, and nobody's bloody perfect anyway. Love's about loving and accepting someone for what they are, you know? Just go out, get pissed, meet someone and get it out of your system. Even if it isn't loves' young dream it'd be something to work with.'

'You can't have good sex until you've had bad sex, right? Got to walk across the pebbles to get to the sea, sort of thing...'

'I don't know, I've never had bad sex, except when I've wanted it, and then it's good sex anyway, and I've only ever had Will, and god I really need a drink now. Can't we talk about the weather, or something?'

'Sure, I'm sorry...I mean I'd love for you and I to go out for a drink one night, but you won't go without Will, I suppose.'

'We're not joined at the hip, so I mean sure, if you want.'

'How about Friday..?'

'Sounds as good as any other day...'

'Okay, let's do that. Shall I call for you?'

'We'll pick you up. I daresay Will'll drive us into town.'

Sandra smiled at that notion.

'That makes it all sound rather stupid, doesn't it, dropping us off at the pub door or whatever?'

'Well, it was your idea, but let's go with it, as long as there're no *'saying sorry'* kind of agendas and what - not.'

'I promise, I've said what I came to say, Em, and a lot more besides, actually.'

'Well let's just go out and have a good time then, like we used to.'

'Sure, of course, it's what I really to do need right now. Friday it is then...Thanks, Em, for being so understanding you know?'

'I'm not that understanding, but you're welcome, as far as it goes.'

Sandra Fox stood up, and so did Emily. It had been a quite brief meeting between two such friends, but agendas had been achieved and a way forward agreed, and that for now was enough. They hugged at the door, and Sandra departed, leaving Emily to wash cups and contemplate the last two hours or so of her life. She had a fairly easy afternoon ahead, mostly just packaging up some cheese for one of her regular deliveries tomorrow. She sold all of the cheese that she produced, but she knew well enough that if her little business were to turn anything like a decent profit she would need to find more outlets, and if she did that then she would have to produce more cheese, which meant buying more goats and getting them in milk. Still, so far so good, and at least her confidence in her products was increasing, particularly as regards her soft cheeses. For now, however, she sat down and finished her cup of coffee, and considered that that had been an interesting interlude in her day. There had been too much talk of death, one of her callers seeming to be convinced that hers was not far away, and the other having already been dead by her own volition, but she had nevertheless been glad to see both people. She hoped that Daphne would be okay, and didn't really understand what she had been talking about regarding wills and so on. She wondered briefly where that conversation might have gone if Sandra had not interrupted it. And did she now trust Sandra? Saying that she would behave from now on was something different from actually behaving from now on, but she supposed that she should give the vixen the benefit of the doubt. If she tried it on with Will again, however, then that would be the end of their friendship, particularly having made such a proclamation; the she – fox was on her last warning, best friend or no best friend. The afternoon was waning before she set about the rest of her days' work, but she did so now with a light spirit. She had a date to go out somewhere, which was a rare thing these days, and anyway Will would be home soon, which always made everything alright in Emily's small but mostly happy world.

She had been a girl that he had known from school. Peter Shortbody had first attended an all – boys senior school, which had gone co – educational during his fourth year, with the resultant hormonal upheaval which had inevitably swept through such a collective of young men and women. Peter Shortbody, however, who had been rather a reserved and retiring youth, had eschewed very much contact with the newly arrived girls, aside from casual, somewhat shy conversations and light friendships, which did not reach far into his young and quite studious soul. Nevertheless, four decades and more after he had last seen her, there she was. They met quite by chance at some unspecified and vague location, and without thought or hesitation had thrown themselves into each - others' arms, where they had whispered intimacies. They were at the same time their actual ages and the age at which they would last have seen one another, as can happen in dreams, and indeed can only happen in dreams, and he had carried their brief conversation into the waking world, and it was she who had spoken first;

'I thought I'd lost you forever.'

'Yes, so did I.'

'We're okay now though, aren't we?'

'Yes, we're okay now.'

'And you'll never leave me again?'

'No, I'll never leave you again.'

He had awoken with a start, and with such an intense feeling of love and having been loved that for a moment he was quite at a loss to order his emotions. In his waking moment he had kicked Tizer off the side of the bed, the cat barely hanging on to the duvet with its' front claws before regaining its' former position, where it settled down again in somewhat disgruntled fashion; it had not appreciated being so rudely awoken, although it had not been the first such time. Peter Shortbody looked at his bedside clock, which told him that it was ten minutes past five in the morning. He sat up in bed, then lay down again and closed his eyes, but somehow the dream or the image or memory of the dream was still there, and would give him no peace; he would, it seemed, sleep no more this night. He got out of bed and put on his dressing gown, went to the bathroom and thence downstairs to his kitchen where he set the electric kettle to boil. He sat at his kitchen table and put his mind to the matter of his dream, and the subject thereof. Her face and her words during their so brief time together had been as vivid as if she had actually been with him, but what on earth had been her name? Mary, Margaret…? It began with an 'm', he was sure. Madeline; that had been it; Maddie…Maddie Young; mid – length, mid – brown hair for most of the time that he had known her; pretty, as young girls are, quite short and slight of stature, and he remembered that she had smiled at him from time to time if they had come upon one another or passed in the corridor, but he could not recall their ever having a significant conversation. No, that wasn't quite right; he had stayed behind at school on occasion and helped her with her mathematics homework, something which he found very easy, but she apparently did not. And then…And then on such occasions they would walk home together, or at least part of the way home, until their respective ways parted. Peter Shortbody had not been much for school discotheques, or any discotheques for that matter, but he had attended one at the end of a particular summer term, and he remembered her being there, and that she had looked quite different out of uniform, and had been wearing sparkly eye makeup. But otherwise, apart from such random and apparently pointless details, there had been nothing, this being the sum – total of everything that he could for now recall about her, aside from her generally being around for his last three years of school. But thereafter he had thought nothing of her, and certainly could not recall the last time they had met, or ever having said goodbye to her. He had left school leaving virtually all of his fellow students behind, and had found a job as a clerk in an accountancy firm for part of the summer before he began his accountancy course at university. And even so, what of any of it? It was just a dream, after all, and it would quickly fade from memory. But it did not fade from memory. He went about his morning rituals of doing his ablutions, feeding his feline companion and eating his breakfast whilst reading the newspaper which had always by now been delivered, and the image of Maddie Young and her words to him were as vivid and wonderfully distracting as ever. So from whence had they come? Some aberration on his part, no doubt; an invention of his subconscious self, nothing more, and he should put the matter quite behind him; yes, that would be the thing to do. In any case, what could be done? He could look her up on the internet, but that was just being silly, was it not, and in any case even if she had a website or whatever she would no doubt be married by now and would likely have changed her surname. Certainly in any case she would not remember him; the quiet, studious young man who had never been in the mainstream of the social or sexual aspects of the school. On the other hand, where would be the harm in it? He had time before he left for number thirteen; Alice was working in London today but she was not leaving until mid – morning. Only to put his mind at rest, and to put the whole ridiculous idea behind him he took his cup of tea upstairs to his spare bedroom where he kept his computer, and turned it on. He typed in her name, and got an immediate result. Madeline Young, or Maddie Young, as she apparently still called herself, had written a novel, which was entitled *'Far away from Everywhere'*. It was a love story, apparently, which had been published three years previously, and there, along with a brief synopsis of the book was her brief autobiography and a photograph, by which it was easy for him to confirm that he at least had the right Madeline Young. Her hair was shorter now, but the years had been kind to her; her prettiness had aged with her, of course, but she had kept it nonetheless, and she smiled out at him again from the screen as she had done in a school corridor so long ago. She lived *'in the south of England'* and there was a means by which she could be contacted to discuss or comment upon her book. He would not write to her, of course, but it might be quite amusing to read her novel, might it not? He paid for and downloaded the book, which he would read over the course of the next few days; he might even read it to Bron and Beth, since he quite often read them to sleep. Thus satisfied with his research, he closed down his machine and went about the more mundane business of preparing for the rest of his day. It was such an odd thing that he should dream of her, of all people, after such a long time, and the nature of their meeting again had been strange indeed, although it was of course in fact only he who had met her, and then only in a dream. On the other hand, once met, and once a connection has been made, in one important sense at least, people never really lose one another, do they?

Chapter 2

THE LIMITS OF ENDURANCE

In the normal run of things, and in an ordinary English village, the arrival or presence of a single and quite young woman would not perhaps attract very much attention beyond vague and casual interest. Our story takes place, however, in the village of Middlewapping, which in truth could scarce now be regarded as an ordinary village, and where things for certain of its' residents had not run normally for some time. Even here, nothing in particular if at all was thought about the woman during her first visit one evening, when she sat alone at the bar of the Dog and Bottle public house, and attempted to engage Nigel Hollyman, the worthy if somewhat sullen landlord in occasional pleasant and convivial conversation, the pleasantry and conviviality being in truth mostly on her part. The village was, after all, no stranger to strangers. Astronomers, geologists and lay – people merely showing an interest would still with some regularity come to see the famous Middlewapping meteorite, whilst others would come in search of a certain Mister Ashley Spears, just to see if the rumours of his living here in the village church really were true. Still others would come merely to see or to photograph the village in all of its' rare and undoubted period beauty. The woman returned, however, two evenings later, and now, by dint of a quite accidental conversation between Keith and Nigel, the first gentle alarm bells began to ring within a certain faction of the small community. Word spread amongst those who should be told, which first included Meadow, Percival and Sophia. The woman was probably in her third decade, casually dressed and apparently without agenda, but Nigel could not say from whence she had come, or why she chose their particular pub in which to pass her evenings. There could of course be nothing to the matter, and certainly Nigel was at a loss to know why she should be of interest to anybody, but the killing of the witches at Farthing's Well, which was known of now within this tight and secretive group, was ever at the back of their thoughts, and not all of the witches had been killed. Rebecca still did not know how she had escaped the inferno, or how she had arrived on that night on the steps of the Manor House, and still nobody had heard of or from Helena. The witch Megan had fled the village, but there may yet be others, and so all agreed that the woman's presence should not be entirely ignored.

Nigel Hollyman knew nothing of any business pertaining to witches, so Keith invented a pretext by which he wished to know if the woman returned, and asked Nigel to telephone him if he saw her again, a request which was reluctantly agreed to.

'I really shouldn't go spying on or reporting my customers, you know.'

'Yeah, I know, but I think she may be looking for someone, and I'd like to help her.'

'Who's she looking for then?'

'I'm sorry, I can't tell you that. It's no big deal, but it's personal, you know?'

'Well, if you want to be bloody mysterious about it.'

'Just call me if she comes in again, that's all I ask.'

'Well it's quite irregular, but I suppose since it's you, and beyond that I want nothing to do with it.'

'Sure, of course.'

In the event no telephone call was needed. It was several days before the woman appeared for the third time, and by chance when she did so Keith was in the Dog and Bottle with Damien, enjoying a mid – evening pint of Old Thumper, and discussing matters pertaining to the work at Orchard House, when Nigel made an unusual point of clearing glasses from their table.

'That's her, at the bar...'

'What…?'

'The woman you were asking about.'

'Oh, right, thanks.'

'And I didn't just tell you that, alright?'

'Yeah, you're cool.'

Neither Keith nor Damien had noticed the woman's arrival, but now there she sat, looking natural enough, but Keith knew well enough that if she were indeed a witch then she could and would hide her identity and intent. Damien was the next to speak.

'So, what now..?'

'I'll go and talk to the lady.'

'Want me to join the conversation?'

'Probably best if I do it alone, two of us might be intimidating.'

'Ay, you're probably right. Anyway I might cramp your style, she might fall for my lilting Scottish accent and rugged good looks.'

'Yeah, then there's that.'

'Think you can handle her then? She might think you're trying to pick her up.'

'I'm a happily unmarried man.'

'She doesn't know that.'

'Anyway I'm quite a lot older than she is, and she probably wouldn't fancy me anyway.'

'Don't you think this is all getting a wee bit paranoid?'

'Probably, or I would have thought so before witches started appearing around the place and people started getting killed. This used to be a nice quiet village.'

'Before my time…She doesn't look like an evil witch.'

'Does Sophia look like a witch, evil or otherwise?'

'I would never have known.'

'There you go then.'

'So what are you going to say to her?'

'No idea yet….I'll just try and sound her out. Pity I left my witch detection kit in my other trousers. Still, here's to it.'

'Good luck. Let me know how it goes in the morning.'

The two men drained their glasses, Damien departed and Keith walked to the bar, looking as casual as he could.

For Michael Tillington these were heady days. The uncertain and sometimes anxious transition between his love for Rose and now for Elin was all but over; the mist which had hung over his life and his thoughts during that which seemed to him to be such a long time had lifted now, or been blown away by new and different emotion. Were he to liken his love for Rose to a tempestuous storm, then his love for Elin was as a gentle and calming breeze, but however such things may be considered the mist was gone now, and he could see so much more clearly the way forward.

He could nowadays look at the portrait of his beautiful and now deceased wife without a lump coming to his throat, or tears threatening the back of his eyes. She was as beautiful as she had ever been, and now would ever be, but now her painted form was becoming just that, and all else of her was fading, and departing with the mist to somewhere else, wherever such things found their place, and their final peace. The painter had done her work well, and the eyes that he had known so well still looked out at him from the canvass, but they were calmer eyes now, and less sad, most of the time.

He had taken a chance, perhaps with most important part of himself, and he knew this, as he had known it at the time. He had put his love and his future somewhere where in truth he had not been certain that they would find fulfillment, but as his love for Rose had by degrees passed on, his new love for Elin had come into the void, and granted him the happiness that he had so wished for. Whether he loved Elin as much as he had loved Rose was something which he no longer asked himself, for all love was different, was it not, and bore no true or fair comparison. In this most important respect Elin was his future now, and with this he was by now quite content.

Nathaniel had grown away from the trauma of his early life, and was as strong and bonny a baby as ever there was, and this was something which Michael could now accept, and believe in, and was daily a source of happiness for him. Abigail attended to his son well, and he knew this, and he would miss her when he moved from the Manor House, but here was something which also daily preoccupied his thoughts. He and Elin had looked in depth at their joint finances, and although they would be left with less money than he had assumed would be the case had Orchard House been sold on, and his business would likely now need further financial support from his bankers, they could afford to live there, assuming that Elin found similar employment closer to their intended home. This was still to an extent dependent on the final and actual cost of the renovation, but there was sufficient financial latitude to make him quite confident that they would manage, somehow. Elin in any case had quite set her heart on living there, and any resistance on his part to the idea had quickly become academic, quite aside from the fact that he very much liked the idea of it himself. It was a beautiful house, or would be once Keith had done his work, and the process had given him and his newly beloved a mutual and wholly positive interest and focus. Almost daily and even at this early stage in the work, she would ask for updates of progress, or proffer new ideas as to how she wished the house to be, and Michael's visits to the house would increase in their frequency from now onwards. It would in any case be a fine place in which to pass the years and to raise his son, before he took his fathers' place at the Manor House. Thereafter the house could be sold in any case, but that was long into the future and need not be considered for now.

This new future for the house had conversely also prompted Michael to take a greater interest in its' longer history. History, after all, was in a sense his life, but thus far he had had no success in this regard. He could find no record of exactly when or by whom the house had first been built, but this was for him and for now a distraction rather than a priority.

For now Michael basked in the warmth of his new circumstance and his new love for Elin, whom he would see once or twice a week, whenever they or more accurately she had the time, and she would now more often make the journey west to see him, and to see the house, her visits to the Manor House thus becoming more frequent during the months of spring. This in turn would prompt his parents and in particular his mother to speculate as to the nature of her sons' new relationship, particularly in terms of its' potential longevity. This could no longer be regarded as a casual acquaintance, or passing fancy, but any efforts on her part to press her son on the matter fell on deaf ears, and he would not be forthcoming on the matter, or commit to any statement of intent. Michael would tell his parents of their intentions in due course, and thereafter make public and formal announcement of their engagement, but for now their betrothal was a secret shared only with Victoria, and herein lay perhaps the only cloud to hang over the life of Michael Tillington during this otherwise happy and heady time. His sister had seemed more distracted of late. She was quicker to anger, and more withdrawn into herself, and Michael hoped that this was not a foreboding of some further or deeper deterioration in her emotional or mental state, for if so, it would not be for the first time.

Keith stood beside the woman and placed his empty beer glass on the bar, which was sufficient inducement for Nigel to pour another pint.

'One for the road..?'

Keith stood considerably taller than the woman, who in any case was sitting on one of the quite high bar – stools. He glanced down at her and smiled enigmatically, or so he hoped, and in any case after only a brief hesitation the smile was returned, whilst she surveyed and assessed him with quick, female eyes. She was drinking something with tomato juice, which was almost finished.

'It's not often I get the chance to buy a lady a drink these days. May I have the honour, just out of politeness, of course?'

Now there was scarce a seconds' delay before;

'Sure...Why not?'

Keith decided that this was a good start, he seemed to have passed that which his daughters would probably call the '*creep test*', and he was at least glad not to be regarded as a creep, however such a thing might be defined.

'One Bloody Mary coming up...' Said Nigel, who was studiously avoiding eye - contact with Keith.

'Name's Keith, if I might make so bold.'

The smile came again; nice eyes; nice face actually, and not in the least bit witch – like, but then what did a witch look like? Rebecca looked every inch the witch, she had dark, witches' eyes; windows onto her dark, witches' soul, but Sophia did not, and if anyone ever said that Rosie looked like a witch he'd punch their lights out. Best then not let her appearance be indicative of anything.

'Georgina, Georgie to my friends.'

So she had friends, which went rather against her being a witch, but then Rosie had friends, but if she had friends why was she drinking alone for three nights in a place where she had probably never drunk before now?

'Georgina it is then, us not being well acquainted and all, at least until you tell me otherwise.'

A gentle laugh now, but not a witches' laugh, whatever that was...

'Well, whatever...'

So far so good, but this was tricky, and Damien had raised a salient point. How to look as though he wasn't trying to pick her up, which he wasn't, but how would she know that he wasn't? And then again supposing she thought he was anyway and was amenable to the idea; that would further complicate matters, would it not? Keith had remained faithful to his beloved Meadow since they had met and made love for the first time, which as far as he could recall had been the first time that they had met, but he had had his opportunities of a certain nature with other women, some of whom were clearly attracted to that somewhat rough, hippie biker look, and Keith could charm if he so wished. So, best all 'round not to be too charming then, but that became even more complicated, having to veer away from ones' natural state of being. And then again supposing she was attracted to the rougher types, women, as Keith had learned in life and by living with one of them and having two daughters, being inherently complicated creatures. In any case his first dilemma was what kind of a conversation could one begin with a total stranger without sounding corny? In the end and all things considered, Keith decided just to launch in, as it were, and see what happened.

'Not from 'round here, are you?'

Which was the best he could think of; corn apparently could not be entirely avoided.

'No, but I don't live that far away.'

'Right....'

Okay so now what? She wasn't helping with the interrogation, but then why should she; she who had been sitting at the bar minding her own business, but what business was she minding, that was the thing. Keith of a sudden felt rather like an idiot, and wondered whether after all this had been anything akin to a good idea, and what his beloved Meadow would make of his performance so far. If this was as far as the discourse was destined to go then so be it, but he now had a pint of ale to drink, which he supposed he could take back to his table and drink alone, but that might also now look rather idiotic. He seemed to be caught between two forms of idiocy, and must now weigh up which was the lesser of the two evils. Fortunately, however, two things now occurred which reduced the tension of the moment somewhat. The first was that her Bloody Mary was delivered to the bar, which gave some distraction, and then of a sudden the lady seemed to have made a decision, and now appeared to rather enter into the spirit of things, whatever that might be.

'You're from the village, though, yes?'

'Man and boy....This has been my local pub since I was old enough to have a local pub.'

'So you must know everything which goes on in the village then.'

'Well, quite a lot of it I suppose.'

'It's an interesting village, isn't it, apart from being extremely picturesque, of course.'

'Well, we have our meteorite.'

'Yes, that really made you famous, but it's the people who make a village interesting, don't you think?'

'I suppose so....'

'I mean for a start there's Ash Spears. Does he really live in the old church?'

'Well yes, that is to say he stays there sometimes.'

'But he's not there now?'

'He's currently on tour with the band.'

'So he is, of course...I read a write – up a couple of weeks ago. So is the church like some kind of a retreat for him then, away from the limelight, sort of thing?'

'I suppose so. He composes music there and such, so I've heard.'

'So do you know him personally?'

'Yeah, we've met, a couple of times...He's a nice guy.'

'I'm sure….And then there's Tara Knightman, of course. The village has a famous daughter now, as well as a famous son.'

Keith did a momentary reassessment of the encounter. It appeared as though she was now interrogating him, which wasn't how it was supposed to have been, but he supposed that he might glean something from her questions in any case before he tried to turn the tables, so to think. The reference to Tara being a daughter was quite coincidental, he was sure, but anyway he wasn't about to impart any information regarding his own beloved and actual daughter, particularly if this seemingly innocuous enough woman was indeed a witch, even if his other daughter was in fact a witch. It was all getting a bit confusing, but Keith thought he could handle it okay.

'What about her?'

'She lives here too, doesn't she?'

A direct question, to which there really was no point in lying.

'Yeah, she lives hereabouts.'

'She's famously rumoured to live on an old bus, is that really true?'

'I wouldn't believe everything you hear…'

'So she doesn't live on an old bus then?'

'I think she's the kind of person who prefers to keep herself to herself, you know, and I respect that.'

'So you're closing ranks on me, are you? I mean I love her voice, I've heard both of her albums, but nobody seems to know anything about her, or they aren't letting on, anyway.'

'Well, as I say, I think she prefers to keep it that way.'

'An enigmatic young lady, indeed; a famous rock musician who doesn't want to be famous…So how well do you know her..?'

'Not that well, just, you know, in passing.'

She took a long drink from her Bloody Mary, of which she was making short work. Keith on the other hand had barely touched his ale, but now he saw his opportunity to move into the temporary silence, which was at least not now so deafening as it had been at the start of their encounter.

'So what brings you to our small village?'

'Oh, I just like seeing new places, you know?'

This was a lie, but the lady was rather good at lying; it was an ability which out of necessity she had learned over the years. Keith, however, who considered himself rather good at reading people, was less than convinced, and since she was apparently less than forthcoming, he decided to let her retake the initiative. If she had an agenda other than discussing the village, then she might give herself away eventually, and now she said something which Keith regarded as being significant.

'So, what about the witch then..?'

'What witch…?'

'Oh come on, you must have heard of the witch of Middlewapping, practically everybody else I've spoken to around here has, and other places as well. Her fame is spreading far and wide, whoever she is.'

So she had been speaking to other people, so why had she been doing that?

'Yeah, well I've heard the rumour, but people who live here don't put much store by it, in fact no store at all.'

'I've even heard it suggested that Tara Knightman and the witch are one and the same person.'

So now she was accusing his daughter of being a witch, and how dare she do that? On the other hand he supposed that it was not so unreasonable, given that one of his daughters was in fact a witch, she just had the wrong daughter.

'That's a quite ridiculous notion, if you don't mind my saying so.'

'Say whatever you like; I'm just telling you what some people are saying, you know? So where do you think the *'rumour'* came from then? I mean I never thought that witches existed either, but then there was that business in Kent, where the house burned down and they found all of those buried women.'

'Yes but that was in Kent. That had nothing to do with our village.'

'So there's no connection, then?'

'Nope, don't reckon there is.'

'Well you should know, I suppose, but I read about the body that was found on the village Green. That was strange, wasn't it?'

The body of Florence, Rebecca's mother, and this was now too close to witch business. The lady had been researching the village, and making connections, and asking more questions than she should have been. This, as far as Keith was concerned, had now gone beyond casual conversation or enquiry. He became convinced that the woman, whoever and whatever she was, had a better or at least other reason for being here than she was admitting to. He decided against confrontation, however; better finish his beer and withdraw. Keith could drink a pint of ale quickly if he so chose, and now he did so. His departure, however, must seem to be as casual as had his arrival, the better not to arouse suspicion as to his own motives; he had also been lying, after all. The conversation thus far had been founded on lies and half – truths, and probably neither had believed what the other had been saying, but anyway, it was time to leave.

'Yeah, well strange stuff happens, you know, but people putting two and two together and making five doesn't help. That's how rumours start, isn't it?'

'Is it? Well perhaps, but I don't think you're telling me everything, not by a long way, actually.'

'What makes you say that?'

'I can just tell with people, that's all.'

'Well good for you…Anyway it was good to talk, but I should be going.'

'There, and I thought we were just getting to know one another.'

'Well I'm in here quite often so you never know....'

She smiled again, mostly to herself, and finished her drink at the same time as did he.

She stood up and they walked to the door together, which oddly enough seemed like the natural thing to do. He opened the door for her; outside the evening was quite chilly, but the worst of the winter was now over.

'Well, it was nice to meet you Keith.'

'You too, I'm sure.'

'And thanks for the drink, I hope I can return the compliment some time.'

'Sure...'

One final smile and then she turned from him and walked across the track and onto the village Green; perhaps she had a car parked somewhere, or maybe she would catch the last bus into town. In the end he had to conclude that the meeting had been inconclusive in all regards. He still knew next to nothing about her, or why she was here, or even whether she had indeed thought that he had an ulterior motive in approaching her. Keith watched until her form was lost to the darkness before heading along the track to the main road, and thence home to the bus, the location of and way to which for now remained a well – kept secret. Whoever she was, she was not who she said she was, or at least she was being far from entirely honest, he was sure, which could of course in itself be nothing of significance. Damien had been right, they must avoid becoming paranoid about every stranger in the village who didn't quite add up, but Keith remained unconvinced regarding the motives of the young woman who was called Georgina, whose friends called her Georgie.

Victoria Tillington had of late been feeling an ever – increasing need for distraction, and to be in a place where she could better order her increasingly disparate thoughts. She could shut herself in her room, and this she did with increasing frequency, but even her room seemed now to her to be a stale and claustrophobic environment. She loved her London, and in general felt most at home in cities, and thought that she might go abroad soon, if only for a few days, perhaps to Rome or Naples, both places which she loved and had not seen for a long time. This, however, would need a little more organization and some time off from the gallery, and her need to get away was rather more immediate. So it was that she awoke early on a particular and quite fine morning, showered, saw to it that Abi had all that she needed and told her of her intentions, took her swim - suit from her drawer and a towel from the airing cupboard, and left the house before her parents were abroad. She got into her car and drove through the gates of the Manor, with little or no real idea as to where she was going, other than that her journey would end at the ocean.

She headed west and drove for most of the morning, ending up three counties away, and at a cove where she had been once before many years ago with her family, when they had been visiting friends in the nearby town, but she had not been back here since. She parked her car at the seaward end of the Municipal car park at the head of the cove, changed rather awkwardly into her swim – suit, wrapped herself in a beach – towel and walked barefoot the short distance across the mostly sandy beach to the waters' edge. The small, narrow cove was entirely empty apart from her, and there was no sign of life in the few houses which were situated above the beach. Most of them would likely be guest – houses, and it was not yet the beginning of the tourist season. She sat against a quite large rock at the waters' edge and lit a cigarette, keeping her towel wrapped around her against the light, landward wind, which had lost its' bite now, though the spring was still young. After a few moments she stood up, left her towel on the rock, and walked the few remaining paces into the water, wading out until she had enough depth of water in which to swim. The weather may have by now have been warmer, but the sea was still winter – cold, and she had to catch her breath as she dived into the next wave, and left solid ground behind her.

Victoria had always been a good swimmer. She had almost always been placed in the top three at inter – school swimming galas, and on occasion she had won her free – style events. She carried very little by way of body – fat, her slim body thus offering little resistance to the water, which made up in part for her lack of significant physical strength, and she had a good stroke. Beyond the breaking – point of the quite moderate waves she found her rhythm, and headed directly out to sea, trying to work – off the coldness which threatened to numb her head and limbs. And now, in this alien environment, she let her thoughts go where they would. She had not seen Rebecca since the night of the revelation that she had bewitched and seduced Michael, and had thus become pregnant with Florence. Rebecca had 'phoned her twice, but she had not returned the calls, nor had she been to the village, despite the fact that she wanted to see Percival. Her reasons for wishing to see him were in any event not specific, other than having the pretext of wanting him to know how Henry was doing, but despite everything she believed that Percival had a different way of seeing the world, and she needed a different perspective on all that had happened before she next saw Rebecca. And then there was Michael, who had also at times been foremost in her thoughts. She had watched her brothers' slow emotional recovery after the death of Rose, and the steady improvement in his state of mind and being, which had now culminated in Elin accepting his offer of marriage. And then of course there was Orchard House, where Victoria had been once with her brother, and which promised his eventual departure from the Manor which she knew he so wished for. In any event Michael was happy again now; happier in fact than she had seen him for a long time, so how then could she tell him that his son was not his son, or that he had a daughter of which he knew nothing? And if not now, then would she ever be able to tell him? Would the passing of time and changing of circumstances ever make the matter easier, either for the giver or recipient of such news? Should she let him remain ignorant of everything, wherein lay the danger that if he ever did find out by other means then he would rightly accuse her of deceiving him, or at best not being honest with him regarding such ever so important matters? Even if, for her brothers' sake, she were able to live with the deception, the truth had its' own way of finding the light of knowledge, and in that case would the situation not be so much worse? Rebecca had said that she would never tell Michael, but never was a long time, and Rebecca was hardly to be relied upon. Her life currently had some kind of stability; she was working hard and attending well enough to Florence, but with Rebecca nothing was ever certain, and Victoria did not believe for a moment that the business of the witches was over. And now into the sphere of her own emotions had come Pandora. They had by now spent two nights together, and it had just been sex, but feelings had begun to stir within her which made her question whether after all it had just been sex, and Pandora would not yet be leaving the Manor. Her fathers' portrait was all but finished now, but Victoria had agreed that Pandora could paint her portrait, and this she had told her father, so to this she was now committed. The ancient secrets, the dairies which had been written so long ago remained hidden in her bedroom drawer, and which to say the least of it cast doubt upon the legitimacy of her fathers' title, were something which also occupied her thoughts from time to time, but this was not something for now. She had let the matter be, whether out of cowardice or concern for her father and brother, and still only she and the coven of witches knew of the deception which had been perpetrated back in the mists of long forgotten time, but Victoria could not now forget, and the knowledge at times felt like a weight on her soul.

So did the thoughts of Victoria Tillington go as she swam, and by now she was swimming hard, and for a short but significant time she became quite lost in her reverie, for it seemed to her that no matter how many times she asked these questions of herself, there were never any answers. Finally she stopped, and trod water. She had swum further than she had thought, and was now out beyond the headlands which enclose the bay on either side. The coldness of the water was biting hard now, and her legs had begun to cramp. Her skinny frame, which aided her swimming technique also offered little insulation against the near freezing water, and for a moment a feeling of panic began to threaten her. The beach was now a long distance away, but the rocky headlands were closer, and these had given her a sense that she was not so far from land if she became too tired to make the return swim. The wind, however, was blowing stronger now, and the waves were bigger, and they now crashed with white foam against the rocks below the cliffs to both sides of her; it would now be difficult and dangerous at least and perhaps impossible to try to make landfall anywhere between her and the beach. So, to the beach then, which would provide her only safe landing, but she did indeed feel very tired now, and of a sudden her limbs felt weak, but she had to move before her body seized up completely and the cold and the ocean take her.

With a great effort of will she forced her body to action, and ducked her head once more into the coldness, and swam. Speed was now of the essence, but conversely she knew that to swim too hard would be a grave mistake; she must conserve her limited reserves of energy for the long swim, or she perhaps would not make it. There were no thoughts now, other than that she must survive, keep the rhythm steady and keep breathing the cold air; time and distance meant nothing, it was just about the next stroke and the next breath, and she must forget the fact that her muscles were now cramping badly and screaming for her to stop, for to stop now would surely mean her death.

The next moments of Victoria's life were lost to her; she was just flesh and willpower now, and she had nothing for anything else, but by painfully slow degrees the beach and safety drew closer, until at last she rode the waves to their breaking point in the shallow water. The last wave broke over her as her feet touched solid ground, and she staggered and crawled through the surf to dry land, and finally to her rock. She sat down on the sand and wrapped her towel around her; her body was shaking violently and uncontrollably, and the warmth was slow in coming, but within a few moments she could at least and at last feel her exhausted limbs again. A few more moments and she was able to take a cigarette from her packet, and finally she regained sufficient control to use her lighter. She now realized that she was desperately thirsty; her mouth was salt – dry and she could scarcely swallow, and she cursed herself for not coming better prepared, but she was safe now, at least, and as she looked out over the now deep grey ocean, Victoria laughed into the wind.

'High Sweet - Pea, how was the pub?'

'Yeah, okay, I sorted some things out with Damien.'

'Good…'

Meadow was about her needlework when Keith arrived home, making a dress for Rosie, who along with Basil had by now retired to the trailer.

'I also had a drink with a woman who was there on her own.'

'Oh yes, was she nice?'

'Yeah, well, I think so. She's the woman who's been in the pub a couple of times.'

'Oh I see. I thought she'd gone.'

'As did we all, but she's back now, and asking quite searching questions about the village, actually.'

Meadow put down her needlework; her eyes were getting tired anyway, and the conversation might need her undivided attention. Keith sat at the small dining table opposite her.

'What sort of questions?'

'Well, it started with Ash, then we got onto Tara, and ended up discussing witches, all in the space of about twenty minutes.'

'What was she asking about Tara?'

'Just the usual; did I know her, did I know where the bus was, that kind of thing. There didn't seem to be anything heavy about it, but then we got onto witches, and that's when I began to think that she had some kind of an agenda, and by the end I was convinced of it.'

'Why, what was she asking?'

'Had I heard of the witch of Middlewapping, to which I said no, but I don't think she believed me. She just seemed too know too much without really knowing anything, as though she'd been making enquiries, and she was definitely trying to get into it with me, and I kind of perceived that she perceived that I wasn't telling her everything I knew.'

'So there was a lot of perceiving going on then.'

'Yeah, and then she told me that she didn't believe me, which, you know, confirmed my perception, if you see what I mean.'

'Yes, I think so....But if she's talking about Rebecca, which I suppose she must have been, then if she was part of the Farthing's Well coven then she would surely have known who and where she was, wouldn't she?'

'I don't know, maybe, and she didn't seem like a witch, you know, not that I know what a witch seems like, I mean Rosie doesn't seem like a witch, does she? I just think we were both lying to each other throughout the whole conversation, so it was all a bit pointless, really.'

‘Right…So did you find out anything about her, like where she’s from?’

‘She didn’t say. All she said was that her name was Georgina, at least that’s what she told me, but I suppose even that isn’t necessarily true.’

‘Oh well, I don’t suppose there’s much to be done about it, apart from putting the word about that she’s still around. It may all be nothing, of course; perhaps she’s genuinely interested and naturally inquisitive. I mean rumours of a witch abound, and we already knew that.’

‘And if she really has come with bad intent, she would hardly make herself so obvious, would she?’

‘No I suppose not…Mind you, Megan made no secret of her presence, and she fooled everyone for a while. It was only by chance, you know…’

‘Sure…Anyway as you say there’s nothing we can do about her, but at least I’ll recognize her again if she ever comes back.’

‘So how did you get talking to her, anyway?’

‘I went up to the bar and said hello, or whatever.’

‘That was bold of you.’

‘I can handle my women.’

‘Well I can’t argue with that, I suppose.’

‘I mean I don’t think she thought I was trying to, you know….’

‘Make advances of an inappropriate nature?’

‘Yeah, that kind of thing...’

‘No, I’m sure she didn’t think that for a moment, Sweet – Pea, any more than I thought so when you first spoke to me.’

‘That was different though, I mean I was, then….’

‘What were you then?’

‘Trying to get inappropriate with you…’

‘Well, you certainly had me fooled, I would never have known.’

‘Are you taking the piss…?’

‘Now Keith, as if I would do such a thing.’

Meadow smiled to herself, put away her needlework and man and woman prepared for bed. Of the woman called Georgina and of her purpose we will hear more as our tale moves onwards, but for now we leave the bus to its' secrets, and Georgina to her particular agenda.

Victoria drove home in a quite different frame of mind than had been the case on her outward journey. Once she had recovered herself sufficiently and had felt able to walk again, she left the shelter of her rock and walked to her car, where she dressed as quickly as she could. She was by now not only very thirsty but also ravenously hungry, her body crying out for sustenance after its' ordeal. The only source of food within walking distance and probably quite a long way beyond was a cafeteria which had opened early for the season, and to here she went and found a table, which was not difficult since she was in fact the only patron. She ordered two bottles of sweet, heavily processed orange juice, coffee and a full English breakfast, which was advertised as being available all day, and which she consumed hungrily. Victoria had rarely during her life eaten in such a place, and there was little in truth to recommend the fare, but to Victoria it tasted like manna from heaven. There were moments, after all, during her very recent life when she wondered whether she would ever eat again, but now she had been through her rebirth and baptism in the ocean, and the salt – sea had washed away her doubt and uncertainty, and cleansed her of her darkest thoughts. So what if Rebecca had done as she had, and Rose had fallen for Percival's undoubted charms? This was none of her doing, and none of her business, so let them to it and its' consequences. She was Victoria Tillington, daughter to nobility and mother to little Henry, and she had her own life to lead. Even the sins of her forebears seemed of far less consequence to her now. The moment when she had turned around in the water to face her uncertain fate would stay with her and have influence upon her for a long time to come. She had been stupid to have done as she had, and this she knew well enough. She had died once before, and now she had been at the edge of her life once again, but once again she had survived, and sometimes only in moments of such adversity can a person gain a new perspective on their lives, and upon the world.

In the cafeteria, after she had finished her meal, she had lit a cigarette.

'Sorry, I can't let you smoke in here.'

Victoria had looked around her, and then at he who she assumed was the manager or owner of the establishment, and had shrugged her shoulders. He had shrugged his shoulders, they exchanged smiles and he brought her an ashtray.

On the journey home she asked one more question of herself; how much if any of that had been deliberate? Had it really been by accident that she had swum out so far, and no further, where it would surely have been beyond her to swim back? Had she really been so stupid, or had she if only subconsciously been testing herself and her resources of willpower and stamina? Had she pushed herself to the edge of herself, in order to be able to see the insignificance of things which did not threaten her life, or the lives of those whom she loved? Well, perhaps, and perhaps after all she had just been lucky, but anyway it was not a question which she had dwelt upon for very long. She was alive, after all, and that was really all that mattered was it not, and so long as she was alive she could face her demons and her doubts, as she had done before.

The motorway on her way home in the waning light of the late afternoon, and Victoria Tillington smiled to herself, and to nobody else.

Chapter 3

GOING OUT

There can sometimes be occasions in the lives of people, where any benefits which may be derived from a given action or event are not immediately obvious. Indeed it may sometimes be true that only by slow degrees and over time may anything positive which is taken away from such an action or event become apparent, especially if the action or event was at the time distasteful or even traumatic. The same may of course be said of adverse effects arising unexpectedly from seemingly innocuous or beneficial occurrences, but it is with the former of these phenomena that our story will for now concern itself, and the person whom it will for now concern is a certain Isabella Baxter.

Isabella had come away from her meeting with Barnabas Overton, one of her four abusers, with a sense that she should never have agreed to the meeting, and during the days which followed immediately thereafter she became convinced that having done so she had failed, in some significant way, and indeed that she had made a fool of herself. She had after all when presented with the opportunity been quite unable to say any of the things that she had intended or wanted to say to him, and although she had in her minds' eye felt the knife in her hand, and had imagined herself doing him grievous injury, the truth and actuality of it as she now perceived it was that she had behaved like an idiot. Her usual intellectual and emotional functions had malfunctioned, leaving her quite incapable of any rational or constructive reaction to the seeing of him, and she silently and roundly berated herself for having so failed.

But then, once these feelings had been worked through over and over again until she could scarce bring herself to think of them, something quite different began to emerge from deep within her, which had begun to make its' slow way into her conscious thoughts. In the first place she had been brave to have met him at all, and the meeting had not been her idea, but had rather been brokered by his wife, Rachel, who had herself called Isabella brave, in that which Isabella assumed had been the last hope that she might see her husband in a better light, and that they might somehow be able to put the whole sordid affair behind them. So it was not she who had in this respect failed, and Isabella expected that now or quite soon Rachel would begin divorce proceedings against him. She had liked Rachel, and none of this had been her fault, but that was a matter between them and was no longer any of her business. Having written her letter of accusation, most of that which occurred thereafter had been and was in any case now beyond her to control. The point was though, that she had met him, and he had not been the swaggering, self – confident monster that she had come to imagine him to be, but rather someone who had wept, and the tears had been real enough. He had said that he was sorry, and asked for her forgiveness for that which he had called his '*unforgivable act*', so what more, really, could he have done? There was after all no compensation which he could have offered her, and all parties to the meeting had known this, so by the same token what could Isabella really have said, other than to hurl pointless abuse at her assailant, and to what end would she have done so?

There was a question, which Isabella had begun to ask herself once she had regained something like emotional stability after the meeting, which was whether or not and given the way that the first meeting had gone, she should or could meet him again. Rachel, she supposed, would not now contact her; this had been her one chance to salvage her marriage, and how anyway could anyone continue to love or to live with a person who could do such a thing? So it had always been a slim chance, which had ended as it had, but Isabella had her 'phone number.

So all things were still possible, given that in a sense all parties to the meeting were now she assumed on borrowed time; how long, after all, would Rachel wait for the 'phone call, which in truth she would probably not even be expecting? It was also the case that she had done this alone, as she had dealt with the entirety of this horrible business. She had not sought or received any professional help or counseling after her ordeal, and Isabella lacked the social networks which other people of her age would likely have had; she had no best friend or friends upon whom she could have called for support or even comfort. After Jed she had become a sexual predator, using her young sexuality to prey upon and then do harm to the lives of those who might be called her victims, but that was over, now, and that had been different in any event; they had had a choice, she had not. Her newly found revulsion at the idea of having intimacy with any man under any circumstances was something which she must one day try to overcome, but that was something for the longer term. In the meantime she must try to once again walk abroad amongst people, and particularly amongst men, without the fear or loathing which had been so much a part of her life since the attack, and the feeling which now grew within her was that the meeting with Barnabas Overton had after all been a very significant step in this direction.

She must draw a metaphorical line in the sand now, not in the more commonly used sense that it be a line which she must not cross going forwards, but rather that it be a line behind her, and one behind which she must never again step. She must not go back to the darkest days, but would look forward now; she had met him and he had said that he was sorry, and that would be the place where she would start. She was not to blame, he was suffering now for his misdeeds as were the others, and Isabella became now determined that one day soon her own suffering would end, once and for always.

Our story now moves forward to Friday, and to a happier and certainly lighter situation, where Emily Cleves is preparing herself to go out for the evening, and is deciding what she should wear. Even here, however, a slight tension has arisen, and Emily is having a conversation with Will regarding her final choice of clothing, and in particular the length of the skirt which she has elected to wear, which does not in his opinion reach far enough toward the ground.

'Em, that's a bit short, don't you think?'

'I thought you liked me wearing it.'

'Yeah, but I'm not going to be there to see it, or to see you, or whatever. Anyway that's at home, you're going out among the general public.'

'I daresay you'd have me going out looking like a nun, or something…'

'There are degrees of decency between dressing like a nun and wearing that, that being in my opinion the lower limit, or rather the upper limit of decency.'

'It's okay, my love, I can take care of myself, and I promise to behave.'

'It's not you I'm worried about, it's all the men who are going to be, well, you know…I'm looking at this from a male perspective.'

'So you're worried about people like you…'

'Exactly...'

'Well I can't help people like you, and anyway not everyone's like you when it comes to me.'

'I'm talking in a more general sense.'

'Yes, I know, but look, you'll be dropping me of at a wine bar, and picking me up from the same wine bar about four hours later, so nothing's going to happen. I'm not going to be walking the streets, am I?'

'It's a bit more than a wine bar, they have dancing and such.'

'Okay club then, but I don't expect I'll be doing any dancing with anybody. Anyway Sands'll be there, and she will no doubt look totally stunning. Everybody's going to be looking at her.'

'I wouldn't be looking at her.'

'Yes, but you're you, and you're in love with me, and that's different.'

'I'm not talking about love. I mean of course I'm in love with you, but what I'm talking about is, well, you know...'

'Lust...Yes, I know.'

'Sexual desire; that kind of thing, and I don't think I'm the only male who has that.'

'You seem to have more than most.'

'Only when it comes to you...'

'You're very sweet, but I'll be fine.'

'And women dress to please themselves, right?'

'Exactly...'

'Well I'm not convinced...Why does she want to go out with just you, anyway?'

'I think she just wants to do some girlie bonding; talk about stuff, you know?'

'Last time we did any girlie bonding she turned up at a most inopportune moment, if you remember.'

'I'm not talking about that kind of bonding, as you very well know.'

'What does she want to talk about anyway, that she can't talk about when I'm there? What it feels like to try to kill yourself; that kind of deal?'

'I don't know, we just haven't been alone together for a while, you know?'

'I mean she can't want to talk about her love – life, since she doesn't seem to have one.'

'Apart from quite possibly being in love with you, my love...'

'Well that's not much of a love life, is it, and anyway you're not going to be talking about me all evening, that sounds a bit creepy.'

'No, of course we're not, and she knows she can't have you, in any case...Anyway you and JJ go out sometimes.'

'That's different.'

'Why?'

'Well for one thing I don't think either of has ever worn a short skirt, not as far as I can recall anyway. Couldn't she just come here? I could go out for a bit, go down the pub or whatever, then you could both be stark naked as far as it matters. In fact come to think of it that doesn't sound like such a bad idea...'

'William shut up, I really don't need to hear about your fantasies right now. Anyway it wouldn't be the same...'

'What, being naked you mean?'

'You know perfectly well what I mean. Anyway come on, we'd better get going.'

'This is your last chance to change into the habit...'

'What are you going to be doing with yourself all evening anyway?'

'Oh don't worry about me, you just go out and enjoy yourself; don't even think about me sitting here on my own.'

'If you're trying to make me feel guilty, try a bit harder. Anyway you've got Monty for company.'

'That's hardly the same, is it; supposing I want to discuss the meaning of life, or whatever?'

'We can discuss the meaning of life over breakfast tomorrow.'

'I might not feel like it then.'

'Well then we can discuss the meaning of something else, breakfast for example.'

'Come on then, your carriage awaits, except it's a Land Rover.'

'You certainly know how to show a girl a good time. So how do I look, really?'

'Devastating, that's the problem.'

They made their way to the Land Rover, she wearing heels which were also too high to meet with Will's approval, and Monty jumping with some assistance into the back of the vehicle, a place which he had made his own, as Will made ready to drive the short distance to the village Green to pick up the other member of the small party. In truth Will was not adverse to the idea of spending an evening on his own; he could not imagine life without Emily, and would not have tried to manufacture such a situation, but if the opportunity arose and the isolation was finite and brief in nature, then he would make the most of it. His indulgencies were simple at such times; he would languish in a hot bath for longer than was usual, and play his own particular favourite music at a louder than usual volume, and tonight he would await a telephone call to let him know that Emily was ready to return home. It had been suggested by Emily that she and Sandra take a taxi home, but Will had volunteered himself and his Land Rover, since tomorrow was not a working day, and the evening would likely be expensive enough in any case. His indulgencies would thus not include alcohol, but with this he was content, if his abstinence meant the safe return of his beloved.

For Isabella, the next step forward, and thus away from her imaginary line and back into that which might be called normal society would, she concluded, need to be practical in nature. It was all well and good beginning to establish something like emotional equilibrium, whereby she might finally begin to consign that which had happened to history and experience, but this must now be translated into something more tangible. Her school work at least had not suffered overmuch as a consequence of her trauma, because school work had always been easy for her, as far as it needed to be. Her teachers and in particular her form – mistress were beginning to apply some pressure in terms of her longer term education, in regard to her choice of university, and her father had raised the matter with her on more than one occasion. She therefore must, she concluded, be ready in every respect for this, and for her eventual departure from the family home; she could not embark on any kind of new life in any more nervous a condition than it was her natural tendency to be, which was in any case nervous enough. She must henceforth begin to once more use her young energy in a positive and constructive way, the main difficulty being how this might be achieved. After due consideration during the days after her meeting with Barnabas Overton, she concluded that a good first step, and leaving aside for now all matters of a sexual nature, would be to at least in other respects establish her life to the point where it had been before the assault, and a significant element to this had for a long time been her chess club. Here she could be in the company of men, within a tightly controlled and safe environment, whilst pursuing a favourite pastime of head to head intellectual combat with a given opponent. This would scarcely represent a full return to normality, but it was somewhere to begin, at least.

So it was that upon a certain evening, Isabella caught the omnibus into town, and walked once more into the so familiar surroundings of the club. She came now without disguise, pseudonym or any ulterior motive, but only to play the ancient game of chess which she still loved so much, and most significantly, she had come here alone.

The scene is now a small nightclub in the town, which boasted a quite intimate and sophisticated ambience, and a small dance – floor. It was not a club which would have been a regular haunt during former days, when the group of friends had been larger, but now two young women were sat together at a table against the wall, and in intimate conversation, the subject matter likely revolving around their few mutual friends, their families, and their lives in general. It would not in truth have been Emily's choice of venue, it being an establishment which by repute was a place where single young women might meet single young men, and visa - versa. Emily was not, after all, attempting to attract a mate, but Sandra had suggested the place and Emily was here and had dressed up for her friend, who, as Emily had speculated, did indeed look stunning, in her eyes at least. She wore a quite modest dark blue, partly sequined dress, which showed her tall, slim, hourglass figure to its' best advantage, and Sandra could do things with makeup the subtlety of which Emily had never acquired. They had arrived at the establishment at a little after nine o'clock, by which time the place was only moderately attended, most of the clientele usually arriving once the local public houses had closed for the night, which would be approximately two hours later. Amongst those patrons who had arrived here early, however, were two young men who stood at the bar, and who were doing their best not to be too obvious in their interest and intent towards the two young women, their interest and intent nevertheless being obvious enough to the subjects thereof. Emily was the first to broach the subject.

'Don't look now, but I think we're about to be approached.'

'Yes I know.'

'I'd give it another beer, maybe two…Christ I haven't done this for a long time, I feel about sixteen years old.'

'You were never picked up in a club, were you?'

'No, but it wasn't for want of people trying, back in the day, you know? So which one do you fancy, then?'

'Em, for heaven's sake…'

'I'd go for blondie if I were you.'

'Look, I didn't come here for that.'

Here was a statement which Emily did not for a moment entirely believe, or one at least which she believed could not be taken at face value. For better or worse, Emily was convinced that Sandra was looking for the fulfillment of a particular part of herself, something in which Emily had been partly instigative, and whilst it may not have been the entire point of the evening, it was certainly high on the list of possibilities. Emily had thus come prepared and happy to act as running – mate should the need or opportunity arise, and it appeared as though it had just arisen, or was about to do so.

'Well it looks as though you're going to get it anyway.'

The approach, which had in fact taken two further beers and about forty five more minutes, was predictable enough. One of the young men, who had perhaps drawn the shorter proverbial straw, came to the table and made himself known.

'Me and my friend over there couldn't help noticing that your glasses are almost empty, and wondered whether you would allow us to buy you another one.'

The young man had short, dyed white – blonde and heavily jelled hair, and a winning smile; his friend had longer, darker hair, but neither was unattractive on a superficial level, and both had clearly put considerable thought and effort into their appearance. Emily could not but be struck for a moment by the contrast between the two men and her Will, who put almost no thought or effort into his appearance whatsoever, and would doubtless have called them posers. In such moments as this, subtlety and perception are paramount, and Emily noted that the smile had been more directed at her than at her friend, and in any case it was Emily who acted as spokesperson.

'Sure, if you want, one Vodka and Tonic and a Bloody Mary….'

'Coming up…'

The young mans' temporary departure gave a moment for comment and consideration.

'Em, are you okay with this? I mean what about Will?'

'It's only a drink, Sands, so come on, enter into the spirit of things for Christ's sake, I don't want to do all the talking.'

Both men now approached, and apparently felt that they had earned the right to sit at the other two available seats at the table, upon which they now placed their beer bottles.

'Name's Mat, and this is Duncan.'

Mat with the dyed – blonde hair had made the masculine part of the introduction, and had sat opposite Emily.

'I'm Emily, and this is Sandra.'

Introductions completed and according to tradition it was now beholden upon the young men to make further conversation, and it was thus that Emily and Sandra learned that both young men lived locally, and both worked at the plastic – coatings factory, Duncan as an engineer and Mat in the administrative and promotion department. Duncan was apparently the more reticent when it came to the business of talking to newly – met young women, and since Sandra remained currently and characteristically unforthcoming, Emily for now continued to represent the feminine faction of the still somewhat awkward encounter.

'Sandra here's a brilliant research scientist, and I milk goats for a living.'

'You do what…?'

The question and tone thereof were not perhaps unreasonable, since anyone currently looking less like farmer or milk – maid than did Emily was hard to imagine.

'Well actually I make cheese; *'Jacob's Field'* cheese, which I don't suppose you've heard of.'

'Sure we have, or I have at least, it's brilliant cheese….So you make that?'

'Well yes….'

And so it was that for the next few moments the conversation revolved around the subject of cheese, and goat husbandry in general. Emily had done her initial best to play up Sandra's intellectual and academic prowess and to play down her own, but cheese it seemed was a more interesting and approachable subject than was scientific research, which was not the way it was supposed to have gone, but there it was. If it was true that Sandra's physical presence spoke loudly enough for itself, her intellectual and emotional self required somewhat more coaxing to find its' voice, and Emily would have to try harder to shift the focus away from herself towards her friend. What was the matter with them, anyway, could they not see that Sandra was without doubt the most attractive female in the place? Or then again, perhaps this was a mainly female perception, and for a moment Emily wondered whether Will had been right, and that the skirt had after all been a mistake. Perhaps after all men really were that superficial in their observation and perception of women, but anyway, since cheese was clearly such an interesting thing to discuss, she must try to change the subject, and to this end Duncan now came to the rescue.

'So, what do you research, anyway?'

Enter Sandra into the conversation, and Emily hoped that she would not blind them too much with her science; dazzling them with her beauty would suffice for the occasion, but at least she was up and running, and Emily could perhaps now take a verbal back seat.

With the remainder of the evening we need not concern ourselves overmuch, the meeting and departure being the significant elements to the process, and of Emily's departure we will hear shortly. Suffice to say that during the ensuing time, further alcoholic consumption made for more easy conversation, and eventually to dancing, as the establishment became full and the music more upbeat. Mat clearly had further designs upon Emily, whilst Sandra and Duncan found a quieter way to one another, but find their way they eventually did, at least as far as the dance floor. At some juncture, once the partnerships had been well enough established, Emily, who was by now feeling quite intoxicated, retired to the lady's room and 'phoned Will;

'Yeah, hi…'

'Okay lover - boy, it's rescue time, come and get me.'

'On my way…'

Sandra then entered the room and joined Emily by the wash - basins, where a brief conversation ensued, Sandra also by this time clearly feeling the effects of the several alcoholic drinks which she had by now consumed, and it was Emily who began the discourse.

'So how's it going, girlfriend?'

'It's going fine Em…He's nice, don't you think?'

'Doesn't matter what I think, if you're into him then go for it, girlie…'

'What about you?'

'I'll be leaving soon; Will's on his way.'

'You're going already? It can't be much after midnight.'

'I know, but I don't want the blonde one to get the wrong idea…'

'I think he's already got the wrong idea, if that's what it is. What are you going to say to him?'

''*Goodbye*', I expect. I'll deal with Mat, you concentrate on Duncan, only don't concentrate too hard. No analysis, that kind of thing…'

'Right….'

'Just go with it, you know, if you really do like him.'

'Go with it…Okay I can do that.'

'So you're going to be okay then?'

'I think so…I think I'll be fine, actually.'

'Good girl, just relax, okay?'

'Okay…I'll 'phone you tomorrow.'

'Whatever, just do tonight, the rest'll look after itself.'

In truth, Mat by now to some degree had Emily's sympathy. Not without some justification would he no doubt be surprised at her imminent and sudden departure, but Emily wanted to go home now, feeling that she had done enough, and that she had played the dummy – hand rather well. In the event the time that she and Sandra had actually had together had been limited, but this was that kind of place, after all, and they had both know this to be so before the evening had begun. Anyway she had done all that she could, and it was up to Sandra now to make what she would of the remainder of the night.

Upon entering the chess club, Isabella was met with muted and polite greetings from some of her fellow players and club members. The combination of her age and gender still made her unusual in this rarified and quiet setting, and eyes were raised from Chess boards as she walked to the desk which served as the focal point of the room, to make her presence officially known. During former times she had earned the respect of these people, most of whom had a lower chess rating than did she, although a quick glance at the roster told her that certain of them had overtaken her in this respect during her absence, and that she was now ranked fifth at the club, where before she had been second. All that anyone here knew of Dusseldorf was that Isabella had given good account of herself at international level when she had represented the club and her country, but aside from that it was as though nothing had changed, and this was how Isabella wished and indeed needed things to be. Only Richard Templeton, who remained the highest ranking player at the club, had known that anything had otherwise occurred there, although he did not know the nature of it, and had acted as her unquestioning guardian angel during her return journey. She was part disappointed and part relieved as she noted his absence on this particular evening. On the one hand he was the only person who would in any way remind her of that night, but nevertheless she found herself wanting to see him, and to feel the comfort and security of his familiar presence, whether or not he and she played chess together.

She was quickly in any case allocated an opponent, whom she beat quite easily, and during the evening she played a total of four games, two of which she won and two she lost, so she had done nothing to improve her rating as a result, but this had not really been the point of it. She was not yet in any case match – fit for playing over the board, this being a different discipline from playing in her on – line chess club, and she would need more evenings here to bring her game back to its' former level. But still, by the end of the evening and on the journey home, Isabella felt that she had achieved something far greater than victory at chess; she had travelled a short distance abroad on her own and without fear, and nothing bad had happened. She had taken the first tentative steps away from her imaginary line, and whatever her journey through life might be from here on, she had a strong sense that tonight the journey had begun.

Before we return to the nightclub, and to the conclusion of Emily's evening, and before we leave this particular Friday once and for all, we might take a moment to hear of something else which had happened earlier in the day, and at the delicatessen, where Meadow had received an air – mail letter. It had come from Los Angeles, and was in fact addressed to Keith, so she took it home with her at the end of the working day, Keith arriving home soon after her, by which time she was preparing the evening meal.

'Hi Love, good day..?'

'Yeah, okay, and we've agreed to take the weekend off, which is cool. I thought we might go for a ride somewhere on Sunday, if the weather holds.'

'That sounds nice….There's a letter for you on the table, I think it might be from Ash; looks like his handwriting anyway.'

'What….? What the hell's Ash writing a letter to me for? He's got our email address hasn't he?'

'Of course, and I don't know.'

Keith opened the letter, inside which was a smaller and rather disheveled piece of paper, upon which had been written some words in Ash's somewhat eccentric hand, the writing having faded over that which appeared to be long course of time. Keith read the brief letter, after which;

'Bloody hell, this is weird…'

'What's weird, sweet - pea?'

'Well, he's sent me some song lyrics. Listen to this;

'Hi Keith man, I found these words buried deep at home and I meant to give them to Tara to give to you but I forgot, so I'm sending them. It's something which I wrote, like decades ago, but it never made it into a song, so there's no tune. I thought maybe you might be interested in working on it with me. Maybe we could use it on Tara's next album; it's a bit dark, written in my angry – youth years, but anyway, whatever; see what you make of it. Maybe it needs a chorus? Or maybe it's crap, I don't know, I can't get my head around it. Anyway see what you think.

By the way your daughter's singing her soul out; I think she's finally getting it; I'm glad she came along. Say hi to Meadow and that witch daughter of yours,

Ash'

'That's ummm, interesting, isn't it?'

'I mean is he really asking me to co –write a song with him?'

'Sounds like it, doesn't it?'

'In the middle of a world tour…? Guy never stops, does he?'

'Well you know Ash...Anyway it's a good thing, don't you think?'

'Well yeah, I mean it's very cool, of course, it's just a bit....I don't know...'

'Weird...? So when was Ash anything else?'

'Sure, I know, but why didn't he just email the words to me?'

'I don't know, maybe the piece of paper's the thing, or the writing. Perhaps he wanted you to see the original version.'

'Yeah, could be. So do you think he's asking me to play guitar on Tara's next album?'

'Again, I don't know, but if the band really are breaking up after the tour then he might be looking for a guitarist, and we know he rates your guitar playing.'

'Sure....'

'You're really taken aback by this, aren't you, which isn't like you.'

'I'm amazed, actually.'

'You played guitar on his symphony, Keith, and Tara's getting herself established in the music world, so perhaps it really isn't so strange, when you think about it. Maybe Tara had some influence on the matter.'

'She didn't say anything to you though?'

'No, she didn't, but however it's come to be it's, well, good, isn't it?'

'I've never composed a tune for a song in my life.'

'You've never had any words before, but you have a unique style, everyone says so including Ash, and most of what you play is original, isn't it? Don't forget that Tara had never sung in public before there was Ash, and now look at her. Ash sees potential in people, Keith, and he's impulsive. He took his sister on tour on a whim, according to Tara, it's just how he is.'

'Sure, I guess....Anyway that's put a different slant on my weekend.'

'So what's the song about, anyway?'

'Here, read it. It's definitely dark....'

Meadow read the scrawled lyrics, which in places had been crossed through and re – written, whilst Keith washed brick – dust from his hands, and looked for distraction by taking over the preparation of food.

'Yes, I see what you mean...It doesn't have a title.'

'He must have been feeling pissed off when he wrote that. Looks like he wrote it in about ten minutes, judging by all the crossings – out, which is how he writes, I think.'

'Yes, it's probably the only version. I'd better photocopy it at the deli tomorrow, I case you lose it.'

'I don't lose things, do I?'

'Yes, you do....'

'Original words by Ash Spears...It's probably worth something, you know, I mean just as a piece of paper.'

'Probably, but that wouldn't occur to him, would it...'

'No, I suppose not.'

'I mean Ash is one of the foremost rock – music composers of all time...'

'That wouldn't occur to him either.'

'No...No, you're right, of course.'

'So are you going to do it then?'

'What...? Oh, sure, I mean I'll try, you know, it isn't every day, is it....? I've just, you know, got to get my head around the idea, that's all.'

'Yes, you do that, but first could you get your head around how many potatoes you're peeling?'

'Sorry...?'

'I think that's enough, Keith. Actually I think it was enough before you took over.'

'Oh, right, sorry, I wasn't concentrating. My mind was elsewhere, you dig?'

'Yes my love, I dig.'

Meadow smiled to herself. This was something which over the years with her man she had become used to digging, but on this occasion she supposed there was more than usual justification for his distraction, and anyway, this was definitely something to smile about.

We return now to the nightclub, the final scene in fact taking place outside the door on the street, where a light rain had begun to fall. Emily had by now fetched her coat, which Mat was rather surprised to see her wearing.

'Are we going somewhere? I live a couple of Streets away…'

'Well I'm going somewhere…Thanks for a nice evening but I should be getting home.'

A final parting smile from Emily, which apparently did not suffice as a farewell gesture, and he followed her to the door and thence to the street.

'So what gives, I thought we were getting on so well…'

'We were, but like I say, I have to go.'

'So what's this then, some kind of Cinderella syndrome, where everything goes to shit at midnight?'

'It's past midnight, and my lift's arriving in a minute, so please don't make this difficult.'

'It isn't me who's being difficult, and you were being…'

'What was I being?'

'Well, you know….Do you always lead guys on like that?'

'I'm not sure I was leading anybody on, and I really don't know what made you think I was.'

'Jesus, I don't believe this….So don't I even get a 'phone number?'

'Better not. Thanks again though, I did enjoy the evening.'

At this point and in timely manner a Land Rover pulled up across the street, and Emily crossed over somewhat unsteadily on her heels and got into the passenger seat, being glad that that particular conversation was over. Mat's parting gesture was to shrug his shoulders and raise his hands to the heavens, by which point the young man had Will's full attention.

'Who the fuck's that..?'

'He's just some guy, he's nobody…Take me home.'

'Looks like he's a guy with a problem, you want me to go and sort it out for him?'

'That won't be necessary, let's just go home…'

'Yeah, might mess up his hairstyle anyway, and he'd look rather stupid with his head stuck down a man hole.'

'Come on Will, forget him, let's just go.'

'Right…Where's Sands, anyway?'

'She's going home later, maybe…'

And so Will drove home, wondering perhaps more than he should how Emily's evening had been, whilst Emily was having trouble staying awake. It had been a long day, and she had been in a state of high alert for most of the evening, and had drunk more spirits than she was nowadays used to. On their arrival home, however, the young lady underwent something of a revival, and as Will closed the door behind them and was about to set the kettle to boil for a nightcap, she came up behind him.

'Thanks for the lift home, hero – boy.'

'You're welcome.'

'I hope you weren't too lonely without me…'

'I managed, and you should get some sleep.'

'Of course I should, but here I am all dressed up and nowhere to go, and gosh, look what a short skirt I'm wearing…'

Will's evening of sobriety had put him in relaxed frame of mind, but here and encapsulated within a single sentence was perhaps a different take on that which remained of the night, and he turned now to face his beloved.

'Which you only wore to please yourself, of course...'

'Of course, but if it has other consequences beyond my control then I'm hardly responsible for that, am I..?'

The hour was already late, and both had responsibilities in the morning, but for now those would be forgotten. Will had had reservations about Emily going out so dressed and to such a place with only the vixen for company, which he felt were quite justified, and he had not been happy with the situation, but there are times in peoples' lives when the benefits of any given action or event are not immediately obvious, at least not to all parties involved.

'He's the man who pays the piper,
but he never calls the tune.
He's waiting for the ending,
but it always comes too soon.
He's never at the scene of crime,
but always takes the blame.
He's a man of many faces,
but he always looks the same.

He's as happy as a sand – boy
when he cries himself to sleep.
He's looking for an answer
but he's going in too deep.
He's watching from the audience
when he's playing in the band.
His head is full of something
which he doesn't understand.

He eats in fancy restaurants
and lives on bread alone.
He stands accused of nothing
but never casts a stone.
He's a coat of many colours

but he's always dressed in grey.
He wants to tell you something
but he's nothing left to say.

He's wishing for forgiveness
for the ideas in his head.
But it's hard to wish for anything
when you wish that you were dead.
He's standing in the background
but he always spoils the view.
And when he's looking in the mirror
all he sees is you.'

Lyrics by Ashley Spears

Chapter 4

THE CALL OF THE SHE - WOLF

For Pandora Winterton, there were certain significant moments during the painting of any portrait. From the moment that the subject sits for the first time, and she stands before a blank canvas, a process begins which must end somewhere, the end having a particular significance of its' own. By now the subject will likely have been dismissed, perhaps for two or three days; they are no longer needed whilst the background is worked on, and the finer and final details seen to. Now it is just the painter and the painting, and between them they must decide when it is time to clean the brushes for the last time, and to seal the paints in their containers, the raw materials of the artists' work put away until the next time they are needed.

The end cannot be planned in the same way as can the beginning. There is no thought that the painting will be finished tomorrow, or the day after; the moment will come when it is ready, the image of someone immortalized and frozen in time, at a certain age of their lives, which will be presented to the world for as long as the painting exists. Look closely, walk away, roll a cigarette and study the painting from a distance and for a longer than usual time; is the essence there, has she got it right, and is it time to stop? This process may happen several times, each time, which may be separated by hours or sometimes days, bringing closer the moment when all is done, and when to return to the canvass would be a mistake. This subject is a Lord, and the painting will be hung not in somebody's lounge or bedroom, but in the grand dining room of a grand Manor House, the next in an historical sequence, the latest in the line of ascendance. This had made no difference to the way that the portrait had been painted, but there was significance to the matter nonetheless, and there was perhaps a longer than usual pause before the final end. Somewhat world – weary eyes, with a hint of amusement at the whole business of life which underlay the serious matter of his having been a person of significance during his life; a man of substance, who had done his best for his family; for his wife, for his gentle and one remaining son who would one day inherit his title, and for his sometimes wayward and sometimes difficult daughter, a lover of women and of the painter herself, which was a matter apparently quite unbeknownst to the subject. When the end came, Pandora thought that she had captured the essence of him well enough, and that it was a good painting.

She would go home now for a few days. She needed to attend to some personal matters and just to be at home, to rest, and perhaps to release some tension and give vent to the less well controlled side of herself in the bars and clubs of Brighton, but she would return here very soon. She had other commissions, but these would wait, for there was someone else now to be painted. The next in the blood – line and a young woman this time, whom Pandora had come to know quite well and certainly intimately during her tenure at the Manor House, but first she needed to rest, and to gather herself, and to lose herself in decadent indulgence as she had done so often before; to live her other life.

Before she left, however, there was one more significant moment to be got through, for the subject, his Lordship, had not so much as glanced at the painting since its' beginning, and it was time now for him to see the image of himself which she had created. Pandora put out her cigarette, cleaned her tools, took a shower and made herself ready for the last part of the process, which was perhaps the most significant part of all.

If Percival had hoped that this time of his life would be characterized by a state of emotional tranquility and at least stability, then he would perhaps best summarize his efforts of achieving this condition as disappointing. He had, after all, cast his love for Louise to the four winds, by writing her an email loudly and definitively proclaiming the end to their relationship, and so far as he was concerned that had been a done thing. He had made his decision and would live with the consequences thereof, and there was an end to it. So then there had been Sally, who seemed now to be instigating quite radical changes to her own life, but this was something which he thought he could deal with easily enough, the changes being of a more practical and financial rather than emotional nature. She could bring her undoubtedly successful career to a sudden and for him at least an unexpected halt if she so wished, and enter the more uncertain state of self – employment, without it otherwise affecting their lives together. Her motivation for so doing was still unclear to him, particularly in regard to himself, but these were her decisions to make, were they not? She was a woman, after all, and women were far more acutely and instinctively aware of their emotional and general state of being than he could ever be; Sally knew her own mind, and it was in the end her mind to know.

But then, upon a certain morning, Louise had knocked at his door, which had been a portent of something which had thrown his man – made and so well – considered and well - laid plans into a state of utter chaos. Of a sudden the four winds had changed direction, and seemed now to meet at a vortex, or whirlwind, at the very centre of which stood he.

She had driven him to the coast, they had drunk bad coffee and smoked too many cigarettes at a seaside café, and walked on the cold and otherwise deserted beach together, throwing beached driftwood and other detritus for Lulu to fetch back from the waves, and then she had driven him home. They had not talked of love, or heavy matters. They had not kissed passionately by the waters' edge, or declared that they would never part again; this was not the stuff of romantic novels, but then that had never been their way. That which they felt for one another could not be put into words, and so could not be spoken of in any way which would make it possible for them to better understand. It just was, and they just were, and she had his soul as he had hers, and she had told him so, and by the time he once again closed the door of his home in the late evening he knew this to be the truth of it, however difficult or inconvenient that truth may be. It wasn't part of the plan, after all; the plan lay now like so much used and now obsolete paper on his desk as he sat down to drink the now cold cup of coffee, which he had been drinking when she had walked through his door at the beginning of this day of days. She had driven away in her borrowed car, and they had not arranged to meet again, nor even that they would 'phone one another. They had not made love, or even kissed; she was not asking him to be unfaithful. That which she asked of him went far beyond mere faithfulness; she had asked nothing of him, but everything of him; whether or not he could in the end live without her, and for what price would he betray his soul, and she had said all of this without words.

Percival finished his cold coffee and closed his eyes for moment, perhaps against the glaring light of realization of what a fool he had been, and this he could see this just as well, if not better, with his eyes closed.

Pandora had decided to wait; she would sleep one more night at the Manor House, and would fetch his Lordship in the morning. She wished him to see his portrait in its' best light, and the light was better in the morning, and she wished for one more night alone with the painting. Victoria would likely not come tonight; there was a greater significance to her coming now, and she no longer came every night. So Pandora spent the last night of her current tenure at the Manor alone, and in the morning she left her accommodation, and walked through her internal door and into the older parts of the Manor House, something which she had rarely done, and went in search of her subject. She first came upon Molly, who informed her that she would find his Lordship in his study under the grand staircase, so here did she knock gently upon the door, and this for the first time.

'Come....'

'Good morning your Lordship.'

'Ah, Good morning, Pandora, to what does one owe the pleasure...?.'

'The painting is finished.'

'Oh, right, well I'd better take a look at it then, don't you think?'

In Pandora's considerable experience, the first viewing of a newly completed painting was done in different ways. Sometimes whole families would gather around a portrait of a child or grandparent, or man and wife would stand together for the unveiling of her portrait, for it was usually she who had been painted, he perhaps wishing to capture her in her young beauty, and rarely had Pandora painted two people together. In any case however it was done, Pandora would make herself absent from the moment; this was private affair, and her part in it was over. First reactions were also different; they might be muted or excited to any and varying degrees, but in any case in this instance his Lordship came alone, and Pandora went outside and rolled herself a cigarette. She knew her subject well enough to expect no extreme reaction, and she also knew that Lord Michael had only with reluctance and out of a sense of duty to his line of ascendency had his portrait painted at all, so these were somewhat nervous moments for her, as she awaited his first words. After only a few moments he came out and stood beside her, looking not at her but at the quite distant views of the village which could be glimpsed through the trees which grew on the land which he called his land, and she followed his gaze.

'I believe we owe you a final payment; I'll see to the transfer this morning.'

'Thank you.'

On the scale of reactions this was about the most muted that she had yet encountered, and she looked for any other signs of his pleasure or displeasure at her work, but none was forthcoming, his face remaining deadpan and unreadable.

'So I suppose you will be leaving us now, at least for the present.'

'Yes, I'll go immediately.'

'And how will you go?'

'I'll take a bus to the railway station. I've been unable to arrange for anyone to collect the painting today, so it'll be taken away for framing tomorrow, if that's alright?'

'Yes, of course, just tell me who's coming and tell them to bring some means of identification, we wouldn't want anyone making off with it, would we?'

'No, of course...His name's Paul Summersdale.'

'Very good then, we will expect his arrival tomorrow… Anyway let me pay for a taxi to the station, shall we say in one hour?'

'That would be perfect, thank you.'

'And when will you yourself return, do you suppose?'

'In a few days I would think. I believe Victoria is at work today so I'll call her to see when would be good for her to start.'

'Yes, that would be for the best….I hope you find her a good subject.'

'I'm sure I will.'

'I believe that you two have become close during your time here.'

Which took her rather by surprise, and now, aside from her uncertainty as to his feelings regarding the painting, she was left to wonder how much he in fact knew of her relationship to his daughter.

'Yes...Yes, we have become friends.'

'Indeed...Anyway, I will leave you to your preparations for departure.'

He left her to her cigarette and to her speculation, and Pandora went about packing her few possessions into her suitcase. Her easel, paints and brushes she would leave here; she would not need them before her return. Within the allotted time she was ready, and she carried her small suitcase to the front door as the taxi arrived, and she closed the great front door behind her as she descended the steps. Her progress was arrested, however, by the door being opened behind her, upon the threshold of which stood his Lordship, who looked ready to speak but did not do so, so she spoke for them both.

'Well, goodbye then....I'll see you soon.'

'Indeed...The taxi is paid for.'

'Thank you.'

'I believe it is I who should be thanking you; it's a very good painting.'

He smiled now for the first time since he had seen the portrait, his expression changing completely.

'Good...That is to say I'm so glad you're pleased.'

'Yes, I believe that one's essence has been well captured, and please forgive my initial reaction. It is not often that one sees a window into ones' own soul, so to speak, or perhaps better say a reflection thereof, and it takes a moment, you know?'

'Yes, of course.'

'Well, there it is then.'

'Indeed.'

A final, parting smile and the door was closed once again. The driver put her suitcase in the trunk and Pandora took a back seat. As the car drove through the iron gates, Pandora was left with a somewhat unexpected sense of relief. In large part she supposed that this was due to his last words to her, which had been important words, but she was not in any case sorry to be leaving, at least for a short while. Aside from the heaviness of the commission, and the grandeur of the setting in which it had been painted, her emotions had been stirred in other ways by someone whom she had not painted, but she soon would. Soon Victoria Tillington would be sitting where her father had sat, and she would stand before another empty canvass, and upon that she would in a sense paint her feelings, and this time it would be different.

We now once again enter the bus which is hearth and home to Keith and Meadow. The bus would never run again; it no longer had wheels, and the engine had been removed some years ago, the space under the vehicles' hood now being used for storage, since storage space was always at a premium in such confined and limited accommodation. Keith had been quite ingenious in constructing a shower and toilet beside the bus, and had built shelves and cupboards inside wherever there was wall – space, so in fact the family had wanted for nothing in the provision of its' always modest needs. Common law man and wife had at times considered moving to larger, more conventional and perhaps more convenient accommodation, particularly when the children had been growing up, but they loved their bus, and they awoke each morning in isolated splendour amidst woodland and fields, and now the birds were once again in full song, and they awoke each day to the dawn chorus, which to both seemed to be the most wonderful of sounds. So they had not moved, and for the most part they were glad of it. In any case on this particular evening there was a knock upon their modest door, which Keith answered, and there before him in the by now semi - darkness of the evening stood somebody who he would not have expected, since she had not been here before.

'Hi…Hello Keith…'

'Sandra, this is a pleasant surprise, come in.'

'Thanks.'

Sandra climbed the two steps into the bus, and for the first time looked around the place which Emma must know so well. Meadow put down her needlework and stood up to greet the visitor.

'Hello Meadow.'

'Hi Sandra, you are most welcome. Can I make us all some herbal tea?'

'Yes, thanks, that would be nice.'

Keith put the kettle to re - boil on the hob, and Sandra was offered a seat at table.

'So, to what do we owe the pleasure of this visit?'

'Well, in the first place I want to say thank you, for helping when I was, you know, sick.'

'We didn't do very much,' said Keith 'we just took Basil to the hospital, or rather I did.'

'Which helped Emma, of course, when she must have needed it, but it's more than that, I mean thanks for showing so much concern, when, well, I really don't think I deserved it.'

'Everyone's deserving of concern, aren't they, Keith.'

'Sure….'

'Even stuck – up bitches like me, yes?'

A rather direct and provocative question so early in the discourse, which Meadow deflected somewhat by pouring tea for them all, leaving any response to Keith, who was for a moment also lost for words. This had in fact been Tara's quite vocal take on the lady in question, but perhaps fortunately Tara was not present at this particular encounter.

'I don't think anyone here ever accused you of being that.'

'Well perhaps not, but you would be forgiven if you had, is the point, and well, I also came here to say sorry, actually.'

'You've done nothing to be sorry for, we're sure.' Said Meadow

'I think I have, actually, at least I do feel sorry, for well….I mean the thing is, I also want to say that I'm happy that Emma and Basil are together. They're great together, anyone can see that, it's just taken me a long time to realize it. Much too long, in fact...'

'She's your younger sister,' said Meadow 'so you would naturally be concerned for her, in all regards.'

'Everyone being deserving of concern, and all.' Said Keith

'Well, perhaps, but anyway I hope you won't think too badly of me because of….Well, because of everything.'

'No, of course we won't, will we Keith.'

'Not at all...We take people as we find them around here, consider any past misdemeanors be they real or imagined to be forgotten….Water under the bridge and all that, let bygones be bygones, that's what I say, never one t…'

'Yes, I think we get the idea, Keith. So anyway, you're back at university now then?'

'Yes, well back to the research, anyway, which is the reason that I've been living at home recently, of course. I've got a few more weeks yet, they've let me extend the project for a bit longer, which is good, in a way.'

'Make up for lost time, sort of thing.' Said Keith

'Well partly that, yes.'

'That's good then….So why did you try to top yourself?'

'Keith, for goodness sake…'

'Sorry, I thought we were having a 'cards – on – the – table' kind of conversation, talking about stuff, you know? No point in beating about the b…'

'Keith dearest, do shut up. Sorry, Sandra…'

Keith was clearly now enjoying himself, and indeed was doing so a little too much for Meadow's comfort, at least a part of her discomfort stemming from the fact that she wanted to burst out laughing, and was having difficulty maintaining a serious demeanor, despite the serious turn that the conversation had just taken. There was little, after all, more serious that a young person trying to take their own life, but the desire to laugh was there, nonetheless, for which Meadow quietly berated herself, whist also berating Keith, who would know of her discomfort. If the fact that Sandra had come here at all was surprising, then the conversation having become so intense so soon was more surprising still; she had hardly so much as spoken to either of them before, and now there was this.

'It's okay,' said Sandra 'it's a fair enough question, and we are being honest, I suppose.'

'My point exactly...So why did you do it, then?'

'Honestly, I don't know…I mean I hadn't intended it, not really, but I sort of get these black moods, you know? Times when whatever I do just seems so pointless, and worse than pointless, actually…I just can't see any good in myself, and well, I don't know how else to say it, really. I don't remember very much about the night that it happened, other than, well, it must have been worse than usual, I suppose. I went to see Will and Emily, and after that it's all a bit of a blank; a complete blank, in fact.'

'So have you always had these black moods?' Said Meadow

'Yes, I suppose so, although I think they've been getting worse lately, over the last couple of years or so. To be honest I don't think I've ever been what you might call a happy person.'

'So have you, like, never been happy then? Said Keith

'Yes…Yes of course I've been happy, sometimes.'

'So what kind of thing makes you happy, would you say?'

'I don't know, I mean life isn't really like that, is it? It's a state of mind, I realize that, and everyone's supposed to be happy on birthdays and at Christmas or whatever, and sometimes I am, and sometimes I'm not, so the circumstances don't seem to make any difference. Anyway, look, you don't want to hear all of this, it really isn't what I came here for.'

'It was me who raised it,' said Keith 'and whatever help we can be we will gladly be, won't we, Meadow?'

Better, Keith.

'Yes, of course we will.'

'I mean the thing is,' continued Keith 'that you start off from a good place, if you know what I mean.'

'What do you mean, actually?'

'Well, you're good looking for a start. Some people are like, really ugly, you know? Short, stubby legs, face like the back of a bus, that kind of deal. I mean imagine carrying that through life.'

Meadow was now unsure whether Keith was on the whole being serious or not, but in any case Sandra laughed, lightly, which gave Meadow license to do likewise.

'Well, I suppose there's that, at least, or so I'm told anyway, but it's more than that, isn't it?'

'Yeah, well there's the fact that you're clever, I mean not everyone can do rocket science or whatever it is that you do. I can't even add up the grocery bill.'

More gentle laughter, before;

'What I mean is, being attractive is not just about looks, is it, it's about being a whole person, and well, being somebody that people can love, I suppose.'

'People love you,' said Meadow 'there's Emma, for one, and I know you're good friends with Will and Emily.'

'Yes, Will and Emily....People do love me, I suppose, but I sometimes think that they love me in spite of myself, rather than because of myself.'

'I'm sure that's just a perception.'

'Sure it is,' said Keith, 'and anyway that's true of everyone to an extent, there aren't many angels around. Everyone has good things and bad things about them, and everyone knows that instinctively, the same way as they know they aren't perfect themselves, if they think about it. People love other people because they want to, and need to, actually, the same as they need to be loved in return, that's the way we are, and it's how everyone gets by. People need you, you dig, and you have to try to be there for them, and love them back. At least that's how I see it.'

'I think that's a very nice way to see it.'

'I mean sure, people blow each other up, or whatever, but that's not people, it's politics, and it really isn't anything personal. We're told who the enemy are, and told to go kill them, or somebody kills them on our behalf, but if we actually met them we'd make them a cup of tea, or whatever.'

'Keith, I think we're drifting off subject, rather.'

'Yeah, sorry, but you know what I mean. Anyway you're still young, you know, and you can't expect to get everything right yet, or get to grips with yourself, it isn't what young people do. That's why they take drugs and such, just to make it through all the confusion. I mean I took a load of drugs when I was young, and got myself in some horrible conditions, and I used to get pissed and beat people up, which was, you know, dead against what I actually believed, or what I eventually became. I mean it's still work in progress, and always will be, I suppose, but I think I've got a better handle on things now, so it'll come, you know, you've just got to make it through the hard years.'

'And for that I need other people, yes?'

'Sure...No one can do it alone.'

'I take drugs, the difference is that mine are prescribed.'

'Yeah, you need to kick those....'

'I intend to, really I do.'

'Better to go out and get wasted sometimes, but don't do that alone either. Phone a friend, and you know, you can always come here if the walls start closing in. The thing to remember is that you're as good as anyone else, and as bad as anyone else, and no one at the end of the day is anyone special, we're all just ordinary people getting through all the crap that life throws our way, the best way we can.'

There was silence for a moment on the bus. Meadow was looking with something like admiration and in any case love at her man, who had in the end taken on the matter of their unexpected visitor better than she could have done, and given her the benefit of his take on the world, which she had always known to be a good take. Sandra was for a moment lost for words, and she said as much.

'I don't know what to say really.'

'Well then,' said Meadow 'best not say anything, but you really are always welcome to come here.'

'Sure,' said Keith 'I mean we've got one sister so we might as well make it the full set. You ever been on the back of a fast bike?'

'No, actually...'

'Well next time you start feeling hacked off, call over on a weekend morning and I'll take you out for a ride, that usually blows some cobwebs away,'

'I'll remember that, thanks. Anyway I suppose I should be going.'

'So soon..?' said Meadow 'You're welcome to stay for a while if you'd like to.'

'I've said what I came to say, and I've got some data to write up for tomorrow.'

'You will come back and see us though, yes?' Said Meadow

'Yes…Yes, sure, I'll come back, and I mean thank you, really, for making me so welcome, I hadn't really expected that, and I don't know why.'

'Well then take it as read, we've enjoyed your company, haven't we, Keith.'

'Sure we have, brief though it has been.'

Sandra stood up to leave, a final, parting smile and she was gone into the evening.

'Poor girl…' Said Meadow

'Yeah, well I hope we helped.'

'I'm sure we did, especially you, actually. You even made her laugh, and I don't suppose she's done much of that lately. I mean I really can't imagine what it must be like to have just attempted suicide, for your life to seemed so bad that you just wanted it to end, it doesn't bear thinking about.'

'Well, end of the day it's up to her to get past that. I suppose some people are just made unhappy, it's in the genes, or whatever.'

'Yes, I suppose so. Anyway I'm tired, think I'll retire.'

'I'll be right there.'

'I wonder if Emma knew she was coming.'

'No idea, I guess they must talk to each other. Is Emma here tonight?'

'I think so, yes. Should we say anything to her, do you think?'

'Well, we'll have to let her know that big sister's called 'round for tea, but I don't suppose we have to go into details.'

'No, best not…'

'I wonder if she's still *'virgo intactus'* so to speak, Sandra I mean.'

'Well I didn't think you were talking about Emma.'

'Not with Bas around. Like father like son, eh?'

'Yes well anyway, what's virginity got to do with anything? Why are you so interested in whether she's a virgin or not?'

'Well, sexual fulfillment, you know? It's a big part of growing up, don't you think? Personal development and all…'

'It was a big part of your growing up.'

'And de facto yours too, since as I recall you were there at the time.'

'Anyway, as I believe I have said before, how would I know whether she's still a virgin, and we don't even know whether she was in the first place.'

'I expect she was in the first place, most people are.'

'Yes, well anyway, I'm to bed.'

Meadow yawned, kissed her man for no particular reason, and made for the bedroom.

Sandra Fox walked up the lane in the now complete darkness. There was no moon, so she used her mobile telephone as a torch to get to the main road. That had been an interesting hour of her life, and Emma had been right; despite everything they had welcomed her with open arms, or open minds, anyway, and despite everything she felt that she had just made two new friends, which was a happy thought.

After Emily had left the nightclub, Mat had returned thereto in intemperate spirit, his clear and particular designs upon Emily having been so quickly and unexpectedly frustrated, and the evening had not gone so well from then onwards. Of the two young men, Mat was clearly dominant, and he voiced his displeasure and desire to leave, and so they had left within the hour, Sandra leaving Duncan her telephone number with two of the numbers reversed. Her evening had been pleasant enough, but nothing more. They had kissed goodnight, she had refused his invitation to come home with him, but said he could telephone her; in the end she had had no wish to see him again. But still, she had been out for the night, which had been the important thing, and she supposed that she had enjoyed herself in a quite superficial way. The next day she had 'phoned Emily, who had voiced her disappointment but understanding that Sandra had gone home alone; she hadn't particularly liked either of the young men either. On the night in question Sandra had found her own way to fulfillment, and had awoken the next morning with a hangover, but a feeling that life at least had the potential to get better, even if that potential had yet to be realized.

On this night she turned off her bedside light and closed her eyes with a sense that it had been a good day, and that every day which separated her from her death – wish was a step nearer to happiness, or at least some kind of contentment. She had made her peace with Keith and Meadow, better, she had made them her friends, and would try to do the same with Basil when next she saw him, which would no doubt please Emma. She concluded that being in their company even for so short a time had been better than any therapy that money could have bought. Keith had played the buffoon, for such seemed to be his way, but in the end there had been wisdom in his words, and meadow had a presence which had been as a balm to her soul, and she had liked both of them more than she had expected to. Tomorrow would be another day, and for Sandra Fox each day that she lived was a victory over herself, and today she had left her pill – bottle unopened, and this for the first time.

The question was obvious and simple enough. Percival had made fresh coffee and poured himself a Scotch, after which he took a shower and put on his dressing – gown, then he sat at his desk whilst Lulu settled in her comfortable place in front of the fireplace, which this evening contained no fire. He had not spoken to Sally today, and she had probably 'phoned, and had probably wondered why he had not answered. He had a mobile telephone somewhere, although he was not certain where, which would have made him available to everyone at all times, but Percival had no wish to be so available, and Sally knew this well enough. At some point during the late evening his house telephone rang, and it was almost certainly her, 'phoning from a hotel room somewhere, but he let the 'phone ring until it became silent again. What could he say to her, after all? *'Oh, hi Sal, guess who came to see me today, and guess what we did…'* No, he couldn't do that, but nor could he lie to her, so best put some thinking time and at least some sleep between now and that conversation. He it was who had contacted Sally after their long estrangement, and thus had put a lit match to something which had burned ever since. He would have settled for friendship, or at least some kind of reconciliation, but her love and desire for him had burned stronger than that, and he had walked willingly into the flames. And now she was about to undo a part of her life, at least in part to keep that flame alive, and he could not condone the doing of that, could he, not now. So, the question was obvious and simple enough; what to do now? Louise would not expect him to 'phone her in some kind of lovers' haste; she at least understood that it would be more complicated than that. If she were to have him again then it must be to the exclusion of all others, and she knew full well that he may never contact her again. They were damaged goods, he and she, who might contrive somehow to put the best parts of themselves together to form something like a whole relationship, but that would not be an easy thing, and she knew that there was an easier way for him.

So then, what to do? Put the day down to experience; call it an unasked for aberration and don't mention anything to Sally. Yes, that would be a possibility, of course; tell her one day long into the future, and reassure her that nothing had happened, really, and that he had not even come close to leaving her as a consequence. Carry on as though nothing had happened, stay on the by now well – trodden path and don't stray into the wildwood, where lay danger and uncertainty.

And yet, on the other hand, was this not how he had always lived his life? He had taken risks in his younger years which saw to it that he had become quite wealthy, but he could equally well have lost all of his money, as others had done, and it had had all happened under and through the influence of cocaine and alcohol, and he had been lucky, really, to survive himself. He could have left the bridge one night in his more recent past and left Rebecca behind to her fate, either to kill herself or be killed, and so could have avoided confrontation with the people from the west country, and thus very nearly being killed himself. He could have thrown the airline tickets to the Far East in his waste – bin, and then he would never have been to the beautiful island, and never met the beautiful assassin who had probably saved his life, but he had gone, when in his heart he had known the risks. He could have walked away from his meeting with Tony Blackman, or he could not have gone there at all, and having done so he could have left the beast undisturbed, but instead he had made the telephone call to Eddie Michel, and unleashed his particular brand of hell and damnation upon those whom he perceived as being his enemies, with no real idea as to how that would end. Eddie had done his work well, but it had been perhaps the biggest risk of all, and who knew whether it was over. Two days ago he had received a letter, or better say note, via private courier, which had read; *'It's over, you win. Call the dog off.'* So he had 'phoned Eddie Michel and arranged the final pay – off, and Tony Blackman would return to his burgled home and his dead house – plants, his passport, money and wallet intact, as Percival had as good as promised that they would be. Percival had won the battle, but would be foolish indeed to assume that the war was over.

And so, what was he, really? He was older now and perhaps had less stomach for the fight. He had told himself that what he wished for now was a quiet life; a place to do his writing and to let his life catch up with itself, but the way that he continued to live went so far against this philosophy that perhaps after all he was only fooling himself. And then had come Louise, just when he thought that that part of himself at least had found safe haven. He had in a sense given himself to Sally, and in so doing had cast his soul into the wilderness, where Louise had found it. So sure, he could stay on the path, and perhaps he would, but the she - wolf was howling now from the wildwood, and for how long could he resist her call? So this then was the so obvious and so simple question; the answer, however, lay somewhere deep within himself, in a place whence he had not been for the longest time, but it was to there that he must now go, and this at least Percival understood well enough.

Chapter 5

LOVE AND DECEPTION

Sally Parsons returned home early upon a certain Friday evening, having travelled that day from the west – country via the London offices of her bank, where she had been called to a meeting of the banks' directors. She first went to her house, unpacked her things and took a shower before walking to the cottage down the lane, where she found Percival about his writing. The two had had a quite brief and quite nondescript telephonic conversation the evening before, and although both looked forward to seeing the other, on this occasion both had particular reasons not to do so.

'Hi, love, it's me, finally.'

'Hi…Good week at work..?'

'Yes, it was okay.'

'Coffee….Wine…?'

'Nothing for me, thanks. Look, I'm really sorry but I have to go out again, I'm running late, in fact.'

'Oh, right…Meeting someone?'

'Polly. She 'phoned and wants to see me.'

'No doubt to discuss her matrimonial issues.'

'Yes, no doubt.'

'Right, well I'll see you later, then. Will you come back here?'

'Sure, as long as it's not too late.'

'Well, whatever.'

They kissed, and she left, and something was off. Clearly she had not yet given her notice at the bank, that she would have told him, but perhaps still the right moment had not presented itself, and Percival felt some relief at the lack of news in this regard. Percival had made the decision not to tell her about his day with Louise, at least not yet, but beyond that he had made no firm plans as to how to proceed. The horns of his dilemma had grown, now, and he was still at a loss as to quite how to order his emotions, and indeed his life in general, but this he had not expected. Sally was behaving in uncharacteristic fashion; usually and particularly having been away she would have slept with him, and woken him up regardless of the hour, and in any case an evening with Polly was unlikely to see her return late. Still, perhaps she was tired, or something, and perhaps he was reflecting his own state of being onto her; his life had after all changed since he had last seen her. For the first time he must deceive her, or at least not tell her the whole truth, or anything like the whole truth. She was the person to whom he was currently the closest, and yet she was the last person that he could speak honestly to; an unfaithful lover who had not been unfaithful, but he could not bare his soul to her, as lovers will do. His soul, after all, was quite elsewhere. Louise had it now, and Percival had woken up this morning to the blatant realization that with it she had taken his love, stolen away like a thief in the night, although it had all happened during the broad daylight, and he had scarce noticed the going of it. So he must deceive, but deception can at times go both ways, and sometimes the deceiver may also be deceived, for in a way, during their brief encounter, both had lied to the other.

Earlier in the day, Sally had made a telephone call.

'Hello...'

'Hi Polly, it's Sally.'

'Oh, Hi Sal; everything okay..?'

'I'm in London, coming home tonight.'

'Right...'

'Look, I was wondering whether we could meet up this evening.'

'Ummm, sure, I can do that. Where and at what time?'

'How about The Dorchester, eight o'clock..?'

'Sure, I'll be there. Is everything alright?'

'I'm not sure, really, but I'll explain everything later.'

'Oh, okay, see you this evening, then.'

After her brief visit to the cottage down the lane, Sally went home and made final preparations for the evening, and whilst doing so she 'phoned for a taxi. This would mean further delay, and she would be late for the rendezvous, but she needed alcohol and there was no way that she would be driving home; that which she needed as much as a drink was somebody to talk to, and she and Polly had become closer of late, and presently she could think of no one else.

'Keith, look at this.'

'What's that, my beloved?'

This was somewhat earlier during the same evening on the bus, Meadow having just returned from the delicatessen to find Keith already at home. During the day one of her regular customers from outside the village had brought her a copy of a particular upmarket monthly glossy magazine, which concerned itself with country matters, and which he supposed might be of interest to her, and he was indeed correct in his supposition. Meadow handed Keith the magazine, which was open at the page in question, and the following is that which he read, the article having been embellished by scenic photographs of an English village. The author of the article was a certain Georgina Hamilton

'A Village which keeps its' secrets.

There's something odd about the village of Middlewapping. Located amidst open, fertile farmland, woodland and heath, the village has existed in one form or another at least since the reign of

King Henry VIII, who, as history tells us, bestowed the first Lordship upon the house of Tillington, and it was then that the first parts of the Manor House were built by the first Lord of that name. And where there is a Manor House there must also be a village, to provide accommodation for those once employed to serve the Lord and his Lady, and this it seems is as far back as the history of the village which is now known as Middlewapping can be traced, though its' roots may be set much further back in time.

The quintessentially quaint and predominantly white – painted and black – beamed houses which nowadays constitute the village were built in the seventeenth century, and more or less, it seems, they were all built at the same time, give or take a few years, and to walk through the village now is to be struck by the sense of history which pervades the place like an aura, and oozes from every not quite upright wall, and every not quite level rooftop. Rarely indeed does one find so fine, complete and well preserved an example of period – England, and for a long time people have come here just to look, and to take photographs, and perhaps to drink a pint of good ale at the village pub, which nestles to one side of the village Green. The pub itself is a piece of history, having once been stabling for the Manor House horses, and one can still almost sense their equine presence behind the smoke which nowadays emanates from the huge, open fire. In a more modern establishment one would expect the place to carry a health warning, but here it sort of fits, and anyway nobody seems to complain.

So what then of this village, and what makes it so unique? There are after all older buildings in our fair land, and finer Manor Houses, and the 'B' road which takes its' share of commuter traffic to the town, and which forms the fourth side of the square which surrounds the Green sees to it that there are quieter villages, but there is, it seems, something special about this particular piece of English heritage.

Everyone, of course, who now lives on these islands and quite a few who live beyond it have heard of the 'Middlewapping meteorite', which landed here one fine summers' night some three years ago. It is, after all, about the most famous piece of extra – terrestrial rock in the islands of Britain, but other than the extraordinary nature of the rock there is nothing essentially mysterious about the matter, and the fact that it landed nearly at the dead – centre of the batting square of the village cricket pitch is no more than a matter of pure chance, all be it extraordinary chance. What beggars belief, however, is that nothing has since been done about it. Surely such a rare piece of outer – space should long since have been behind glass in some museum or scientific institution, or at least be protected in some way, but there it sits, in the middle of a village cricket pitch, for all to see and to touch. Since its' landing, an ongoing battle has it seems ensued between certain scientific organizations and the local and regional councils as to what should be done, but other than the cricket pitch having long since been declared an area of special scientific interest, no agreement has been reached nor any solution found. The village is, in the first place, a conservation area, and the buildings and thus it seems the land between them are listed and cannot be disturbed, nor can their use be changed, and digging up the cricket pitch even in the interest of science is apparently not yet an option. This, one feels, could only happen in England; our beloved national summer sport must go on, regardless of the inconvenient arrival of such an uninvited interloper. The powers that be in the local and regional councils are in any case it seems quite happy for the rock to stay exactly where it is. What better way, after all, to attract people to the village and keep the place on the map than for it to boast its' very own meteorite, and this it was which first brought Middlewapping into the wider public eye.

Since then, however, other things have happened in the village which have only added to its' infamy. On the opposite side of the Green from the public house stands the ancient village church, which is older than the rest of the village, and which in common with so many other rural places of Christian worship has now been deconsecrated. This church, however, was not bought by a developer and turned into a family home preserving many of the original features. Oh no, nothing so mundane or ordinary for Middlewapping; this church was purchased by none other than Ashley Spears, one of the foremost rock composers and performers of his generation, and probably of any other generation, with a view to turning the building into a recording studio. This has not happened, not yet anyway, and the old church stands empty, the man himself being currently on tour with the band which made him famous. 'Dead Man's Wealth' have it seems undergone a late rebirth, and Mr Spears is not at home, and in any case he is apparently only an occasional visitor, but he comes here sometimes, or so I'm told.

Furthermore, if that were not strange enough, it is rumoured that this is the building wherein the singing career of a certain Ms Tara Knightman began. Here it was, or so it is said, that she of 'Tara' and 'All that I will Ever Be' first sat or stood with Ash Spears whilst she sang and he played his guitar, and here within these ancient walls were thereby laid the first foundations of another successful singing career. She lives here somewhere, so they say, in an old bus, and it is further said that this bus forms the cover of her first album, upon the steps of which sits Ms Knightman herself, but on my few visits to the village nobody will tell me the whole truth of the matter, or indeed if it is true at all, and if it is true then nobody is saying where the bus is located. It is, like so many things about the village, a well - guarded secret, and nobody is saying anything. That said, nobody is denying it, either, which leads me to think that it must be true, though by now one must assume that the young lady could afford a whole fleet of double - deckers. Ms Knightman is as I write this on tour with the band, giving the music loving world the unique blend of the old and well – worn songs of 'DMW' with the fresh young voice which has apparently become a part of the ensemble, so that's probably a first as well; a bit of much more recent rock and roll history in the making, which blends seamlessly with the older history which is everywhere about in this strange and beautiful village.

And then, of course, there is the witch of Middlewapping. Quite how the rumour of her started is shrouded in a characteristic fog of mystery, and although her infamy has not yet spread far beyond the county borders, most people within them seem to have heard of her. I mean witches, in this day and age? I for one assumed that they had died out with fairies and vampires, and such other superstitious nonsense, and perhaps it is after all just that, but having been to the place even this skeptic has been persuaded to keep an open mind on the matter. Everyone, of course, denies her existence. From the landlord of the 'Dog and Bottle' to the lady who runs the village delicatessen, everyone that I talked to said that it was nonsense. One gentleman with whom I passed a pleasant hour or so in the pub, who bought me a drink and who sported a long, blond pony – tail, and could have himself have come from any age, was particularly vociferous in his denial. I even had the sense that his approaching me in so polite yet forward a fashion was less to do with his wishing to spend time with me and more to find out why I was there, and why would he have done so? In any case certainly nobody in this instance is talking up their witch, perchance to raise the profile of the place still further, as one might perhaps have expected. Quite the opposite is in fact true; to a man and woman, all are quite categorical that she definitely doesn't exist, which leads one as suspicious as yours truly to wonder whether they protest too much, and to think that their denial merely reinforces the likelihood of there actually being some hidden truth to the strange matter. There is, after all, no smoke without fire, and the smoke around here seems to be of the thick and impenetrable kind, within and beyond which who knows what might be hidden?

A murder was committed here, or at least the slain body of a woman was found one morning on the village Green, and this murder remains unsolved. This may of course have nothing to do with witches, but here is another mystery to add to the catalogue of mysteries which surround the village of Middlewapping.

I came to the village with an open mind, and left in similar vein, having got frustratingly little closer to the truth regarding whatever may have happened or may be happening here. The good people who dwell behind her quaint and uneven walls, at least those whom I have managed to speak to, have perhaps closed ranks around something, or perhaps they have not, and my journalistic imagination may be working overtime, but there is something about the place which defies any firm conclusion one way or the other. One merely has the strong sense that something is going on here of which only the few have knowledge, and those few are keeping that knowledge to themselves.'

'Bloody hell, so she wasn't a witch after all.'

'Apparently not...'

'She was a reporter, or freelance journalist or whatever.'

'So she was. I don't think she's a regular columnist, I think it's a one – off.'

'Yeah, well whatever....What does she mean, I could have come from any age? Anyone could come from any age; bloody cheek. And I wasn't *'vociferous in my denial'*, not as far as I remember, anyway. I mean of course I said there wasn't any witch, but I wasn't being vociferous about it.'

'Journalistic license, I suppose.'

'Funny that we both get a mention...'

'Sounds as though you left the greater impression on her, though...'

'At least she used her real name. She's got a nerve though, making out she was just someone having a drink.'

'Did you ask her why she was there?'

'Well no, of course not, I mean I was trying to work out whether she was a witch or not, and she was hardly going to own up to that, was she?'

'She might have told you she was a journalist though, writing an article about the village, had you asked her, you know?'

'The point is that she didn't volunteer the information, which was sneaky, don't you think? And then she quotes me in a national magazine without asking my permission.'

'I suppose that's what journalists do. Anyway she didn't quote you as such, and your name isn't mentioned.'

'Yeah, but I mean so what, anyway? It's an article based on nothing but rumours.'

'Most of it's true, though, about the meteorite, and Ash, and Tara of course. And there is actually a witch here; more than one, as it happens.'

'Yes, but to imply that Tara might be the witch was really going too far.'

'Was it? Rosie's a witch, Keith.'

'Yes but only a kind of part – time witch. Rosie's not a full – blown in your face kind of witch like Rebecca.'

'No, I suppose not....'

'I mean Rosie's still at school for heavens' sake.'

'She didn't say anything in the article to imply that Tara was a witch, and anyway we both know that it's Rebecca, or the rumour of Rebecca that she's talking about, and I wonder how that started.'

'And where it'll end up... And I mean to drag up the business of the dead woman, you know? Clutching at straws, don't you think?'

'She was Rebecca's mother, Keith, so it's all connected, it's just that nobody outside has made the connections, not yet, anyway.'

'Yeah, well let's hope they never do. I wonder if she met Rebecca...'

'I doubt it.'

'Rebecca would probably have worked some voodoo on her anyway. That would have been ironic, don't you think? To have actually met the witch in person without realizing it...'

'And to have been bewitched by her...'

'Irony itself…'

'She ought to be told though, didn't she?'

'Who..?'

'Rebecca of course; we should at least make her aware of the article.'

'Yeah, I guess, although there's nothing to it, is there, when it comes down to it. It's just an article about a village when there wasn't enough other stuff to fill the magazine.'

'Still, we ought to tell her. I'd quite like to visit her anyway, see how she's settling back in and so on.'

'We can call 'round later if you want.'

'Sure…Why are you home so early, anyway?'

'We got to the end of banging off the old plaster, so we thought we'd leave early to celebrate. We start on lifting the floorboards on Monday, so god knows what we'll find.'

'So you're not working tomorrow then?'

'Nope, I decided to give everyone the weekend off, including myself. I'll probably sit down and start getting a serious materials specification going, pipes and so on. I'll put an order in for next week.'

'So Michael's serious, is he, about moving in?'

'Seems that way, although nobody's supposed to know about that yet'

'Why the secret, I wonder?'

'I don't know, perhaps he doesn't want mater and pater to know about Helen, or whatever she's called.'

'Elin…'

'Yeah, that's her. She seems like a nice enough kind of chap.'

'Yes, so you said. I expect I'll meet her sometime, but they must know about her, surely.'

'You would have thought so. Maybe it's not the relationship itself but the seriousness thereof. I mean he'll have to marry again eventually.'

'Yes, I suppose…'

''Course he will, there'll have to be a lady Tilllington, kind of mother to the second Lord in waiting and all, so why shouldn't it be Helen.'

'Elin....Her name's Elin, Keith.'

'Right....Guy deserves a bit of happiness after what he's been through.'

'That's true, poor man.'

'Still, at least he's got a son now, to carry on the title.'

'It seems unfair that Victoria's child can't take the title, he's the eldest boy, after all.'

'This is ancient lore, writ before the days of gender equality.'

'Theoretical gender equality, anyway...There's still somc way to go, Keith.'

'And it'll take the English aristocracy a few centuries to catch up, no doubt, if it ever does.'

Sally entered the public house, which somewhat enigmatically was named *The Dorchester Arms*, despite its' being nowhere near Dorchester. The establishment provided better than average pub food and offered a quite sophisticated atmosphere, and it was a place that both Sally and Polly had frequented infrequently in the past. Polly was already seated at a small, quite distant table when Sally entered, and had placed her coat over the opposite chair, thus reserving it in the somewhat crowded atmosphere, where not everyone could be seated. Sally waved hello, and mimed a drinking motion, Polly waved in the negative: she already had a drink, so Sally bought herself a vodka and tonic and made her way to her seat.

'Hi, sorry I'm a bit late.'

'It's okay, I've not long been here myself.'

'So, how are things?'

'Oh, you know, about the same with my dear husband, if that's what you mean.'

'Right….So have you seen anything of the others, Fiona and Ray and so on?'

'Not much. You haven't missed any dinner party invites lately, anyway. Do you know that Claudia had the bloody nerve to 'phone me the other day?'

'Christ, really..?'

'She's helping to organize some charity event at the weekend and wanted me to do some baking, would you believe.'

'So it was like, please bring a chocolate cake and by the way I'm banging your husband most weeks…'

'Yes, that kind of thing, although she didn't actually say as much.'

'I hope you said no?'

'I said I was too busy at the moment.'

'Well good for you. Anyway, cheers, god do I need this…'

'Cheers…'

'So, still no confrontation with George, then..?'

'Not yet, but it's coming. I'm just putting off the evil hour, you know?'

'Sure, of course…It can't wait forever though, Polly.'

'I know….Anyway, how are things with you? It all sounded very mysterious on the 'phone.'

'Yes, well, something happened in London today.'

'You gave in your notice?'

'Not quite, no. I've been so busy and working away that I just haven't had the chance, and I saw todays' meeting of the high and mighty as my opportunity.'

'An opportunity which you didn't take, apparently...'

'No, I didn't.'

'Right….So what did happen, then?'

'They offered me promotion, sort of, although it's better than that, actually.'

'Well you said that might happen, but I thought you'd made your mind up to leave.'

'Yes, well I had, and I still might, but the thing is, the bank's expanding into Scandinavia; Stockholm, Copenhagen, Oslo, and god knows where else from there, they're really making a big push for investment, and well, they want me to carry it forward; oversee the expansion and whatever.'

'Become their Nordic representative, so to speak.'

'Exactly…'

'So will this mean more money?'

'A lot more, and I'd be on expenses, of course. I probably wouldn't have to touch my actual wages, and now I don't have the mortgage anymore, well, I wouldn't know myself, financially. They also made it clear enough that if I perform well then I'll make the board of directors, probably within a couple of years, all being well, but that's not the point, really; it's just such an exciting project, and I've never even been to Scandinavia, would you believe?'

'So will language be a problem, I mean I know they all speak English…'

'Yes, they do, but anyway wherever I was I'd have a bi –lingual assistant on hand if I needed one, or if things get technical, you know?'

'I see, so what did you say?'

'I said I'd give them my answer on Monday morning.'

'But surely you can't refuse, can you?'

'I told Percival I was quitting.'

'Yes I know, but surely it's not an either – or situation, is it?'

'I'd be away a lot, probably all the time for a few months at least, and probably longer, maybe years.'

'Yes, but Scandinavia isn't that far, is it? You could come home weekends or something.'

'Yes, of course I could, and Percival's said he'll support me in whatever I do. It's always been my idea to go self – employed, or to somehow change my life, anyway.'

'Well this would certainly be a life - changer, so what's stopping you?'

'It's just…It's just so different to how I'd imagined the next years of my life to be. A big part of why I was quitting was to be at home more, you know?'

'Yes, I know, so have you discussed any of this with Percival?'

'Not yet, no...'

'So have you seen him today?'

'Only briefly, but that was my doing. I just need a sounding board before I say anything, just to talk it through with someone.'

'Someone apart from Percival, who aside from you will be the person most affected by it.'

'Yes, I suppose…'

'There's no '*suppose*' about it, is there? So do you think he'd react badly to the idea?'

'No, I don't think he would. I mean he'd be pleased for me, I'm sure, but otherwise I really don't think he'd care either way, which is the point, really.'

'Sorry, I'm not getting this.'

'Well, you know how Percival is.'

'I don't know him that well, but I'm still not getting the point, or where the problem is. Is it that you don't want to be away from him for so much of the time?'

'Yes, I really don't want that, of course.'

'Well, in that case I begin to see your dilemma.'

'It's not even just that though.'

'So what else is it then?'

'It's that…Well, if I go ahead with this, I think I'll lose him, you know?'

'I see….It wouldn't be permanent though, would it? It may only be for a couple of years.'

'A couple of years is a long time with Percival. Christ, a couple of days is a long time with Percival.'

'Right...Well forgive me for saying so, sweetheart, but this doesn't sound like a good basis for a lasting relationship.'

Sally laughed, and drank the last of her drink, which would not be her last drink of the evening.

'What's funny?'

'I'm sorry, but you really don't know Percival, do you?'

'So enlighten me.'

'Percival's...Well, he's a very passionate man, but he's a kind of one day at a time person, if you see what I mean.'

'And he's not too particular where he puts his passion from day to day, is that it?'

'That wouldn't be fair, really, I mean I don't think he'd be unfaithful, and I think I'd know if he was, because he'd probably tell me, but, well, if I wasn't around not to be unfaithful to...'

'So it's about commitment, then, or lack thereof.'

'It's a lot to ask of anyone, Polly, I mean it's not like we're married or have been together forever, and he left me once before, remember?'

'So in order to keep him, you would have to sacrifice a wonderful career opportunity and all the money that goes with it, is that it in a nutshell?'

'Put in its' simplest form, yes.'

'So it really is either – or then.'

'In a way, yes it is, I suppose, potentially anyway.'

'So otherwise you'd leave the bank, set up in business with all the risks that that would imply, without by the sound of it being certain that the reason for your doing so would be around for very long anyway, is that it?'

'It's not even that simple, I mean I really wanted to do it, you know? To be independent; I wasn't doing it all for him, or for us, in fact it was mostly for me.'

'The continuation of your relationship being a kind of fringe benefit, is that it?'

'He was always behind me, Polly, and he said he'd support me financially, whatever happened.'

'For as long as he was around.'

'That makes him sound like a terrible man, and he's not, and I do love him, and I'm sure he loves me, in his way. I mean I was a mess when he left me before. God I was so angry for such a long time, although I wouldn't admit it to myself at the time, but now I really don't know what to do. I was quite determined not to make the bank the rest of my working life, you know?'

'And then this happens.'

'Exactly....I mean you know I'm not well – travelled, and the thought of working abroad, well, it puts a whole new perspective on it. I even considered the possibility of renting the house out for a year or two. Just stay with friends or something when I was in England.'

'Well you'd always be welcome at ours, but you love your house.'

'I know, but as you say, it would probably only be in the short or medium – term, at least I'm sure I'll come back one day whatever happens.'

'And then you'd have even more money, if you rented the place out.'

'I'd be raking it in, which would mean I could travel more. The other thing I'm determined to do is to see all of the big world that I haven't seen yet, which is most of it. I'm ridiculously untraveled for someone my age, and this could be my big chance, you know?'

'Sure, and you'd do that alone?'

'Well, if I have to, yes.'

'The way things are going I might jump on board sometimes.'

'You'd be welcome, of course. Maybe we could become travelling companions.'

'It's a thought, isn't it....So, what it comes down to for you is a glowing career and seeing the world versus a relationship which you don't seem to have a great deal of faith in anyway.'

'I do love him, Polly.'

'Yes, I know you do. God what are we doing? You're thinking of ending a relationship that you don't want to end, and I'm trying to stay in one which I'm not sure I want to be in anyway. It's all bloody ridiculous really, isn't it?'

'Well, at least none of us has any kids to think about.'

'Yes, well there's that I suppose.'

'Anyway I need another drink.'

'I'll get these. Have you eaten?'

'No, but I'm not hungry, you?'

'Me neither. If I'm going to be out there in the big romantic world again soon then I'd better start looking fit for it.'

'Oh come on, you're stick – thin anyway.'

'Well I'm not hungry anyway, so let's just drink, shall we?'

'Sounds like a plan.'

The numbing effect of the alcohol consumed during the rest of the evening did nothing to clarify the thoughts of Sally Parsons, in the so significant matter of how her life should proceed from here on. The banks' decision makers had in fact decided some months ago to expand its' operations into the Nordic countries, and most of the infrastructure was already in place, but at the eleventh hour the person whom they had I mind for the job of coordinating the project had been made a better offer by a rival bank, and only then had Sally's name come into the frame. Even then not all of the board had been in her favour, but they had needed a quick decision, and Sally was young, smart, highly presentable, totally reliable and single, and in the end she had won the day, provided, of course, that she took the job, and was able to pack her bags within two weeks at latest, and preferably within the week. So she had the weekend to decide, and by Monday morning she would either accept the post, and by doing so accept the consequences of her acceptance, or she could more or less say goodbye to further progress at the bank in the foreseeable future, in which case she had better leave and begin her career as an independent financial advisor, or fitness trainer, or whatever else she may decide to try to become. At the end of the evening she took a taxi home, undressed and fell onto her bed. She would see her beloved Percival in the morning; perhaps by then and by dint of having spent most of the evening discussing the whys and wherefores of the matter with Polly, she would be able to come to a decision. She had waited a long time for him to come back into her life the last time, and she knew in her heart that there would not be a third time. This time she would lose him forever, and that thought lay heavy on the soul of Sally Parsons, as she drifted into an uneasy but drunken sleep.

It was quite late in the evening by the time Keith and Meadow arrived at the front door of number seven, The Green, which was currently the residence of Rebecca and her infant daughter, Florence. For the most part Rebecca bought her vegetables, fruit and other basic provision in the town, which was more convenient for her studio, and she had little need for the more luxurious and costly fare provided by the village delicatessen, economy always being a consideration for her. It was thus the case that Meadow had seen Rebecca only twice since her return to the village, and then only briefly, and Keith had not seen her at all, so the meeting of these three had a certain significance, although the significance was difficult to specify. The last time that Keith and Meadow had been here was in search of another witch, who had by then made good her escape on the night that Rebecca had burned down the coven, so now they knocked on the door with somewhat less trepidation; this witch they knew, at least. Rebecca opened the door and was pleased indeed to see who was calling. She lived now in a constant state of awareness that every caller could signal danger to her and her daughter, and she always checked before opening the door.

'Hi...This is a nice surprise; come in.'

Meadow kicked off her shoes and they walked across the threshold, noting the Spartan but perhaps surprisingly tidy and always clean way that Rebecca lived. Florence was asleep in her drawer on the table which Megan had used for her needlecraft, and which was now for the most part Rebecca's dining table, which had only one chair beside it.

'I'm sorry there's nowhere to sit, really, I don't get many callers, but it's great to see you both. Can I offer you tea; I've got three cups at least, and I was just making some for myself.'

'Tea would be nice, thank you.'

Rebecca retired briefly to the kitchen, whilst Meadow instinctively went to Florence, who was sleeping soundly, only stirring slightly as Meadow adjusted her bedding.

'She's a great sleeper....'

'She's beautiful, isn't she?'

'Yes she is, well I think so, anyway. So, is the floor okay?'

'The floor's fine.'

The three people sat cross – legged on the carpeted floor, Lady lay down beside them, Rebecca poured tea for them all, and they smiled for one another in a quiet moment of reunion. They had been through certain significant times together, not the least of which had been the night that Meadow had confronted and killed the witch Eve on the steps of the Manor House, when Rebecca had taken Victoria's child, Henry, into her safekeeping. They did not speak of such times, there was nothing to be said, really, that had not already been said, and all of their lives had moved on, but none would ever forget their shared experiences.

'Look,' Said Rebecca 'I'm really sorry that I haven't been to see you. Life's been rather busy lately, not that that is any excuse. Time just seems to go, you know, and I've hardly seen anyone really. When I'm not looking after Florence I just seem to work and sleep at the moment.'

'Of course,' said Meadow 'and don't even think about it, we absolutely understand.'

'Thanks, that's done then, so anyway it really is good to see you both. Are the children well?'

'Very well, thank you.'

'Yeah,' said Keith 'Tara's busy taking the musical world by storm on her world tour, Basil's still up to his eyes in love and can't wait to leave school, and Rosie can't get enough of it, school that is.'

'She's the academic, then, and Tarragon's doing so well. About the only luxury that I've allowed myself since moving back is a half – decent second – hand music system, and I play her albums a lot. Florence loves them too; they get her out of bad moods every time…'

'I don't suppose she gets many of those, does she?'

'Not really, she's a contented little soul, on the whole. Makes you wonder where she gets it from.'

'Well, I'm sure you're a good mother.'

'I'm learning, I think, although they soon tell you if you're doing something wrong, don't they?'

'Don't they just…' Said Meadow

'Yeah, that applies at any age,' said Keith 'and the older they get the better they get at telling you, and the more stuff there is to get wrong.'

Easy conversation, and this was on the whole a happy reunion. Meadow had never trusted Rebecca, or been happy with Keith's involvement with her, but she trusted Keith, who this evening had the magazine article in his jacket pocket, and it was not until some while later that Meadow thought they should get around to the ostensible reason for their having come here, Keith having probably forgotten.

'So, Keith, have you got, you know…'

'Sorry..?'

'The article, dear heart...'

'Oh right, yeah, I'd forgotten about that. Someone gave Meadow this, which we thought you might want to read.'

He took the now single sheet of glossy paper from his pocket and gave it to Rebecca, who read it quickly, after which she smiled, and then laughed, gently. Then she became serious again.

'Christ, who the hell's this? I wish I'd met her and known her intent, I'd have shown her where the witch is, and what it's like to meet one. She'd never have asked again.'

And there, just for a fleeting moment, both Keith and Meadow saw the other side of Rebecca, the side which could massacre her enemies, and murder people in their beds. She who could almost at will control the thoughts and actions of others, unless those others were stronger than she, or had the depth and purity of spirit which Meadow possessed, and which nobody but she could control.

'I mean, there's nothing to it though, right?' said Keith 'It's just some bullshit, isn't it?'

'No, there's nothing to it, but thanks for showing me.'

'Someone, somehow, knows that you're here though, and word seems to be spreading' said Meadow 'and doesn't that concern you?'

Rebecca smiled again, but it was a different kind of smile.

'I have concerns, of course, but I'm not the only witch here, am I?'

Neither Keith nor Meadow knew whether she referred to Sophia, but both assumed so, since she couldn't know of Rosie's involvement in the sisterhood, could she?

'In any case, whatever concerns I may have don't include this kind of idle nonsense. I have greater enemies than this, believe me.'

'Do you refer to the chicken stranglers,' said Keith 'or other ones' of your type?'

'Both, I expect. In the former regard I'm sure that Percival is up to something, although he won't tell me what, so I have to trust him. You know Percival well, has he said anything to you?'

'Not to me.' said Keith

This was quite untrue, since Percival had indeed taken Keith into his confidence, but it would be Percival's decision to tell Rebecca, or not to tell her. In any case Keith decided to move the conversation forward and away.

'So what about the dark witches then? I mean we know there's at least one of them at liberty, since she liberated herself from this very house.'

'Yes,' said Rebecca 'there's at least one…'

'So you think there might still be more of them?' Said Meadow

'I don't know, but after the fire…There's a gap in my memory, you see. I don't know how I got back here, or rather back to the Manor House, and that makes no sense to me, unless I was brought there, and I don't know who would have done that.'

There was still no word from or of Helena, and Rebecca was by now as good as certain that she was dead, killed on the night of the fire, and if that were true then somebody else had saved her, and the only other possibility, hard though it was to fathom, was that one of the coven had brought her back from Farthing's Well. The motivation for doing so was quite unclear to her, but she had become increasingly convinced that this was what had happened, and if so then at least one of them had got away.

'I'm sorry,' said Meadow 'but I don't really understand.'

So here for Rebecca was something of a dilemma, should she tell them or not? They had always been nothing but friends to her, and to Percival, and whatever strange power Meadow possessed, Rebecca knew well enough that it was beyond her or probably any of them to bewitch her. Charlotte she knew was a very powerful witch, and for a fleeting moment she wondered what would happen if these two ever met in confrontation, but equally she knew that both had always been a power for the good, and so that was never likely to happen, and she found herself being glad of that.

'Nor do I, but….My accomplice has disappeared, you see, and I think she may be dead, so, well, I now think it likely that it was a black witch who brought me here.'

'I see, I think…'

'Yes, it's hard to see sometimes, isn't it, and I don't pretend to understand, but one day I will.'

'Right…' said Keith 'so we remain vigilant, then. I mean the only reason that I talked to what's her name…'

'Georgina…' said Meadow

'Yeah, her, was to find out whether she was a witch or not.'

Rebecca smiled.

'And now we've found out that she wasn't. That must have been an interesting conversation.'

'Well, not really, as it happened.'

'So did you ask her?'

'No, I never really got the chance, to be honest. Anyway it's not the sort of thing you can just come out and ask somebody, is it?'

'No, I suppose not. I don't think even you would do that.'

'We kind of spent the whole conversation lying to each other, and now I know why she was lying, but it doesn't make for constructive dialogue.'

'Lies can be very informative,' said Rebecca 'and thanks for doing that, but a witch would never be so obvious, and if this witch is as good as I think she is then you would never have known until it was too late. Be careful, Keith.'

'Yeah, I'm beginning to see that…Think I'll stick to blokes in future, you know where you are with them.'

He looked at Meadow.

'Maybe you should do it next time, you're better at witches than I am, although it might have looked a bit weird, a woman kind of chatting up another woman, not that I was chatting her up, as such, in the traditional sense of the phrase, but I bought her a drink, which might have given out the wrong signals. I kind of had to watch myself, remain kind of calm and aloof, like I was just being friendly, or whatever.'

Now it was Meadow who exchanged smiles with Rebecca.

'I'm sure you did fine, sweetheart, and I'm sure she was flattered.'

'And I'm flattered too,' said Rebecca 'and grateful that you took the trouble.'

'The whole village are being vigilant, Rebecca,' said Meadow 'at least those of us who know, and you must be careful, too.'

'Always, and I have a mothers' instincts to protect now, so yes, I'm careful, and I know you're looking out for me and I really do thank you for it, but if you have any suspicions about anybody again, please tell me.'

'Yes, that would be better.' Said Meadow

'Anyway,' said Keith 'I suppose we should be getting back.'

'Yes, I've got a deli to open tomorrow, and I'm sure you must be tired, Rebecca.'

'I'm glad you came.'

They departed, and Rebecca closed and locked the door behind them. Keith and Meadow held hands as they began their short journey home in the darkness.

'That went alright.' Said Keith

'Yes, but I still think she's far too exposed, if anything serious did happen.'

'Well, she must know the risks, and I wouldn't bet against her if it comes to it. I still think we should check people out first though, she might start killing people again just to be on the safe side.'

Meadow smiled at her man and took his arm, just as a taxi pulled up outside number three, and Sally Parsons walked somewhat unsteadily to and then through her front door. She did not see them as she fumbled somewhat with her door key.

'I wonder how that particular relationship's going.' Said Meadow

'Lord knows, I mean I don't see how it works anyway, they're chalk and cheese, you know? I mean she's Ms Conventional herself and Percival, well, we all know what Percival's like on a bad day, or even on a good day.'

'Yes, it does seem unlikely, and she's obviously drinking again, which apparently she wasn't before.'

'That's not a good sign. I can't see it lasting, can you, her and Percival I mean?'

'Who knows, Keith my love, love works in mysterious ways.'

'Not that mysterious, she's probably got him by the balls for the moment, and what happened to what's her name, anyway, I thought she was the love of his life. You think it's really over between them?'

'If you mean Louise, then I really wouldn't like to guess.'

'No, me neither. I liked her though, the little I saw of her. She was kind of off – the – wall, a bit neurotic, you might say, much more Percival's type.'

'There's another person you have to feel for, really.'

'What, Perc…? Don't waste you sympathy. I mean don't get me wrong, Percival's a mate, but he has to live his life on the edge of disaster, it's the only place he can function. Show Percival happiness and contentment and he'd run a mile. Guy's only happy when he's unhappy.'

'Which is sad, don't you think? Perhaps they couldn't make it work'

'Who..?'

'Percival and Louise...'

'Naaa, she'll be back, you mark my words. She'll turn up like a bad penny one of these days, then his problems are really going to start.'

'Well if you say so, my love, who am I to speculate about such things, a mere woman…'

'You still love me though, right?'

'What are you talking about?'

'Just, you know, checking in. Our relationship is based on a sound foundation, wouldn't you say?'

'Works for me, most of the time…'

After her visitors had departed, Rebecca prepared herself and her baby for the night, and whilst doing so she gave consideration to the conversation, in particular regard to the woman who had visited the village, and had written the article. By the time she had placed her head on her pillow, she had come to a conclusion, and it would be a conclusion which would have profound impact upon her life in the quite near future; indeed in this regard the impact would prove to be ultimate in its' profundity. Not all things were as they seemed, after all, and witches were seldom so, and Rebecca fell to sleep quite convinced that she had returned. That the woman who had saved her from the fire was back, and she was coming.

Chapter 6

THE BLUSH OF THE ICE MAIDEN

Quentin Forbes – Dolby had, for as long as he could recall, been fascinated by the deep history of his own species, and by other species of ape which formed the chain of ascent which had either led thereto, or which had formed their own branch of the evolutionary tree of that which were collectively called hominids. It was commonly enough known that humankind was so genetically similar to chimpanzees that their common ancestor cannot have been very far back in geological time, just as it was by now known that certain of his own species had some genetic material inherited from Neanderthals, a recent and quite separate species of hominid which had not long ago and for unknown hundreds of thousands of years shared the earth with homo sapiens. These two species had met one another, and had indeed interbred, before by some quirk of fate, fortune or by dint of some acquired or learned advantage, his own taller but much weaker species had become dominant, and the last Homo Neanderthalensis had died their lonely death. And if they had interbred, what else had they done? Could they have understood one another? Did they have verbal communication as well as physical union, or even share something of a common language? Did they sit beside the same fires in the cold nights of the Pleistocene, sharing their hunted meat, afraid of the same darkness? Such things, he knew, would never be known. The voices of these ancient people had died long ago, but the echo of them lived even now, in the way people looked, and behaved, and such things had always held a fascination for the man who had been named Quentin Forbes – Dolby.

His own species had, as climatic conditions had allowed, migrated from the savannas and forests of Africa along the coastlines of the ancient world, eventually moving inland, where communities and later populations had become isolated, and had by degrees and by process of natural selection adapted to their new environment, by perhaps growing taller, or by changing their skin pigmentation, and here they had made their own languages and ways of living, and had developed their own beliefs. After long course of time, and with improved technology and learned abilities to survive, vast oceans could be spanned, and mountain ranges could be crossed, and such by now diverse peoples had come together again, with sometimes good but often devastating results. And still, in the enlightened times in which Quentin lived, they held distrust for one another, and held hatred for one another even as they began once again to interbreed, and so to soften the racial boundaries which had for so long kept them apart, and unaware of one another. African blood was now mixed with European blood, and the great genetic reunion had begun, and would continue, a coming together of those who after all shared a common ancestor. That ancestor was now dust, but she had once walked the earth, and through hard and dangerous times had raised the children from whom everyone is descended. 'Mitochondrial Eve', who was by now a concept in a textbook, had once been flesh and blood, and had laughed, and wept, and unbeknownst to her had left her so significant legacy, for she and the issue of her womb had been the beginning of everyone.

Quentin's deeply held interest in such things led him quite naturally to his choice of university courses; Geology, with a specialism of Paleontology, and later a post – graduate course in Human Evolution, which served to satisfy his intellectual quest for knowledge, but did not serve him so well in the competitive world into which he had been born. He had some money on deposit, bequeathed to him by his parents, who had divided their worldly goods equally between the three brothers, but he had to work to pay for his rent and his daily needs, and to this end he had recently secured employment as a warehouseman for the local supermarket. The post was at least in part supervisory, but the hours were antisocial, and involved early mornings and some night – work, but he needed the money, whilst he kept alive the hope and ambition of finding work more commensurate with his considerable qualification. He saw himself one day taking part in archeological excavations in far – flung, exotic locations, perhaps thereby finding fossil evidence which would fill another gap in the still so scant knowledge of human evolution, and perhaps change once again the accepted and established wisdom of how things came to be as they are, but this was a hard world into which to break, and for now he must do as he must.

Quentin lived in a modest, one - bedroom flat on the third floor of a three story apartment block, which was conveniently located close to the town centre and railway station. He cooked for himself, or else bought takeaway food from one of the numerous local outlets, and spent his evenings surfing the internet for articles on subjects which interested him, or watching the television, or doing crossword puzzles, and once or twice a week he would frequent one of the local public houses. He had friends whom he saw occasionally, mostly people that he had known from his post – graduate year at Oxford, and he had made acquaintances within the local community, but otherwise he largely kept himself to himself, and was for the most part content with this state of being. Recently, however, something far less cerebral and pertaining absolutely to the here and now had begun to occupy Quentin's thoughts, as he went about his daily business, and that something, or better say someone, was a certain Rosie Knightman. As we have learned these two had met twice on the same train, whilst the train had been going respectively in different directions, and he had subsequently invited her to meet his two brothers, Tarquin who was commonly called Freddy, and Tristan, but he had not seen or contacted her since, and this had now been more than a week ago. We have also learned that Quentin had lost his virginity whilst at university, and had female as well as male friends, but had never thus far had anything which might be called a girlfriend, since in truth he had never thus far felt the need or desire for one. It was also the case that his brothers, having met the young lady, had not been unanimous in their approval of her for one particular reason, and Freddy had voiced his disapproval, as and in a way that Freddy was wont to do.

'What the fuck are you doing, Quen, she's a fucking schoolgirl for Christ's sake. I mean you're not serious about her, are you? And if you're not serious then leave her the fuck alone, you know?'

Tristan had been somewhat more sympathetic.

'She's damnably good looking, Freds, I can quite see the attraction. She seems mature for her years, and girls grow up quicker, you know, which kind of narrows the age gap somewhat.'

'Anyone can see the attraction,' Freddy had said 'but can't you pick on someone your own age?'

His brothers had departed three days subsequent to the funeral of their grandmother, Tarquin to France and Tristan to India, having incidentally reached no agreement as what should be done with the family home, but the words of his eldest brother had found traction in Quentin's thoughts, and he had hesitated before contacting Rosemary again. She had 'phoned him the first time, and it was his turn now, but for now he was hesitant, and needed a little time to think on the matter. She had told him that she was in her last year at school, and he had no reason to disbelieve her in this regard, so that would make her seventeen, or perhaps eighteen. Quentin was twenty four, so there were perhaps six or seven years separating them. Quentin was used to thinking in geological time, in which the entire evolution of humankind was but a relatively very recent event, no more than a blink of the geological eye, really, so six or seven years did not seem very long to him in that context. They were, however, important, university years in the life of a modern – day human being, who counted their years more carefully, and no doubt held them in greater significance than had their less socially aware forebears. The fact remained, however, that he had certain feelings for Rosie which he had not felt for other young women of his acquaintance, and whilst a young man without a mate may on occasion find his own way to non – specific sexual fulfillment, Quentin found that his thoughts in this regard were now very specific indeed, and all were directed toward the young woman whom he had met on a train. He had never seen her anything but fully and modestly clothed, nor had they had any significant physical contact, but he had a young mans' imagination, and this was currently working overtime. So there was that, but it was also true that he had liked her, and believed that she had liked him in return, and he had enjoyed her company on the two occasions that they had spoken. And Tristan had been right, she did seem mature for her years, and had held her own in the company of he and his two brothers, who were he knew not always the easiest of company. He had the excuse of the presence of his brothers for not having contacted her immediately after their last meeting, but that excuse was now running rather thin, and he must make his decision soon, one way or the other. Should he do the perhaps sensible and decent thing and delete her 'phone number from his telephone, putting their brief encounter down to pleasant if frustrating experience; let the memory of her fade, as it would doubtless do. Or should he disregard the respected words of his elder brother, who was after all no expert in matters of love and relations between men and women, and continue the journey of mutual discovery with Rosie Knightman, always assuming, of course, that she also wished to make that journey with him. Such thoughts occupied the mind of Quentin Forbes – Dolby as he went about his work at the warehouse, or in the quieter and more reflective hours of his evening, and there came to be a certain nervousness about the matter, which he knew was ridiculous, but there it was. So perhaps after all it was best left; best leave her on the train to continue her journey without him, but they had moved now beyond their train journey, had they not, and she would be expecting him to 'phone her. In any case, that which was best and most decent was not always the best option, was it? What it came down to, he concluded, was how much he wanted to see her again, and the degree of indecency which he was prepared to accept in himself, and on these criteria would he make his decision, but the decision must be made soon.

Peter Shortbody had read *'Far Away from Everywhere'* within two days. It was a quite intense, fairly well written and to Peter's mind quite charming story about a boy and a girl who become close friends when they are respectively nine and eight years old, and both spend a summer at the same orphanage, before both are found adoptive parents. The book was in three approximately equal parts, the first part being concerned with the summer in question, and was in Peter Shortbody's opinion quite touchingly written, the final scene being one in which he gives her a single Buttercup as a parting gift. The second part covers their growing up in their respective families, neither of which transpire to be happy environments, indeed the girl, who is called Lily, becomes the victim of abuse by her adoptive father when she reaches her early teens, and the boy, whose name is Edwin, fares little better in other regards. The final part of the novel finds the two characters in their third decade, by which time both have been married and divorced, their early lives having it seems made it as good as impossible for them to form lasting and loving relationships. It is now that quite by chance Lily, who by now works as a travel agent, notices Edwin's name on the passenger manifest of a cruise liner. She books her passage on the same ship, and here she contrives that they meet. During the next chapters, which take place on board ship and at various ports in the Aegean Sea, he does not recognize her, and for reasons best known to herself she is using a pseudonym. Nevertheless there is something about her that makes Edwin convinced that they have met before, and in any case the two people find emotional solace with one another, and become close once more. In the final chapter, Lily leaves an old and faded card in Edwin's cabin, upon which are the remains of a pressed flower, the Buttercup which he had given her when they were children. All then becomes clear to him, and the flower is the catalyst to their falling in love, the final scene being the two people leaning over the railing of the ship, looking out over the ocean, and travelling to their new and unknown future together.

So, Peter Shortbody had enjoyed the novel, but thereafter had thought little of it, or if he was honest with himself had tried to think little of it, but at odd and unguarded moments he found himself thinking that after all, where would be the harm in leaving a message on her website? This feeling was reinforced by the fact that the novel was concerned with two people meeting after a long absence, and although the parallels were extremely tenuous, there was the ghost of a similarity between the essence of the book and his having not seen Madeline Young since they were at school. One evening therefore, which was three days after he had read the novel, and having given Tizer his supper, Peter sat down and sent a message, which read as follows;

'Dear Madeline. Doubtless you will not remember me, but my name is Peter Shortbody, and we were at school together during the last years of our secondary schooling. Anyway this is just to say that I have recently read your novel, and enjoyed the reading of it, so congratulations, and I hope that the novel has proved a success. Best regards, Peter.'

That done, Peter brushed his teeth and made ready for bed, with no real expectation that he would receive reply to his message, and in this regard at least he was correct. After count of several days without response, he would quite give up on the idea, and was somewhat surprised by a quite strong sense of disappointment; he would have liked to have spoken to Maddie Young once again.

On the morning after her evening out with Polly, Sally awoke quite early, took painkillers for her only fairly moderate hangover, made coffee to aid the awakening process, and did a half – hour work - out on her cross – trainer, in an attempt to put herself in a more relaxed frame of mind. She then showered, applied some light make up to eyes and lips, dressed in jeans, casual shirt and a light jacket, and walked out into a grey, overcast but mild morning. The trees were still bare, but early spring flowers had begun to bloom by the side of the track and in her small front garden; the long winter months were all but over, at last. The short walk to the cottage down the lane was one which she knew so well, and this morning, perhaps for the first time, she wished that the distance were longer. She found the side door to the cottage open, and Percival sitting on his side step, smoking a cigarette with Lulu beside him. The dog gave her its' customary canine welcome, she kissed Percival hello and concluded that her not crossing the threshold on this particular morning was rather symbolic.

'Hi...Have you walked her this morning?'

'Not yet, I was sort of waiting for you.'

'So, shall we go for a walk then?'

'Sure, I'll get a jacket.'

She waited outside, and without further words they set off through the field gate and down the side of the field. They would often walk to the lake if they had things to talk about, and for both of them this was such a morning. They sat on one of the rustic benches which overlooked the water; Percival lit a cigarette and offered her one, which she refused. The awkward silence between them became deafening, as both tried to find a way to begin a conversation which neither wished to have.

'Reginald's ducks are doing well, aren't they?'

These had been his words, but they now struck him as funny in the context of that which he was about to tell her, and he laughed quietly as he exhaled his cigarette smoke.

'What's funny?'

'Oh I don't know, life, don't you think? Anyway I've got something to tell you, Sal.'

'I've got something to tell you, too.'

'You first then…'

She had probably given in her notice, and if her new life had anything to do with him, then that part of it at least lay in pieces before it had so much as started.

'I had a meeting with the board of directors yesterday.'

So here it was then, and this would not make his news any easier for her; everything had just been so badly timed.

'Oh yes, so how did that go?'

'Differently to how I'd expected, actually… They've…Well, they've offered me a new job, in Scandinavia.'

Percival was looking out over the water, and the water suddenly looked different. He had no plan, really as to how he would tell her, but of a sudden any plans that he may have made in this regard looked somewhat obsolete.

'Scandinavia..? So is this a temporary post, or what?'

'I don't know, I mean probably not. Could be a long post, months at least, and maybe years, you know? I suppose it would depend on how much I liked Scandinavia, and how up to the job I am.'

'Well it's a growing financial market over there, so I can see the logic in it, and of course you're up to the job. So have you accepted?'

'I'm letting them know on Monday.'

'I see…'

'I wanted to talk to you first, of course.'

'Just not last night...'

'I needed to talk it over with someone.'

'Anyone in particular..?'

'I really was meeting Polly, somebody who isn't a part of it, you know?'

'So when does the job start?'

'They want someone there next week actually, or as soon as possible, anyway. I…I mean I haven't said yes, Percival.'

This conversation was definitely not now going as he had expected, nor anywhere near it, and Percival took a moment to make the necessary adjustments.

'And I mean, I could come home some weekends, so we could still….'

'See each other? Sure, that would be nice.'

The adjustments were nearly made, but not quite.

'So, say something, you know?'

'I am saying things, and I don't quite know what you want me to say, but you have to take it, I realize that. I mean if you throw this one up you'll never forgive yourself, will you?'

'I think if I take it I'll never forgive myself either, that's the problem.'

'Don't stay for me, Sal, I couldn't live with that. This is your future, you know?'

'It's not our future though, is it?'

So there it was; the statement of something which they both knew to be true, and which she had apparently come to accept, and Percival must now choose his words carefully.

'Nobody has a future outside themselves, Sal, I think that's what I've been trying to tell you. If somebody else comes along for the ride then so be it, but it all comes down to ourselves in the end. In the end if we deny ourselves then it can only end one way, and it's not a good way.'

'I don't want to leave you, Percival.'

'I know you don't. I do understand that, Sal, but life's just like that sometimes, don't you think? We can only do so much, you know, life does the rest. So go. It's the bright new future that you were looking for, don't throw it away.'

He lit a cigarette, and this time she accepted. He put his arm round her, and now her tears came.

'Don't do that…'

But he held her anyway, and she made no move to resist, but rather she put her head on his shoulder.

'I wasn't going to cry.'

'None of us is ever going to cry until we cry.'

'We can still love each other though, can't we? I mean we can still be friends?'

'Of course, call in for a cup of tea any time you're passing. I might even buy some biscuits.'

She smiled now through the tears.

'Idiot man...'

'That about sums it up. Just, you know, no more anger, okay?'

'No my love, no more anger...'

'Well then, that's a good way to end, don't you think?'

'Yes, it's a good way to end. It's not too late…I could still leave the bank. I could still try to do all the things we talked about, or I talked about.'

'Of course it's too late.'

'I thought…Well, I thought you might try to talk me out of it.'

'Did you, really?'

'No, I suppose not, and thank you, you know, for not trying to, although damn you at the same time.'

She stood up.

'I have to go.'

'Of course...'

'I'll see you again though, before I leave.'

'That's what friends do.'

She turned to walk away, but then turned to face him again.

'What was it that you were going to say to me, anyway?'

'What…? Oh, nothing, really. I was just thinking of going away for a while, and now I certainly am. Get things straight in my head, you know?'

'I don't suppose there's any point in asking you where you're going, since you probably don't know.'

'No, probably not...'

'Don't be alone, Percival, you know you're hopeless on your own. I don't want to think of you on your own.'

'Well then don't think of me. Before you know it you'll probably meet some rich, handsome Norwegian anyway.'

'I'll still think of you. I'll always love you, Percival.'

'I'll always love you too.'

She turned now and walked away along the footpath, before the tears really started; the first steps into her new life, and they were unhappy steps. Percival sat where he was for a while longer. Well, that had been unexpected, and very sudden; the guilt now became entangled in a deep sense of loss that he had not been expecting either, and for a few moments it tied his stomach in knots. He had heard it said that the price that men pay for sex is intimacy, and the price that women pay for intimacy is sex, and there might be some truth in that as far as he and Sally had been concerned, but he did love her, and would miss her presence in his life. He had wanted her friendship, and she had given him and taken from him more than he had asked of her, but they were equal now, at least, in so far as these things can ever be equal.

Would he now 'phone Louise? He thought not, although he should tell her that he was going, and why he was going. He needed time now, and some time with nobody, before he saw her again. He would go and see Keith and Meadow before he left, and Will and Emily, and Rebecca. He should go to the Manor House as well, and see Victoria, if only for Henry, his Godson. He would need to find somewhere for Lulu, anyway, and the probably unfinished business with the witches and the chicken – strangers would just have to wait. Better that he was not here, in all such regards. Sally was leaving, and this was something which he had not factored with any certainty into any way that he had seen his life going, and he would feel the loss of her too acutely if he stayed. No, better that he be gone. He stood up, and as he began to walk home he was overcome for a moment by an acute and almost overwhelming sense of sadness. It wasn't Sally, not really, nor was it even just his own life; he had made all of that happen, after all. It was the whole bloody mess of it; of Rebecca, and the danger that she was in; of Victoria Tillington and her illegitimate son, and the death of Rose, and her child, who was his child, and how had all of that come to be, really? How had such people, himself included, contrived to make the decisions that they had made, which had brought them to such a pass?

He put his hands deeper in his jacket pockets and wrapped it more tightly around himself. A light rain had begun to fall from the grey sky, but that was not the only thing from which at that moment he considered that he needed greater protection.

The final scene of this chapter takes place on the bus in the wood, where Keith, Meadow, Rosemary and Basil are unusually enjoying a quiet evening together, Emma having made other arrangements to stay with a friend for the night. In our homely and familial scene, Rosie and Basil are sitting on the cushioned floor playing a card game, Keith is playing his guitar quietly, and Meadow is at the dining table reading her electronic mail.

Nobody had spoken for a few moments, and it was Meadow who broke the contented silence, without taking her eyes from the screen.

'Oh my god…..'

'What's up?' said Keith, who now abruptly ceased his playing. His beloved was not one to over dramatize, and something had clearly provoked this unusual and spontaneous outburst.

'This is….Oh good lord, Keith, look at this, in fact everybody look at this, it's from Tara.'

'Is she okay?'

'What…? Oh, yes, I think so, but…Well, read it.'

Everyone now stood behind Meadow and read over her shoulder, and the following is that which they read;

'Hi everyone, well you're not going to bloody believe this, so prepare yourselves…We're going to be playing the concert at Hyde Park, which I'm sure you must have heard about, you know the 'Famine – Relief' *one. I mean Christ it's in less than two weeks' time, on Saturday, and loads of the big names will be playing, for nothing, of course, but it's all completely insane. Nobody invited us until now because we're on tour, but yesterday Ash had a 'phone call from the organizer, who must have looked at our concert – schedule and decided it was possible, and well, long story short, we had a band meeting and we decided to do it, or rather Ash decided that he wanted us to do it. So we come off stage here and have to be on a 'plane in the early morning our time, and the concert's the next evening, your time, then we have to catch a 'plane back the next morning, your time, and then be on stage again our time in the evening, which is all madness, really, but there it is, we'll just have to sleep on the flights, but apart from that, it's great news, don't you think? I mean we won't be topping the bill or anything but we'll be up there somewhere, I expect, I don't even think the band order has been decided yet, but the really scary news is that I'll get a mention in the program, you know* 'Dead Man's Wealth' *featuring* 'Tara'

or whatever, and well, since we'll already be on stage as DMW it means that I'll be doing some of my songs at the same time! I mean talk about singing out of your grade…

So anyway, I'm a bit confused with my time – zones at the moment, so you'd better check this, but the whole thing's being rather thrown together and there was some kind of last – minute legal cock – up with the ticket company, and I think the tickets go on sale at twelve – midnight your time tonight, so pleeease try and get tickets. Tell Bas I haven't forgotten about O2 but he'll have to be on – line and waiting when the tickets go on sale, they're going to sell out very quickly.

We're leaving the road – crew here, so we'll just be travelling with three guitars, and Evie'll bring her flute, but the rest we have to borrow.

So there it is, but I mean Hyde Park, you know?!! I don't think I'll even have time to come home but I'll see you there somehow before or after our session, and I miss you all so much, so do try, won't you?

Love and hugs from Bluegrass Country, how did life ever get this crazy? T xxxxxx'

'Okay, I'm on it,' said Basil 'I'll check when the tickets go on line, and I'll need a credit card.'

'I haven't got a credit card.' Said Keith

'Use mine.' said Rosemary 'Oh bloody hell, who's this?'

Meadow and Keith exchanged looks, which was all that was needed, really. With any luck they would quite soon finally see Tara perform live, and at such a venue, and both knew how they felt and how the other would feel about this. Somewhat to her annoyance, Rosemary was unable to share the moment with her family, as her mobile telephone was ringing and she retired to the other end of the small room.

'Hello…?'

'Yeah, hi, this is Quentin.'

'Oh, hello...'

'Uuum, well look, my two brothers have departed these shores now, so I was wondering whether we could meet up again, you know? If you wanted to, that is.'

'Yes, sure, let's do that.'

'How about I come over to the bus sometime?'

This, Quentin had decided, would be his strategy. If he were to go to her in her home environment and thus perhaps meet her parents, then he would be more certain of her and of their reaction to him, which would tell him whether there really was any future in the relationship. If on the off – chance she turned out to be some sixteen year old runaway who lived on a bus because she had nowhere else to live then this would soon become apparent. He didn't think that this was the case; her accent and general demeanor spoke otherwise, but he wished to dispel his reservations, and particularly his brothers' reservations, once and for all, and so he had formed his plan. It was also the case that he was interested to see what manner of people lived on a bus, and to put the young lady in some sort of domestic context. The young lady in question, however, had reservations.

'You really want to do that?'

Why would he want to do that? Since they as yet hardly knew one another it seemed to Rosemary to be somehow inappropriate, but perhaps he had his reasons.

'If it suits, you know? We could go to the pub, what's it called, the Dog and Bottle, yes? I've not been there and I hear good reports of the ale from people I've spoken to.'

'Well, if you want to I suppose, although it's not easy to find, the bus, I mean.'

'I'll 'phone for directions on the way. So how about Saturday night..?'

'Sure, okay.'

'So anyway, how's life been for you since we last met?'

'Okay...We've just had some good news actually; Tara's performing at Hyde Park, at the Famine Relief concert.'

'What, Tara as in your sister, Tara?'

'As in my sister Tara...'

'That's amazing news. Are you going?'

'Well, Basil, that's my brother, is going to try to get us tickets tonight.'

'I don't suppose he could get one for me, could he? I'll pay for it, of course, in fact I'll pay for both of us to go if you want.'

'I'm going with my family, but…Yes, sure, I'll ask him to get another ticket, or try to anyway.'

'That would be very cool. So, I'll call you on Saturday then.'

'Okay…'

She returned now to the atmosphere of quiet anticipation, although nobody was yet assuming that Basil would be able to secure tickets, so reactions must for now remain muted, aside from the excitement generated by the news that Tara would be singing in front of an audience of so many thousands, which was reason enough to be excited on her behalf. Things had just happened rather quickly for Rosie, and in retrospect she now suffered a moment of doubt as to whether she should have invited Quentin to join her family, but having told him that she was going she could hardly have refused, could she? Basil would be bringing Emma, after all, but that relationship was somewhat more established than her own. Aside from Tara, with whom she had had only brief conversation, nobody in her family knew anything of Quentin, and now she would have to tell them, and this was sooner than she had expected, but there was nothing to be done now. She considered having a quiet word with her brother, but what was the point in that, really?

'Bas, could you try to get one more ticket.'

'Who's coming?'

'A friend of mine just called.'

Keith and Meadow, who knew their children well, noted the too – casual nuance and the non – specific nature of their daughters' last statement, and more information was required.

'Might we know the name of this friend?' Said Keith

'He's called Quentin.'

Brief looks were again exchanged between parents. This was now certainly not enough information, and Meadow continued the gentle enquiry.

'We haven't heard of Quentin before, have we?'

'No, he's a new friend, you know?'

'So what kind of friend is he?' said Keith

'What do you mean?'

Rosie was clearly uncomfortable. The ice – maiden was even looking somewhat embarrassed, and had a slightly red blush about her, which was a rare thing indeed, and she was becoming somewhat defensive, which made her discomfort still more apparent.

'I mean is he a boyfriend or what?'

'Well he's a boy, and he's a friend, so I suppose you could say he's a boyfriend.'

'So who is he, then?'

'He's someone I met on the train when I went to see Charlotte, okay?'

'You met him on a train…'

'Yes, and why not, people have to meet somewhere, don't they?'

'Of course they do,' said Meadow, who thought she should try to diffuse the tension 'and we look forward to meeting Quentin, don't we, Keith.'

'Sure…Sure we do…'

Which was as far as both parents thought that they should pursue the matter; Basil, however, was not of the same mind. Of a sudden he felt oddly protective toward his elder sister, and considered himself by now to be something of an authority when it came to the business of relationships, his own being by now well established.

'So like, what's he like then?'

Rosie felt that she had dealt well enough with her parents, and did not appreciate her brothers' intervention.

'What do you mean, what's he like?'

'So…How old is he, what does he do, that kind of thing.'

'I don't know how old he is, I've only met him once.'

'So that would be on the train then…'

'Look, I've met him once since then, we went for a drink, okay?'

'So any general impressions as to how old he is, I mean have you got it narrowed down to the nearest decade?'

'That's enough, Basil.' Said Meadow

'I'm just asking, you know….?'

'Okay…He's just post - university, his first degree was in geology and he went on to Oxford to study human evolution, he lives in town and has two brothers called Tarquin and Tristan, and now you all know about as much about him as I do, so can we talk about something else?'

'Nope,' said Basil 'not until we've dealt with the names, I mean Quentin, Tristan and Tarquin? What the fuck sort of names are those?'

'Basil, language…' said Keith

'Exactly my point, I mean what kind of language are we talking here?'

'Leave it Bas,' said Keith

'I'm sure we're all looking forward to meeting Quentin next week.' Said Meadow, 'so let's all calm down, shall we?'

'I'm perfectly calm,' said Rosemary, 'and you might meet him before that. He's picking me up from here this Saturday, and do you still want to borrow my credit card, Basil?'

'Yeah, okay, I was out of order, I'm just not used to the idea of you having a boyfriend, or man – friend; got to get my head around it, you know?'

'Well try a bit harder, and anyway he's not anything, yet, he's just someone I had drink with, so let's all go back to being happy for Tara, shall we?'

'I've got that one nailed,' said Basil 'and I'm cool with staying up all night on my lonely vigil while the rest of you sleep soundly in your beds, so, you know, none of you give it a second thought.'

'It's only until midnight, for goodness sake.'

'Pray do not so belittle my self – sacrificial gesture.'

'Basil, fuck off.'

'Father, did you hear that, she used that language word again.'

Meadow laughed. Basil was not the most academically gifted of her children, but he was clever in his dealings with people, and nobody could be angry with him for long. The subject of the Hyde Park concert dominated that which remained of the evening, and it was not until Keith and Meadow were alone in bed that the subject of Rosie's new acquaintance was raised again.

'Did you see her,' said Keith 'she actually blushed.'

'I know….'

'He's a bit old, isn't he?'

'Not really, I mean Rosie's mature for her years, Keith. Don't pre – judge, and I need hardly remind you th….'

'Yeah, I know, you were sixteen when we f…..'

'Yes, well enough said.'

'I was going to say when we first met.'

'Anyway she's only been for a drink with him.'

'I just wonder why she didn't tell us about it.'

'You mean about him, well it doesn't sound as though there was much to tell, and anyway she's old enough to have her own life.'

'Yeah, I know.'

'You have to let go sometime, Keith, although I know she'll be the hardest for you when the time comes.'

'She's still at school, you know? We're still responsible for her.'

'Sure, but not for much longer, and then she'll be gone, and I think she'll be more independent than Tara.'

'Which is kind of ironic when you think of what Tara's doing now, isn't it?'

'I know, bless her. I sometimes try to think what it must be like, you know, to stand up in front of so many people and sing.'

'She's got the band behind her, and Ash especially, but they're all good people. It sounds like she's having a gas. I just hope Bas can get the tickets.'

'Well, we'll know in the morning.'

'That's too long.'

'Where are you going?'

'Think I'll wait up with him, I mean it's nearly eleven now anyway, and it's not often I get my son on his own these days.'

'Okay, well, let me know if he gets them.'

'Shall I wake you up if he does?'

'Of course...'

'How long is it since you and I went to an outdoor concert?'

'Not since Tara was small. We don't even know who else will be performing, do we?'

'No idea, Basil'll probably know by now. Anyway what the hell, there'll be some big names there, and there's only one person who really matters.'

'That's true…'

They smiled for one another in the semi darkness; she turned over and he went in search of their son.

Chapter 7

A Moment of Spontaneity

The hanging of the portrait of the first Lord Michael Tillington in the grand dining room of the Manor House was in the end a thing of little pomp or ceremony. Here would the painting reside, actually as well as historically the next in line to his Lordship's forebears, for tens and perhaps hundreds of years, where it would from now on gather the same dust in the small fissures of its' quite modest but intricate frame as did all of the portraits which had preceded it, but still, the hanging of it was a thing of little circumstance. He who would one day be the second Lord Michael stood on a step - ladder and drilled and plugged the hole, then inserted the large, brass hook into the wall upon which the sturdy metal chain would hang, and with some assistance from ground level he heaved the painting into place, and there it was, done. She who was sister and only surviving sibling to the next Lord then stood a little distance away, on the other side of the great dining table, and gave her brother final instruction.

'Top left corner up a bit….A bit more….Okay, that's it...'

There was a schism, of course, genetically speaking. The first portrait was undisputedly that of the first Lord Tillington, who had been called Henry, but thereafter there was a gap, although there was not literally a gap, and all of those who came thereafter were sons, grandsons and on to an interloper; a pretender, who quite unwittingly and through no fault of his own had no place being here, any more than did any of his ascendants, but of those present only the daughter to the current Lord knew this. She and the witches were aware of the lie which had been perpetrated so long ago by Edward Tillington, the second Lord, whose son had been murdered at the behest of the first in line, and his sister, Anne, but none would yet speak of it.

Also present at the hanging were the current Lord himself, and his wife, Beatrice, and all at least agreed that it was indeed a fine portrait. Even Lady Beatrice, who had had almost nothing to do with the painter herself, stated without doubt or reservation that she had done an exceptional job. The matter of blending her paints and the subtle art of their application, which had taken Pandora Winterton years of her life to perfect, and were the essence of her very particular craft, lent the painting a timeless quality. It could equally well have been painted yesterday or a hundred and more years ago, and there was no apparent difference between her subject and his descendants, save that her subject was still very much alive, and stood watching as his image was hung upon the ancient wall of Middlewapping Manor.

There had been some small controversy regarding the painting just prior to this day. Since its' completion, Lord Michael had mooted the idea that the portrait not be hung in its' final place until he had, as he had put it *'popped his clogs'*, suggesting the compromise that the portrait be for now hung elsewhere, perhaps along the grand corridor. He had no wish, he had said, to stare at an image of himself, no matter how fine an image, whilst he was eating his breakfast or evening meal. His wife and daughter, however, would hear none of it, and they had, not he had to confess for the first time, won the day, for against such a united feminine front there was seldom any victory. In any case he was pleased to note that mother and daughter had actually agreed upon something, which was a rare enough occurrence, and so he had let the matter be. And so there the portrait would hang, until history caught up with itself as it surely would, and the entire life of the man in the picture became a part of that history.

The last two to leave the grand dining room were his Lordship and his daughter, who stood beside her father and took his arm.

'There, Papa, you look very grand indeed, don't you think?'

'Well, perhaps.'

'You know you do. It feels as though we should have opened a bottle of Champagne or something.'

'Does it, why, to celebrate the future demise of the next in line of the rogues' gallery? One feels rather like the undead, as though since one is up there, one should not be down here, as it were.'

'Stop being so morbid, dear Papa. How about celebrating your life, you know, and all the wonderful years that are left of it?'

'There are days, Victoria, when one searches for very much to celebrate.'

'Oh come on, that's not true, I mean there's me, for start, is there not?'

'I rest my case. In any event, what, pray, has put my beloved daughter in so positive a frame of mind?'

'Oh I don't know, I just think....Well, why not be happy, you know?'

'An admirable philosophy I'm sure, and one which one should perhaps try emulate. Anyway, you're up next...Any idea when our painter will return?'

'Soon, I expect, I believe she is waiting for me now. Are we really going to put me up there next to you?'

'Most assuredly, if I have to be there then so will you. You will in any case be company for me.'

'I'll be the only woman.'

'A fitting endorsement to the age in which we live, I daresay.'

'I'll also be the only one under the age of about fifty, I would think, and I won't feel in the least bit dead.'

A moment of coldness passed between father and daughter, and though neither spoke of it, she held his arm more tightly until the moment had passed. She had been dead once, after all, a moment of far more recent history which both had tried hard to forget, but the memory would never completely fade, and probably best that it did not. Despite her unintended poignancy of her words, Victoria Tillington was indeed now feeling in positive frame of mind. Her brother had noted that her general state of being had improved since she had taken herself off to the coast one recent day, although she had not spoken of the day, and nor had he enquired of her, or made any direct connection, for how could he?

On the previous evening Victoria had had a caller, and she was pleased indeed when Molly, who was working later than usual that day, informed her that a gentleman by the name of Percival was waiting for her in the drawing room. She put down her novel, went to the nearest bathroom to check on her appearance, and went to join her visitor.

'Percival, this is indeed a pleasant surprise.'

They smiled for one another.

'Shall I have some tea sent, or coffee I suppose, or can I offer you a drink?'

'Scotch would be fine, of you have some.'

'Of course...'

'Just as it comes...'

She poured two glasses of whiskey from a cut – glass decanter and handed one of them to him. They touched glasses, Percival noting that the quality of the Scotch did not quite live up to that of the vessel which had contained it, but it would serve its' purpose well enough.

'Look, I'm sorry, we can't really smoke in here, should we go outside, do you think?'

'Sure.'

They walked together to the front door, and sat on the steps, she taking up her time – honoured place and he sitting beside her. They lit cigarettes, the evening was mild for the season.

'You really should allocate yourself a smoking room, the house is big enough, after all. What do you do in the depths of winter?'

'I freeze…So, you don't need a reason, of course, but does anything in particular bring you here?'

'Not really. Well, I'm going away for a while, so I thought I'd check on Henry before I left, and see you, of course.'

'That's sweet of you. He's sleeping by now, of course, but I'll take you to him if you want.'

'No, it's okay, just news will be fine.'

'In that case he's very well, thank you, in all respects, as is Nathaniel, which I'm sure will be of at least equal interest to you.'

'I make no distinction, Victoria, and Henry is my Godson, after all.'

'Of course….So, when and where are you going, and for how long..?'

'I've not the least idea yet, in any regard. Well, I'll be off in a couple of days I expect, and probably heading south rather than north, but beyond that…'

'I see. So has anything in particular prompted this sudden departure?'

'I just need to work some things out, you know?'

Victoria laughed gently.

'I think we could all do with some of that, I might try it myself. Do let me know if you succeed, won't you? Anyway I think we know each other well enough for me to ask if anything specific needs to be worked out?'

'Well, for a start I'm…I'm at the end of a relationship, Sally's leaving the village and de facto leaving me.'

'Ah, I see, and I'm very sorry to hear that, of course. Might I ask where she's going?'

'North, and for what it's worth I'm sure she's absolutely making the right decision. She's been offered a job in Scandinavia, and has no idea how long she'll be gone.'

'Oh well, one never knows quite what to say in these situations, does one? I don't really know Sally, of course, but anyway I hope things work out for you.'

'Thanks...The other thing is that I think I'm at the beginning of another relationship, and I need to get away from that, as well.'

This made Victoria laugh again, and Percival could also see the funny side of it.

'So it's what one might call complicated, would that be an apt description of your present romantic circumstance, do you think?'

'Yes, I suppose one could call it that.'

'So would you care to elaborate, or would that be pressing the enquiry too far, even between friends?'

'I hope to be able to elaborate better when I get back, but as far as I understand it so far, it seems to me that there are different kinds love, not all of which are necessarily constructive.'

'Yes, well I can't do other than agree with that, Rebecca and I have been destroying each other with depressing regularity since the beginning, and I think I need another cigarette.'

He gave her a cigarette, and lit one for himself.

'But you still keep going back to each other?'

'So far, yes, although our current estrangement runs deeper than usual.'

'For which I assume there is a particular reason, but I won't ask, unless of course you want to tell me?'

'It's....complicated.'

'I'll show you mine if you show me yours.'

A moment of female hesitation followed; she liked Percival, and trusted to his integrity. He was Godfather to her son, after all, but as confidences went this was a big one. On the other hand, why should she not share Rebecca's sordid little secret with her friend, and had she not decided that she had been giving the matter more significance than it deserved?

'You first then...'

'Her name's Louise, and we've tried to be together before, more than once in fact, but things didn't quite work out the first time, or the second time for that matter.'

'I see...Yes, I've heard of Louise.'

'All the evidence so far is that we can't be together, the problem being that we don't seem to do so well apart, either.'

'This all sounds so familiar; you love her, she loves you and the tricky part is putting that together in a way that works, is that about it?'

'It and all about it, actually...'

'So what will you do? I mean sure, you're going away, but I assume and hope that you'll come back, so aren't you just putting off the moment?'

'Probably, but that isn't always a bad idea, and I need some time out, I think.'

'To work some things out...So what is it that you're trying to work out, actually?'

'That's what I need to work out, before I start working stuff out, you know?'

She laughed again.

'God, you sound nearly as bad as me...Just, you know, don't be too long, will you? I know we don't see very much of each other, but, well, I like to know that you're around, if that doesn't sound too stupid. I mean we draw strength and happiness from people even in their absence, do we not?'

'Of course we do.'

'Perhaps you just need what I believe is commonly called *'closure'*, with Sally, I mean, before you can move onwards?'

'Yeah, maybe that's it then. Anyway you don't have to play by the rules, but it's your turn, I think.'

'A deal's a deal....My current problem with Rebecca relates to Florence, and not to Florence herself, of course.'

'Are we talking about the paternal part of the gene – pool?'

'Yes, we are.'

'And you know who he is?'

'Yes, she told me recently for the first and only time.'

'So I assume that you know him.'

'Yes, I know him very well...Do you know, it once even crossed my mind that he might be you.'

'Well, that isn't an unreasonable hypothesis, stranger things have happened, but I'm off the proverbial hook, time – wise.'

'Well, if you say so, and anyway it isn't you this time, not that it has ever been you, of course.'

'Perish the thought...It isn't too late, you really don't have to tell me, you know?'

'Well then, let's just say that I'm closely related to him, and that you know him as well. You might have even played cricket with him.'

That took only a moment to work out, and a slightly longer moment to come to terms with.

'Jesus....That takes some sorting out, doesn't it?'

'More so when I tell you that he doesn't know he's the father, or that there's any possibility that he's the father. He's totally innocent, if you can believe that.'

'She did that...To he who shall remain nameless?'

'Yes, she did.'

'Christ....'

'Exactly my reaction when she told me.'

'Okay, well the first thing to say about that is that I can empathize. I know it's a hard thing to understand, but it can happen, so you have to believe the guy.'

'I do. As I said, I know him about as well as one human being can ever know another, and he would never willingly have done such a thing.'

Victoria hesitated for a moment. Something about his words of reassurance had struck her, and needed clarification.

'So, she did it to you, then?'

'Let's just say that I speak from first – hand experience. But really, what do you do with that?'

'That's been my dilemma, until now.'

'So what's happened now to undo the dilemma?'

'I've changed my mind, that's all. I mean people do things, don't they, which are quite beyond our control, so why concern ourselves with them?'

'We can't entirely ignore our feelings about things though, can we?'

'No, we can't ignore them, but surely we can control them, and act accordingly.'

'So how will you act, will you forgive her?'

'That I haven't decided, yet, but it's my choice, that's the point.'

'Yes, well that's true, I suppose.'

The thought that this was not the only time that Rebecca had practiced this so particular aspect of her witchcraft had become lodged now in Victoria's mind. Not only that but she had done it to Percival, of all people, and she could not for the moment let the matter be. Aside from anything else, perhaps she could now learn something of how such a thing could possibly happen.

'So, have you forgiven her?'

Percival smiled, and finished his drink.

'Well, in the context of everything that I've had to forgive Rebecca for it was hardly a hanging offense, so yeah, I suppose so. It was different with me though, in one fundamental sense.'

'How so..?'

'I remember it, in some detail, actually. She left the memory of it for me, and from a male perspective it isn't a bad memory.'

'I see...The other fundamental difference is that she didn't become pregnant as a consequence. Was she trying to, do you think?'

'No, at least she told me that she wasn't, and I believe her. In our case it was just, you know, sex for the sake of it.'

'She might have asked you first though, don't you think? You two were...Well, you were close for a time, were you not?'

'You could say that, and I said the same to her. The thing is, though, and without going into detail, I don't think that under more usual circumstances I could have contrived to do the things that we did. It was the very stuff of male fantasy, you might say, which makes forgiving her all the easier. It was a fairly intense experience; no heterosexual male would have stood a chance against it, if you understand me.'

'I'll take your word for it. Of course there are moral issues to be considered, aren't there?'

'I try not to think too much about those.'

'I mean accepting the idea that men cannot be made to have sex with a woman against their will, and therefore can't be raped, as such, if someone is controlling the will of another person, then it becomes a different matter altogether, does it not?'

'It certainly gets a bit fuzzy around the edges.'

'Yes, it does, doesn't it?'

Both had finished their drinks by now, so it was time for Percival to leave, or to stay. When it came to matters to be forgiven, it appeared that she had forgiven him for as good as certainly being father to her brothers' child, and thus being indirectly responsible for Rose's death, which were no small things to forgive, after all. And now there was this; her sometimes lover and soul – mate, and in any case the most important person in her emotional life, had seduced her brother, or however one might describe it, and Victoria's own child had been born of unknown paternal parentage to anyone but herself, and despite the intimacy of their conversation, this was not something which Percival felt sufficiently emboldened to ask her. Nevertheless it appeared that the most private aspects of Victoria's life were everywhere complex, for which he was in no small part responsible, and not for the first time Percival felt a wave of sympathy for her. It was she, however, who broke the silence, perhaps in an attempt to bring the conversation to its' conclusion.

'So, it seems that we both have decisions to make, then; you whether and how to be with Louise, and I whether to forgive Rebecca.'

'Yep, looks that way.'

'I still think that you're putting off the inevitable, if you really love her.'

'Yes, well perhaps we're both guilty of that, don't you think?'

'Well, let's see, shall we? Come and see me when you've worked it all out, okay?'

'That I think would be too long an absence.'

'Well then come and see me anyway, when you get back.'

'I'll be sure to do that.'

He stood up.

'Could you leave me one more cigarette, I've left mine indoors and I want to stay here for a bit longer.'

He lit her cigarette for her, and descended the grand steps of the Manor House, to the place where a witch had once died.

'We're hanging my father's portrait tomorrow.'

The thought and the words had come from nowhere in particular, and for no particular reason, but they had come anyway.

'Right, so that's two of you done, then.'

'Yes, in somewhat contrasting pose, you might say.'

'Well, the subjects were somewhat different, weren't they...'

The past tense was deliberate, and noted, and the two shared a moment of sadness for the first to be painted.

'You met Pandora I assume?'

'Yeah, we met.'

'Any impressions..?'

'I don't know her well, but she seems sound enough, for an artist, you know? She's a bloody good painter anyway, which I suppose is the main thing.'

Victoria smiled to herself.

'Yes, I suppose it is. I've agreed to have my portrait painted by her, she'll be back here soon, I expect.'

'I look forward to seeing the results of that in due time, if you want to show me, of course. Well, good night then.'

'Goodnight Percival, and thanks for coming, it really was good to see you, and it's helped, you know? Don't be a stranger, will you?'

A final parting smile in the darkness, and Percival walked away, turning back only once to see the small figure set against the grandeur of the Manor House, seated on her step, where she had sat so often before at important moments in her life.

If the emotional horizon of Mister Percival Saunders was currently obscured by a mist of his own uncertainty, a certain other gentleman, who lived at number twelve, The Green, was during these days undergoing something of a transition in the romantic aspect of his own life, or perhaps better say that romance had entered his life for the first time. Here was no grand passion, and in truth the matter was more akin to a deep friendship than anything more, but in any case his weekend in Venice with Gwendolyn had been an experience which Reginald would never forget. In the first place there was the city itself, with all of its' aging charm and history, and they had spent long days sitting in coffee houses, and evenings in restaurants, avoiding the worst of the somewhat inclement weather. Even the matter of sharing his twin – bedded hotel room with a woman had in the end been a quite easy matter, which perhaps bore testament to the depth of friendship which had quite quickly and mostly unconsciously taken form between them. Their mutual interest in things historical saw to it that there was never very much awkwardness between them, and Gwendolyn, who was at heart a perceptive and careful person, saw to it that the way into their continued friendship was made easy for the male part of the ensemble.

Their short time away together had indeed been quite definitive, and had given wings to the evolution and further development of their relationship to one another, and upon their arrival back on home soil it was by now an easy matter them to arrange their next meeting. Aside from the odd occasion when his sister had stayed overnight with him, Reginald had never before shared his home with anyone, and perhaps the final part of their coming more closely together occurred one day when they were considering visiting the ruins of a thirteenth century abbey. The abbey was located not far from the village, and whilst Reginald had been there and knew something of its' history, Gwendolyn had not, and knew nothing of it. In any case during their discussions they decided that having visited Holmbrook Abbey, for such was its' name, they would dine at a restaurant in the locale.

'Of course,' Gwendolyn had said 'it might be the easiest thing if I stayed at your house for the night, since we would be so close, if that would be convenient, of course. It would save my having to get a bus or taxi home.'

It took only a moments' consideration, before;

'Yes, of course, that would be for the best. I will make up the spare bedroom, nobody has slept in there for a long time.'

'I'm sure I can help with that, after all I do know your house very well, don't I?'

This was true, of course, since Gwendolyn had cleaned Reginald's house with consummate thoroughness, and knew every part of it intimately.

'Yes, well, that's settled, then.'

So it was that on the appointed day, Gwendolyn arrived with her toiletries and a change of clothes, and for the first time since Reginald had bought the property, someone other than himself or who was not related to him by blood slept there, and ate breakfast at the same table as had Reginald each morning of his later adult life.

She did not stay for long on this first morning, as she had been commissioned on that day to clean for several of her regular clients, but it had been a beginning. After her departure Reginald sat for a while beside his fish – tank, and watched the always quick Zebra – Fishes playing at the surface, ever it seemed in a rush to be somewhere else, and the Harlequin – Fishes who preferred to live at the deeper levels, and who scarce moved at all, being apparently quite content to be wherever they were. This morning after her departure there had been two cereal plates and spoons to wash and dry, and two coffee cups. Small matters, perhaps, in the grander scheme of things, but such small things can sometimes have significance disproportionate to their own dimension. Reginald had never in truth felt lonely, in a way because he had never had anything with which to compare his state of being, until now, but if perhaps from now onwards there would be a different way to be, and if all of his years of living always alone were to end, then Reginald considered this to be a good thing, and the washing of extra dishes to be a small inconvenience indeed.

For another of the people who have become enwoven into the fabric of our tale, life had already and perhaps for the first time found a place in which it could be content. Damien Fotheringay could never have predicted when he had first come to the village, and had walked about the ancient graveyard in search of its' history, that here would be a turning point of such significance for him. From his youngest years passed beside the bleak and rugged Scottish coast, where his life had been every bit as bleak and hard as had his surroundings, to the theatres of London where he had sought solace and escape by for a short time by becoming other people, who were not real people but the invention of play – writes and directors, he had never until now felt so at one with himself. He had come here conversant enough with the skills required to build gardens, and worked hard and diligently at his craft, and now these skills had, with the help and support of Keith, crossed over somewhat into the craft of building houses, which was a different discipline in essence, but required similar skills and no more or less dexterity. The hardness of his early life had instilled in Damien an inherent hardness with his dealings with others, and he and Keith, whose underlying, masculine essence was no less hard than his own, had faced each other down, and found their way to friendship rather than conflict, and such friendships once there can run deep, though they are seldom if ever spoken of between men. Keith had, as Damien realized well enough, been his way into this small community of southern English people, whose lives had not been as his had been, and here indeed and on the whole had he found a soft landing. And then, as we have learned, Sophia Cutler had found her way into his soul, and the two had travelled north of the border together, and thus had he found a way to finally lay that part of his life to rest, forever. Sophia, the historian and the witch, who was, he in the end concluded, moderate in her witchcraft. Every so often she would travel west to a place which she called the white house, a place where he would never go, and here she would meet with others of that which she called the sisterhood, who were people that he would never meet, but otherwise he would never really know that he lived with a witch, which had made him see the whole business of witches in general in a new light. There were others, of course, who used their craft to different and sometimes devastating effect. There were those who had lived in the coven called Farthing's Well, where Damien had indeed been, and where the dark witches had lived their secretive lives and fostered their cruel ambition, and now Rebecca had returned to the village, and of her deeds he knew as much as he wished to know. A woman she was, and now she cared with feminine gentleness for her infant child, but there burned within that soul something which made her far more dangerous than he could ever be, for all of his maleness.

Of those who were presently his work colleagues, Keith Knightman and Will Tucker, we have heard at various times throughout our story, and each working day these three would cross the county border together, and engage together in the business of turning a partly derelict house into a place where people could live once again. For the most part, dialogue between them was confined to that required to carry out their appointed or self – appointed tasks, or they might share insubstantial anecdotes of their lives since last they had met, but the depth of their unity remained unspoken, for none had any need to speak of it. Their work for now was concerned with the more mundane business of the lifting and relaying of floorboards, which had suffered from the neglect of years since anyone had lived in Orchard House. Some indeed were past the reuse, and these they would put aside for burning or to be used for some other purpose, and others would be laid more carefully aside for treatment and to be relayed, but thus did they now pass their working days, in the mess and noise of a construction site, where any kind of unnecessary conversation was in any case difficult. And then, upon a certain morning in the mid - week, Damien came across something which warranted cessation of work, and which required discussion.

For the most part, the boards had been nailed directly onto the old timbers which supported them, and as the boards were lifted they could see through to the ground floor below. In places, however, there was a second layer of boards below the first, creating a narrow void, and it was in such a place that Damien made his discovery.

'Hello, what's this…?'

The others stopped their work and joined him, as he pulled out from under the floorboards a flat, leather container, about A4 size, which had been sewn with thick leather thread around three of its' edges; a wallet, in fact, which he handled with care and placed on the floor. Keith picked it up, and carefully removed some of the dust and grime with his shirtsleeve. There was no mark or writing on either side of the leather, but through the open side it appeared as though the wallet contained several sheets of paper, which had apparently fused together, and had become stuck to the leather container itself, rendering their removal without damage all but impossible.

'Looks like some old documents or something.'

'Must be bloody old then,' said Damien 'these floorboards haven't been up for a very long time.'

'Yeah,' said Will 'and leather hasn't been the material of choice for folders for a long time either. So like, how did this get under the floorboards?'

'Someone must have put it there,' said Damien 'this looks like deliberate concealment. These could even be the original boards.'

'I think we'd better leave well alone,' said Keith 'we'll give it to Mike when he comes, he should be here later today. Anyway, seems like a good moment to stop for tea, don't you think?'

'I'm on it.' Said Will

None present could know the historical significance or otherwise of the discovery, or whether the documents, if indeed they were documents, would be retrievable, but it was definitely a tea moment. The wallet was carefully put to one side, whilst the three men made their way across the remaining floorboards, and made for the stairs.

Within two days of his visit to the Manor House, Percival was in all but two respects ready for his departure. Lulu was safely ensconced with Will and Emily on the smallholding, where she would temporarily be canine company for Monty, and he had been to see Keith and Meadow on the bus. This latter had in fact been a fairly protracted meeting, as they had wished to know why he was going, which perhaps inevitably led to a discussion regarding his current romantic status; why his relationship with Sally was over, and why therefore his relationship with Louise could not once again begin, the former being easier to answer than the latter, since he was not certain of the reasons for the latter himself. There had also to be discussion regarding the cult from the west – country, and how that particular situation currently stood, and any available information regarding witches was exchanged, although from both sides such information was insubstantial.

He and Sally had met once more, and here was a matter which neither found easy. Louise had still not entered the arena of their conversation, in this regard Percival had decided that this would merely add unnecessary complication to their parting; better that she think she was wholly responsible for it, partly if he was honest for his sake, but partly for hers also. Here therefore was an unusual situation. Nothing had apparently happened between them which should end their relationship, other than her going, so it was in a sense anticipation of their break – up rather than its' actuality, which in fact amounted to the same thing, the more substantial reason in any case remaining hidden to one of the parties involved. They drank coffee together one evening at Sally's house, whilst she made her preparations for her now imminent departure, although in fact it was he who would be departing first. Neither thought it a good idea to drink wine, to perhaps better symbolize their parting from one another, since this would make it more likely that they would symbolically make love, one last time, and neither wanted the pathos of that, or the weakening of resolve which might also follow. Better to let the matter be, and to move on, but both bore the guilt of it. She felt guilty because as far as she knew it was only she who was the cause of their separation, and he felt guilty for the same reason, so he did not stay for long, their parting words being as stilted as was the situation.

'Well, I suppose I should let you get on then.'

'Okay, well, I'll see you sometime. I'll be coming back every so often for while at least, until I sort out what's happening with the house.'

'Of course, well let me know when you're around.'

'I will.'

He left. There was no final kiss goodbye; even that was beyond both of them, and her resolve that there would be no more tears proved to be pointless as soon as he had gone.

And so in any case there remained now only two things for Percival to do. The first was to establish where on earth he was going, and to that end he now set his computer on line and began to research available flights and accommodation. In the end this proved a quite easy matter, since within certain bounds he did not particularly care where he went, it was the going that was the thing. The second and now final part of the business was the part which he had put off until now, but it had to be done. Thus it was that quite late of the evening he poured himself a large Scotch, lit a cigarette, and 'phoned a certain mobile telephone number, the recipient answering almost immediately. He had no idea as to the reaction that he was about to receive, particularly in view of that which he had just done, which had been an act of pure and uncalculated spontaneity, and was quite against all that had come before, but now the next few moments of his life would decide a great deal as regards the rest of it.

'Hello…'

'Yeah, it's me.'

'Hello you, you took your time.'

'Well shit's been happening, you know?'

'What kind of shit?'

'Sally and I have split, for one thing.'

'I see…Because of us?'

'Actually no, although actually yes, in a way, but I'm not getting into that.'

'So, Percival my love, what are you getting into?'

'I'm going away for a short while, or maybe a long while, I don't know yet.'

This brought a moment of silence; a pause for thought, perhaps. It cannot have been what she had been expecting.

'I don't see anymore.'

'Nor do I, and since we're both shooting blind, I thought it best we hold fire for a while.'

'So is this a sort of trial separation is it, before we're even together?'

'If you're to be believed we've never been apart.'

'I was talking spiritually, but spirituality doesn't always cut the mustard; I want to see you, and the fact that I also want to fuck your brains out comes secondary to my wanting to see you. I've given up London for you, Percival.'

'Looks like we've both made some sacrifices then...'

'And all so that we can't be together…What sort of sense does that make?'

'What sort of sense did we ever make? Sense doesn't come into it, Louise, which is why I'm going away, try to make some sense of it, you know?'

'You'll never do it on your own, there're two of us in this mutually assured destruction, don't forget.'

'How could I forget, since you seem so good at reminding me? I just needed time out, you know, away from, well, whatever....'

'So this is a fly – by then, is it, before you decide whether to engage?'

'I don't know what it is, but I thought I should tell you, that's all.'

'Well thanks for telling me. A woman could take this personally, you know?'

'Then she'd be right to do so.'

'So you're going away because you think you want to be with me but you're not sure yet, is that how it works?'

'Stop asking complicated questions.'

'Don't go, Percival.'

'Why not..?'

'Because I love you, and I'm sick to my soul of being without you, can't you see that?'

Percival wasn't certain, but he suspected that the gentle sensation that he had just experienced might have been his heart breaking, so perhaps after all he had been right to do as he had done.

'So why did you leave me?'

'Now who's asking complicated questions? Anyway I thought we'd dealt with that, at least, and now I'm asking you not to go.'

'I've just booked tickets, it's too late.'

'Cancel them....Wait, so what, you've booked your return flight as well, so you know when you're coming back?'

'No idea.'

'You said "tickets", you're not going alone, are you? So who's going with you?'

Even now it was not too late, he could return to his original plan and she would be none the wiser, and she was right, tickets could be cancelled; one of the tickets at least. He thought he could even get his money back.

'Nobody, perhaps, but that depends.'

'On what..?'

She was on to him now, so now it was time to decide, once and for all.

'Hello, are you still there?'

'I....Look, I've done something, okay. It was kind of an accident. At least I probably wasn't thinking straight at the time.'

'What was an accident? What are you talking about now?'

'I just found your passport number, and I already knew your name, so, well, like I say, it wasn't thinking logically.'

'Fuck are you talking about? You booked tickets for me? No, you didn't do that....Did you?'

'Call me a fool, but sometimes I just can't help myself.'

More silence now, this would be even less that which she would have been expecting, but her recovery was quick enough, under the circumstances.

'When...? I mean where are you going, or where do you think we're going?'

'A small island in the Maldives, twelve cottages and nothing but ocean for miles'

'Christ....When?'

'The day after tomorrow...'

Okay Louise, focus, and try to say something sensible, or at least to think something sensible.

'I'm...I'm working.'

Not bad....

'So get someone to cover, it wouldn't be the first time.'

Okay, got me there, try again, one more time.

'I might have made other plans.'

'Cancel them, just like you wanted me to cancel the tickets.'

She looked now to her resolve, but her resolve had just melted away or otherwise deserted her, but she was not to be won over this easily, was she?

'This isn't the first time you've done this to me, you bastard. You made me follow you around the world once before.'

'I suppose I'm getting predictable. Anyway this is different, I hadn't bought the tickets last time, and this time we'd be going together, so now it's your choice. Either I go alone or it's you and me on a small island, and we see how it goes from there.'

'And if you go alone then that's how it stays, yes?'

'I hadn't thought that far ahead. I didn't even know how you'd r…'

'Shut up, I'm thinking. So this is an ultimatum…'

'Call it what you will.'

'We don't do confined spaces well; we could end up hating each other.'

'That's what we have to find out, don't you think?'

'Death or glory, right..? One last chance to reach for the fucking stars.'

'So, are you in, or what?'

'And for that you expect me to just drop everything and come when you call, is that it?'

'I hadn't quite seen it like that, but however you want to see it, are you coming or not?'

So here it was then, the moment that Percival had been awaiting with some anticipation, and resolve…? Who said anything about resolve?

'Hell yes, of course I'm fucking coming, bastard though you are.'

Both now were silent for a moment. Both felt as though they had just lost control of something, though neither knew the nature of it, or why or how it should ever be controlled, but somebody had to speak, and it was his turn. So, what to say then?

'That's my girl.'

'So what do we do?'

'What do you mean?'

'We have to make some arrangements, don't you think?'

'We meet outside Gatwick departures, the flight's at around ten a.m., I'll be there an hour or so before.'

'Where will you be?'

'Drinking coffee somewhere, I'll wait 'til the flight's called.'

'Any chance of a flight number..?'

'I don't have that information to hand, it's a flight to Dubai, departs at 09.55 I think. Our final destination's Male, and from there we go by boat.'

'Well that'll do I suppose. Can I 'phone your mobile, on the great day, you know?'

'I don't carry a mobile.'

'No, of course, silly of me…So, do you have any other surprises for me or are you done?'

'I'm all done, I think.'

'Well go away then, I've got some thinking to do.'

'Don't think too hard, I'm not.'

'No, you're just acting on instincts, yes?'

'You know me….'

'Do I? Sometimes I wonder.'

'Well there's something we have in common then, let's start from there, shall we?'

'I'm going now.'

'So go…'

The line went dead. Percival finished the last of his Scotch, and poured himself another one. He tried to imagine what Louise would be doing now, which was an exercise in futility since he didn't even know where she was. As to what she would be thinking, that was something else which he couldn't get close to, so he gave up the chase. Perhaps he had been unnecessarily brusque with her; his had not been lovers' words, but still, she was coming, and he supposed that everything else would follow from there, whatever that might be.

Michael Tillington arrived at Orchard House in the mid – afternoon. Discussions were had regarding floorboards, the agreement being that since not all of the boards were in sufficiently good condition to be re - laid, the best of them would be used to board the main rooms upstairs, and new boards bought for the bathroom, and perhaps one of the bedrooms. Michael, and especially Elin, wished to keep the old boards exposed where possible, using strategically placed rugs as opposed to full, fitted carpeting. Also under discussion was the final position and number of electrical sockets and light fittings, since those existing would be insufficient for a modern home, and conduits for electric cables would have to be placed in position along beams before the boards were replaced, and to this end colour – coded pencil marks were made on walls. In the event, however, the most significant occurrence of the visit was the handing over of the leather wallet, which was once again examined as closely as possible. By now Keith and Michael were outside at the front of the house, and Michael was about to depart.

'I think,' said Keith 'that you might have to take this to some sort of specialist historical document restorer, or whatever; get them prized apart.'

'Yes, well I'm sure Vics will know somebody, at least she knows painting restorers, but anyway I'll work on that. I wonder what on earth they could be...'

'Could be nothing, of course, and there may not be much left of whatever it is when it comes to it, but somebody took the trouble to hide them under the floorboards, and quite a long time ago, I would say.'

'Yes...Fascinating...Anyway, thanks Keith, I'll see you in a couple of days I would think, buy whatever you need in the meantime.'

'Sure...See you soon then.'

Michael turned to leave, and Keith to continue his work for that which remained of the day, but then Michael had something else to say. He had been waiting for the right moment, but that moment had not come, so now seemed to be as good a time as any.

'Keith, I never said thank you.'

'What for..?'

'For our conversation in the pub...'

'Which conversation in the pub..?'

'About there never being a right time to start one's life again...That one should stop looking back, but rather one should look to the future.'

'Oh that conversation, well, it was probably just the ramblings of an idiot.'

'Not at all...In fact, to be quite honest I doubt whether I would be where I am now had we not spoken, so, you know, thanks, that's all.'

'You're welcome, for what it was worth.'

Michael got into his car and started the engine for his return journey, having placed the leather wallet carefully on the seat beside him. Whilst he walked back to the house, Keith was left to ponder the somewhat enigmatic words of his current employer. He assumed that he had been referring to Elin, the woman with whom Michael would one day quite soon be cohabiting, although this was apparently still a secret known only to the few.

Chapter 8

THE MEANING OF LIFE

Of the myriad and various events which occur daily in the lives of people, most will be considered insignificant, and will for the most part be forgotten, and will be consigned to the place where mundane memories pass beyond need of recall. From the moment of awakening begins the highly complex and little understood business of being self – aware, and of being aware of others, and other influences, all of which come to bear on all that people do, and which makes them unique among all living things, and yet for the far greater part such things are taken for granted in the interest of their continuation. People may awaken to familiar surroundings, and have routines which do not require much thought or consideration, which will ease their passage into and later through the new day, but beyond that their own influence even upon their own lives may be said to be limited. Practical matters must be thought of; the day ahead will perhaps have been planned in advance, and perhaps written into diaries, events which may include meetings with others for business or pleasure, which may in turn be said to give any given day mutually assured significance to those who will meet. Such things give focus to the business of life, and help to imbue it with at least a semblance or impression of meaning, but they will not be the end of it. Thoughts or emotions will come unbidden into the minds of people which will not have been predicted, chance meetings which have not been planned may occur, or a letter may arrive by post or by electronic mail which was not expected, and these people must deal with and process each day, for such is their genius, and so have they learned to be. And the process will continue, as it must, for something must always happen. There can be no void or cessation of thought, until sleep take them again, and all things once again become subconscious. Notes in diaries will soon enough become a part of history, and a new page in people's lives will be turned, and new things will be done, for such is the lot of people, and in this way do people gain reassurance that there is indeed some point to it all, for there must be, must there not? So much intelligence and consideration, and so much co – dependence surely cannot after all be for nothing, can it? So, let this chapter in our tale begin at the start of such a new day, for some things will not be forgotten; some things may be called significant, and be worth the remembering, and the author begs your leave to make such judgment in this regard as he may, and to impart certain events which happened during the days after Percival departed from the village. Of his adventures we will hear in our next chapter, but even the absence of people will have influence, and people will always leave something of themselves or their lives behind.

So, then, let this chapter begin on a certain morning in the life of Sally Parsons, which is a particular day in her life, for later today she will take a short flight north, to Oslo, where she will for an indefinite period take up residence. Temporary accommodation has been found for her, from which she will discover a city to which she has never been, and in time find her own place to dwell, but here will be somewhere from which to start, and to travel to the other destinations and cities which will be within her working remit. From now onwards hers will be a world of overseeing the installation of corporate décor, computer systems and cash – machines, and the hiring of staff to sit behind counters, ready to greet and to do business with the local populous on the banks' behalf. A world of competitive interest rates and easy – start loans, where customers must be convinced that money invested with this particular bank will be wisely invested, and money borrowed will be wisely borrowed; a world which Sally Parsons had so nearly left behind.

For now, though, her day is concerned with leaving rather than arriving, and saying goodbye to the house which she so loves, and for which she has worked so hard and sacrificed so much. She will come back here, of course. Soon, if all goes well, she will be employing the services of a removal and storage company, whereby the stuff of her former life will be put away until it is needed again; her table and chairs, her cross – trainer and her bed, in which she has for so long slept, and made love, and felt the loneliness of separation from the one from whom she is now separated once more. Others, who will be strangers to her, will one day soon be sleeping here, and via a rental agency will be paying her to do so, but these are not matters for today.

Today, Sally is saying goodbye, and to this end did she walk the short distance beside the village Green, along the main road and down the lane toward the field, where she knocked on the door of the old cottage, just in case. Percival had already gone, as she knew in her heart that he would have done, and the cottage down the lane stood empty, and silent. There had been no final farewell, no last – minute words to even now try to persuade her to stay, or even that he would come and see her, sometimes, and she would come home, sometimes, and of course she could stay at the cottage. No, it was over, and he had not even tried. There was nobody else in his life, at least as far as she knew, for surely she would have known, would she not? She had imagined conversations where he had asked her not to go, and she had agreed in a moment of existential love and passion, and later she had 'phoned the bank and apologized, but she would not be taking up the position after all, and she had further imagined the chaos which would have ensued among the board of directors. But these were silly thoughts, which must be put away once and for all, because he had already gone, and his letting her go had in the end it seemed been an easy thing for him. A line had now been drawn from which there was no going back, and the sweetness of her memories of the good times with Percival would at once be a solace and torment to her in the months and years to come, but she would always at least have the memory of them.

Later in the day she had unplugged appliances, made one final check of windows and doors, and walked from her house by the Green, closing the door behind her. A beautiful, clever and still young woman wheeling only a suitcase and carrying a shoulder bag into her new life, and tonight, at the end of this most significant of days, she would be sleeping somewhere quite else. There had been one final telephone call to Polly, but with the others who formed her closest group of friends there had been no contact. Polly would tell them, of course; yes, Sally had gone to Norway, and yes, it was over between her and Percival, and this time she had left him rather than the other way around, and of this they and particularly Ray could make what they would. The next time she saw them, and who knew when that would be, she would have a different story to tell.

On the appointed evening that Quentin Forbes Dolby was to meet with Rosemary Knightman, it took two brief telephonic conversations between them en his route to assist his navigation to and thus ensure his timely arrival at the bus in which she lived. She had emphasized to him the importance of his arrival before nightfall, since to arrive thereafter would have rendered his task all but impossible. Landmarks would not be so marked in the darkness, and he could have become quite lost even quite close to his destination. Rosie was still not certain of the merits of or motivation for his wishing to so meet, his given reason that he wished to drink ale in the Dog and Bottle public house seeming to her to hold very little water in terms of its' logic, or in terms of their new and still uncertain relationship. But still, coming he was, and she had of course told her parents of his planned arrival, which was looked forward to with a certain degree of anticipation. Here, after all, was the first gentleman friend that Rosemary had made her parents aware of, and certainly the first that they would meet, so there was some matter to it.

For Quentin it was also a thing of some import, since it would in large part determine whether his undoubted and singular feelings toward the young lady would prove to have foundation in terms of their future possibility. Since their first and particularly their second meeting, he had had to admit to himself that these were feelings that he had never before experienced, and was even open to the strong likelihood that he may in fact be in love with her, but he would not allow such feelings to get away from him or to find further definition until he had further explored their implication. It was thus with some anticipation on all sides that Quentin approached the bus and trailer, in the twilight of the early evening, where this particular part of his immediate future would better find its' metaphoric way. He took a moment before he made his final approach to the door of the old bus, taking in the somewhat ramshackle accommodation in its' nonetheless certainly idyllic setting. He observed the overhead power cable which would have provided their electricity, and the somewhat home – grown plumbing system which appeared to service an outdoor shower and standpipe. Ashley Spears had approached the bus in similar fashion as Tara had been singing whilst washing the dishes, and thus had so much begun, and thus would Rosie's sister soon be singing before the multitudes in a park in London, but now the standpipe stood alone and unused. Washing hung discretely to dry to one side of the bus, hidden in the woodland upon a rope strung between two trees, a clearly home – made table and chairs set formed the main focal – point beside the bus, waiting for warmer months, and the whole scene had a homely self – sufficiency which appealed to Quentin's sensibilities. His own upbringing had been one set against a backdrop of upper middle – English ambition, imbued with the motivation to get on with the business of life, and to do so as quickly as possible, and his young domestic circumstances had not been without tension, sibling rivalry certainly playing its' significant part. Here was a different feeling; gentle and well – played guitar music emanated from within the bus, and a sense of peace and contentment pervaded the air, before he had so much as met the people responsible for its' creation. With these thoughts in mind did Quentin knock on the door of the old bus, whilst doing his best to quell a growing sense of anticipation which had started somewhere in the pit of his stomach.

For Michael Tillington, these continued to be heady days. Elin was once again working long hours during long days, and rather to her frustration was unable to find sufficient time to travel west to view that which she was certain now would be her future home, and to be with he who would be her future husband. Michael therefore during this time travelled east to Canterbury about once a week, and during such visits they would spend evenings or nights of passion together, before he was dispatched once more to be her eyes on the progress being made at Orchard House, despite his assuring her that for now there really wasn't very much to see, aside from the lifting of floorboards and drilling of holes for cables and pipes. Their lovemaking continued to be something of an enigma to him, and this despite his having been married to a prostitute, who had been well enough versed in the art of making love. With Elin, it was rather a matter of calculated and pre – ordained experimentation, the preordination being always on her part, and he never quite knew what to expect. She would perhaps say '*Tonight I would like to have sex in the kitchen, I will lay on the kitchen table and you will be standing upright.*' and afterwards they would have discussion on the relative merits of any given experience, and to what extent, comparatively speaking, they had both enjoyed the matter of it. In truth during such conversations it was she who did most of the talking, he being not particularly particular where or how the business went on, so long as it went on somewhere. She thought nothing of buying high – end, softly pornographic magazines in his absence, which they would read and look at together, during which times she might enquire of him as to whether he would like her to wear a certain type of lingerie, to which he would almost invariably say yes, since to him all of the lingerie looked rather nice. Otherwise their conversation revolved for the most part around the renovation work at Orchard House, and how the house would look when all was done. When they were apart she would almost daily take photographs of things which she saw, or from pages of design magazines, and these she would send to him on his mobile telephone. These might be images of bathrooms, wherein she would ask his opinion on various types and shapes of baths, taps or washbasins, being sure to offer her own opinion whilst she was about it. Michael, meanwhile, being somewhat more linear in his thinking, concentrated upon the more practical matter of getting the house into any sort of shape to receive any kind of bath, or colour of paint, before such finer points were settled upon, being certain that in any case she would change her mind several times before it came to the final stages of renovation. But still, it was a happy and fulfilling process for them both, and so far as he was concerned she could offer as many opinions as she wished.

During these days, Michael's thoughts turned ever and anon to the leather container which had been recovered from below the floorboards, and the rather mysterious paper which it contained, and in this regard he one evening during this week received a telephone call whilst he was at the Manor House.

'Hello, is this Michael Tillington?'

'Yes, it is he.'

'My name's John Forester, I'm a sort of colleague of Victoria's in London, and I'm sure you're aware that she has given me some old papers to try to bring into the light of day. I believe you found them in a house that you're renovating?'

'Oh yes, of course....'

'Well anyway, I've managed to get them apart without inflicting too much damage. In fact I've got them spread out in front of me, five sheets in total.'

'Gosh, that was quick...So what have you discovered?'

'Well, in one respect at least we've been fortunate, I mean these are definitely old, the paper's flax, and of high quality, but they must have been kept in fairly ideal conditions. Usually paper of this age degrades a lot quicker than this; too wet or too dry and there would have been nothing left of it.'

'I see, so how old is it, do you think?'

'It's hard to date it precisely, but this kind of paper hasn't been around for a long time, I would say we're looking at eighteenth or maybe even seventeenth century.'

'Good grief...'

'Yes, well the leather container gave us some clue as to the age, it's hardly the sort of thing that documents are carried or stored in these days...'

'No, of course...So, what else can you tell me?'

'Well after that the news isn't so good, I'm afraid. The ink has degraded as one would expect, and there's nothing legible anymore, at least with the naked eye.'

'So the paper was written on, then?'

'Oh yes, that much at least is clear. I would say these are letters of some kind, but as I say, beyond that it's impossible to tell.'

'That's a pity.'

'Yes...Fortunately however, all may not be lost. I know someone who might be able to work some magic with back – lighting and magnification and such, if anyone can make anything of it, she will, she's got the patience of Job when it comes to this sort of thing. I mean it depends how far you want to take this, cost – wise and so on, and nobody can guarantee anything, of course.'

'No, of course not, but I want to take it as far as possible, if you think it's worth a stab...'

'Well it's always worth a go, in my opinion. Her name's Pat Wagstaff, she works out of Exeter University. If you like I'll have the papers sent to her via specialist courier, and after that it's between you and her. I'll have to send her the originals, it's partly at least to do with the relief, you know. Pens leave an indentation on paper, and a lot will depend on how hard the person was pressing when they wrote, it might all come down to that, I'm afraid.'

'I see, yes, well that would be splendid, then, and thank you for everything that you've done so far. This is all rather exciting, for a layman such as myself, I mean.'

'Well, even us professionals never tire of the thrill of the chase, so I'm glad this isn't the end of it, although I really wouldn't set your hopes too high, not even the best of us can work miracles.'

'No, of course...'

'Tell you what, I'll send my invoice to your 'phone including the courier, and I'll include her contact details so you can get in touch directly. Cash would be good, if possible.'

'Of course, I'll ask Vics, that is Victoria, to settle the bill immediately.'

'Well I see her fairly regularly, so thanks, you know, and good luck. I mean it could be shopping lists or whatever, even if we do manage to read them.'

'Well, at least they'd be old shopping lists...'

'Sure, well, goodbye then.'

'Goodbye, and thank you again.'

The call was ended, and Michael was left to ponder the possibilities of that which may have been written, when, and by whom. It may even shed some light on the older history of the house, which was ever frustrating in its' absence, but in any event somebody had written upon the old paper, and then taken the trouble to conceal their writing under the floorboards in a leather wallet, so there must be something to the matter, must there not? All now depended upon someone called Pat Wagstaff, and all for now that he could do was to wait. In a moment he would 'phone Elin to tell her the news, and go to see Victoria, since she had been instigative in the process of possible discovery, but for now he leaned out of his bedroom window and lit a cigarette. The evenings were milder, now; long awaited spring had come at last to the counties of England. Keith was making a good job of Orchard House, and his decision to offer him the work to the exclusion of all others seemed to have been vindicated, at least so far, and Michael was in love, and one day, sometime in the future he and Elin would be married. All things considered then, life was moving along in a nothing but positive way for the next Lord in waiting, even if the pursuit of the words apparently written so long ago did finally prove to be a dead - end.

'Hi, you must be Quentin.'

The door was opened by a quite tall, slim woman wearing a long dress and no shoes; she had fine, long blonde hair and a winning and welcoming smile. The thing which struck Quentin immediately and above all else, however, was a palpable aura of calmness which was about her, which overlay a sense of undefined strength, or power perhaps, which he had seldom if ever come across, and from which it took him a moment to recover. Her quick, clear blue eyes took him in, and he felt open or exposed in a way that he could not recall feeling before, as though she looked not only straight into his eyes, but into his very soul. Here would be a very hard woman from which to hide oneself or ones' feelings.

'Yes, hi…Hi, and you must be Mrs Knightman.'

That smile again, and gentle laughter behind the words; here was a clearly extraordinary person.

'Well, something like that, I'm Meadow, anyway, Rosemary's mother. Come in, won't you? Rosemary will be here in a moment, I'm sure, in the meantime may I introduce Keith, Rosie's father.'

A tall, broad – shouldered man stood up and placed his old and clearly well – used steel – strung acoustic guitar on the floor beside him. He had slightly darker, much thicker but still blonde hair, which was tied up in a ponytail, and the hand which was extended and now took Quentin's had strength of a different kind. Rosie had told him that her father was a builder, but it was immediately clear to Quentin that here was a man who was rather more than that. Rosie had told him, for instance, that her father had played the guitar on a symphony which Ashley Spears had written and recorded, and this he could now more easily believe. Whatever or whoever Quentin had been expecting to meet, it had not been people such as this, and he noted in passing that there was absolutely no physical similarity between Rosie and either of her parents. Still, he had not been turned away at the door, which was one scenario which he had imagined, and from this the young man took encouragement.

'Name's Keith…'

'Quentin, very pleased to meet you, sir.'

'Likewise, I'm sure.'

'May we offer you some herbal tea?'

'Ummm, sure, that would be nice, thanks.'

Enter Rosemary, wearing a loose – fitting and quite unfashionable top, and quite short skirt and heels, who nevertheless stood considerably shorter than any of them; Quentin was struck once again by her prettiness. Rosemary had quite short, dark hair, and a young and immediate energy which broke the tension of the moment.

'No thanks, we're going to the pub…I see you've met my parents.'

'We were just getting introduced.'

'Good, well that's done then, so let's go, shall we?'

'Sure…'

Quentin exchanged parting smiles with Meadow, and a more serious look passed between Keith and himself; he was about to leave with the man's daughter, the first ever to do so, and this was a matter to be taken nothing but seriously between men. Rosemary took a warm, winter jacket from the back of a chair, and Quentin followed her out into the now quickly fading light.

'I might join you later for a pint.'

This was Keith, who stood in the doorway and watched their departure.

'Please do…I mean that would be great…'

'Must you, father dear…?'

They walked away together, the door of the bus closed behind them.

'They seem like good people, your mum and dad.'

'They have their moments. Anyway, what were you expecting?'

To which there was no answer, really, since he had not known what to expect, so for now they continued their progress in silence up the rough track toward the main road, and thence to the village Green. Rosie now made somewhat more sense to Quentin, as did the fact that her sister was a now famous musician. The fact of their having been born and brought up on a bus had not sat easily with his middle – English way of seeing the world, but that was before he had met their parents. Exceptional people, it seemed, could sire exceptional children, regardless of their circumstances, and perhaps even because of them.

Behind the closed door of the bus, Meadow decided that something should be said.

'He seems like a nice young man, don't you think?'

'We hardly met him, and he's not that young, don't forget.'

'He's not that old, Keith, and he's certainly good looking.'

'Looks have got nothing to do with it.'

'Really..? Would you have asked me out if you thought I was ugly, then?'

'That's a ridiculous hypothesis, since you weren't. Anyway, that's different.'

Meadow smiled.

'If you say so…Anyway regardless of what he looks like he's obviously intelligent, what with having degrees and all.'

'Clever is as clever does, as my old dad used to say.'

'Your dad never said that, did he?'

'No, but I just said it anyway. Rosie was wearing a short skirt, and shoes.'

'Rosie usually wears shoes.'

'Not like those shoes, and tights, she never wears tights out of school, and those aren't school tights, are they…'

'Yes, it's unusual to see her dressed up. You aren't really going for a drink with them, are you?'

'Absolutely…'

'Do you think that's a good idea?'

'Yeah, I do. Why do you think he wanted to meet her here?'

'I really don't know.'

'Guy came here for a reason, I mean of all the pubs in all the counties, you know?'

'No, I'm not sure I do.'

'Guy's checking us out, obviously.'

'Perhaps he wanted us to *'check him out'* too, seeking parental approval, one might say.'

'Could be, in which case he won't be disappointed, I mean about the checking out part, the jury's still out on the approval, that he will have to earn.'

'Well please try to curtail your protective paternal instincts toward your daughter. He's alright, Keith, trust me, I can tell with people.'

'I know, but I want to be certain, you know, get to know the guy a bit better.'

'They're going out for a drink, Keith my love, that's all.'

'They won't mind me joining them then, will they?'

To which there was really no counter argument, so Meadow let the matter be, and decided that perhaps she had better go too, four people at least being better than three. She had almost absolute trust in her man not to embarrass their younger daughter, but her being there would put the final seal on his trustworthiness in this respect.

If there is anyone in our tale who could be said not to draw succor and reassurance from the company of and cooperation with others, that person is surely Isabella Baxter. Perhaps by chance inherited characteristic, but in any case for whatever reason, Isabella had been born into the world with an intellect far above the average for those of similar age to herself, and perhaps those of any age. Thus has she ever found herself set apart from others, and thus does this singular young woman see the world through different eyes, something which could be said to be at once a blessing or a curse. To be the exception rather than the rule, even if a person has exceptional gifts, is not always an easy place to abide, and this is something which cannot be talked of with others, as they would not understand. Perhaps in more godly times Isabella might have found solace in a godhead, but Isabella believed in no god, and to perceive or understand with such clinical and absolute certainty and at such a young age that there is in the end no meaning to any action beyond the action itself, and yet to be driven by the same instinctive and hormonal influences as anyone and everyone, is to be in a particular place, and a place to which few could follow. It would be an easy and perhaps understandable thing for others around her to see Isabella as cold and unfeeling, and yet she is none of these things, but rather she is someone who is ever at pains to try to rationalize the irrational, and to try to make sense of the ultimately senseless, and such inner conflict can at times drive such a person to distraction, or to actions which seem to others to be heartless and even cruel. For someone such as she, who does not enjoy the comfort of close friendship, or the giving and receiving of love from those around them, something else must be found to fill the place where such things abide, and on her journey back to at least some semblance of a normal life after the trauma of her having been raped, Isabella looked now increasingly to the game of chess for something upon which to focus her thoughts. Here, in the all but infinitely complex movement of pieces around a chess board did she find simplicity; here was only cold calculation, and the simplest of ambitions; to out – think and so win against her opponent, whoever they may be.

So it was that during these days Isabella went sometimes to her chess club, which at once paved her way back to the world, and gave her exceptional mind a way to find expression, and so it was that on the evening that Quentin and Rosemary met with the so different ambition of becoming closer to one another, Isabella found herself sitting alone once more on opposite sides of a chessboard from her newest opponent. By now, she had by dint of her having won most of her most recent games, improved her rating and thus her ranking at the club, until once again only Richard Templeton stood between her and the position of highest ranking player. Since her return to the club she had seen him only once, and then only from a distance across the room. They had exchanged looks, but he had left when she had been mid – game, and she had not spoken to him until now, but now he stood on the opposite side of the table, where she sat awaiting her next opponent.

'I suppose it's about time you and I had a game, don't you think?'

He smiled, and she found herself smiling back; here was a man, and men were her enemy, and yet here was Richard Templeton.

'Yes, I suppose so…'

He took the seat opposite her and picked up two pawns, one of each colour, which he concealed one in each hand, and held them out for her to choose. She chose his right hand, and so drew the black pieces, which would give him the advantage of the first move. He played his queen's pawn to d4, she played d5, and his second move of pawn to c4, offering her his C pawn, would likely develop quickly into an open and combative position, and so it proved to be. In the end the game would take sixty three moves and would last for somewhat over an hour, by the end of which others who had completed their last game of the evening had gathered around the board; here was a confrontation between their best player and the strange young woman who threatened to usurp him, most of those gathered had played against both of the players, and most had been beaten by them, so here was a game worthy of the watching.

The audience were not disappointed; here was indeed a battle – royal, fought on different fronts, with each player living on the edge of instant defeat if a false or less than perfect move were made, and yet by move fifty three only kings and six pawns remained on the board, three pawns each, and he had a slight positional advantage and looked set to win. And then, on move fifty six he made that which appeared to all to be an erroneous pawn move, which as far as any could see was the first error which either player had made, but it was enough, and any advantage was lost. Thereafter it was just a matter of kings capturing pawns, until in the end only the two kings remained on the board, and the game was drawn.

A palpable release of tension and a low murmur of voices spread through the small crowd of onlookers, and the two players looked at one another, and smiled again. He stood up and took his raincoat from the back of the chair, and without thought as to why, she did likewise and followed him outside onto the damp street, where a light rain had been falling. They stood together on the roadside, both distractedly looking out at the passing headlights, and listening to the sound of tyres on the wet road. After such a confrontation and such prolonged intensity of thought, players will often take time for heads to be cleared, and to engage once more with the world beyond the sixty four squares of a chess board, and so they did, until he was the first to speak.

'Well played...'

'Not as well as you...It seems I can't beat you yet.'

'Your time will come.'

A moment of silence followed, before;

'You don't have to tell me what happened in Germany, Isabella, it's none of my business, of course, but if you ever need to talk to anyone, well, I'm here, so, you know...'

The words had been quite unexpected, and took a moment for her to process. He had helped her on the day after the assault; without him she was uncertain as to how she would have made the journey home, but this was the first time that he had said anything of the matter, and the first time to her recall that he had addressed her by name. She couldn't tell him, of course; she couldn't tell anyone, but the fact that he had asked, and after so long a time, had taken her quite unawares.

'I see...Well, thank you.'

The moment was almost lost. They would part company and meet again in the indefinite future over the chessboard, but such moments do not often present themselves, and she had just as good as affirmed that something had indeed happened, as if it had not been obvious enough. But why had he spoken now? Had she not covered her tracks and her emotions well enough? No, of course she had not, but she said nothing, for no words would come, but neither did she walk away. In truth and for reasons that she was not sure of, she did not wish the moment to end, and apparently neither did he, and now he spoke again.

'You haven't been the same since Dusseldorf, that's all.'

So what, was he reading her thoughts now, and how had she not been the same, and how well did he suppose that he knew her to make such comparison? She was Isabella, and she was doing okay, and needed nobody's help, so why would she even think of telling him, but the words came anyway; her words, at last, for such moments, as rare as they are, should not be lost forever.

'I…I was raped. They drugged me unconscious, and raped me.'

The words hung in the air as though they had substance and form of their own, and might escape if they were not caught quickly, and quickly understood. Now it was his turn to process, but the words were as strange to her as they were to him; she had never heard herself speak them before to anyone who had not been a part of it.

'Christ…'

He took a pack of cigarettes from his pocket and lit one.

'Do you…?'

'No, and I didn't know you did.'

'I don't, not really, unless somebody whom I regard as a friend tells me that she's been…Even my wife doesn't know I smoke, sometimes.'

His words went in somewhere, but could not for a moment find anywhere to settle, so again he was the next to speak.

'Who….?

'Other members of our team, actually...'

Richard made a swift mental inventory of the others in the British team, none of whom he had seen or spoken to since the contest.

'That's why…It's why they took a different flight home.'

So that was it then; all now became clear to him, or at least began to do so, and there had been four of them, although their names for the moment escaped him. He took a long draw on his cigarette.

'Have you…I mean have you spoken to anyone about this?'

She laughed, and it was not a happy laugh.

'Oh yes…I found them all. I think they're all getting divorced, now, or most of them anyway.'

He exhaled his smoke in a long breath, which gave him long enough to once again collect his thoughts, and to find the next and obvious question.

'But no legal action was taken?'

'No, that was the deal, when I found them, or rather when they found me…'

He did not for now question her somewhat enigmatic words, he did not wish to press his enquiry further than it should go, but there was another obvious question.

'Have you sought any professional help?'

'No, actually you're the first person…I haven't spoken to anybody apart from them, and it was only one of them.'

'Not even to your parents?'

'Especially not to my parents, for different reasons...'

More time, and more passing cars, whilst he searched for something to say in the face of this revelation, but there was nothing really, for now, anyway.

'Well, then….As I say, if there's anything I can do.'

'Of course, thank you. Just please don't tell anyone, you know?'

'Not a soul.'

He threw his cigarette into the wet gutter, and turned to leave, pulling the collar of his raincoat tighter around his neck as the rain began to fall again, but now she had a question.

'Why did you do that…?'

He did not turn around, but he stopped, and he was listening.

'Why did I do what?'

'You know what you did, you could have beaten me.'

'It was a mistake. Everyone makes mistakes.'

And with that he was gone, lost to the wet evening, and Isabella was left alone once again. She had told someone, and now she had a friend, because he had told her that it was so. Something good had happened in her life, and although she knew well enough that there was no meaning to it all, that was enough meaning to be going on with.

It was somewhat after nine o'clock in the evening as Keith and Meadow entered the rather dimly – lit and always comforting environs of the Dog and Bottle public house. Rosemary and Quentin were sitting in quiet and intimate conversation at a table away from the bar and near the fireplace, which was emitting its' customary gentle pall of smoke. Nigel Hollyman, the landlord, had given assurance to certain of his customers that he would have the matter seen to during the spring, whilst giving assurance to certain others that he would not, opinions on the matter being approximately equally divided among his regular clientele. In any case, this would prove to be one of the last fires to be lit during the still early spring months.

As Keith and Meadow entered, Rosie shot her mother a '*Really…?*' look across the bar room, to which Meadow could only reply with a look of apology and a subtle glance at Rosemary's father, who had made directly for the bar, where

Ron and Barbara were well established in their position on bar – stools. Quentin got quickly to his feet;

'I'll get the beers in, Mrs…Meadow, what's your poison?'

'Just orange juice, thanks...'

'Right…'

Quentin made for the bar, Meadow sat at the table momentarily with her daughter, which in the event would prove to be rather more than momentarily.

'We won't be long; I made your father promise that this would be a quick pint only.'

'I don't know why he had to come at all.'

'He has a right to do so, Rosie, and this was Quentin's choice of venue, after all. You might equally well ask why Quentin wanted to come here, of all places.'

'I don't know, I think he wanted to meet you and Dad.'

'Yes, your father thinks so too, which I suppose is no bad thing, after all.'

'No, I suppose not.'

A quick glance over to the bar saw Keith, Quentin and Ron in already earnest conversation.

'I wonder what they're talking about…' Said Rosemary

'Lord knows.' Said Meadow

'I hope dad's not asking him what his prospects are…'

Which made both mother and daughter laugh, and Rosemary offered her mother her drink.

'You can help with this if you like, it's only lime cordial.'

What the men were in fact talking about was cricket. The reader may recall that Ron was captain of the village cricket team, and he had begun to make preliminary enquiries as to who would be available to play this season.

'Sure,' said Keith 'I'm in, of course.'

'What about Percival, he around at the moment..?'

'No, but he'll be back. You ever play cricket?'

The question was addressed to Quentin, and Keith was not expecting a positive response.

'Yes, actually, that's to say I was captain of the school team for a while, back in the day, then I used to play a bit at uni. I even made the first team at Oxford during the one season that I was there.'

Keith and Ron exchanged looks, and Keith began a quiet reassessment.

'Batsman or bowler..?'

'Well, you had to be a bit of an all – rounder to make the grade, but I never made it past number six with the bat, bowling was always my thing. Medium to quick, as it went, and given the conditions I could move the ball through the air a bit. Used to bowl a mean in - swinger, as it happens, and I could get some movement off the seam on a good day.'

Which in terms of ingratiating himself with the present male company was about as good as it could get, and it was time to press home his unexpected advantage.

'How about you..?'

'Ron opens, I always bat number two.'

'So I'm in haloed company then, who bats number three?'

'Guy called Percival, lives in a cottage nearby, he's our best batsman.'

And so the conversation was set, and any awkwardness to the meeting between father and boyfriend to Rosemary vanished beyond recall. The discourse moved on to a critique of the current England international squad, and their chances of victory against the West Indies in the forthcoming test series. Also covered were the relative merits of test matches and the one – day game, and anybody not intimately familiar with the game of cricket would have been quickly and completely lost to the technicality and particular nature of the conversation. Meadow at a certain point came over to claim her orange juice, which Quentin had bought but quite forgotten to deliver to her, for which he apologized profusely.

'It's quite alright, as long as you men are enjoying each other's company.'

'Quentin here's a cricket player,' Said Keith

'Well, fancy…' said Meadow, who together with Barbara returned to join Rosemary, and to report that all was well between the men in their respective lives, but also to warn her daughter that she should not expect very much more of Quentin's company during that which remained of the evening.

In fact it took a diplomatic intervention by Meadow about half an hour before closing time to break up the small, male gathering.

'Keith, dear, I think we should be going, don't you?'

Goodbyes were said, and Quentin returned to the table near the fire.

'Sorry about that, got talking to your dad and Ron.'

'Yes, I noticed…You seemed to be getting on very well.'

'Yeah, he's a great guy, and your mum's seriously cool, too.'

'I'm glad you think so.'

On the walk home, Meadow saw fit to gently chastise her beloved.

'That was supposed to be a quick pint, Keith, we disrupted their evening completely.'

'It was only two pints, and the guy didn't have to stand there talking to us.'

'No, I suppose not….So what do you make of him now, then?'

'Yeah, he's okay, you know? Thought he was when I first saw him.'

Meadow said nothing, but shot a quick smile into the darkness.

Only a little later, Quentin walked Rosemary to the door of the trailer. 'So, this is where you sleep, then.'

'Yes, this is where I sleep.'

'Well, goodnight, then.'

'Goodnight…'

They moved closer to one another and met halfway, where they kissed farewell, although for both of them it felt rather more like a beginning than an end to anything.

'I'll call you then, shall I, about arrangements for London?'

'Yes, do that...'

'Unless of course...Can I see you once more before then..?'

'That would be nice, but let's meet somewhere else next time, shall we?'

'Of course...'

'Well, 'phone me then.'

He turned away into the darkness; she climbed the steps into the trailer and closed the door behind her. She undressed as she pondered the evening, which had not been as she had expected, but then again perhaps it had. She also considered the fact that had their genders been reversed, he could have invited her into the trailer, and she might even have accepted the offer. Basil slept with Emma here, after all, with the full knowledge of their parents, but it was different for girls, and if she and Quentin were to spend their first night together it would have to be at his flat, if she could get away for the night. But still, they were not yet at that stage of intimacy, it seemed, and the fact of his wanting to come here at all still struck her as strange, and not entirely a good thing, despite her enjoying his company for the time that they had had together. She liked him, but he would have to do better than this, and he would, she was sure. The two most important men in her life had this evening rather stolen the agenda, both for their own ends, but that was done, now, and next time perhaps the girl who was the reason for both agendas would get somewhat more of a look in.

Quentin had missed the last bus into town, so he began walking along the main road with the vague expectation of being able to hail a passing cab. He had an application on his telephone which would have allowed him to call for a taxi at any time, but he was content to walk, and in the event he walked the whole way home; he was not working at the warehouse until tomorrow evening, so he could sleep in. He had met her parents, so that was done, and although he was aware that Rosie had not been at one with the idea of his coming to her home, he was glad that he had done so, and that he had even, he thought, met with at least initial and general parental approval. Just as importantly, perhaps, he could from here onwards ignore any doubt expressed by his eldest brother; Freddy could think now what he wished, the matter of Rosemary's age and situation was closed in Quentin's mind. As regards his feelings toward the young lady in question, to these he could now and over course of time he hoped give full expression, and he began to wonder how they might go on from here. They had met three times, now, so this could be called his first relationship worth the name. No longer would his life just be about himself; Quentin Forbes Dolby was in love for the first time, and the ever complex business of life had for this young man just become a great deal more complicated, and a great deal more meaningful.

Chapter 9

LOVE ON A SMALL ISLAND

If a body were perchance to find themselves in the geographical region of southern India, and if they became of a mind to take a short – haul commercial flight to the small, busy capital city of Male, they might then make for the portside, and from there they could if they so wished charter a fast boat northwards into the Ari Atoll. If they were further, with the aid of a good captain, to navigate their way through a maze of small Maldivian islands, until it may seem to them that they are leaving civilization far behind, they may eventually arrive at the small island of Bathala. The island is not untypical of the thousands of islands which make up this unique archipelago; palm – fringed, sun drenched white – sand beaches offer views out over a shallow lagoon onto azure – blue seas, across which one may glimpse other coral atolls, or one may not, so isolated are some of the islands, many of which are uninhabited, since there is in truth no point in inhabiting them. Human life cannot be independently sustained in such a place, and nothing can be commercially grown or manufactured on these small, coral uprisings which have over millennia lifted their heads just above the surface of the ocean. There is no naturally standing fresh water here, and no soil worthy of the name, and no point to coming really. Historically, fishermen may have come in their small canoes to fish the surrounding waters, for here exists a rich and diverse ecosystem which belies the arid and mostly deserted land above, where only lizards and other hardy creatures have in the past made the journey on driftwood or man – made vessels, to colonize the dry, harsh environment.

At least, this was the case until the still so recent advent of mass tourism. Reliable and affordable air – travel, and a wish to escape at least for a short time from busier or colder lives, has seen the recent arrival of a quite different life form. Nowadays an island may be leased, some quite basic chalets and a landing jetty may be built, a generator installed to supply electricity, and thereafter if a reliable and frequent supply of fuel, food and fresh, drinkable water can be negotiated, then a sustainable living can be made where none was before possible. A motorized boat will also likely be needed, as will diving equipment to be hired and a compressor to fill metal tanks with the correct mix of gases, and by this means may one facilitate and satisfy the still growing demand for people to reclaim the shallow ocean, from which their ancient ancestral species emerged billions of years ago. They do not stay for long, these people, but from islands such as Bathala they must stay for one week at least, until the small but quick ferry - boat arrives and then leaves once more on its' journey through the archipelago to the port of Male.

On such days there is always a sense of quiet anticipation among those few people who nowadays live and work here, who are variously employed as cooks, cleaners or dive – guides, and on this particular day, as the weekly boat appears on the horizon, it carries two people who have come in search of such beautiful isolation, and perhaps of each other, and after their long and protracted journey on three airplanes have reached their journeys' end. Percival and Louise will by now have caught their first glimpse of the island which will be their home for the coming week, and will shortly disembark on the narrow, wooden jetty, and from there, in terms of their thus far torrid and unpredictable relationship to one another, all things may be possible.

'Peter Shortbody, well my goodness!'

So began a message which Peter read quite early one morning on his mobile telephone, which Alice had bought him for his last birthday and of which he was still learning the rudiments. The message continued;

'Sorry for my tardy response, but I don't visit the website very often these days, my one attempt at literature sort of died a death in its' early life. Anyway of course I remember you, you used to help me with my maths homework, and we used to walk home together sometimes, if you remember. (My maths never improved, by the way…) Anyway here's my telephone number if you want to call me for a chat any time. Hope to speak soon and it's amazing to hear from you! Maddie.'

Having by now made his mind up that he would probably not in fact hear from her, Peter was if truth were told somewhat taken aback by the enthusiasm of the reply, and was in truth not certain how to react to it. Peter Shortbody had always been a man of numbers, in which there had always been safety, giving a new meaning to the time – honoured saying. Numbers were immortal, indestructible and unchanging, and their behavior could always be predicted, whereas people could not, and nor indeed could ones' own emotions. Only once before and still quite recently had the emotional part of him quite by accident found expression, when he had for a short time been in love with Alice, but he was of an age now when such feelings have only so long, and the thought or idea of Madeline Young had stirred something within him which he was not entirely at one with. So much time had elapsed between this and his having last spoken to her, whenever exactly that might have been, and so much life had happened, that somehow the thought of actually speaking to her again was a strange and somehow worrisome thing. He had seen her photograph, of course, but the dominant impression of her in his mind was still as an eighteen year old girl, with a nice smile and sparkly eye makeup, as if the intervening years had not really happened, which he knew was a ridiculous notion, but there it was. In any event the delay in her reply gave him just cause to wait before he responded, if he responded, although better perhaps not to respond, as this might unleash more strangeness into the already often strange world of Peter Shortbody. He knew full well that it was he who had first contacted her, because he had dreamed of her, but still, he was presently still in control of the situation, and could still walk away, which might after all be the better thing to do. Perhaps at least this inaction would bring time back into its' proper context again. Anyway he would do nothing for now, but would think further on the matter, and a more immediate priority was in any case the fact that Tizer was waiting for his breakfast.

Upon arrival on the island, Percival and Louise were shown to their chalet accommodation, where they unpacked their few belongings, took a mostly cold, salt - water shower in the enclosed, outdoor bathroom, and changed into clothes more appropriate to their new surroundings.

They had arrived in the late afternoon, and after a slow walk around the island, which took a little under fifteen minutes, they made for the small restaurant to drink the no better than average coffee on offer, and thus to await the evening meal, which was daily served at seven o'clock. The food was basic but acceptable, and so it would remain throughout their stay, and the beer was kept acceptably cold. They would also learn that the generator was turned off for some hours of each day, which for these hours rendered obsolete their air – conditioning unit and all electrical appliances, and left them temporarily without running water, but they would learn to live around these inconveniences. During their first evening meal they learned that for the most part the rest of those staying as tourists on the island consisted of a group of ten early middle – aged German SCUBA – divers, who were of mixed gender and would complain most vociferously if all things were not to their liking or convenience. Otherwise there was only an Australian husband and wife, who did not complain at all, and whose teenaged children, who were one boy and one girl, were taking to the sub – aquatic world for the first time. All of these people were beginning the second week of their two – week stay, and all of them for the most part ignored the newly arrived English couple, a situation which suited the English couple well enough. It was also now that they were introduced to the manager of the island, who was a quite short man who called himself Captain George, whose lack of height was made up for by his not inconsiderable girth. They suspected that George was in truth not his real name, and they would never see him so much as step onto a boat during the whole of their stay, but such did he call himself. Otherwise Captain George was a person of somewhat enigmatic and quite flamboyant character, who apparently liked English people very much, as he seemed not to tire of telling his newly - arrived guests.

After supper and before returning to their chalet, Percival and Louise took a stroll out onto the deserted sandy beach, where a light breeze was blowing, and here they sat together watching the sun go down over the clear horizon. Thus far their time together had been for the most part taken up with the practical matters of catching just about connecting flights, or watching on – board movies when they were not sleeping their way through time zones, so this was their first suitable opportunity to speak of more intimate and personal matters, and it was she who spoke first.

'Well, here are then. You weren't kidding when you said that it was a small island…'

'I don't expect they come much smaller.'

'And you were really going to come here on your own? I almost didn't come, you know.'

'I almost didn't ask you.'

'What the hell would you have done here?'

'I don't know, sorted out the secrets of the universe between dives, I expect, or I might have made a play for one of the Germans.'

'Which one..?'

'The tall, blonde one, probably...'

'Male or female..?'

'Female, preferably...'

'She's with the tall blonde male with the attitude, they're the only couple.'

'How did you work that out, you had your back to them most of the time, and they were speaking German for Christ's sake.'

'It's obvious in any language, and typical of you to go for the unobtainable. Anyway I speak a bit of German these days. The skinny, dark – haired woman fancies the balding guy, by the way, but he's not interested, so you might have stood more chance with her.'

'You worked all of that out over one meal?'

'By the end of the week I'll tell you their life history. Well, I suppose we should get it out of the way, then.'

'Get what out of the way?'

'The end of you and Sally...Was it messy?'

'No, not really, she had Scandinavia on her mind.'

'She was lucky that turned up out of the blue, so were you for that matter.'

'Yeah, it made it easier.'

A thought then struck Louise, and this for the first time.

'It was out of the blue, wasn't it?'

'What do you mean?'

'Her getting the right job just at the right time...'

'Complete coincidence.'

She would have let the thought go, but now he lit a cigarette, which tipped the balance in favour of her not quite believing him.

'Percival, tell me you weren't behind it.'

The silence lasted a second too long, and she was on to him.

'I can't think what you're talking about.'

No, this was wrong, she always knew when he was lying, and he knew that she knew, so better limit the damage.

'That is, I might have made a couple of 'phone calls, you know?'

'What the fuck kind of 'phone calls?'

'I still know people, in the city.'

'That is insufficient information. What did you do?'

'Look…I mean I didn't do anything, really. It was just easy for me to find out who was the big cheese at her bank, that's all, so I sort of put the word out.'

'Which word did you sort of put out, exactly?'

'I just made it known, through others more influential than myself, that she was about to leave unless they offered her something…Made it worth her while staying, that kind of thing.'

Louise took a moment, and then she laughed at the ocean and at the setting sun.

'You know what, you are unbelievable. So what are you now, some kind of puppet – master?'

'It wasn't like that.'

'It sounds exactly like that…You manipulated the situation to your advantage so that she would get the job…Tell me that you didn't do that.'

'You make it sound worse than it was. I didn't know anything about Scandinavia, and she wouldn't have got the job had she not been up to it. They could have let her go, and she wanted the job, you know? It was actually to her advantage.'

'That's not the point, without your intervention she wouldn't have even have been offered the job in the first place.'

'You can't know that. She probably wouldn't have done well, you know, being self – employed.'

'How do you know that?'

'She's a corporate kind of person, sort of good at working independently but in a larger organization.'

'So now you do psyche tests in your spare time...'

'I just know Sally. All I did was to give her choices, indirectly. It was her decision to take the job.'

Louise laughed again; this was getting worse or perhaps better by the minute, and for a moment she couldn't decide whether his behavior had been utterly despicable or admirably clever, or both.

'Did you even tell her about us?'

'It was the next thing I was going to say, but she beat me to it. The pieces were already moving before you came to see me, it wasn't all about us.'

And now a long exhalation of breath, whilst she made further and deeper assessment, but she still couldn't quite work it out.

'My god, Percival, you really are something else...You let her believe that it was she who was leaving you, so now she gets to take the blame and have all the guilt, is that it?'

'She did leave me, technically speaking, although in a way it never officially ended, it was just a given, you know?'

'And poor, innocent you are the injured party. So how did it go; *'I'm so sorry Percival, but I've been offered this job, so I think it's over between us', 'Oh dear what a pity, off you go then...'* Christ....'

'As I see it, I gave her control of the situation.'

'No, that doesn't work. What you did was to give her an illusion of control over the situation.'

'Which amounts to the same thing, doesn't it? At least this way she doesn't know there was anyone else involved, which there wasn't really anyway, at the time.'

Louise was still smiling as the sun faded completely, and the beach was transformed in the moonlight, every shadow of every slight undulation in the sand now had dark definition.

'Well clever old you....I think that's the neatest sidestep I ever heard of.'

'If that's how you want to see it.'

'I'm not sure I want to see it at all, but having seen it I can't see any other way of seeing it.'

One final laugh as she yawned.

'Christ I'm tired.'

'Me too...'

'So no sex on the beach tonight then...In fact no sex at all. If you brought me here to have sex you might be disappointed. Did you bring me here to have sex with me?'

'I can't say I thought about it in quite those terms.'

'Pure as the driven snow, you, right?'

'I wasn't expecting a total ban, if I'm honest.'

'That's all we ever did, have sex.'

'That isn't true. We did other stuff as well, between the sex.'

'Well, from now on it has to be making love, or it isn't going to happen.'

'I'm not sure I can tell the difference.'

'Then let me be your guide...I'll know when the time comes, if it comes.'

'Well, as long as one of us knows.'

'What I'm saying is that you and I have to start again. We need to put all of the bad things behind us, all of the you leaving me, me leaving you bullshit. This time we have to get it right...'

'I'm up for that.'

'Well then, you've got a week to fall in love with me, do you think that's enough time?'

'I'll be working on it.'

She took his hand and they stood up together. He held her waist and she put her arms around him as they kissed. She pulled away, breathing heavily.

'Well that wasn't a bad start, mister puppet master.'

'I'm a quick learner.'

'It's all about incentive, my love. Come on, let's sleep, you never know, the island might look bigger in the morning.'

They walked hand in hand across the beach. Theirs was the only chalet with a light showing inside, everybody else was already sleeping.

Upon a certain evening, which was a Wednesday, Victoria did not make for the underground station which was her normal habit upon leaving the gallery. Instead she headed westward, and emerged into the dull twilight of the London evening at the station nearest to her destination. This was a rendezvous which had been arranged by telephone on Monday, and as she entered the restaurant she saw that Jessica was already seated at their pre – booked table. She had still not spoken to Rebecca since the night that she had walked out on her, but if nothing else certain practical matters would eventually need to be seen to, such as payment of electricity and gas bills. Victoria was after all the point of contact between Rebecca and her brother, and the lack of contact with Rebecca could not go on indefinitely, any more than could Rebecca's tenure at number seven, The Green. Sooner or later, and preferably sooner, she would have to find her own feet and find rooms to rent in the town, which would be nearer to her studio anyway. Victoria may have in her mind come to terms with the fact that Florence was her brothers' child, but taking this coming to terms to her next meeting with Rebecca was quite something else, and not for the first time it was in the ever pragmatic and practical hands of Jessica that she had decided to try to find solution, if one could be found. These two were in fairly regular telephonic communication, but not everything could be discussed by telephone, and in any case, even if in the end she decided that it was better not to tell her, she had not seen Jessica for a while, and there was always comfort and undefined reassurance to be found in their meetings.

She approached the table, and Jessica smiled her ever reassuring smile, and Victoria was glad indeed to see her friend.

'Hi, you...'

'Hi, not late, am I?'

'Not much. I ordered you a G and T.'

Victoria gave her overcoat to a waiter, took her seat and then took a long drink from her alcoholic beverage, which immediately made her feel more relaxed, and made distinction between this and her working day, which had in fact been a busy one.

On the first morning of their self – imposed exile, Percival awoke before dawn. He had slept passably well, given that it always took him two or more days to work off this degree of jetlag, and given that he had been sleeping beside a beautiful woman without the possibility of a certain fulfillment, which so far as he was concerned he might reasonably have hoped for. He took a cold shower under the still starlit sky, and resisted any temptation to imagine that which had not happened; that would be ridiculous, and anyway he must maintain a state of preparedness in this regard, in the event that she decided that that having slept upon the matter they were in fact enough in love. There could as yet, however, be no resolution to this, as Louise was still sound asleep as he dressed in T shirt and swimming shorts, and walked along the dimly lit, sand – covered pathway to the jetty, at the end of which he sat and lit his first cigarette of the day. They had watched the sunset together, and now he sat alone as the first light appeared over the eastern horizon. The dive – boat lay moored beside him in the darkness, air - tanks filled and in their racks in readiness for the days' diving. He and Louise had dived together before, when he had been on his journey of self - discovery in a part of the Indonesian archipelago, where she had come to meet him, and they had made love once underwater, or perhaps it had been having sex, since he had now learned that the two were apparently distinct from one another even between the same two people. In any case, no doubt they would dive together here, but not today. The boat would leave after breakfast and not return until the afternoon, and they needed a day to recover themselves before they took to the water. He smiled inwardly to himself as he considered his current situation. Not so long ago he had thought that it had finally been over between them, and that Sally would be his future, but that had been before he had seen her again, after which any resolve on his part had melted in the warmth of the spring days, and there had been an end to something, and a new beginning. And Louise was right, of course; they had to get it right this time, and these were in a sense the best and the worst of circumstances in which to try; if they couldn't do it here in so idyllic a setting then they had better not try again, and if it went wrong then there would be no distractions and no escape from one another until the next ferry boat arrived. They loved each other, and this was something which she knew well enough, but they had hurt each other before, and there was only so much pain that a soul could take, and this also she understood. So then, put all of it behind you, Percival. Your humble and impoverished beginnings, your often difficult school days, and then all of the years of money and cocaine which almost broke your spirit, and everything which had come thereafter; your near – death at the hands of the still mysterious sect, and all of the women who had been a part of it. Rose, and Rebecca, and Sally; lay the ghosts to rest once and for all and let yourself be in love with the woman who loves you, or let your capacity to love die in the trying, for there could no longer be any compromise. She had his soul, she was right about that, as well, so if they failed now let her keep it; without her it was of no use to him anyway. He put out his cigarette and put the butt – end back in the packet, took off his T shirt and made a shallow dive into the clear but still dusky water off the end of the jetty. He swam across the lagoon and back, whilst thinking that this reminded him of a different time spent on another island in Indonesia, when again he might have been assassinated but for the intervention of a beautiful woman, whose name had been Sandi, and who as it turned out had had her own particular agenda. He was to this day uncertain whether Philippe had invited him there and paid for his airline ticket in order to murder him, or to make him his friend and confidant, and this was something which he would likely never know, since Philippe had had his throat cut before any confidences were shared. He had been close, that time; close to perhaps understanding more of the mysterious people from the temple, who might perhaps be Satanists, but he thought not, and had never really thought so. Tony Blackman, the one of them whom he had come to know the best, seemed nothing like a Satanist to Percival, but what did he know, really, and that was a chapter in his life which had likely not ended yet. He could travel to the most remote island in the world, but one day soon he would have to go back and close that particular chapter, one way or the other.

These were not thoughts for now, however, and by the time he had turned and was halfway back to the jetty, she was standing at the end of it, wearing a sheer sarong over her bikini, the sarong blowing about her in the light morning breeze, the shape of her silhouetted in the growing light. It was an image which brought his thoughts swiftly and absolutely to the present, and by the time he reached the jetty she had dropped her sarong onto the timber boards at her feet, and now she sat on the end of the jetty.

'Good morning.'

'Coming in?'

'Is it deep enough for me to jump?'

'It's deep enough.'

'Should I trust you, do you think?'

'That's up to you.'

She jumped in, neither of them entirely missing the symbolism of the moment, and they swam now together across the shallow water, until at the opposite shore it became shallow enough for them to sit together on the sand, from whence they had a view back to the island. They heard the quite distant sounds from the kitchen of breakfast being prepared, as the island made ready for the new day.

'Did you get any sleep?'

'Yeah, I did okay, I just woke up early.'

'So, having brought me to this island paradise, what do think we should do today?'

'I don't know, I thought we might go for a bike – ride later.'

She smiled.

'So, do you love me this morning?'

'Yep…'

'Are you sure you're not just saying that?'

'Nope…'

'Is that no you're not sure, or no you're not just saying that?'

'I'm not just saying that.'

'How do I know I can believe you?'

'It's a tricky thing to prove, especially before breakfast. Sometimes you just have to trust people and jump in, you know? Anyway I thought you could tell these things.'

For a moment she said nothing, so they sat and watched the first guests emerge from their chalets and make for the restaurant. Two of the staff went onboard the dive boat and began setting up for the day, one attaching dive gear to tanks and the other filling the engine with gasoline.

'So, nothing else you want to tell me about your recent life then? No dark little secrets that you're keeping from me?'

This was harder than Sally. To be with Sally was to live apart from the other things which were currently happening in his life. It had been enough for them to share a part of themselves, but to also live apart, literally as well as figuratively. But then he knew that this was not entirely true, either. Sally for her part had been an open book, and would tell him everything which occurred in her life, even relaying insignificant conversations which she may have had during any given day, perhaps because this was Sally's life, simple and uncomplicated; Sally carried no excess baggage through life, and it was this simplicity and lack of complication which had been a part of her attraction for him. Sally had never asked him searching questions, and so he had not told her about his hiring a hit – man to kill on his behalf, or that this would quite likely put him in danger, eventually. And then there was the one about his in all probability being father to a son, and a son who would one day become Lord Tillington, and that the birth of that son had killed his mother. Only so far had he allowed Sally into his life, because she had asked no more of him; they had been as they had been, and they would likely have gone no further. But now had come Louise, who would demand to know everything, and he would have to tell her everything if they were to have a future; there could be no more secrets or half – truths, she demanded no less of him than he put his life and his soul in the full light of exposure, not perhaps to be judged, but she had to go with him to his darkest places, and he knew full well that he would have to take her there, and it would have to be soon. They had a week to get it right, and if they could do that then his love for her and hers for him would take him to higher places than he could ever have gone with Sally; truth or falsehood, death or glory, and this was the choice that he had made. It would be an easy thing to be in this place and to forget for this short time about everything else which was constituent of their lives, but now she had asked him the question, and he would have to answer; there was now no escape from it, not on an island as small as this.

'You've gone quiet…'

'There are a couple of things that you should know about.'

'I thought so.'

'Why did you think so?'

'Because I'm talking to you.'

'It might need cigarettes and alcohol.'

'Well, not now then. I'm hungry anyway, let's see if we can beat the rush to breakfast.'

She stood up and walked back into deeper water, being careful to avoid the beautiful but sharp coral which grew everywhere in profusion. He followed her and they swam back toward the jetty.

'So, how're things at the Manor?'

We return now to a very different place and a different time of the day; a London restaurant, where Victoria and Jessica are just beginning their evening together.

'Oh fine, much as ever anyway… Michael seems to be making progress with the conversion, but it's still early days, you know?'

'So no more secret wedding plans?'

'Not that he's told me about. I think that's a long way in the future anyway. Elin comes over occasionally but I think she works long hours most of the time.'

'He still hasn't told their Lord and Ladyships of his marital intentions, then? I mean I take it that he still intends to marry her, eventually.'

'Oh yes, he'll do it properly when the time comes, I'm quite sure, but it's still a secret we have to keep.'

'Right, well as long as I know, it's getting hard to keep track of who knows about what about whom where your family are concerned. So you don't get to see much of Elin, then.'

'Hardly at all….'

'So no more impressions of her, or rather of the current manifestation of her..?'

'No, but she's good for Michael, I'm sure. I think the Lady's got her feet firmly on the ground, solid, no – nonsense Nordic roots, you know, and he's got a real spring in his step these days.'

'She probably hasn't got her feet on the ground all the time then. Oh gosh, sorry, I really don't know where that came from.'

They laughed, and ordered their food, and it was a happy reunion of old and dear friends.

'So what about Ginny..?'

'No change, really, except she's getting really big these days, you would hardly recognize her, Vics, she's taken comfort – food to some kind of extreme, and she still can't seem to settle to anything, job – wise.'

'She must deeply regret leaving Africa, don't you think?'

'In a way, of course, although she wasn't happy there, either…It's hard to know what would make her happy, to be honest.'

'At least living in Africa has some romance about it.'

'I think the romance died a long time before she came back.'

'So still no significant other?'

'I think she's given up on the whole idea, anyway it's hard to see anyone taking her on in her current state of mind, not to mention her current state of body.'

'Jess…'

'I know, I really don't know what the matter is with me this evening, I obviously don't get out enough…'

More gentle laughter, and another change of subject, but not yet the subject which was most on Victoria's mind. That would need more alcohol, and the wine had only just been delivered to the table.

The remaining daylight hours of the first day on the island were for the most part spent swimming in the lagoon, and sleeping. Despite the beauty of the beaches this was not a beach resort, and there were no sun – loungers, so Louise spread her towel and herself in the sun, whilst Percival stayed steadfastly in the shade, but neither felt the desire to do otherwise than to rest; the journey and time difference had taken its' toll on them both, and so they contented themselves with one another's company and light conversation. The day was only punctuated by lunch, which they ate alone, all of the other guests having left on the dive boat in the morning, and they had the small, open - air restaurant to themselves. Otherwise the only notable occurrence was a moment during the early afternoon, when Captain George took Percival to one side, said simply to him '*I like the English*' and gave him something which Percival would never have expected, nor did he have time to react or speak before Captain George was gone. Captain George was in fact a remarkably lithe and agile man, given his size, and such a large man hid well on such a small island, and was seldom seen except when he wished to be seen. Every evening, however, he gave Percival the same, small gift which he had given him on the first day, and each day Percival accepted, though the surprise barely lessened with the passing days. On this first day, Percival and Louise awoke from an afternoon sleep in the early evening, and by now an awkwardness between them which had been building upon itself all day had become manifest. If there were things to be talked about then better get it done, but better it be done in the hours of darkness, and with beer to lubricate the thought processes, and both of them knew this. The evening meal was thus a quick affair, and whilst the other diners stayed to drink beer and no doubt discuss the days' diving, Percival and Sally took their bottled beer and made once again for the beach, this time having found a more secluded place away from any of the accommodation, or any likelihood of being disturbed or overheard. It was another clear, breezy evening; the moon had not yet risen and the sky was ablaze with stars. Both sat down on the still warm sand, and Louise was the first to begin the by now somewhat impatient dialogue.

'Well, come on then, what is that you think you should tell me?'

'There's quite a lot, actually.'

'We've got all night, my love, and I'm not tired anymore.'

'Well, for a start there's the chicken stranglers….'

Louise was all too aware of the cult, and all that had previously happened from the last time that she and Percival had been together, so only the latest developments needed to be conveyed, and she listened to his monologue until he appeared to have finished.

'Okay, so just to be clear, you hired this hit - man, Eddie, and he's killed how many people so far?'

'Three, as far as I know...'

'You're not even sure?'

'Eddie's a bit of a law unto himself, to be honest.'

'So were you paying him per hit, or what?'

'It was more of a general kind of agreement, Eddie and I go back a long way.'

'Oh well, so what's a couple more dead people between friends, right?'

'Something like that….'

'And this Tony Blackman character is now released from his protective custody, or however one might describe it?'

'Yeah, he's out.'

'And you don't know what's going to happen next.'

'At the moment one can only speculate, maybe nothing. It just depends, you know, whether the wish for revenge is greater than the danger inherent therein. Rebecca killed some of them and she's still alive because of the threat of further extreme violence, or more importantly the threat of revelation, and now they've seen what can happen.'

'When you get cross with people....'

'They drugged me, imprisoned me and nearly killed me, Louise, leaving aside anything which they did to Rebecca.'

'I know....'

'And he wouldn't give me final assurance that we were safe.'

'Yes, well I bet he's kicking himself about that now.'

'So I thought something had better be done.'

Louise laughed gently, despite the seriousness of the conversation.

'Well something was certainly done, and there was I thinking that London was where the action was.'

'It's surprising what goes on in small towns and villages.'

'So it would seem. I'll say this much for you, you don't do things by halves, do you?'

'No point in beating about the bush, as they say.'

This made her smile again.

'Well Christ, Percival, tell me something ordinary. I need to get my head around all of this, and I need to know that your life isn't all so bloody dramatic.'

'What sort of ordinary?'

'Tell me what's happening in the village, how's Mea....Where the hell did you get that?'

Percival had just pulled something from the pocket of his shorts; a marijuana cigarette the dimension of which Louise had not seen for a long time, and nor in truth had Percival.

'It was a gift from Captain George; he likes English people, apparently.'

'Jesus, Percival, even here on this godforsaken sand – spit in the middle of nowhere you manage to find the only drug – dealer for a hundred miles, and on the first day.'

'He found me, and like I say, it was a gift, no money changed hands.'

He lit the spliff and gave it to her.

'Are you sure you know what it is?'

'It smells like dope, but right now I don't think it matters, do you?'

They took a moment to adjust as they shared the first intoxication, after which the world was the same, but it seemed and looked different. The stars were brighter now, and infinitely more mysterious, and the nearly full moon which had just risen once again bathed the beach in its' first gentle light, and spread its' glow across the wide, quite calm ocean.

'Anyway, you were saying…'

'What was I saying?'

'I think you were about to go ordinary, but that might be more difficult now.'

Ordinary things, from Percival's perspective and within the sphere of his knowledge, Percival's interest and involvement in general village matters being limited to occasional and chance meetings with others, but he did his best. Rebecca was back in the village and living at Michael Tillington's house with her infant, who was called Florence, Keith was converting an old house somewhere for Michael, and Tarragon's singing career was going well. The eldest Fox girl had been taken critically ill but was okay now, apparently, and Reginald had a lady – friend called Gwendolyn. Percival was unofficial Godfather to Victoria Tillington's child, Henry, and Rose's child, Nathaniel was doing okay having very nearly not made it into the big world, and Rose, of course, had died a tragic death. And so on, this being essentially a monologue, interspersed occasionally by Louise for more detail or clarification as to who was who. She had lived in the village herself, of course, but wished to be brought up to date, and at the end of the monologue she seemed satisfied that this was the best that she was going to get, and both agreed that he had in any case done a passably good job. By now they had smoked the marijuana, and had all but finished their beer, so it would be time to move on soon, but their current state of mind made both reluctant to go anywhere; the marijuana had been of high quality, and time was stretched now beyond its' actuality. Neither spoke for that which seemed like a long time, but finally it was she who broke the silence.

'So is that it then, or is there anything else you want to tell me?'

There was one more thing, but that would be betraying a confidence between himself and Victoria. On the other hand, if this really was to be the beginning of their future, then how could he have such secrets from her, and if it was not then the matter would be academic in any event. It was also the case that sitting here in the darkness on this tropical beach with the woman that he loved, and currently having a somewhat shaky sense of reality, the village and the Manor House seemed like a long way away, in all senses.

'Yeah, there's something else.'

'Go on…'

'There's a fairly good chance that Michael Tillington's son is illegitimate.'

'Christ, that's a good one….So Rose was spreading her affections elsewhere, was she, and spreading her legs for that matter. Being married to a future Lord wasn't enough for her then?'

'She's dead, Louise.'

'And I shouldn't speak ill of the dead, right?'

'Well I've never entirely agreed with that philosophy, but this was Rose, you know, and she was a friend of mine.'

'I know, and I'm not condemning her, but anyway how do you know the child's illegitimate, or might be illegitimate?'

'Yeah, well that's the other thing…'

'What?'

'Rose and I had, well we had a close relationship for a while.'

'How close?'

'About as close as it gets...'

Another moment of silence as this new intelligence was taken in and processed, before;

'Okay, I know I'm stoned and everything, so you'd better just clarify. What you're saying to me is that you are the father to the future Lord Tillington, is that right?'

'Looks that way, although it's not been verified, and as far as I'm concerned it never will be. I've made it clear that I'll never make any claim to him, even if it was ever proved, and I don't see how or why it ever should be.'

'So does Michael Tillington know?'

'No, he doesn't know.'

'So who have you made it clear to, then?'

'Victoria. She and I are the only two who know that there's even a possibility, and we've come to an understanding.'

'So how or why does she suspect?'

'She found out, or guessed, maybe, that Rose and I were, you know...'

'Lovers...'

'We were never that, not really.'

'So you were just really good friends, yes?'

'We just got a bit too boy – girl sometimes, and I know it sounds trite but it was mainly on her instigation. I'm not disclaiming any responsibility, and we agreed that it had to stop, but it was a bit late by that time, and if I'd thought that there was the remotest chance that she would get pregnant it wouldn't have happened at all. I thought she'd have it covered, particularly in view of everything.'

'You mean in view of the fact that she'd been a hooker?'

'Actually I meant in view of her illness. She'd had cancer, you know, and the doctors told her she should never even try to have children.'

'And yet she went ahead with the pregnancy, and as a result of that she died.'

'I suggested she have a termination, and she agreed, and then never did. After that I didn't see her again. It was her choice, and I don't need to say that I wish to God it had never happened.'

'Bloody hell, Percival…'

'That's what it felt like, sometimes, but you know what, the sky hasn't fallen in yet, it's just stuff that happens, you know?'

'I know…I know, and I'm trying really hard to get some perspective on it, but I find myself wondering why so much stuff seems to happen to you. I mean if it ever came to light that the future Lord of the Manor was a bastard there'd be hell to pay, wouldn't there?'

'That's why neither Victoria nor I are in a tearing rush to prove anything, one way or the other. We've sort of agreed that since nobody actually knows, we can pretend that nothing's wrong. Like I said we have a kind of understanding, and now you now as well, so that's three of us, and she would condemn me for telling you. This must never get out.'

'No, I can see that, and I'm not going to tell anyone, for heaven's sake. Who the hell would believe me anyway?'

Percival lit cigarettes for them both, which gave them both a moment, and intensified the effect of the marijuana. The moon had risen low in the sky by now, and the moonlight had once again begun to cast shadows on the beach. The only sound was the gentle breaking of waves on the reef beyond the lagoon, and this time it was Percival who broke the quietude.

'So, there it is; all of my darkest secrets revealed.'

'There's nothing else, then?'

'I think that about covers it.'

'It's enough to be going on with, anyway. You haven't led a boring life since the last time it was you and me, have you?'

'Never a dull moment…..'

Louise was processing as she drank the last of her beer, then she seemed to come to a decision.

'Why is everything with you so bloody complicated?'

'Makes you wonder, doesn't it?'

'It's okay, Percival…'

'What's okay?'

'Everything's okay. You shouldn't have got me stoned, though, that isn't playing fair.'

The next thing that she did was something which took Percival completely by surprise. She removed her sun – dress, beneath which she was naked, and she lay down on the sand with her hands above her head, looking up at the stars. He removed his T shirt and shorts, and lay over her; she opened her legs and he was inside her, but there was something that he wanted to know.

'So just to be clear, what are we doing, having sex or making love?'

'I love you, Percival, you idiot.'

'Despite the complications..?'

'Despite the complications…'

'I love you too.'

'Well then, who gives a damn?'

'So, when's the great portrait to be painted, then?

'Please don't let's talk about that…'

As we rejoin Victoria and Jessica, they have just completed their main course, and have ordered only coffee to follow. It was a time – honoured and quite unconscious tradition between them that they would initially skim over all matters to be discussed, before either of them decided that any given subject was worthy of further development or in – depth analysis, but this was the first time that the upcoming portrait had been mentioned.

'Oh come on, it'll be an experience, I wish someone would even want to paint my portrait.'

'You'd make a better subject than me, anyway.'

'Nonsense, you just don't appreciate your own beauty; you never have.'

'Anyway we start this week, actually. Pandora arrives at the weekend, so we've got Sunday, and I've even agreed to take time off work next week so we'll have a couple of days of daylight to get things moving, so it'll be long sessions on those days. She likes to paint by natural light, as far as possible.'

'You saw quite a lot of her when she was painting your father's portrait, didn't you?'

'Yes, we spent some time together. We got quite close actually, in a way.'

'In what way did you get close? You weren't shagging the painter, were you?'

This was said mostly in jest, but Victoria drank her wine and said nothing, and whilst silence does not always speak volumes, it can sometimes say enough.

'You were, weren't you…Bloody hell, Vics, so what's she like then?'

'She's quite bohemian, I suppose you might say; rolls her own cigarettes, that kind of thing, and she shows great dedication to her work. I think she's a person of extremes, when she's not working she gets drunk, and so on.'

'I see, well there's a thing then…Girls will be girls, I suppose, and now Bex is absent from your life…So is she completely, you know, gay, or what?'

'I don't believe so, no.'

You're not in love with her, are you?'

'Christ no, why do you always think I'm in love with everybody, just because…Well anyway, I'm not.'

'Do I think you're in love with everybody?'

'You thought I was in love with Percival…'

'Yes, well I can see how that could happen, he's rather lovable, isn't he, in a roguish kind of way.'

'Well I'm not, with either of them.'

'If you say so…Anyway that's going to give new meaning to the painter – subject relationship, isn't it?'

'I'm sure we're both big enough to deal with it. She's a superb painter, Jess.'

'Yes, well I suppose that's what matters in the end. So is Percival still with what's her name?'

'Sally, no, that particular relationship is over, I believe, and he's gone away now.'

'Gone away where?'

'He didn't know. He does that, I think, just kind of takes off and sees which way the wind takes him.'

'A free spirit, you might say.'

'I suppose you might, although he doesn't act like a free spirit. Percival carries the weight of the world on his shoulders, when he doesn't need to, I'm sure. He's his own worst enemy, the stupid man.'

'That was said with feeling.'

'Was it? Well anyway, let's change the subject.'

'Okay, so what's going on then, between you and Rebecca?'

Victoria had been quite certain that here was a subject which would eventually be put forward for further discussion, but she had made it through to coffee without having to make a decision, and despite her love and respect for her dining companion, it was a decision that she had not yet made.

'What do you mean?'

'What I mean is, she's busy, you're busy, blah - blah - blah, but you've hardly mentioned her all evening, which leads me to think that something has happened between you, quite aside from your being unfaithful to her, which isn't a first, I know, but there she is living a ten minute walk away and you haven't seen each other, so I ask myself what's going on? Is it to do with Florence?'

'It's nothing, really…'

'Yes it is, and if you'd rather not talk about it then that's fine, but I know you well enough to know when you're keeping something from me.'

She was homing in, and Jessica was clever, and underneath the bluster and jocularity she was probably about the most perceptive person that Victoria knew. So now it came to it; should she tell her, or should she not? Victoria after all had convinced herself that she had quite come to terms with the situation, but in the process of so doing she had nearly drowned herself, and what had that been for if not to allow her to unburden her anger and uncertainty on her best friend? But now of a sudden there was something else that she needed to do first.

'Look, I badly need a cigarette. Can we pay up, and I'll tell you about it outside.'

'Sure, okay…'

Ten minutes later they were walking together through a small London park, which despite its' reputation was usually safe enough during week - day evenings, and they were two, after all. They sat on a bench in the semi darkness under a street lamp, which spread its' glow into the park from the road outside. Victoria lit a cigarette, and waited a brief moment for the nicotine to find its' way into her nervous system. Jessica waited for what on earth was about to follow.

'Okay….Okay, it is about Florence, in a way, but before I tell you, you have to give me your solemn promise that you won't say a word of what I'm about to tell you to anyone. Nobody at all, is that clear?'

'Okay, I promise, of course. What is it, sweetheart?'

'It's about her father….Rebecca told me….She told me who Florence's father is.'

'Right….'

Tears now, from nowhere and quite unbidden; perhaps it was the moment, or the alcohol, or the relief of actually telling somebody, or the love of the person who sat beside her, but for a moment Victoria was quite lost. People can sometimes hide the deepest of things, even from themselves, and until this moment Victoria had not realized quite how deep her anger had gone.

'Sorry…Sorry, I'm okay. Do you have a handkerchief?'

A handkerchief was duly provided, and Victoria wiped her eyes and blew her nose, and still Jessica waited.

'She saved my life, Jess, and you know how much I love her, but sometimes I hate her so much…There are people who want to kill her, you know…Other witches and the people from the temple, and who knows who the fuck else, and there are times when I could gladly do it myself.'

Aside from the remarkable nature of the statement, it was such an unusual thing for Victoria to use such an expletive that Jessica was quite taken aback, and made further aware of the seriousness of the conversation.

'So who's the father, Vics?'

'It's Michael.'

There was only one Michael that Jessica knew of, but she had to be certain.

'Michael your brother..?'

'Yes…My beloved, stupid brother, and here's the best of it, he doesn't even know, Jess. You know…You remember that night in the pub, when Rebecca told Ginny that it was cold, and Ginny started shaking and whatever.'

'Yes, of course.'

'She has such power over people. She can even fuck somebody without their having any memory of it, can you believe that? I mean can you really believe that she can do that?'

'I don't know…'

'Well she can, and she has, believe me.'

'My god….So I mean, she must have seduced him then.'

'She bewitched him, there's no other way I can think of putting it. I mean it doesn't make sense, does it, that a man can be an unwilling participant in, well in that, but she must have had complete control over him. She used a man's most base instinct to her advantage, and to her own ends. It was a quite deliberate act, just a means to an end, and the end is Florence. And now, well, I really don't know what to do with that, you know? I mean I thought I'd come to terms with it, but I clearly haven't.'

'No...No, well, I can why that would be.'

'She made some lame excuse, you know, about her wanting her baby to have my genes, so it would be like her and me having a baby. Christ, I feel as though I've been raped, or something, but to do that to Michael....So now I want you to play devils' advocate, and tell me all the reasons why it isn't as bad as it feels.'

Victoria threw her cigarette end onto the pathway, which was something which Jessica had never seen her do before, and now she lit another one immediately, Jessica noting that her hands were shaking slightly as she did so, which was less unusual.

'Well, okay, off the top of my head, and given that I've had about five seconds to think about it....I mean she told you, which is one thing, and she didn't have to do that, so that's a couple of points in her favour.'

'I wish she'd never told me, but okay, so let's give her points out of ten, ten being forgiveness; two so far.'

'And presumably she's never going to tell Michael?'

'So she said...Not that he'd ever believe her anyway.'

'No, but it must be possible to prove these things, so I suppose she gets a point for that, two, probably. I mean he must have the memory locked away somewhere, so I suppose if she could make him forget she could also make him remember, and I'm sure she won't do that.'

'Okay...'

'And I mean she's not exactly the first, is she? Women have been seducing men to their own ends since sex was invented, men are so gullible and weak in that way, and she just found a better way of doing it, and one where the male involved doesn't have to know and thus feel guilty about it. How am I doing so far?'

'Not bad. Carry on…'

'And….And if you look at it from a different way, it's actually quite sweet that she wanted Florence to have a part of you in her. I mean I know it's a bit spooky, but if you get past the spookiness then you can see why she would have wanted that. And I mean there's Florence, you know, and although I've never met her you tell me that she's a beautiful and happy baby, and without any of this there would have been no Florence, so there's that, don't you think? I suppose it comes down to whether the end justifies the means.'

'Yes, I suppose so, and don't think she's got to ten yet, do you?'

'No, probably not….It also comes down to how much you love her, and you have to bear in mind all of the good things that she's been to you, and that you've been to each other, and if she saved your life, well, you could look at it as a life for a life, in a strange kind of a way.'

Now there followed a moment of contemplation, for both of them. Victoria found that her anger and unexpected reaction had subsided in the cool and conciliatory words of her friend, and Jessica was still trying to get her thoughts in order so that she herself could work out how bad an act it had actually been.

'Another thing is that men have been raping women forever, so if you look at it from a more detached perspective, this is one back for the girls, isn't it?'

This made Victoria smile, despite herself.

'I mean how would you feel about it if it was anyone apart from Michael?'

'Differently, I suppose, and it was somebody else, I mean she did do it to somebody else, only this time there was no issue from the encounter, and she let him remember.'

'That must be even worse, mustn't it, I mean remembering it?'

'He didn't seem to care very much. I can't tell you who it is, Jess, it wouldn't be fair, but he actually seems to enjoy the memory of it.'

'It's different for boys, I suppose.'

'I suppose it must be, and you're right, of course, the thought of it doesn't affect me in the same way.'

'And I mean, Mike will be none the worse for any of it, as long as he doesn't find out. Don't get me wrong, I think she's a scheming, devious cow for even thinking about doing what she did, but that's nothing that we didn't already know, is it, and I think you're a saint for putting up with her for this long, but it's always been what you might call complex karma between you two.'

'Yes, well I can't argue with that. Anyway, if I'm going to get the last train home I'd better go, but thanks, Jess, this has really helped.'

'You can stay over if you want.'

'No, it's okay, I think a train journey might give me some time to think about everything again, and I've actually got some preparation to do for tomorrow, but thanks anyway.'

'I'll call you tomorrow evening, then.'

'Yes, do that.'

They walked together until their ways divided, then they hugged goodbye.

'Thanks, Jess…'

'You're welcome. She loves you, Vics, despite what you must now be thinking. Don't forget that.'

'Does she get any points for that, do you think?'

'Probably not, but it's up to you. I don't know, witches eh? They're a law unto themselves…It was only sex, Vics, despite it being a very weird kind of sex. She didn't steal the family silver.'

'No, she stole something much more precious. At least that's how it feels to me at the moment.'

'Well anyway, see you then, and 'phone me anytime, you know?'

'Of course…'

A final parting smile, and the two women went their separate ways along the dark but lamp - lit London streets, both for different reasons thinking that the evening had in the end not been as they would have expected.

The rest of the week on the island passed in something like a dream for Percival and Louise. The dive boat was crowded each day, and both wished to avoid crowds, so on the second full day of their tenure Percival spoke to the manager of the small dive centre, and persuaded him to rent them scuba gear and let them dive the island from the shore, and alone. This was quite without the policy of the dive centre, but when additional money entered the equation the persuasion was complete, and so each day thereafter until the last day they donned scuba gear once or sometimes twice a day, and found their way through the deepest water channel and out into the open water. By the weeks' end they knew the waters around the entire atoll, and everything that grew and lived there, and this was enough. Each day, at about the same time of the early evening, Captain George would quietly pass Percival a marijuana cigarette, a favour apparently reserved only for the English people, and for which in the end Captain George would be justly and generously rewarded. Each evening after supper Percival and Louise would find some quiet place, and drink beer, smoke and talk, sometimes long into the night, and each night they would make love in their chalet, and sometimes not in their chalet. For this short time the small island became their world, and a place where their love could find nourishment and begin to take new root, and to grow once again, to the point where they could perhaps take it together into the bigger world beyond.

On the day of their departure, the somewhat enigmatic English couple whom nobody had seen except at mealtimes, boarded the transfer boat with the rest of the tourists. On the previous evening they had taken their customary stroll out onto the beach, where they had sat for the last time, drunk their last beer and smoked their last joint together.

'Well, I never thought I'd say it,' said Louise 'but I'm going to miss this small island.'

'It got bigger, didn't it?'

'It got huge. I don't know what I'd expected, Percival, when you invited me here, but whatever it was it was better than that.'

'So, what now, then..?'

'I go home, I suppose, which in my case is a room in a shared house. Not much to go back to, is it? So what about you; where will your adventure take you from here..?'

'I haven't decided yet, believe it or not.'

'Oh I believe it.'

'I've been rather distracted these past few days; haven't really given much thought to the immediate future, or any future for that matter. I mean I might stop off in India for a bit since we'll be flying that way, and I've never been before. So what about your job..?'

'What about it?'

'I mean where will you work?'

'It's a nationwide organization, so within reason I can work anywhere, I suppose. It's not much of a job but it has that going for it, and most places are looking for people.'

'Anywhere but London, right..?'

'Not really. I mean sure, I can leave London now, but I need somewhere to go, and a reason to go there.'

'Somewhere that you won't walk out of, with no warning whatsoever.'

'That was…I'm sorry, Percival. That was then, you know…?

'Sure, it was just one in the series of fuck – ups that we've made of everything so far.'

'Yes, I suppose so.'

There was a bigger sea today, and the waves crashed more noisily against the distant reef. The pause was pregnant with anticipation; both knew what needed to be said, but neither could say it, and Percival knew that it was beholden upon him.

'So what say you we try again then?'

'I thought you'd never ask. Where..?'

'I've only got one house.'

'That isn't true.'

'Yeah okay, but it's the only one I live in.'

'You'd have me back again?'

'Well you know, these holiday romances are all very well, but we're worth more than that, don't you think?'

'A lot more...Forever more, if we can make it work this time...'

'I've still got some stuff to deal with, you know?'

'Like weird cults and probably secret illegitimate babies, and people who probably want to kill you.'

'That kind of thing...'

'Rebecca's child; that isn't yours as well, is it?'

'No, that one's not down to me.'

'Well that's something, at least. Are you sure, Percival? I mean about us. I'm still as fucked – up as ever, you know? Do you really want to invite me back into your life?'

'It was your idea. It was you who came to see me, remember?'

'I was pointing out the folly of your ways, I still haven't dealt with the folly of mine yet.'

'I'll take a chance on that, if you will.'

One final moment of silence, and a last deep breath before the plunge. That which they had had before was something precious to both of them; precious and delicate memories which they held now between them, and if either let go then there would be an end to it, and they would lose them forever.

'Okay...Okay, if you're really sure. No more *'dear Louise'* letters?'

'I promise...'

'You break my heart again and I'll kill you, you know that, don't you?'

'Sure, and you might even succeed where others have tried, in fact I'll hold the knife for you.'

She smiled in the semi darkness, and this time her smile was returned.

'You'll have to let me know when you're home.'

'If I'm to expect a house guest I think I'll give India a miss, anything else would be rude, don't you think?'

'So you're coming home then?'

'We'll do India together sometime. From now on it's you and me.'

'Death or glory, right..?'

'Death or glory...'

'Well then,' she held up her beer bottle 'to us and our fucked – up future together.'

They touched bottles. A small sound, which was quickly lost to the waves and the warm, tropical air, but sometimes small things may have significance far beyond their dimension, and just then a bright light appeared over the horizon. Tonight there would be a full moon, and tomorrow they would leave their small island to others, but even on small islands, big things can sometimes happen.

Chapter 10

THE WRITING ON THE WALL

On about two or three days during each working week, and on no day in particular, Will Tucker would take Monty to work with him, and on such days the young dog would amuse himself in the derelict and semi – wild gardens of Orchard House, whilst the three men went about their tasks. On the other days he stayed with Emily on the smallholding. Emily liked having Monty around her, but both she and Will thought it better for him to have a change of routine to avoid his becoming bored, particularly as they did not habitually take him for walks on weekdays, or any days for that matter. Perhaps on a Sunday morning they might drive to the winter coast, or to nearby woodlands, and let their charge discover new places, but it was by no means every Sunday, and as they were to increasingly discover there were in any case restrictions as to where dogs could be taken. Such restrictions were something which oft times caused Will to vent his ire; he might for example say;

'What's the matter with this country, here we are on miles of open land without another soul in sight and we can't let a puppy off the lead. Man is born free but is forever in chains, Em, and it's the bloody bureaucrats from the council that are doing it.'

To which Emily might reply;

'Never mind, let's go somewhere else', omitting to mention that it was actually the dog which was on the chain, but she knew what he meant.

In any event, on this particular day Monty had stayed with Emily, and on his arrival home from work Will was greeted with customary canine enthusiasm as he alighted from his Land Rover and walked to the kitchen door, and for now he also had Lulu to contend with, whose only slightly lesser and more mature enthusiasm was made up for by her considerable size. Building can often be dirty work, and on this day Will had arrived home in a particularly filthy and disheveled condition, something which Emily noted as she went about preparing the evening meal.

'Hi Sweet - pea, good day at the office..?'

'Yeah, not bad…Had a bit of trouble with the photocopier, but my affair with Maurine from accounts is going okay, although I think she may have some commitment issues to get past.'

'Oh dear, I'm sorry to hear that.'

'So how was your day?'

'Interesting, actually… I've got some bad news which I'll get out of the way, then I'll tell you some interesting news.'

Will poured himself coffee and sat at the dining table, and waited for the bad news.

'I went to the village today and spoke to Meadow. Daphne's in hospital again.'

'Oh dear, what's wrong this time?'

'She's had a recurrence of the cancer, apparently.'

'I thought she'd been given the all – clear.'

'She had, but…Well it seems to have come back, and it could be more serious this time.'

'Christ….'

'I'll have to go and see her tomorrow. I'll probably go in the afternoon.'

'Sure…I'll take Monty tomorrow then.'

'Okay…I hope she's going to be okay, Will.'

'Yeah, as do we all…Anyway, what's the interesting news?'

'I had a visitor today, someone from FareMart.'

'Oh yes, what did they want?'

'They want to buy my cheese.'

'Really…? I thought it was only the oppressed poor and those just about hanging on to the fringes of society who shopped at

FareMart, not the sort of market for posh cheese, I wouldn't have thought.'

'That's not true anymore; the middle classes are flocking to FareMart these days. They've worked out that they can buy about everything they need for a lot less money. It's becoming quite the place to be seen nowadays, so FareMart are trying to further woo this market by stocking some local produce and what not. Trying to change their image, you know?'

'I see…So this is good news then, isn't it?'

'I don't know…I mean the thing is, they want to buy all of my cheese and stock it at all of the local outlets in the county and beyond. They'll even send a van once a week to collect it, but I have to enter into an agreement that I'll supply a minimum of so much cheese for a fixed rate for one year, and the rate is a bit less than I'm being paid now.'

'Isn't it negotiable?'

'Apparently not...I mean I'd save money on the deliveries, so it probably wouldn't make much difference, profit – wise.'

'So a couple of quid here or there would be neither here nor there, if that makes any sense.'

'No, not much, to be honest...'

'No, well economics were never my strong point. Thing is, though, this is just another example of large companies trying to control their suppliers, isn't it, and what about all the other places that you supply to currently?'

'That would all have to go past the board.'

'You mean go *by* the board.'

'Well whatever…Whether one is going past it or by it, the board is still the thing.'

'Never forget the board…So supposing you were to increase production and keep everyone supplied? I mean you've been talking about doing that anyway.'

'I don't think it works that way. I think the more I produce above the minimum the more they'll buy.'

'So they want exclusive rights?'

'I think that's the general idea.'

'And what do you feel about that?'

'I don't know, I mean on the one hand it's a guaranteed market regardless of how much I produce, which would make commercial sense in years to come, and it would save my having to go around looking for places to sell, and I wouldn't have to deliver, which would save us both some bother, wouldn't it?'

'You know I don't mind doing that, and I don't lose that much time every week, so that's not really an issue. So you wouldn't even be allowed to sell anything to Meadow at the deli?'

'I don't think so, no.'

'Well I don't know, Em, it's your business, but if I were you I'd tell him so stick his agreement where the sun doesn't shine.'

'Actually it was a she.'

'Well that gives her more options as to where to stick it then, but I mean it goes against the general philosophy, doesn't it?'

'Yes, I suppose it does. I mean I don't mind who eats my cheese, or where they buy it from, but I actually enjoy meeting all of the small people that I supply to, it makes it more personal, you know?'

'Of course it does, and the fact that they came to you indicates that there will always be a market for it anyway, and you're still trying different cheeses, so you haven't even got the full range of products yet, so to speak.'

'I haven't got enough goats, either, I mean it would only take a batch to go wrong and I'd miss my target.'

'And that would put you in breach of the agreement...'

'Yep...'

'Well then sleep on it and accept the endorsement, but I don't think it's a runner, do you?'

'No, probably not...'

'So what was she like then, this buyer woman?'

'She was nice, you know, and she only had good things to say about the cheese. It was her idea, you know, to stock the cheeses and what not. She bought some in town and fell in love with it, apparently.'

'Everyone loves your cheese, Em, but that shouldn't give anyone exclusive rights to it. Cheese for the people, you know? Support the small retailer in the face of the threat of takeover by large corporations.'

'Small is beautiful, yes?'

'Why do you think I fell in love with you?'

'I'm not that small, and I hope you're not comparing me to cheese?'

'Thought never crossed my mind....Anyway is dinner ready yet, I'm starving.'

'I'm just waiting for the potatoes.'

'What are we eating anyway?'

'I have attempted nut – burgers.'

'Cool...'

'Don't you think you should have a shower first?'

'This is good, honest grime, the result of an honest days' toil.'

'Even so I'd rather not sit opposite you looking like a street urchin, if we're being honest.'

'I have always seen myself as a part of the great unwashed.'

'Well I prefer you as part of the great washed.'

'Fair enough...'

Will stood up.

'Do I get a kiss first?'

'If you think you're getting anywhere near me looking like that...Shower first, then you can do whatever you want, within reason.'

'Then my shower shall be as swift as the showers in April, and I will emerge smelling of roses.'

'Don't overdo it.'

'And I shall hold you to your promise.'

'It wasn't binding, and hurry up, the potatoes are nearly done.'

The affairs of the heart of Barrington Thomas at this time could perhaps best be described as uncertain. He had not seen his sister, May, since she had proffered her well – intentioned advice as to how he should proceed with the matter of his relationship with and to Miranda Spool, but something had now happened which had brought this particular matter to a head, and Barrington was well enough aware that something further and definitive must now be done. Barrington continued to enjoy his quite menial but to him quite fulfilling job with the Parks Department of his local council, the majority of his modest income therefrom being paid to the letting agents, and from thence, minus commission, did the better part of his earnings find their way into the bank account of a certain Percival Saunders. Otherwise his needs were few, his years as a monk having instilled in him a necessary frugality of living, and with care he managed his financial affairs well enough. About once a week he would allow himself the luxury of a pint or two of ale in the Dog and Bottle public house, and in this way and by occasional visits to the delicatessen did Barrington by degrees become integral to the small village in which he lived, and in which he was for now content to live. His romantic life, however, continued to be a vexatious thing for him, and although he had no wish to be a nuisance to his youngest sister, it was to May that he knew he must turn for further advice, and to this end did he telephone her, and thus did she agree to visit him again at her earliest opportunity.

As we have learned, May's working life was a frantic and frenetic affair, and only between or during breaks in any given television or film production could she spare any length of time for anything else, and so only when filming finished early one day did she spontaneously board a train south from London, on the assumption that her brother would be at home that evening. She would have to catch an early commuter train back to London in the morning, but for now this was the best she could do. In truth her patience with her brother as regards to ordering his own affairs had begun to run somewhat shallow, but his had not been an ordinary upbringing, nor had his time in the monastery prepared him well for an ordinary life. She it was who had met him at Bangkok airport, and she alone had seen how far he had fallen, and how far he had raised himself and his life up since then, and thus did she grant him latitude. In any event, having 'phoned him from the train en route, in the early evening she knocked once again upon the door of number two, The Green, and was admitted by her brother, who had prepared coffee in advance of her arrival.

'Hi Bats.'

'Hi, coffee…?'

'Of course, and wine, both at the same time….'

'Right…Thanks for coming, Maisy, although you really could let yourself in, you know?'

'No key…I came straight from work, and forewent a rare early night and a hot bath, so I hope whatever needs to be talked about is worth the sacrifice.'

She sat at the dining room table, having taken a compact disc from the rack, upon the cover of which she prepared two lines of white powder whilst her brother poured coffee and opened a bottle of red wine, which he had purchased and kept by for just such an occasion.

'I didn't think you did that here.'

'Busy day, you know? Busy life, in fact, and I've not been sleeping well. Anyway this is only my second hit today.'

Which was apparently sufficient justification, and in any case Barrington let the matter go with no further comment. Having taken her stimulant, May seemed ready to engage.

'So, what's happening then, Batty, haven't got her pregnant, have you?'

'No, nothing like that...'

'So what's the problem, then?'

'Well the thing is, I took your advice and tried to, you know, see her more often and so on, and that seemed to be going okay, at least in theory.'

'What do you mean?'

'Well, she agreed that it would be a good idea if we saw more of each other, but in practice we aren't actually...Seeing more of each other, that is.'

'I see...And...?'

'It was just that every time I raised the matter of our future together, and where that was going, she sort of changed the subject, as though she didn't want to talk about it. And then I went to see her one evening last week without prior arrangement, and, well, quite frankly she wasn't at all pleased to see me.'

'Right....'

'She said she wasn't feeling well, but there was quite loud music playing from inside, and I had the sense that somebody else was in the apartment. Anyway I didn't get past the front door.'

'Oh dear, so how was she dressed..?'

'She had a bathrobe on, and probably nothing else.'

'Oh well, better than being naked I suppose. So have you seen her since?'

'No...No, actually...'

'Or spoken to her?'

'Again, no, and then three days ago I received this letter via Meadow at the delicatessen. Somebody had posted it through the letterbox overnight.'

He handed her an envelope, upon which was simply written by hand *'Mr Barrington, The Green'*

May had by now drunk her first glass of wine, and Barrington poured her another. She removed a single sheet of paper from the envelope and read the letter, which had been printed from a word – processor, and read as follows;

'Mr Barrington

We have never met and are unlikely to ever meet, so I hope you will forgive my writing to you in this way. I do not know your first name, and nor do I have your full address, and have heard of you only from a third party. The reason for my writing is that I believe you are involved with a young woman named Miranda Spool. You should know that it has recently come to my attention that this young woman has been having an affair with my husband, and my further enquiries have revealed that she has also been in a relationship with at least one other man within my circle of acquaintances. What you make of or do with this information is of course up to you, but you should know the kind of woman that you are involved with.

Assuring you of the truth of this letter, and with my apologies for being the one to tell you. For my own reasons I wish to remain anonymous.'

'Christ almighty….'

'Exactly…'

She read the brief letter again, whilst imbibing the better part of her second glass of wine, and whilst Barrington awaited her further comment.

'I wonder what tangled web of communication led to whoever wrote this being aware of you, or something about you anyway. I mean they didn't get your name right so they can't know that much, and they must have been only vaguely aware of where you live.'

'I've no idea, of course, and I don't know what to make of it, to be honest.'

'No, well I suppose it all depends on whether you believe it or not.'

'Yes, but why would anyone take the time and trouble to write and then hand – deliver this if it wasn't true?'

'Good point, a rival suitor for her attentions perhaps, but that doesn't make much sense, men aren't this imaginative, and the handwriting on the envelope looks like a woman's writing. All things considered, I reckon we must assume it's true, which would explain why she hasn't wanted to talk about your future, and why she doesn't appreciate spontaneous visits. It appears as though Ms Spool has been playing the field, and it looks, dear brother, as though you are only one of the players.'

'Yes, it rather looks that way.'

'Christ, Batty, I'm sorry. Looks like you got a bad one after all.'

May now took from her bag a pack of cigarettes, some cigarette papers and a small quantity of cannabis resin, with which she proceeded to manufacture a joint.

'What else have you got in there?'

'That's it, I'm clean apart from this. Do you have any food?'

'Yes, of course, it's only pasta left over from last night, but I wasn't expecting you. I've got bread and olives.'

'Pasta sounds great, left over or otherwise. I haven't eaten all day apart from a beef burger which was so awful I could hardly eat it. Give me a minute to think about this, then let's have a smoke and some food. We need to think about what you do next in view of this revelation.'

The artist Pandora Winterton had had a long – running love affair with the coastal town of Brighton. Her house was located in the far quieter and more gentile environs of Rottingdean, a small, historical village separated from the town by a couple of miles of open downland, and a good stones' – throw from the so prestigious girls' – school of Roedean, where Victoria Tillington had completed her schooling, and where Rebecca had begun her secondary education before her parents had moved her to the Convent School. Rottingdean was nowadays where Pandora had her small studio, which was integral to her small house, and here she painted many of her subjects, and practiced her art, and here did she become somewhat reclusive by habit and nature, but between commissions she would oft times spend the better part of her time in Brighton, where she was anything but. Here she became a socialite, in a town which lent itself easily to such a lifestyle, and here she had open agreement with certain friends whereby she could sleep in their various spare bedrooms, or on lounge floors if none were available, and of this facility she would avail herself whenever she was frequenting the bars, public houses and nightclubs which the town offered in abundance. Thus it was that for three nights just prior to her departure to Middlewapping Manor she gave free reign to the darker and more debauched side of her nature, but on the final day she returned home. This was in part to allow her nervous system sufficient time to recover itself from the abuse that it had suffered, for she must regain her steady, artists' hands for the task ahead, but it was also in order that she make practical preparation for her next commission. To this end she once again stretched canvass over wooden frame, washed and packed such clothes as she would need, and gathered herself and her few belongings for her tenure at the Manor House. Soon she would stand once again before a blank canvass, upon which this time she would attempt to paint the image of Victoria Tillington, a woman with whom she had been in certain respects as intimate as it is possible for two women to be. Thus would there be a certain nervousness about the matter, and this she must overcome in order to ply her craft, and thus would the three paintings which she had been commissioned to paint by the Tillington household be so very different in essence. When she had painted the image of Rose, the essence had been the simple beauty and complex sexuality of a young woman, whereas her intent when painting his Lordship had been to capture the image of a man in his twilight years, with all of the wisdom and pathos of a man such as he. And now there would be Victoria, who it seemed to Pandora was not yet wise, but who carried the weight of her still young life as a heavy thing, and kept a good part of herself and her knowledge of the world hidden, even from those closest to her. Victoria had secrets, and one of these she shared only with the painter, but there were deeper secrets than this, Pandora was sure, and this would be a hard thing for her to express through her paints, for how does one paint a secret?

On the evening before her departure she retired early, and would rise early the next morning, and from that moment on her energy and focus would be solely on her next painting, which may prove to be the most difficult of all.

'So do you think I should confront her?'

Barrington and May had by now eaten their repast, she more hungrily than he, and had smoked the joint together. Barrington had not taken any form of illegal drug since returning from Thailand, but decided that the occasion justified his doing so now, and he needed to be in at least a similar state of mind to his sister, who would otherwise doubtless have smoked the whole thing. The events and letter had been discussed until nothing further could be gleaned, and now it was time to look forward.

'Pfffff...Well there's the question, dear brother. I mean you obviously can't see her again unless you do, you can hardly ignore any of this, can you?'

'No, I can't'

'So that has to be the big question, then. Whether in view of this you want to see her again or drop the lady like a hot potato.'

'Don't you think she should be given the chance to explain herself, or deny that the accusations in the letter are true?'

'Yes, I suppose so, you might owe her that, at least. You say there's been no contact between you since you were turned away at the door, and that's a bit odd, unless she really is ill. How much time elapsed between the door – shutting evening and the letter?'

'Three days, I think.'

'So six days without a word, and you haven't tried to contact her?'

'Well no, I was pretty pissed with her, to be honest, even before the letter. We know each other well enough not to let illness prevent our seeing one another, even if she was actually ill, but I now think there's more to it than that.'

'Sure….Sure, and if this was a normal situation you would reasonably expect that she would have at least 'phoned you to apologize for or at least explain her behavior. On the other hand if she really has been caught with her knickers down in somebody else's bedroom then who knows what the fallout from that might have been.'

'Indeed…'

'The problem for me is that I've never met her, so it's hard for me to have any kind of opinion about her. I mean, what's she like, Bats, when you're, you know…Without going into unnecessary detail.'

'What do you mean?'

'I mean how does she make love? Is she warm and demonstrative, does she scream the place down or is she sort of cold, quiet and detached?'

'She's….Well, more of the latter than either of the former, I suppose, why do you ask?'

'I ask because, well, it's always struck me as a bit odd to say the least, the way she as it were introduced her sexual self to you. I mean walking around stark – naked in front of men she hardly knows isn't exactly normal female behavior, is it?'

'No, I suppose not.'

'Trust me, it isn't.'

'So what are you saying?'

'What I'm saying, and I'm only postulating, is that she might be some kind of sexual psycho, you know, not quite all there in the emotion department.'

'I've never really thought of it like that. I mean I don't have much to compare it to, or rather her to. Only prostitutes really, you know?'

'Which isn't much of a comparison, is it? Sorry, Bats, this is all getting about as personal as it gets, and I may be way of the mark, but I think if we trust the letter then she seems to be making free with her affections despite being in an apparently loving relationship with you, and that isn't usual for a woman either, and certainly not a nice, Catholic girl like Miranda purports to be.'

Barrington took a moment to consider his sister's words, whilst his sister lit a cigarette.

'You never said that before…That you thought it was odd behavior.'

'We never doubted her feelings for you before, did we? I mean as a one – off thing she could maybe have got away with it, but who knows how many other men she might have walked about in front of?'

'It doesn't bear thinking about.'

'Well you'd better start thinking about it now, Bats, and preparing yourself for a confrontation with her, if that's what you want to do.'

'What would you do?'

'Not a fair question, it's got to be up to you. I'm not the one who's in love with her, always assuming of course that you're still in love with her?'

'It's wearing a bit thin, to be honest.'

'That might have a bearing on what you do.'

'I mean I could just wait and see if she contacts me.'

'That's the other option.'

'Do you think she will?'

'I've no idea, how would I have? I mean if she does then there's your opportunity to get her side of the story, and if she doesn't then you'll know for sure, won't you, only don't wait forever, Bats. If you're going to spend the rest of your life wondering what might have been then better you go and see her, you know?'

'Even if I do, the letter was written to me anonymously, so I can't really quote from it, can I?'

'No, not really, anyway I would keep the letter out of it unless you get into deep and meaningful conversation about the whole thing. I can't write the script for you, Batty.'

'No, of course you can't….'

'Just concentrate on the evening that she turned you away, tell her how you feel about that and see how it goes from there. Anyway like I say, I'm sorry if things don't work out, but she's not the only woman in the world, and if nothing else your obsession with our Miranda got you away from the priesthood, for which I believe you owe her an eternal debt of gratitude, no matter what happens from now on.'

'It wasn't only her, Maisy.'

'No, of course it wasn't, but it helped, didn't it, so try not to think too badly of her. You probably had to go through your Thailand in order to end up where you have, and if she was the catalyst then you owe her for that, and for making you see that a life of celibacy wasn't such a good idea after all. Christ they fucked us up, didn't they?'

'Who, our parents..?'

'Mum, dad, the church, all of it. Our father's avowed intent that his only son should be the priest that he never was, and mum encouraged him in his ambition by proxy, or whatever you might call it.'

'You turned out okay though.'

'You think so? I work too hard, Bats, so maybe that's my obsession, and it's all fuelled by coke and whatever else I can get hold of. Keep the show going so I don't have to think about it, but we all carry the guilt. I sometimes think that the Catholic church is about the most evil institution that exists. I mean evil regimes come and go, you know, but Catholics have been around forever, and have always hidden behind a veneer of goodness and Godliness, despite all the misery and pain that they inflict on the world. It's insidious, you know; it's just fucking evil.'

'Erica doesn't carry the guilt...'

'Erica's as guilt – ridden as the rest of us, she just caved in to it a long time ago.'

'What do you think she'll do?'

'In what regard..?'

'Any regard.'

'I suppose she'll devote her life to god, meet some other pious, god – fearing soul, have loads of guilty and unprotected sex in the name of god and have loads of children as a consequence, then devote her children's lives to god to make up for the sex.'

'It's a hard circle to break, isn't it?'

'We do our best, dear brother...So what do you think you'll do then, about Miranda?'

'I really don't know. I mean on the one hand if it really is over between us then I'm wondering why I should put myself through the ordeal of seeing her again, and yet if I don't see her then I'll never know for sure, will I, whether she really did the things that she's been accused of.'

'Even if you do see her you might not be certain, she could lie, you know, and if the letter's true then she's probably quite good at that. Still, if there's a chance that it will put your mind at rest then see her, always assuming that she agrees to see you. If she has any feelings for you at all, which I'm sure she does, she might find the idea of meeting up as difficult as you do.

Even psycho – girl must have feelings somewhere under all the weirdness, and if she breaks down, tells you everything and begs forgiveness then there's another decision for you to make. There're all kinds of ways that this could go.'

'Yes, I suppose…I think I'll sleep on it for a few more days, I'm too stoned to make any sensible decision now anyway. So what about you then? That's the first time I've heard you speak negatively about your work, I thought you loved it.'

'Oh I do, but there's a myth, isn't there, about sharks having to keep moving to stay alive, and I think I'm in shark – mode at the moment. I tell myself sometimes that I should get away somewhere, you know, take a break. I mean I stay in some nice hotels on location, and sometimes I wish I could just, you know, be in the hotel, go lie by the pool for a few days, but I know I'd be bored senseless in about two hours. As it is I barely have time for breakfast, which is crazy, I know, but I don't think I could stop myself even if the opportunity presented itself.'

'I don't think I could lead your life. My life is basically get up, eat breakfast, go and hoe borders or cut hedges or whatever, then come home again. My only variation to that is an occasional pint in the Dog and Bottle, your visits and Miranda, but it looks like even she may have gone now.'

'Perhaps you should get away somewhere, don't you employed people get paid holiday or something?'

'Yes, I'm accruing some days, the problem is I'm not paid enough to be able to afford to do anything with it.'

'You've still got some money on deposit, haven't you?'

'That's for emergencies, like if I lose my job or something. I'm trying to live within my meager means, and I'm content enough, on the whole. I used to be a monk, remember, so I'm used to having a lot of time, I just don't waste it praying anymore, so I've got too much time to think, you know?'

'It seems we have opposite problems. Anyway I'm fading out, and it must be about midnight, isn't it?'

'Not quite.'

'That's close enough, and I've got an early start tomorrow.'

'How early..?'

'I've ordered a cab for six o'clock, I've got to be in town and working by eight at the latest, I've got a heavy schedule tomorrow. We're pre – production, and I've got to get a lot of ducks in line before we go on location.'

'Where..?'

'The Bahamas, probably, although even that's not certain yet, we need a good beach for somebody to get washed up dead on, and someone's out there looking even as we speak. It's all a big bloody rush as always.'

'I'll wake you at five thirty then, shall I?'

'Better had, although that's a horrible thought at the moment...'

'And thanks Maisy, for taking the time to come down.'

'Well it wasn't Thailand this time. Your life crises are getting closer to home, at least.'

'I still owe you for Thailand.'

'When the boat comes in, dear brother… Money – wise I'm okay these days anyway, I just don't have time to spend any of it.'

'Like you say, opposite problems….'

She stood up and made for the stairs, but had one more thought.

'I don't suppose you've met Tara yet then?'

'No, not yet...'

'Or Ash Spears..?'

'Not him, either. I think they're still on tour anyway.'

'You really should get better at networking, Bats, the next woman's out there somewhere.'

'I just have to find her, yes?'

'Go to it, brother.'

She made the stairs. Barrington cleared away the dishes and general detritus from the evening. He wasn't feeling particularly tired, and had some thinking to do, and a particular decision to make. There was no definitive way forward as yet, but sometimes just sharing a problem is help enough, particularly when the help had come from his beloved younger sister. Whether he would ever see Miranda Spool again, however, remained for now a matter for conjecture.

The return trip for Percival and Louise was as convoluted as had been their outward journey, the difference being that this time they had two prolonged periods of waiting time between flights, which they whiled away in cafes and designated smoking areas. The other essential difference was that on the way out their love for one another had been a shy and uncertain thing, whereas now it carried itself with pride, and as much confidence as either could bring to bear upon it; now she took his arm around airport concourses, and fell into contented slumber on his shoulder during flights. In any case, as English time would have it they arrived by taxi at the cottage down the lane at a little after midnight, Percival noting as they drove past the village Green that the lights were still on at number two, the house which he had bought quite spontaneously when Louise had first come back into his life. 'Halfway House' she had called it, and she had even sent him a small plaque with the name engraved upon it. She would have it that he had bought the house for her, something which he had never definitively confirmed or denied, perhaps even to himself. In any case his tenant, who was called Barrington, who had formerly been a monk, and whom Percival had only seen on occasion was apparently not yet abed, but was in fact washing dishes, as his sister May fell into exhausted sleep above him in the spare bedroom, which Barrington called her bedroom.

The taxi pulled up outside the cottage, Percival paid the driver and looked for his house keys, although upon reaching his side door he found that he did not in fact need his house keys, the door standing already slightly ajar. He pushed it open, turned on the light and both entered, neither speaking as they took in the scene before them. Tables had been pushed over, books, ornaments and framed pictures lay strewn and broken upon the floor, and such soft furnishings as there were had been slashed. It was a scene of utter devastation, and Louise was the first to speak.

'My god, Percival...'

'Yeah, I've been meaning to tidy up, but never seem to get around to it.'

He walked into the kitchen.

'At least they left the coffee machine.'

He poured water and put coffee into the percolator and walked away whilst the device went about its' business.

'But who…I mean who would have done this?'

'I don't know; somebody who doesn't like me very much, either that or they don't share my taste in furniture.'

'Can you tell if anything's been stolen?'

'There's nothing to steal, really, I don't exactly collect Ming vases or antique jewellery. The only things I have of value are my passport, credit cards and lap – top, and that only because of what's on it.'

'And you had all of those with you.'

'Anyway this wasn't about theft, they weren't looking for anything when they put a knife through the settee.'

'Oh Percival, I'm so sorry…'

'It's just stuff, Louise, and I probably had this coming, the insurance company will sort it out. I think I need to speak to Rebecca.'

'I think you need to call the police.'

'What for, they'd never catch whoever did this.'

'The insurance company might need to see a police report or whatever.'

'Yes, maybe... I'll call them in the morning.'

'Why do you need to speak to Rebecca?'

'Because if this was the chicken - stranglers they might have come for her, too.'

'And she has a child, doesn't she?'

'It could just be me, but I need to be sure, and Rebecca can look after herself.'

'Percival, what would have happened if you'd been here?'

'Nothing good, probably, but I think they knew I wasn't here. This wasn't about any kind of confrontation, it was sending a message, and it could have been worse. They could have burned the place down, and I wonder why they didn't.'

They walked upstairs together and into the main bedroom. The bedclothes had been pulled back and a large 'X' had been cut corner to corner into the mattress. On the wall above the bed had been painted in red paint the words *'YOU ARE THE LIVING DEAD'*; Louise exclaimed, and Percival spoke.

'Well, there's the message, then.'

'What does it mean?'

'I think it's meant to be cryptic.'

Percival ran his finger over the lettering.

'They were here quite recently, the paint isn't completely dry. It probably happened this evening.'

'Christ....So what are we going to do, we can't stay here.'

'Why not, whoever did this is long gone. It's just words, Louise, designed I suspect to provoke me into doing something.'

'Doing what?'

'I don't know yet, I need time to think, but first I need coffee.'

They went downstairs, Percival poured coffee and two large Scotches, which they drank before the coffee whilst sharing a cigarette.

'Look, I'm sorry about this. Of course if you want I'll 'phone for a cab and we'll get you to a hotel.'

'Won't you come with me?'

'No, I'm staying here. Apart from anything else I need to change the lock in the morning, anybody could walk in and I'd be embarrassed if a genuine burglar came in and saw this.'

'Aren't you afraid?'

'I don't know what to be afraid of yet, and until I speak to Rebecca I can't make any sense of anything.'

'Well you know, just general fear would cover it for the moment.'

'I'm all done being afraid, Louise. That's what they want, this was a terrorist attack.'

'Well then it worked, as far as I'm concerned. It's because you had those people killed, isn't it?'

'I don't know…In a way that doesn't make any sense, if they'd wanted to assassinate me then this wouldn't be the way. Something doesn't add up about this, but I haven't joined the dots yet. Not much of a homecoming, is it? Hardly a good start to our life together, you can bail out if you want; come back when I've got a house to come back to.'

'And leave you again? No, Percival, I won't do that. I wasn't sure what to expect when I agreed to go away with you. I didn't know how I'd feel, or how you really felt, but now I'm certain of one thing, which I decided on a beach somewhere. It's you and me now, whatever happens, and I mean whatever happens. If this is your life now then it's my life as well. Death or glory, Percival, my love, and if that turns out to be literal then so be it. If they kill you then they'll have to kill me too.'

For a moment they held each other, and amongst the devastation both took comfort from the holding, and it was Percival who broke the silence.

'Well then, I'd better make sure they don't kill me, hadn't I….'

'Yes, you'd better had. Come on then, let's start, shall we?'

Between them they lifted the dining table back into its' upright position, took two chairs from the floor and sat down opposite one another.

'There,' said Louise 'and so it begins. So apart from calling the police in the morning and then clearing up this mess and buying you some new furniture, what do we do now?'

He poured more Scotch. They had been tired at various stages during the journey, and Louise had slept through most of the last flight, but different time zones now saw to it that they had pulled away from the tiredness, and they were certainly awake now.

'I need to talk to people in the village, I mean aside from Rebecca. After that I don't know yet.'

'Well I'll try to get a couple more days off work, but I'll have to go home sometime, apart from anything else I need clothes which aren't beach clothes. But I mean will you even stay living here?'

'I expect so, but that will depend on conversations with others. I really haven't got my head around any of this yet, Louise.'

'No, of course…Well, my love, I never thought life with you would be boring, but I didn't think it would get this exciting this quickly.'

'It's a thrill a minute with me.'

'We should have stayed on the island, shouldn't we? I liked it there.'

'There're other islands, but not yet.'

'I know, you have to sort out this mess first, and I don't just mean the house.'

'I can't just walk away, not yet.'

'No, I know you can't, so nor can I, but now I need a pee, then I need you to tell me everything that you haven't already told me.'

She left the room, Percival lit a cigarette. He was at least fairly sure by now that the cult were behind this, but it was a lesser response than he would have expected in view of that which he had done. So perhaps they had come for him and vented their frustration at his absence, but that still it didn't make sense to him. And now there was Louise, which made everything different. He had started all of this for Rebecca, and Rebecca had been worth killing for, and perhaps even worth dying for, otherwise why would he have done it, but he had a son now, and Louise had come back to him, so now he had something far more important. Now he had reasons for living.

Chapter 11

Singing from the Soul

Upon a particular morning, Keith awoke with a strong but as yet undefined sense of anticipation, which was his first emotional engagement with the waking world. Something was going to happen, which would require the intellectual part of him to break free of his sleep state into full consciousness before anything more could be made of it. It took another moment, but then his emotion and intellect met on common ground, and a state of realization was achieved, which now found vocal expression.

'It's today, isn't it…'

Meadow, who was by now somewhat more awake that Keith, was able to confirm Keith's enquiry, which was in fact a statement.

'Yes, my love, it's today.'

Barbara, who was wife to Ron who ran the car – repairs and servicing garage would stand in for Meadow at the delicatessen for the day, as she had done on occasion in the past, they would wait for the commuter rush to have subsided, such as it would be on a Saturday morning, and then Keith, and Meadow, Rosemary and Quentin, and Basil and Emma would board a train to London. The only missing member of the family had been in telephonic communication the evening before, and she and they would meet at an as yet unspecified time and location later in the day, prior to her performing in front of the largest crowd that she had yet sung before, for this evening Tarragon and the band called Dead Man's Wealth would take their rightful place amongst other great and good of the rock – music world, and perform their songs at a concert in Hyde Park. It was early in the concert season, but the day had dawned fine, and there would be no rain.

That Keith and Meadow should be going to London at all was an uncommon enough occurrence, since despite living an easy distance away and quite close to a good commuter line, both could count on the fingers of one hand the number of times that they had visited the capital city before. This was through choice, since as a general principal neither liked cities, but today they had good reason to go, and so there was much anticipation at the thought of their day – trip.

Much to their mutual frustration, Rosie and Quentin had not in fact seen one another since Quentin had last been here on the evening that he had been introduced to Rosie's parents. He had since then been working the evening – shift at the warehouse, and so there had been no sensible opportunity for their meeting, and he would meet them at the bus this morning. They had nevertheless spoken each day by telephone, which had been something good, at least, but this had also served to cast fuel on the fire of their frustration, and they had their own reasons why today would be special for them. Feelings may develop and grow within people even in the absence of others, and by swift degrees did both parties to the matter independently conclude that they were in love, a conclusion which both confirmed to the other, and this was the first time for both that such all – consuming emotion had entered the soul of either, and it was a good feeling. Basil and Emma were by now old hands in the business of being in love, but they and particularly Basil also awoke in the trailer with a sense that today would be special, although it was as usual Emma who was the most vocal on the issue, even before Basil was awake.

'Hey you, wake up.'

'What…? What's going on?'

'We're going to London.'

'Oh, yeah….That's cool then.'

'I'm excited.'

'Yeah…Yeah, I expect I will be when I've come to a bit… What are you doing?'

That which she had done was to straddle him, and a young man who may in any case awaken with a certain sensory sensitivity will likely be further aroused by the sight of a beautiful, naked young woman.

'I told you, I'm excited.'

'Me too, I think….'

'It certainly seems that way.'

'We'll have to be quiet, though, my parents are in the next bus.'

She laughed, they made love, and it was a happy start to their day.

Quentin arrived just as Meadow was preparing pancakes and had made herbal tea, and just as Rosie emerged from the trailer.

'Hi you, you're nice and early.'

'I had reasons for wanting to be here.'

They kissed, and held one another for a moment, which would for now have to suffice in terms of the expression of their new – found love, but for both it was a moment of significance, for neither had been with anybody that they were in love with before, not even each other.

'So, big day for your big sister...'

'Big day for me, too, none of us has ever seen her perform before, and I mean, Hyde Park, you know?'

'Absolutely…'

And so did preparations for the day continue, which were only interrupted at the last moment by the arrival of somebody whom neither Keith nor Meadow would have expected to see, and he came with somebody whom neither would have expected to be with him.

Percival and Louise had fallen asleep in the spare bedroom during the late hours of the night, and had not awoken until just before the eighth hour of the day, and then only grudgingly. Once coffee had been made and they were sufficiently awake for mental faculties to begin to function properly, Percival 'phoned the local constabulary, and then his Insurance Company, and reported the break – in to both. The insurers would send an assessor by the afternoon, which Percival thought was highly efficient, but the police were even more so, a squad car arriving within twenty minutes of his having made the call. The two policemen were shown around the cottage, after which they took notes and photographs and would file a report, which Percival still assumed would be a purely academic exercise, particularly in view of the fact that nothing had been stolen, but it was done now, at least. Particular interest was shown regarding the words which had been painted on the bedroom wall, but since Percival could shed no light on the matter of who had written them, they would be in the report also, but the police would be unable to take the matter further.

In any event it was not therefore until just before ten o'clock that Percival knocked on the open door of the bus, just as the assembled party were making their final preparations for departure, and Meadow was the first to come to the door.

'Hello Percival, we thought you were away, didn't we?'

'Yeah, we got back late last night.'

'Oh, hello Louise, well this morning is full of surprises.'

'Hi Meadow...' Said Louise

'Yeah, we're, ummm, anyway, is Keith about?'

'Indeed he is,' said Keith, who joined the group just as the others were entering the bus 'but we're all just leaving, so what brings you so unexpectedly to our door? Hi Louise...'

'Hi Keith...'

'We're to London; Tara's performing at Hyde Park this evening.'

'Really…? In that case we won't detain you, but I thought you should know that the cottage was broken into while I was away, probably last evening.'

'Christ, man…What did they take?'

'Nothing, I don't think, but the place was trashed, and I was wondering whether you had any news of Rebecca. I just called over there but there's nobody home so I suppose I must have missed her.'

'We've heard nothing from her.'

'Well the house looked fine as far as I could see, so I think it's safe to assume that she's okay.'

'Yeah, I guess…I'm sure we'd have heard by now if anything was amiss in the village. I dropped by your place after work yesterday and everything looked fine, so it must have happened after about seven o'clock, but why are you concerned about Rebecca? You think this might be our friends from the west – country?'

'I think that's a fair assumption. They left a none too friendly message for me, but look, I won't hold you up, I mean it's great news about Tara, she's really hit the big time, has she not?'

'Well, she's singing with DMW, so it's not her as a soloist, but yeah, the girl's done good, but are you guys sure you're okay?'

'We're fine as it goes. The police have been 'round, so I'll get the locks changed today, then I'll have to dispose of some furniture and so on.'

'We can use Damien's Land Rover for that…Jesus, Perc, this has got serious, hasn't it?'

'You might say that.'

'We need a meeting. We'll come to yours tomorrow morning, see what needs to be done. I daresay we'll be late home tonight, always assuming that we make it home, so we'll leave you to get hold of Rebecca.'

'Sure, I'll see her this evening.'

Meadow had been listening to the conversation with uncommon interest, and had exchanged smiles with Louise, whose unexpected and sudden reappearance had not been explained, and nor apparently would it be. Sufficient unspoken information had passed between the two women, however; a question had been asked and had been answered, and Meadow thus felt it safe to make certain assumptions, and in any case felt that she should offer to help.

'Look, we don't have to leave just yet, we were going to spend some time in London before the concert, but under the circumstances…'

'No, you go, we're fine, really, there's nothing anyone can do today, and we aren't going to screw your day up. We'll see you tomorrow, and you know, have a great day.'

Percival and Louise departed, the family and lovers thereof gathered from their discrete distances, and Keith spoke.

'This is bad news…'

'Who were they?' Said Quentin

'It's a long story, Rosie'll fill you in, but we should be leaving.'

'So…' said Rosie 'Louise…?'

'Yeah, what's that about?' Said Keith 'Not together again, are they..?'

'I don't know, perhaps.' Said Meadow

'So what happened to whatshername?'

'Sally; she's gone to Norway.'

'What the fuck for?'

'Work, I believe. She's moved out of the house.'

'Well I suppose she could hardly commute. Jesus, stuff happens around here when you're not looking doesn't it, so is that the end of the line for Percival and Sally?'

'Keith dear, you know as much as I do.'

'Man, the guy doesn't let the grass grow, does he? Anyway, let's go before anything else weird happens, or anyone else turns up with the wrong person.'

The assembled party left the bus to begin their journey, Keith and Meadow walking behind, and Meadow wished to be sure of something.

'Keith, I don't know everything that Percival's been doing, and I know you know more than you've told me, but whatever this is all about, you won't think about it today, will you? We'll do whatever we can tomorrow, but today is for Tara, agreed?'

'Totally...'

'And from now on I want full disclosure, okay? Percival's always been trouble, Keith, and whatever you do don't put yourself in any more danger.'

'I think we'll all learn things tomorrow...Anyway, says she who single – handedly dealt with a sword – wielding witch at Howard's Bench, and went without me into a deserted farmhouse without knowing what the hell was in there. Oh, yeah, and what about the time you faced down the black witch on the steps of the Manor House; that was a good one.'

'That was different.'

'Differently dangerous, perhaps, but dangerous nonetheless... I just beat guys up, you know?'

'And so far you've been fortunate.'

'No, I'm just good at beating guys up, but don't make out you're a shrinking Violet, hiding from every peril.'

She took his arm.

'Keith, just shut up and be careful.'

'I'm always careful.'

'And today's for Tara, okay?'

'Today's for Tara. I never said it wouldn't be.'

They would catch a bus into town and alight in the proximity of the railway station, which would take them quite close to Quentin's apartment, but for his own reasons he had wanted to pick Rosie up from her home. From thence through all stations northwards to Victoria, and they would be in London in just over an hour.

During the time that Pandora had been painting his Lordship's portrait, and she had been ensconced in her temporary studio and accommodation in the new extension, which had been most of the time that she had last been here, it had been quite easy for her to forget where she was. Now, however as she was once again driven up the graveled driveway between the sweeping lawns which led up to the Manor House, she was once again struck by the grandeur of so fine a building. Here was a remnant of a bygone age, when the many were ruled by the very few, and the contrast between them had been so extreme that no bridge could ever link them. Then by slow but inevitable degrees had come the fall of the British Empire, and the rise of industrialization, whereupon thousands upon thousands of those who had once been called peasants were set to work together in factories and warehouses, where in time they had found common voice, and so had begun the rise of the working classes. In further time had come easy credit from banks, whereby even the lowliest could borrow to set up their small enterprises, most of which were bound to fail, but those few who were successful, or had found fame and fortune by other means, could in time dare to call themselves wealthy, and some became wealthier than those who had once ruled over them. And now, in the time in which Pandora lived, in the post – industrial, globalized age, where the economy was largely ruled by banking and commerce, the middle – classes with their valuable properties and expendable income had become the engine room of the economy, and upon them now depended the financial success or otherwise of the nation. Pandora was an only child, and whilst her parents could not count themselves amongst the most wealthy, they had been rich enough to allow her to indulge in her art, and support her when the need had been there. Few indeed of her contemporaries had gone on to be able to make even a modest living solely from their craft, but Pandora had been single – minded enough and in the end good enough to come through the difficult times, and here perhaps was a symbolic culmination of her life to date, and a representation of the times in which she lived; to be able to come to such a place as this and see herself and be treated as an equal amongst those who lived here. Such houses as this had been built upon the toil and poverty of those who had paid for their construction and continuation, but those times were gone now, and the legacy of a former imperial age had in large part become a burdensome thing to those who were left in its' wake.

Some years ago Pandora had researched her family history, and had discovered that her great grandfather, Noah Winterton, who was one of seven children, had been employed as a farm labourer in the county of Norfolk. Her great grandmother, Olivia, had for a time been a kitchen maid, probably in just such a house as this, and had during her quite short life born five children, two girls and three boys. Neither of the girls had survived to adulthood, but the three brothers had together learned the art of tailoring, and had eventually between them established an apparently quite successful business making men's suits in the city of London. Her grandfather, who had been second eldest, had been the last to survive, and he had passed the business to his only son, Pandora's father, who had sold the business and premises to his considerable profit. Via a series of different professions, her father had in the end become a stockbroker, and his earnings from this quite lucrative profession, together with his inherited wealth, had seen to it that Pandora had been born roundly and without question into the middle class of English society.

Thus it was that on this day Pandora was greeted at the front door of the Manor House, this time by Michael Tillington, the next in line to his father's ancient and inherited title, who helped her with her canvass and small suitcase into the new part of the house. Victoria would be home in due course, and in the meantime Pandora unpacked her clothes and toiletries as though she had been to the Manor born. She set up her easel and paints, made tea and rolled herself a cigarette, and made ready for her next subject. Victoria Tillington had burdens enough of her own, and although their financial circumstances could scarce even be compared, Pandora felt by comparison like a free spirit, and the paints and brushes which had given her this freedom now lay in wait, as did the artist who would see to their use.

Aside from Quentin, who had during his life made quite frequent trips to London, Basil and Emma were the most familiar with the ways and workings of the capital city, as they had come here on occasion as time and more particularly money would allow. It was Basil therefore who assumed responsibility in the matter of negotiating his family through the complexities of the London underground system, and thus navigating their way to their various intended destinations, the first of which was the Palace of Westminster and thus Westminster Abbey. Here, and somewhat to the surprise of his parents, did Basil regale the rest of his family with certain facts regarding the fine and extraordinary building in which resided the seat of British government. For example;

'It's a commonly held misconception that the tower's called Big Ben, which it isn't, Big Ben's a bell, the tower's called the Elizabeth Tower. The other tower's actually taller, it's called the Victoria Tower, where they keep the archives, which are like, well old.' Or 'That over there's called the Jewel tower, which is part of the original

medieval palace, most of the main palace isn't that old, it burned down and was rebuilt in the nineteenth century. That's why they call it the new palace.'

When questioned as to how he had come to know such things, Basil merely stated that he '*just knew stuff about London*', and the matter was let be. From thence they made their mostly subterranean way to Covent Garden, where after a quite brief walk around the predominantly indoor markets they found a suitable café in which to eat lunch. This quieter and more interactive time gave the family further opportunity to get to know its' newest addition, and Quentin, who was in his turn observing the others, and particularly Keith and Meadow, was able to answer further polite enquiry as to his life and circumstances to date. For example it became clear to all that he was in fact close to his two brothers, despite his referring to Tristan and Tarquin as 'Intelligent idiots who argued a great deal'. Emma rarely shone in social situations, and was her more usual reserved self, and Rosie had also rather withdrawn back into herself, and was also quietly watching the proceedings, and how her new – found beaux was finding his way with her family. In any case they had all but finished their meal when Rosemary received the expected telephone call; Tara had arrived in central London and was making her way to Hyde Park, and would meet them in about two hours or whenever she could get away. They narrowed their meeting place down to somewhere near the Serpentine, and she would call again soon. The emotional and practical focus of the assembled party thus quietly shifted to the main event of the day, and to their reason for coming to London. Keith paid the bill, Quentin's offer to pay half of it being politely refused, Basil once again took control of navigation, and all made their way to the nearest tube – station, and from thence to Hyde Park Corner.

It was early in the evening by the time Percival and Louise called once again at number seven, The Green, by which time Rebecca had arrived home and was beginning her evening ritual of feeding herself and Florence, and settling her infant for the night. If she was pleasantly surprised to see Percival, she was somewhat more surprised to see him with somebody other than Sally. She knew of Louise, to whom Percival had spoken much of Rebecca, but the two women had never met, and Louise in particular was by now keen to be introduced to the person about whom she had heard such a great deal. If Percival's life was to be her life from now on, then she must begin to accept the existence of witches, and in this context here apparently was a witch of some power, and one furthermore who had committed murder. She must from now on forget images of witches from childhood story – books; this witch was real enough, and aside from her extraordinarily dark eyes appeared to be ordinary enough, as did the domestic setting in which they found her. Only that which she had heard from Percival had made her aware that here was a woman who was very far from ordinary, and the fact that she had checked who was calling, and had to unlock and unbolt her door indicated the way that she nowadays had to live.

'Hi, this is a nice surprise.'

They entered the lounge, which was to say the least of it sparsely furnished; between them Rebecca and Percival now had scarce enough viable furniture to furnish a single room; the infant Florence, however, appeared to be contented enough in her drawer. Lady had known who was there before the door had been opened, and as they entered she did nothing but raise her head in interest from her lying position. Him she knew, of course, but not her, but she was with him so probably all was well. Her mistress was showing no sign of distress or fear, so she put her head back down on her paws, and took no further part in the proceedings other than continue to watch carefully.

'We've come to see if you're okay.'

'I'm fine. Any reason why I shouldn't be..?'

Something passed between Percival and Rebecca which could only have happened between people who knew each other as well as did they; the merest eye contact had begun a conversation before any conversation had begun, to which Louise had not been party, but it had been enough to indicate to Rebecca that all was not well. Meanwhile the two women assessed one another; Rebecca had clean, unadorned hands and bare feet, but her face and forehead, as well as her clothes, which were jeans and a casual smock, bore the marks of her days' work with clay and water. This was something which would doubtless have passed without explanation had Percival come alone, but now there was another woman present.

'Sorry, I haven't had time to wash and change yet, and I wasn't expecting anyone.'

'Yes, well we're sorry to disturb your evening. This is Louise, Louise, this is Rebecca.'

'Hi…'

'Hi, I'm pleased to meet you.'

'So, to what do I owe the pleasure of this visit?'

'Nothing pleasant, actually, the cottage was broken into last evening, and they left the place in an even worse mess than usual.'

Rebecca took a moment to consider the implications of this statement, which was probably an understatement, before;

'Was anything stolen?'

'I don't think so, I think the point was to make the mess, and to leave me a message, which was to the effect that I am apparently the living dead, whatever that means.'

Now came further pause for thought, before she asked the next and the next most obvious question.

'Do you think it was them?'

'I think that's a fair assumption, don't you?'

'They didn't come here…Christ, I'm sorry Percival.'

'You should see the other guy.'

'What do you mean?'

'I mean that it wasn't an entirely unprovoked attack. I sent someone down there to try to disrupt their organization, and he was rather more successful than I'd anticipated. Somehow he managed to infiltrate their ranks, and three of them met with unfortunate accidents.'

'You sent a hit – man?'

'Our mutual friend Tony Blackman's okay, he was kept out of it, but the head has been cut off the snake, and now I think they're rather angry, so I think we should be even more vigilant than usual.'

'Bloody hell….I knew you were up to something, but I didn't think it was that. So, it's war then, is it?'

'It always was. I couldn't get any assurance from Mister Blackman that it was all over, and that we were safe, so, well, the rest is recent history.'

'So what do we do now?'

'I'm meeting with Keith and Meadow tomorrow morning, and I think you should be there.'

'Do they know everything?'

'Keith knows everything, so yeah, they know everything, or they will by the time we meet. The thing is, I've seen Tony Blackman since, and he sent me a note to the effect that it was all over, so this attack makes no sense unless he's lying, or somebody or bodies in the organization don't agree with him. They know we can get to them now, that's the point, so this was a risk, assuming that I or we respond to it, which I don't think we should do, incidentally. I didn't like the furniture much anyway.'

'What about the threat?'

'It's just words, Rebecca, perhaps designed to provoke a reaction, which is another reason why I don't think I or we should react. This could just be a one – off, a '*fuck you very much for everything and goodbye*'. If they'd made up their minds to kill me then they'd have done it by now, and whatever we may think about Tony Blackman, I think he's genuine.'

Florence now awoke in her crib, and Rebecca went to her. Louise of a sudden needed cool, fresh air, and went outside and leant against the doorpost overlooking the Green. From that which Percival had told her during their several conversations, it seemed to her that he could have walked away from all of this, and the reason that he had not done so was presently inside attending to her child, which was not his child, at least, but having met Rebecca and seen them together she could see clearly enough the connection which they had to one another. She did not see Rebecca as a rival for Percival's affections, and this despite the fact that they had slept together, and she did not believe that they were or had ever been in love in the conventional sense of the word, but they were more than just good friends. During and since her time with Percival on the island, her emotional focus had almost entirely been upon their reunion, which had overridden and still overrode all else, but in quieter moments she had given consideration to the moral aspects of all that had happened, and of the rights and wrongs of it all. If all that Percival had told her was true, and she had no wish or reason to doubt him, then Rebecca had suffered abuse by the sect as a young girl, and Percival's motivation since then had been to save her from further abuse or perhaps death at their hands, or at her own hands, which was laudable enough, but he had now put himself so far above the law of the land that this no longer had any part in it. He had explained to her that the sect itself numbered at least one officer of the law in its' ranks, so from the beginning he had had no recourse there, but Louise's thoughts regarding all that had happened were still in solution, and were looking for somewhere to settle.

Inside, during this brief time that they had alone together, the opportunity was taken for a quiet conversation of a more mundane nature between Percival and Rebecca. In fact all that had been required to commence the exchange was an enquiring look from Rebecca as she held Florence to her.

'Yeah, It's over between Sally and I, she's gone to Norway with the bank, as it happens. Louise and I are together now, which has all happened rather quickly.'

'So it would seem, and I'm sorry for you and Sally but I have to say thank goodness for that. Like I said before I don't know her well, but from what I saw you were never right for each other.'

'Yes, I knew you thought that.'

'Anyway Louise seems really nice.'

'You've hardly met.'

'I hardly need to meet people, you know that.'

'Yeah, I suppose so. So how are things between you and Victoria?'

'I haven't seen her for a while. Victoria isn't talking to me at the moment, which is a long story, which I don't want to get into now.'

The small person who was indirectly the reason for Rebecca and Victoria's current estrangement had quickly settled her own small emotional issues, and was placed back into her crib, where she fell into reassured slumber. Louise now reentered the room.

'Look, I'm sorry, can I offer you both tea or coffee?'

'It's okay,' said Percival 'we'll leave you in peace. I just wanted to make sure you were okay.'

'Well, like I say, I'm fine, and I'll certainly come tomorrow morning.'

'See you then, then.'

'It was nice to meet you, Louise, despite the circumstances.'

'Likewise…'

They left, Percival feeling somewhat reassured and Rebecca feeling less so, whilst Louise didn't yet quite know what to feel. She would stand by Percival no matter what, of that she had made up her mind and to that would she hold, but of the three of them it was she who was new to all of this, and the least battle – hardened for the battle which was perhaps to come, despite Percival's attempts to reassure her that all might be well from now onwards.

'Where are you?'

'We're in the Park, near the water.'

'Okay, look, I'll meet you at the north end of the bridge.'

Thus had run a brief conversation between Rosemary and her sister, and the family made their way through the assembled throng to the appointed place beside the Serpentine, a large, man - made body of water which on quieter days was a place for relatively quiet recreation for the denizens of the busy and crowded city of London. Today, however, they already shared the park with tens of thousands of others who had come to watch the show, and to listen to live performances by some of the foremost rock bands of the time. Today the focus was upon the huge stage which dominated the park, and around which the great majority of the crowd had already begun to assemble to watch the first acts of the day. Within this context did Tarragon once again meet her family, and the reunion was a happy and emotional affair. She hugged everyone, and even hugged Quentin as she was introduced to him for the first time. For Quentin this was a moment of some significance, for here was not only Rosemary's sister but a rock – Goddess in the making, and he had never met one of those before, far less been hugged by one. Here was the young woman who could on a whim change her lilting, seductive voice into something far more hard and guttural, for in large part Tara's appeal and success was the versatility with which she could deliver the songs of Ashley Spears, and Quentin had by now listened to both of her albums a great many times. The moment was made still more significant for Quentin by the fact that just behind Tara now walked Ashley

Spears himself, dressed as he always seemed to be dressed, in tight jeans, cowboy boots, partly unbuttoned grandpa vest and loose – fitting jacket, and as ever he wore small, round – rimmed dark glasses. He seemed to many who knew and saw him to be the embodiment of the now bygone age when he and his music had been in their heyday, but the man still had an undefined presence; he was a hard man to ignore under any circumstances, even just walking through a crowd. With him walked Samantha Rodrigues, to whom he was now married, and Aiko, the beautiful Japanese base guitarist who had played her part in their becoming man and wife, and who had played her own so significant part the bands' renaissance. Such an eclectic group of famous musicians was bound to draw the attention of those around them, and so it proved to be, but within the context of an outdoor concert, where famous musicians abounded, they were observed with interest but otherwise left respectfully alone. That which also became immediately apparent to Quentin was the strong bond of friendship which existed between Rosie's parents and Ashley and Samantha, all of whom also now hugged each with the other.

'It's so wonderful to see you all.' Said Tara 'God I've missed you guys…'

'Where're the others?' Said Keith

'I think Rick's off sorting himself out a drum – kit, and Al and Evie are probably networking somewhere, it's like a who's – who of rock music backstage, but look, can I introduce Aiko, who's very keen to meet you all. Aiko was now ushered into the forefront of the assembled group, and she put her skilled hands together and bowed to Keith and Meadow in turn, who each bowed equally respectfully and in turn took her hand.

'I very honoured to meet you.'

'Yeah, likewise…' Said Keith

'Tara speak many good words of you, and you play guitar very beautifully, I hear you on Ash's symphony.'

'You don't play guitar so badly yourself, as it happens.'

They exchanged smiles, and such introductions as would be made had been made.

'So, when are you on?' said Keith, who now addressed Tarragon.

'After '*The Airwaves*', actually...'

'*After* 'The Airwaves'…? Christ that's a hell of an accolade.'

'I know, can you believe it…? We're third highest on the billing, so we'll be on mid – evening sometime.'

'Third highest is good.'

'Yeah,' said Ashley, 'not bad for a bunch of aging fuck – heads, present company excepted, we must be doing something right, I guess.'

'And Ash has promised to try to be on cue this evening, haven't you, Ash?'

'Yeah, I'll try that…Problem is the band's sounding so good now that I sometimes get lost in the music, and kind of forget to sing.'

'And I can't sing until you sing, so do try, won't you?'

'Give it my best shot….'

This brief conversation between the bands' two vocalists caused some amusement among the party; Rosemary smiled, and somewhat to her surprise, Ash's next words were addressed to her.

'So how's the young witch then, still casting spells on the unwary?'

In any other circumstance this light – hearted jibe would have been taken in the good spirit in which it had been intended, but in the circumstance of her standing next to her new beaux, who as yet knew nothing about Rosemary being a witch, the words were less well received, and for a moment Rosie didn't quite know what to do with them, so she did nothing but laugh, and that somewhat half – heartedly. Quentin looked momentarily confused, and Meadow, who saw her younger daughter's discomfort, thought it prudent to deflect the subject.

She had clearly not told him yet then, and so to the first subject which came into her head.

'So….Have you people had any sleep?'

'Most of us slept on the 'plane.' said Tara, who now took her mothers' arm and led her to one side.

'So, are you really okay, sweet – pea?'

'I'm fine, mum…God, have you seen the size of the stage, it's huge.'

'Are you nervous?'

'Well, you know, it's the usual mix of terror and excitement, but I suppose you can't have one without the other, and I'm learning to live with the fear, and it's always okay these days when I'm up there. I just have to keep the adrenalin under control, and this is a different kind of gig, it's like one big outdoor party really, isn't it?'

'Yes, it's the kind of thing your father and I would have gone to when we were your age and younger. We took you to one of these once, but you'd have been too young to remember, and now here you are singing in Hyde Park. Your father and I are so proud of you.'

'Yes, well I'm still pinching myself, and I still wonder sometimes how it all came to this.'

'Still living the dream, then...You're looking thin, honey.'

'I'll eat when this is all over, I mean I'm staying in great hotels and eating loads some days, but I seem to burn everything off, you know? Anyway don't go mumsy on me, I need to get focused. Let's join the

others, shall we?'

'Just one more *'mumsy'* question then, have you actually got anywhere to sleep tonight?'

'Sure….Well no, actually, but I think Evie was going to sort that out with the organizers, she's good at that sort of thing. I don't think they'll kick us out on the streets of London anyway. It'll probably be all party – party after the show, and then it's back on the 'plane tomorrow morning. So that's Quentin then, he looks nice.'

'He is, I think.'

'My beautiful little sister has a boyfriend, who'd have thought it?'

'He doesn't know she's a witch, yet.'

'That should be an interesting conversation, then.'

Their return to the group was briefly impeded by two early – teenaged girls, who approached them somewhat cautiously before one of them spoke.

'Excuse me, you're Tara, aren't you?'

'Yes, that's me.'

'I don't suppose...Would you sign our tickets?'

'Yes of course, who shall I write them to?'

'I'm Liz, this is Bonny.'

Tarragon gave both of the girls her best wishes.

'Thank you, we love your music.'

'Well then, thank you, too.'

Everyone smiled, the girls departed happy, and talking excitedly to one another, and Meadow spoke.

'You must get that a lot these days.'

'Sometimes...'

The others had by now formed a loose circle and were sitting on the still quite cold but at least fairly dry grass, Aiko having adopted the lotus position. Later she would take herself off alone to the quietest place she could find for her customary period of meditation before the performance, but for now she was engaged in conversation with Keith, whilst Basil was speaking earnestly to Ash about some matter or other. The group attracted passing glances from as good as all who passed by, and as Meadow sat down next to her beloved man, she could not help a feeling of pride which rose within her at the sight of her family so engaged. At some juncture, Basil and Emma were sent in search of hot – dogs or their vegetarian equivalent, and so did the remainder of the afternoon and early evening pass, until Samantha suggested that they should rejoin the rest of the band and begin preparation for their performance, particularly since she did not yet have any keyboards to play. All therefore said their goodbyes, and Tara once again hugged all of her family, this being the most emotional part of the farewell. The next time they would see her she would be on stage, and a long distance away, after which they would miss the rest of the show in favour of catching a late – evening train home, so she would not see them again until the tour was over, still several weeks hence. The final farewell was between Tara and her father.

'Well, bye then, Papa.'

'Go give 'em hell, kid.'

'Tonight I'll be singing for you, okay?'

'Don't forget your mother.'

'How could I?'

A final smile and the three musicians turned and walked away, Tara took the arm of Ashley Spears, and waved a final goodbye to her family before she became lost to the crowd.

It was a little after the hour of nine o'clock by the time the compare made the announcement. Having made arrangement to meet by the bridge if any of them became separated, Keith, Meadow and the others moved through and with the crowd to be a little closer to the stage, which was by now all but impossible to get anywhere near close to, but they could see well enough, and there were large television screens to either side of the stage.

'And now ladies and Gentlemen, a band who have interrupted their world tour and travelled a long way to be with us tonight. Ladies and gentlemen, I give you....Dead Man's Wealth!'

The stage lights were lit, and with perfect synchronization drums, keyboard and three guitars played the opening bars of *'Fools' Paradise'*, which was from the band's second album, and the crowd responded with great and universal enthusiasm; this was not dance music, but it was music which could be danced to. Eight bars in, and the man who had been sitting quietly and modestly on the grass but a few hours before sang out to his loving audience, and behind and between his voice and in perfect harmony came the voice of Tara, and for the first time Keith and Meadow saw and heard their daughter sing to a live audience, and both were moved in a way that both had expected, but neither had really expected. She took his arm and he leaned down to her in the darkness and spoke into her ear.

'Do you know, that's my daughter up there...'

'Really....? She's good, isn't she?'

'Yeah, she's good. Are you crying?'

'Of course I'm bloody crying, aren't you?'

'Yeah, man tears, which are the same only you can't see them.'

They smiled and kissed one another, and of the rest of the more than one hour that the band were on stage, which included three encores, it need only be said that three or four songs in, and nobody was really counting, Tara took centre stage and the main microphone, and sang *'Hell Can Wait'*, the opening track from her second album, and throughout the set she was to sing four of her songs, which the audience of who knew how many tens of thousands greeted with seamless enthusiasm. Under the protective wing of Ashley Spears, and within the beautiful sound created by this unique band of now absolutely professional players, Tara had made the big time in rock music. She had been singing quietly to herself whilst washing dishes one day, when the world had seemed to her to be a good place to be, and from there she had got to here, a small dot on a distant stage and an image on two vast television screens, wearing her stage attire of short dress and high – heeled shoes, a young woman in the prime of her life and looking good, and singing from the depths of her soul, the place from which Ash had taught her to sing. And here was a band on tour, which had hit the stage running and performed with their customary polished spontaneity. They didn't always get everything in the right place, but they had played together often enough to understand one another. Ash still missed his cues sometimes, and Al came in too early with guitar solos, but none of it mattered. If Evie hit a rhythm with her flute, which nowadays haunted the songs, or Samantha was playing some particularly excellent keyboards, then the others would give way, and the songs would end by mutual and indicated agreement when everyone was done. It wasn't exactly jamming, but it was close, and everyone who was there and who witnessed it knew that they had seen and heard something special; a rock band in the old – fashioned sense of the word, who in the days of studio – produced perfection were a rare and dying breed.

On the way home, light conversation was had to take care of the practical matters of getting about London, but on the final train journey the family were quiet, and subdued, each having taken something private from the occasion which they wished to keep private, and nothing need be said, really. Everyone knew it had been something special, and understood that which Tarragon had achieved, and all knew that it had been the evening of a day that they would never forget.

Rosemary said goodbye to Quentin at Queenswood railway station, and they promised only that they would 'phone one another. They had been together, but the day had not been for them; they would have other days, and on another day Quentin would ask the question which had been biding its' time at the back of his mind despite the day; why had Ashley Spears as good as called Rosie a witch?

At some time after midnight, Keith and Meadow said goodnight to their children and to Emma at the door of the bus, having made sure that they had all drunk and taken with them sufficient water to counter the dehydration which the day in London and in the crowded park had seen to. They then retired to the inner sanctum of their bedroom at the end of the bus, where they lay together as they had lain together at the start of this day. Neither quite knew what to say, but Keith thought that something should be said.

'Well, what do you think?'

'What do you think I think?'

'Yeah, I agree. Well, goodnight then.'

'Goodnight my love.'

'Were you like, nervous for her?'

'Very….You..?'

'Only for the first hour or so…She's got a hell of a voice these days.'

'She always cried the loudest, maybe we should have seen this coming.'

'Yeah, maybe…'

The silence lasted just long enough for Meadow to reach the edge of sleep, before she was pulled back.

'Makes you think though, doesn't it?'

'What….? What does it make you think?'

'Well, you know, amongst all the money and all the bullshit, there are still higher things…'

'Like our amazing daughter singing amazing songs, you mean?'

'Well yeah, of course, but I don't just mean that. I mean today was like it used to be, you know, when things were different.'

'You were always an idealist, that hasn't changed, at least.'

'I suppose I was just born into the wrong age.'

'You weren't born into the wrong age, Keith, my love, but the age isn't the same anymore.'

'Yeah, I suppose that's it then. Well, goodnight.'

'Is this actually goodnight, or have you got anything else to say that won't wait 'til the morning?'

'I just have to say stuff while it's there, you know, otherwise it kind of goes...'

'Yes, I noticed that. Sweet dreams, Keith.'

Both now lay in the darkness for a moment without sleeping and without words, until finally fatigue got the better of their happy thoughts, Meadow found the shoulder upon which she had rested her head so many times, and both drifted together into contented slumber.

Chapter 12

A SORT OF PRAYER

As can be the way of such things, once the word was abroad regarding the break – in at the cottage down the lane, it spread quite quickly through the village and its' environs, and particularly amongst those who had better know, or whose help would be enlisted in the matter of assisting in the clearing up. To this end, on Sunday morning Keith had seen Damien, and had 'phoned Will at Jacob's Field, and both had immediately put themselves and their vehicles at Percival's disposal. More usually Emily would also have gone to help, but aside from her having to milk her goats, she had already planned to be elsewhere, and it was a commitment which she felt strongly that she should keep. So it was that by mid – morning Will had driven her to and kissed her goodbye at the hospital, from whence she would in due course catch the bus back to the village. She found the ward easily enough, and spoke first to a nurse regarding the condition of the patient, who was apparently now lightly sedated, and on an intravenous drip which provided the sedative and a pain - killer. She approached the bed, therefore, which was one of ten in the Fairfield Ward with some trepidation, and her dislike of hospitals in general was not diminished by the experience. She had been here quite recently to visit Sandra Fox after her attempted suicide, if such it had been, but Sandra was now quite recovered, whereas the prognosis for this much older woman was not so good. The cancer which had been operated upon had nevertheless become malignant, and had quickly spread to places where a further operation could not be medically justified, and with this new and somewhat shocking intelligence in mind, Emily went to her friend.

She pulled up a chair and sat beside the bed, and took Daphne's hand, which Emily noted had become frail very quickly, or perhaps she just hadn't noticed it before, and the two friends smiled for one another.

'Hello Emily, my dear.'

'Hi Missus P, what have you been up to now then?'

'I know, silly old me…I'm so glad to see you, my dear. I felt certain that you would come.'

'Yes, and I'm glad to see you too, but I'll be much happier when you're up and about again.'

'Yes, this has happened at such an inconvenient time, just when the milder weather has come and the garden will begin to bloom, and will need so much attention.'

'Well don't worry about that, Will'll call in and make sure everything's kept under control for when you come out, you just concentrate on getting better.'

'Bless you, I know you'll look after everything for me. I leave the house in good hands, I know that, and that is such a comfort to me. So anyway, enough about me, how are you, my dear?'

'Oh you know, I'm fine, just busy making cheese and what not.'

'And how is William?'

'About the same as ever, just being Will, you know?'

'Of course….You two are very much in love, aren't you?'

'Yes we are, well most of the time anyway.'

'I'm sure it's all of the time, really.'

'Well, he has his stupid moments and I have my silly moments, but yes, underneath we always love each other.'

'Of course you do, and beneath all of the dry humour and self – effacement, William is a fine and good young man, Emily, and you're so lucky to have found one another. You two have done so well, to have…Well, you were neither of you born into wealthy circumstances, were you?'

'I'm sure we'll never be wealthy, but we do okay, I suppose, and we don't really need very much.'

'I know you don't.'

'I mean Will's still wearing the same T shirts as he was when we first met, bless him, so as long as we've got enough to eat and can pay the bills, that's all that matters, really, isn't it?'

'Yes, it is, and you never know what might happen one day in any case, but whatever happens the only important thing is that you are happy, and have a happy and fulfilled life as I have had.'

'Let's put that I the present tense, shall we? You still have a happy life.'

'Alright, have it your way, but I've been very fortunate, and I know that. I'm a lonely old woman now, but I have also found love, in my day, and for that I will always be thankful, and for knowing people like you, my dear. Yes, I have been lucky. I do not fear death, Emily.'

'Stop it, don't talk like that.'

A pressure had been building at the back of Emily's eyes; she had been determined not to cry, but that determination was now a thin veneer.

'No my dear, you of all people should know that I have made my peace with the world, and if God calls me to him then I am ready, so please don't be sad, my dear Emily, for we must all find our way to God in the end.'

The tears came now, there was no helping it, and there was nothing more to be said, really, so the two women held hands more tightly.

'Do you remember, after you had quite by accident killed the man from London? How it was me that you first talked to about it, and how you were feeling?'

'Yes, of course I remember.'

'I have never forgotten that, and that was the first time I knew that, well, that you and I were really friends.'

'Of course we're friends, and I've never forgotten how good you were to me.'

'We all of us need people sometimes, and the thing is that... Well, I think you needed me then, and that is something which I have always kept dear to my heart, and why you have always been special to me.'

'Oh stop it, for heaven's sake, or I'm just going to cry.'

'You already are, my dear, and not all tears are bad, and some things are best said before....Well, I've said my piece now, and now I'm very tired, and you don't want to sit here all day listening to me wittering on. Go, my dear, and live your happy life, and try always to see the good in everything, as I have. Don't worry about me, my dear Emily, for I am at peace, and I know that the Lord is with me, always, and I am blessed. Goodbye, my dear, and God bless you.'

Daphne closed her eyes and rested her head back on her pillow. Emily lifted the hand that she held, and kissed it.

'Goodbye Missus P....'

Emily stood up, and must somehow have found her way out of the hospital. In any case she became aware that outside a cool, spring breeze was now blowing, and it made her eyes feel cold, and as she wiped away her tears she very much wanted to go home, and be with Will, who would always make her laugh, and would anyway always make her feel better. She also knew something else, however, which was that she would not go straight home. She did not therefore walk in the direction of the bus stop, but instead made her way in the opposite direction, and after a few moments she stood before her destination, and walked in through the huge and ornate double doors.

'Christ, this is worse than I thought, and I don't just mean the damage.'

The party which had assembled at the cottage consisted of Percival and Louise, Keith and Meadow, Damien and Sophia, and Rebecca, who had brought Florence, Will having not yet arrived having dropped Emily at the hospital. Percival had by now made coffee for those who wanted it, shown everyone who wished to see it the painted message on the bedroom wall, and given a brief synopsis of the situation to date, and it was Keith who had vocalized his concern.

'I knew what might happen, Keith.'

'What, you knew they might trash your house?'

'Not specifically that…'

'Well it certainly did happen, didn't it, I mean who is this Eddie guy, anyway?'

'He's from London, and he's very good at what he does, and that's all I can tell you, really, and all need to tell you.'

'So now three of them are dead, and they'll be seeking vengeance, so this could only be the start of it.'

'Perhaps, or it could be the end of it, I don't know. Hitherto my life and Rebecca's life have bought my silence, and as far as they know this is still the case.'

'You may have put them in a position where they consider that they've got nothing more to lose by taking you down, and dead men are fairly silent, you know?'

'It's a risk, I know, but I promised to unleash hell and damnation if they killed any of us. They've got a lot more to lose, Keith.'

'So tell me,' said Damien 'what form would this hell and damnation take, exactly?'

'It doesn't exist, but it's the threat of it that counts, and now I've shown them what I can do.'

'So the whole thing's a huge bluff, then?'

'Yeah, it's a bluff, but so far it's worked. The fact that Rebecca and I are still alive is proof enough of that.'

'So why not just leave things as they were?'

'Because in the end they would have come for us, they'd have called my bluff eventually, and on their terms, and without any assurance of peace I couldn't wait for that to happen.'

'So this was a preemptive strike, one might say.'

'Sometimes you have to go to war to achieve peace, Damien. Whatever it is that they hold secret down there must be worth preserving at any cost, and that has always been my trump card. They'll risk anything rather than have their temple exposed to the outside world, or at least this has always been my assumption, and so far I've been right.'

'If you ask me, you're taking a huge and unwise gamble with your life.'

'Of course, but what other choice did I have? I mean I could have left and gone to live in the Outer Hebrides, and so could Rebecca, but there's no guarantee that they wouldn't have found us, eventually, or far worse taken their revenge on anyone who was left behind. I wasn't the only one who went to rescue Rebecca. Keith was there, and so was Emily, and Keith and Meadow were both at the dell the night they drugged and almost killed me.'

'So what you're saying is that you are all that now stands between the chicken – stranglers and disaster for anyone involved, is that it?'

'I'm not saying that for certain, because there are and never have been any certainties about any of this, but I've never seen my walking away as being a good option. I've made certain decisions and I'm still making decisions, but I've always been shooting blind, and I still am, but as far as I can see doing nothing has not been an option either. I tried to talk to the only member of the cult to whom I have access, to at least get a promise of peace, or even the possibility of it, even if that promise proved to be false, but I didn't even get that, so I made the next decision, and I'll take all that's coming to me before I put anyone else in danger. If they're after anyone it seems that they're only after me.'

'Well that's laudable, at least in theory, and I wouldn't recommend the Outer Hebrides, by the way, but I'd like to hear what Rebecca has to say. She must know them better than anybody, and what they're capable of.'

So far the four women present had been silent. Sophia was in any case not yet involved with anything to do with the cult, any more than was Damien, and Louise was still quite new to all of this and was listening intently, but now everyone waited for Rebecca.

'Well, in the first place let me say that I'm only too aware that everything that's happened is because of me. Everyone could have let me die, and that would have been the end of it, and I owe my life and therefore Florence's life to people who are gathered here, to whom I owe what must be I suppose the greatest possible debt of gratitude. Meadow has had less to do with the cult, but she rescued me and Victoria's child from the black witch, and in so doing put herself at great risk, so to her also will Victoria and I be eternally grateful. As to what the cult are capable of, I think we saw that at Howard's Bench. I have no wish to recall or speak of the abuse that I suffered at their hands as a teenaged girl, but we have seen that they are capable of ritual slaughter of a human being, whose only crime was to try to save me from my fate.'

'If what I've heard is true,' said Damien 'you're not beyond slaughtering human beings yourself, in fact you seem fairly good at it.'

'What you've heard is true, Damien, and I will never be able to express to you the anger that made me do the terrible things that I've done, and I have tried, you know, to live a good life since then, but so far that has not been possible, has it?'

'If you say not….Just remind me not to piss you off.'

'My own mother was killed because of me, and her body was left on the village Green like so much carrion for all to see, so if you wish to know what my enemies are capable of then you perhaps need look no further than that.'

'Right,' said Damien 'so there's the cult on one side and the witches on the other. You've certainly made some enemies out there, bonny lass.'

'Yes, there are also the witches, and it was not my wish to go with somebody else and kill them at Farthing's Well, but had we not done so then Victoria's child would likely be dead by now, and who knows what else may have happened. I am a witch, and you all know that, and what I can become capable of, but it was not my choice to become what I have become. My mother rejected the sisterhood and because of that it was easy to kill her, but the sisterhood is in my blood, as was once made very clear to me. I can trace my ancestry back to Jane Mary, her blood is in my blood, and she was killed by the first Lord Tillington, and others have for centuries sought revenge for that one deed, and I have tried to stop that from happening, but I had no wish to kill again, if there was any other way. And Percival is right, there are higher things than the death of people who live now, whether that be a philosophy or a belief, or making the world safe for the generations who will come after us, we must all do what we can and what we must while we have the chance, and such evil as exists in the temple in the west – country must be stopped from doing further harm, and if they will not give that promise then I for one condone Percival's actions, and will do whatever I can to help him. We must all do as our conscience dictates, and believe me when I say that the things that I have done hang heavily on my conscience, but that is something I must live with, and do live with every day, but in the end I would have done nothing different, and my dearest wish now is that my daughter will live in peace, and for that I will gladly kill again, or die, if I must.'

For a moment nobody spoke; none of them, not even Percival, had heard Rebecca expound in such emotive terms as this, and for a moment her words hung in the air, until it was

Damien, who had for now taken up the role of chairman of the meeting, who broke the meditative and contemplative silence.

'Well then, Percival, it seems as though at least one of us is right behind what you did, so what has anyone else got to say? What about you, Keith?'

'Yeah, I mean I can't disagree with any of that, and Rebecca's right, I was there when they carried her out of the hovel unconscious. I picked her up myself and put her in the Land – Rover, so I know what these bastards are capable of, and I can't exactly mourn the passing of any of them, so there'll be no condemnation from me, but what's done is done, anyway, so as I see it it's a question of what we do from now on to lessen the danger to any of us.'

'Well that's admirable pragmatism, I suppose. And what do you think we should do?'

'Well there's the thing, isn't it. I mean you all know that I don't shy away from a fight, I don't think any of us do, but we don't know what we're fighting, so sending in an assassin is one thing, and the guy did his job well, but we can't take them on in open combat, even assuming we got the chance. I think for now to remain vigilant is all we can do, and hope that Percival's right, and that this is just a final statement that they can get to us if they want to, but you know, I also agree that we can't be certain about that.'

'What do you think, Damien?' Said Meadow

'Ay, well I agree with Keith that this isn't some backstreet pub – brawl in Glasgow. That I can handle but this is way out of my league, and way beyond any of us. Whether we agree with what Percival here did or not, it's done now, and we're all friends here, so I suppose we just watch each other's backs from now on, and hope it goes away. And as for the witches, well, I saw Farthing's Well before the fire, and whatever motivation Rebecca had for burning it down, it was a job well done, and if the sole purpose of the black coven or whatever it was called was the death of children, then the sooner that's ended the better, but they're not all gone yet, is that right?'

'There are two of them left, at least,' said Rebecca 'and we can't know their intentions either. Eve, who Meadow encountered on the steps of the Manor House, was the last of the bloodline of the witch Edith, who first put the blood - curse on the house of Tillington, and Eve is gone now, but no, they are not all dead, and in this regard I at least must continue to be careful.'

'Be careful of what? Hi everyone, by the way, did I miss anything important?'

This was Will, who had just entered through the open door which had the day before had new locks fitted, and his entry was as a cool breeze on the heat and intensity of the discussion.

'Not really,' said Damien 'we were just discussing whether it was still too early to plant out Geraniums.'

'Can't be too careful when it comes to Geraniums...' Said Will

'One good frost and they're gone, right?'

'Fucks you're summer – bedding right up.'

'I'll tell you all about it on the way to the tip.' Said Keith

'Ay,' said Damien 'I suppose we'd better get on with the other thing we came here to do, but I think further discussion is needed in due course, when we've all had a bit more time to think about everything. Jesus, if I'd known what kind of a village this was I'd have gone back to Scotland.'

'Then you would never have met me.' Said Sophia

'Ay, well, I suppose at least we've proved that not all witches are bad then.'

Here was another statement which hung rather in the air. Whilst there were those present who knew that Sophia was a witch, there were others who did not, and Sophia had quickly to find a form of words which would let the subject be; she would speak to Damien later.

'I believe that most witches are good, and always have been.'

The next part of the day was devoted to cleaning up the cottage. Percival's settee was too big to fit through the rear door of a Land Rover, so this was first taken into the lane and reduced to its' constituent parts. Keith, Damien and Will worked together each working day, and with their by now well established efficiency and cooperation, all of the bulky items of furniture, including a double – mattress, were quickly loaded and ready to go, whilst the others collected broken ceramics, picture – frames and so on into plastic bin – liners and swept through the house. Soon thereafter the two vehicles departed, carrying the broken remains of that which appeared to be the majority of Percival's furnishings, and Sophia rode with Damien, leaving Percival, Louise, Meadow and Rebecca in Percival's lounge, which now looked and felt rather empty.

'Well,' said Meadow 'it looks as though you two have some furniture to buy, I mean I'm sorry, that is always assuming….'

'Yes,' said Louise 'it looks as though I'll be moving back in, although after what I've heard today I might be having second thoughts. I'll stay at least as long as it takes to refurnish this place anyway. Whatever else you may be good at, Percival my love, your taste in furniture is appalling.'

'You never said that before.' Said Percival

'Well, we're all of us hearing some home – truths today, aren't we?'

'It'll be nice to have you back in the village.' Said Meadow

'Thanks, I'm looking forward to it, I think.'

'We have our good days as well. Anyway I should be getting home, I suppose, I want to have some time on the allotment later, it's that time of year again.'

'I don't think I knew you had an allotment.' Said Louise

'It keeps me fit, sort of, and focuses the thoughts on simple things, you know, as well as providing the family with vegetables. So, I'll see you all, then, it's been an interesting meeting to say the least.'

She stood up to leave, and so did Rebecca.

'We'll walk with you to the end of the lane.'

The infant Florence was picked up and placed on Rebecca's back, and Meadow and Rebecca departed. These two had always had a complex relationship with one another. Rebecca was ever at a loss to know how it was that Meadow was so immune to her influence, and to the influence of the other witches. She was quite sure that nobody but Meadow could have confronted the witch Eve on the steps of the Manor, and therefore saved the life of Victoria's child, and perhaps her life as well. For reasons which she did not quite understand, of all the people to whom she wished to prove that she was a better person now, and no longer a murderess, it was perhaps Meadow that she most wished to convince, but she knew well enough that Meadow's friendship was not so easily won, and this she also understood. For her part, Meadow had never trusted Rebecca. Quite aside from any matters relating to the cult or the other witches, on a warm afternoon at the Manor House she had once tried to seduce Keith, and although Meadow was not by nature a jealous person, and had always granted Keith a certain freedom of which he had never taken advantage, such things can have influence on the way that women perceive one another.

Once Percival and Louise found themselves once more alone in the now rather more empty house, they sat at the dining table, lit cigarettes and finished their coffee. Prior to the meeting, Percival had imparted to Louise the better part of all that had happened to those who had been there, but by accidental omission rather than design he had not told her everything, and experiences are always different when relayed by the people who had actually experienced them. She now therefore had questions, but such had been their time together since their return from the Maldivian island that she fell shy of asking them; there are times when enough information is enough, and the questions could wait. Their conversation thus began on a more mundane subject, and it was she who raised it.

'I'll have to go back, just for a few days.'

'I know.'

'I'll catch a ridiculously early train in the morning and change in London. I'll be back at the weekend, and maybe by then I'll have organized a transfer, I'll have to see what's available, and I'll have to give a month's notice on the room.'

'Of course, I know you can't just drop everything, just as long as you come back.'

'Of course I'll come back, with a suitcase, at least, and then Meadow's right, we'd better start looking for furniture, don't you think, if you can wait until then?'

'I can wait as long as it takes, I didn't use most of it anyway.'

They both now glanced briefly around the room before she spoke again. The paint on the walls was a somewhat different colour where furniture had been, or where pictures had hung.

'Now would be a good time have the place repainted, don't you think? Christ what a mess.'

Whether she was here referring to the paintwork or to Percival's current circumstances was unclear, and in any case he let the statement go unanswered, since in either case he could scarce disagree with her, and it was she who next spoke.

'Still, it's sort of symbolic, don't you think? An empty house and a new beginning...'

'That's a good way of looking at it.'

'Just promise me one thing.'

'What's that?'

'That you'll have that horrible message painted over by the time I come back.'

'Of course, even if I have to do it myself, in fact I probably will do it myself, and I'll have a new mattress delivered tomorrow.'

'Well, that would be a start, then.'

She smiled for him, and they reached for one another's hand over the table.

'They're right behind you, aren't they?'

'They're good people, Louise.'

'Even Rebecca..?'

'I think we've gone beyond making that kind of distinction. We're all of us in it now, for better or worse.'

'Yeah, I get that. I suppose I'd better try to start to like her then, hadn't I?'

'I wouldn't take things too far.'

'Don't you like her, then?'

'Like's not a good word when it comes to Rebecca.'

'So do you love her?'

'No, unless we can agree that there are different kinds of love, I mean I love Keith, you know?'

'Yes, Keith and Meadow are sound, aren't they, and I took to Damien, he looks like good people.'

'They're a….'

'I know, they're all good people, even the ones who kill people, right?'

'Well I can hardly talk any more in that respect.'

'No, I suppose you can't. Christ, Percival, I honestly began to think you'd turned into a country bumpkin living here among the hayseeds, but I suppose it's true what they say, you can take the man out of London….'

'There's life in the old dog yet…'

'Apparently so, and let's try to keep it that way, shall we? Anyway enough, we have an evening together, so where are you going to take me? I love this house, but right now it's creeping me out.'

'I know a few good places in town.'

'Well then, surprise me. After all, it wouldn't be the first time lately that you've done that, would it?'

If word of the break – in at Percival's cottage spread quickly through the village, it was slower to reach the Manor House. The most usual channel of communication between the two had latterly and at least until recently been between Victoria and Rebecca, and this channel was presently closed. The first anyone would know of it would be when Michael Tillington next visited Orchard House, when Keith would mention the matter in passing, but that would not be until the mid of the next week.

In any case, both Michael and his sister had other distractions on this day, and of Michael's news we will hear in a moment, but today was also a day of some significance to Victoria, for today would see the beginning of the painting of her portrait. Whatever image of her was now created upon canvass would hang in the grand dining room for all to see, and to judge, for as long into the future as anyone could foresee. The manifestations of the entirely male and entirely elderly Lords of the Manor in all of their grandeur was one thing, but for reasons which defy easy explanation, and which go deeply and instinctively into the human psyche, the image of a young woman is something quite else.

Any hopes that Pandora had of beginning the painting on the day of her arrival faded with the fading light of the late afternoon; Victoria did not return to the Manor House until mid – afternoon, and then did not visit the new extension until she had done whatever else it was that she had to do. Whether she had done this deliberately was for Pandora a matter for conjecture, but in any case a precedent had been set for their relationship; Pandora was to wait on Victoria's convenience and not the other way around. She was being paid to do a job, and she was being paid well, so waiting was apparently a part of the deal, and their first meeting in the early evening was for the most part quite businesslike; a fairly trite hello, and an agreement that work would commence the next morning. They had slept together during the painting of the portrait of Victoria's father, so perhaps this was Victoria's way of reestablishing the natural order of things between client and employee, or perhaps it was an overcompensation for a sense that she had previously acted inappropriately. For Pandora, their brief and sporadic affair had been little more than spontaneous and opportunistic sex with another woman, but during the evening and during the smoking of marijuana, she began to wonder whether in fact Victoria might have deeper feelings for her, and whether her coldness was another kind of compensation altogether. In any case, on the day of her arrival she did nothing more than set up her workplace, take a brief walk around the grounds of the Manor House, and cook herself a meal from the more than adequate provision which had once again been left for her.

Before we leave the subject, there had been one aspect of their conversation during the previous evening which had raised the matter above the mundane, and this had begun with Pandora asking a short but significant question.

'So, what do you want to wear for the painting?'

For her two previous commissions for the family, this matter had been taken care of with little conceptual intervention from the painter. Rose had wished to be portrayed in all of her young and beautiful sexuality, and Pandora' role thereafter was to ensure that this was tastefully and elegantly done. They had agreed to create the enigma, and the eternal question; had the subject been captured forever in the act of covering her modesty with the white satin shroud, or had she been removing it to reveal the rest of herself, and both in the end had agreed that the enigma had been perfectly expressed. With his Lordship, sex had had nothing to do with it, but here was a different subject, and a different concept. As had been the case with Victoria's father, this portrait was to end somewhere just above the diaphragm, and was to be a quite different embodiment of young womanhood, and yet here was a young woman, so here was a question which must be answered.

'I don't know, and oddly enough I hadn't thought about it…'

'You've got good bones, you should show them off.'

Pandora was not always or indeed often familiar with her subject's anatomy below the neckline, but Victoria's body she knew in the most intimate way possible, which as an artist had given her advantage.

'You mean I'm skinny.'

'I mean you've got good bones. It's up to you, of course, but I think we should paint you wearing an evening dress. If you're to hang next to your father then I think we should make the contrast as great as possible.'

'I see…Well, if you think so.'

Thus it was that the next morning Victoria brought with her to the temporary studio a selection of her evening attire, which she wore occasionally to formal functions with her parents, and the first hour or so was used to model various dresses. Some had sleeves of varying lengths, or a low – cut V – neck, but Pandora was in the end convinced of that which would look the best.

'Straps…We need straps, and the thinnest straps possible.'

'Are you sure?'

'Quite sure, we need to see your shoulders.'

And thus it was that Pandora's final choice was a simple, dark blue dress with the thinnest straps possible, which was quite loosely and a little immodestly cut across the bust.

'That's it….'

'I'm not sure, you know?'

It took a little further convincing, but in the end the artists' opinion began to prevail, the subject in the end only raising one final and specific objection, which was in any case practical and sensual rather than aesthetic or moral in nature.

'It's bloody cold in here, I'll freeze.'

'We can turn the heating up, you'll be fine. Okay, sit down, we need to make some final adjustments, you look too organized.'

Victoria sat down on that which was to be the model's chair, Pandora moved one of the straps of her dress across until it rested close to Victoria's shoulder, and then carefully roughed her hair until she had achieved the desired effect, which brought further comment from the subject.

'This wasn't quite what I'd been expecting. I must look a bit, I don't know....'

'Scruffy?'

'Wanton, I was thinking....'

'You're a young woman. Trust me, you look great. Have you had any thoughts about jewellery?'

'Again, not really...'

'Well you don't habitually wear very much of it, do you?'

'Not really, only stud – earrings as a rule.'

'Well stay with those, then, and no necklace, unless you think otherwise. I think people should see you as you are.'

'Well then, as you think best.'

'Okay fine, I think that about covers it, let's try a few slight adjustments to position.'

Whilst, under instruction, Victoria sat face – on and then with her body slightly to either side, always facing forwards, Photographs were taken on Pandora's mobile telephone and shown to Victoria.

'I think this is the best position. What do you think?'

'I don't know. Yes, I mean it looks okay to me.'

'Well there it is then, that's what you'll look like, approximately. You will be immortalized with one strap half – off and your hair in a mess, what do you think?'

'I...I really don't know.'

'Look, we can cover you up and make you more formal if that's what you want.'

'Show me the photograph again. No….No, let's stay with this.'

'Good…Okay take up position please. Head slightly up, pretend that I'm only painting your neck, and chest out, please, we want you looking dignified as befits your status; defiantly wanton is good.'

Pandora first went to the dial which controlled the central – heating system and turned the temperature to a higher setting, then for the first time she took up position in front of her easel.

'Yes, that's perfect, so, shall we begin then?'

Pandora took up her brush and painted the first, crude outline of a head and torso. She painted it in blue; it didn't matter, none of this would show in the end. An outline of a person, an emptiness within which for the next days of her artistic career, Pandora would attempt to recreate the image and capture the essence of the woman who sat before her.

Whilst Victoria was making ready for her portrait, in another part of the Manor House Michael was reading his emails. He and Elin had not met this weekend, she having had to spend the weekend abroad with her family to celebrate her fathers' birthday. She had told her parents of her involvement with Michael, but not yet of the serious nature of that involvement, their betrothal remaining a secret which otherwise only Victoria shared. Most of the electronic mail was of no consequence, but there was one which immediately caught Michael's attention, from an address which he did not recognize. He opened the mail, and read its' contents, which were as follows;

'Dear Mr Tillington

This is Patricia Wagstaff, writing from Exeter University. Please find attached a transcript of the first of the letters, for we now know that they are letters, which were sent to me by John Forester. I have to say that this was painstaking work, and as you will see parts of the paper and thus the writing are too damaged to be able to read, so we have lost some words, but we have most of it, and we have a date! The first sentence implies that we may have been lucky and have the first letter in the series, assuming that such it proves to be. I have used brackets where there were half – words or where I have made assumptions. I also attach my bill for the work to date, and once you have read the attachment, please let me know whether you wish me to proceed with the rest. I hope your answer is yes, since letters of this age preserved in this condition are a rarity, and the contents of this letter are fascinating, as I'm sure you will agree.

I wait to hear from you,
Regards,
Pat Wagstaff'

It was with some anticipation that Michael opened the first attachment, which he first printed without reading, and he then took the single sheet of A4 paper to his chair by the bedroom window, and these are the words which he read;

'30th May 1665
My (dearest) William

You would no doubt think me witless to be writing these words, since it may come to be that you will never read them. I intend to (adhere?) absolutely to your .... that there be no contact between our houses until you say (otherwise), or I hear news of you, nevertheless I find some comfort in the writing, and in the thought that one day, God willing, I might give this letter to you, ... be a happy day indeed.

John and Margaret) have .... two days since. John grows now into a fine and (handsome?) young man, and takes after his father, and little Margaret is of such sweet countenance. Both do I regard……..were my own children, and this would be a happy time were it not for the reason for their coming.

As………worry for them, for it is said that the sickness can take days to show, and each morning I pray that they will awaken in good health, and so (far my prayers) have been answered.

We……born into the Protestant faith, dear William, and our God is a benevolent and forgiving God……..but wonder why He has sent such a (plague upon) us all, which kills it seems without discrimination. Yet pray I will, since I know not what else I might do. I pray also for you, dear William, and for Rosalind, that she might yet recover, and that you will not fall to so (horrible a) malady.

Your ever loving and obedient……..

Jane'

Michael read the letter through twice. So, the writer, whoever she had been, had lived at Orchard House in the year 1665, and this now became the oldest record of the houses' existence. So, who was she, then, and what was her relationship to the intended recipient, whoever he might be? Were John and Margaret William's children, and who was Rosalind? It was quite clear that the plague referred to must be bubonic plague, or the 'Black death' as it became known, and that the children had likely been sent to Jane for their own safety. So, questions remained, but in any case, of one thing there was no doubt, and having opened and read the second attachment, Michael sent an immediate and brief reply.

'Dear Pat, thanks so much for sending this, your bill is fine, and do please continue with the rest of the letters!

Regards

Michael Tillington'

There are times when even those who do not believe may take solace from being in such a place as this. When a person needs to feel as though in all of the chaos and mundaneness of life there is something higher, which people called god, whether that be the Christian god or any other, but Emily had been born into the Christian faith, and so here she had come, to the vast and echoing building which was St Peter's Church. She found herself quite alone, and here she sat down on a pew, about mid – way down the great aisle, and here she bowed her head and wept a little for her friend, Daphne, who for all of her silly poetry and seemingly bigoted views Emily knew to be a good person, who had been born at a different time, when the world had been so different a place.

She looked around at the huge, stone pillars and vast arched dome above her, and all of the finely wrought stained – glass; at the image of the dying Christ, and of the angels who Daphne was so sure would be waiting for her, and then she bowed her head once again and spoke silent words into the emptiness.

'Hello…I mean I know I don't believe in you or anything, and that isn't because I don't want to, because it would be nice to think that you were there looking after everything, but I can't, because it doesn't make any sense really, does it, and one can't make oneself believe in something, can one? But some people do, believe in you that is, and Daphne does, and so, well, I know it won't make any difference what I say or anything, but please look after her, and well, that's it, really. That's all I came here to say.'

After a moment Emily stood up without raising her head, and turned like a thief in the night back in the direction from which she had come, and walked directly into a tall, well – built figure dressed in white tunic and black robes, who had been standing for a moment watching her.

'Oh, I'm sorry….'

The priest looked at the pretty young woman, who he now saw had been crying, and his heart went out to her.

'Are you troubled, my child?'

'What…? Oh, no, not really. That is to say that, well, a friend of mine's dying, you see, so I came here, which is silly, I know, but I didn't know what else to do, actually, or where else to go.'

'So you have come to the House of the Lord to find comfort…'

'Yes, I suppose so.'

'And did you find the comfort which you sought?'

'In a way, I suppose….I said a sort of prayer, anyway, which wasn't really a prayer, but it was the best I could do.'

'I see…Then be comforted, my child, for God will have heard you, and your sort of prayer, for God hears all things, and God will understand your sadness, and your doubt, just as he will understand your words.'

'Oh, I see…Well, that's good then, and thank you…'

'Don't than me, thank him up there, I'm only the messenger. Tell me, is your friend a he or a she?'

'She's a she.'

'Then she is lucky indeed to have such a friend as you.'

'Yes, she said the same thing, actually.'

'Then it must be true, must it not? And is your friend a believer?'

'Oh yes, absolutely.'

'Then be comforted, my child, for though she may die, yet shall she live, and she will be taken into the house of the Lord, and there shall she dwell in peace, forever.'

'I see, well, that doesn't sound so bad then.'

'No, it is not so bad. Go in peace, my child, for God is with us all, saint and sinner alike.'

'There's hope for me yet, then.'

'There is always hope, my child, and today you have done a good thing, and the Lord will not forget that.'

'Well, goodbye then, and well…Goodbye...'

Emily walked back across the intricate, echoing mosaic floor, and out once again into the fine, spring air. She sat for a moment on a wooden bench outside the church, and gathered herself and her thoughts together. In truth she had not known why she had come here, but one thing was certain; she felt the better for having done so, and the words of the priest had made her cry even more, but she supposed that this was no bad thing. Nothing had changed, of course. Daphne was still very sick, but somehow nothing seemed to matter so much anymore. It was as though she had said a final goodbye to her friend, and sent her off with her blessing, and there was indeed some comfort in that. She wouldn't tell anyone that she'd been here, not even Will. He would probably laugh at her, although he wouldn't really laugh at her, bless him, so she would see, but anyway she now very much wanted to see him.

Later this day, Daphne would drift peacefully into a coma from which she would not regain consciousness, and by the morning she will have passed away.

Chapter 13

THE WITCH AND THE GENTLEMAN

The next time that Quentin and Rosemary were to meet was on the first day that Quentin had changed to the morning shift at the warehouse, which was on the Wednesday following their day in London. On this occasion Rosie arrived home from school, forewent the eating of anything other than bread and cheese to stave off her hunger, showered and changed, and the caught an early evening bus into town, having told her parents where she was going and with whom. It was not until somewhat later in the evening, when Basil and Emma had retired to the trailer, that her parents had the opportunity to once again discuss the current emotional upheaval which had so clearly beset the life and soul of their youngest daughter, and it was Keith who raised the subject.

'She's really into him, isn't she?'

'Yes, it seems so, bless her. Her first relationship...'

'Do you think it is, or rather will be, or would be, assuming that they are, as it were, or will be having a relationship, eventually, that is?'

'What are you talking about?'

'Well, you know what I mean…'

'If you're asking me whether your youngest daughter is still a virgin, then my answer is how would I know? Daughters of a certain age don't by necessity tell their mothers everything, you know?'

'No, I suppose not….'

'Then you suppose right, she's old enough now for it to be her body and her business.'

'Sure....So you never talked to her about the birds and the bees, so to speak, I mean in terms of avoiding pollination.'

This made Meadow laugh, gently.

'Well no, I mean we once had a conversation without really having a conversation, but it was enough to reassure me that she knows what she's doing, so don't you worry about that, girls scarcely need their mothers for that sort of advice nowadays anyway. She's a smart young lady, Keith, she isn't going to do anything stupid, even assuming she does anything at all.'

'No, well, we wouldn't want her to go and get herself pollinated at her age.'

'I seem to recall that you weren't so concerned when it came to me, and I was younger than Rosie.'

'Yeah, well men don't think about that kind of thing so much.'

'Apparently not...Anyway I knew that I wanted children, or at least wouldn't be unhappy if I became pregnant, otherwise it would never have happened with us, either, and things are different these days. Rosie has opportunities which I never had, and she isn't going to throw all of that away, our daughter is far too clever for that.'

'Well, that's alright then.'

'Yes, it's alright, Keith. So, any further impressions having spent the day with Mister Bee...? Our thoughts have been so preoccupied with Tara and with the break – in that we haven't really talked about that aspect of the day.'

'Yeah, you know, he's a nice guy, don't you think?'

'Yes I do, so what do we know about him, then?'

'He obviously comes from money, or a posh background at least. What are his brothers called again?'

'Tristan and Tarquin...And he has a double – barreled surname....'

'I rest my case...'

'We know that his father and mother are both passed away, and his grandmother died recently and left the brothers a house in Clandon, which they can't agree what to do with, and he's massively qualified and works in a warehouse in town.'

'And he plays cricket. Shame about the warehouse job…'

'It's what young people so often have to do these days, it takes a lot longer than it used to establish any kind of a career, and his qualifications aren't exactly mainstream, are they?'

'Nope….'

'Anyway he seems sensible enough, and he seems very fond of Rosie.'

'I just hope he deals with the witch business okay, when it comes to it.'

'What do you mean?'

'She clearly hasn't told him she's a witch yet.'

'She isn't defined by being a witch, Keith.'

'No, sure, but…Well anyway, he's a very fortunate young man to have won our daughters' affections, and I hope he realizes that.'

'I'm sure he does. Anyway, what plans for the rest of the evening?'

'I don't know, thought I might buzz around a bit and see what happens, you never know I might find a beautiful flower upon which to alight.'

'With no thought of pollination, I hope?'

'With man – bees it's the buzzing's the thing.'

'And always assuming that the beautiful flower wishes to be alighted upon, of course...'

'Yeah, there's that….'

Running approximately concurrently with this conversation was another conversation, which was taking place in a small, backstreet bistro in town, which specialized in simple but wholesome Mexican food. Thus did gentle salsa music, bottled beer, enchiladas and vegetarian tortillas form the backdrop to an evening to which both Quentin and Rosemary had been looking forward. Perhaps inevitably, the early part of the conversation had revolved around Hyde Park, and in particular a certain performance.

'Your sister's amazing, you know…? She's got a great voice, anyway.'

'Yes, she has, hasn't she?'

'Was she classically trained?'

'No, nothing like that, it all comes naturally. I think she's been sort of learning on the job.'

'Well she's learned well. So Ash Spears composes her songs, is that right?'

'Yes, well that is the lyrics are all his, then he and Tara work together on the melodies and so on, and once that's done it's a collaboration with Samantha and the others for the instrumentation.'

'It's unusual, isn't it, for a successful solo artist to also be part of an established band, in fact I can't think of another example of it. I mean plenty of people go on to have solo careers once bands have split, but this is different, isn't it?'

'Yes, although I think Ash intends to make this the bands' last tour, and DMW don't record as DMW anymore.'

'But Tara's going to make more albums, I presume.'

'I think that's the idea.'

'So how do you two get along, generally speaking?'

'Oh, we're good, you know, considering how different we are, which is very different.'

'Yes, well you don't look anything like alike anyway.'

'No, she got tall, for a start….And blonde, whereas I stayed short and dark.'

'All of your family are quite fair – haired, aren't they, you must have got the recessive gene, and I'm not complaining by the way. So what about Basil..?'

'Basil takes after our father, or will do anyway, and he's hopelessly in love with Emma, so nobody sees much of him, but he's okay, you know, as brothers go.'

'Yes, well I've got two of those, so I know how brothers can be. Tris was steaming with jealousy about Saturday. I never expected to meet Ashley Spears, for a start. He's more, I don't know, down to earth than you'd expect. He had a real reputation back in the day, didn't he, his drug abuse was the stuff of legend as I recall.'

'Yes, but he survived, and now he's great, in fact the whole band seem really nice, or the one's I've met, anyway. Sam's lovely, and Aiko….Well, she's just soooo beautiful, isn't she?'

'Sure….Sure…As well as being an excellent base – guitarist. Rosie, what was Ash talking about, when he called you a witch or whatever? Is that some kind of standing joke or what?'

'Something like that.'

'Maybe he thinks you're the famous witch of Middlewapping, right?'

This was said in semi – humorous manner, but a serious question lay behind the speculation, and Rosie did not smile.

'Yes, maybe he does, but I'm not.'

'No, of course not...'

Rosemary had known with some certainty that the subject of Ash's casual and impromptu remark would be raised, and so after much thought and not a little prevarication she had made a decision as to how she would react in the eventuality.

'That is to say, I'm not *the* witch of Middlewapping.'

'I don't follow….'

'No, I know…Look, I mean we don't know each other that well yet, but I think I know you well enough to trust you. Can I trust you?'

'Well sure, of course.'

'Because what I'm about to tell you is in absolute confidence, this is just you and me, okay?'

'Okay….'

'Well then, I'm not the witch that everyone's apparently talking about, but that doesn't mean that I'm not a witch, in fact, there's something about me that you'd better know.'

'What had I better know?

'I am actually a witch.'

Quentin smiled, but the smile was still not returned, so the smile faded as quickly as it had come.

'Are you serious?'

'Yes, and it really isn't as bad as it sounds, you know?'

'I'm not…I'm not saying it sounds as bad as anything, but… So, tell me about it.'

'I belong to a sisterhood of healers, which is how witches began, centuries ago. We were women who could heal by using traditional herbal treatments and so on, although there was more to it than that, and the sisterhood itself is hundreds of years old, although nobody actually knows how and when it all began. Of course we became most famous during the witch trials.'

'Yeah, I mean I can tell you more or less what happened if we're talking in millions of years, but I'm crap at recent human history.'

'Well, the worst of it began in the sixteenth century, in Scotland actually, although before that tens of thousands of women had been put to death in mainland Europe, but anyway over here it all began with a bad storm at sea, believe it or not.'

'How so..?'

'Well….are you sure you're interested in this?'

'Of course…'

'Okay, well history tells us that Queen Anne was making her way to Scotland from Copenhagen when a bad storm sunk her sister ship, and the boat she was on barely made it back to port, so King James the sixth, who was then king of Scotland, went over to fetch her, and a rumour was being put about in Denmark that witches were responsible for causing the storm, and thus trying to assassinate the Queen, and certain of us were put to death over there because of it. So anyway James and Anne came home to Scotland, and brought with them the idea of witches, and that's when the witch – hunts began, and the first witches were put to death in Scotland in 1591, after a guy called Edward Seaton accused his maid of being a witch. She confessed under torture, and 'admitted' that certain of her family and other women were witches. These were called the *'North Berwick witch trials'*, and after this witches all over western Scotland and up to Inverness were blamed for all kinds of ill – fortune, and made by various horrible means to confess to being witches, or the 'Devil's Handmaidens' as we were then also called. Then when Queen Elizabeth died in England, James became the first King of England and Scotland, and throughout his reign witch trials and executions became common in England. It became a bit of an obsession of his, and he wrote the 'Demonology', which was basically all that was supposedly known about witches. I mean he mostly wrote the book as an academic work, but others, and it was quite a lot of others, saw it as license to identify and persecute women suspected of practicing witchcraft. Then, when he died his son Charles the first became king, and he outlawed witch trials, but it all started up again during the civil war, although it was by now illegal to persecute or hunt for witches, but nevertheless god knows how many of us were either garroted or burned, or both. And to bring it all closer to home, the first Lord Tillington of Middlewapping Manor became convinced in his insanity that the woman who his son married to was a witch, and that she had bewitched his son, and she died at his hands at the Manor House. Her name was Jane Mary.'

'Christ….'

'I mean the so ironic thing is that some of the women who were executed may even have been witches, you know, but that didn't make them bad people, in fact they almost certainly weren't bad, but anything which went against the accepted religious and cultural norms of the day was regarded with deep suspicion, and because of that people were killed in the most horrible ways. But still, the sisterhood survived, and now there are hundreds of us, possibly thousands, but nobody's counting, and the thing is that we don't necessarily know who each other are, if you see what I mean. I mean it's all connected up, and some of us have formed local networks, and so on, but a lot of us are on our own, like me.'

'So okay, but I'm not getting what it means to be a witch, is it a way of life, or what?'

'Yes, I suppose that's exactly what it is, and people can take it to whatever depth or degree they want to.'

'So what does being a witch actually entail?'

'We learn things, you know, like how to heal with traditional remedies, that kind of thing, and we learn other ancient traditions and rituals, but it's also about ourselves, and learning to be better people.'

'Give me an example.'

'Well, for example we learn how to concentrate better, and to centre ourselves. In a way it's a kind of meditation, and we believe that by making ourselves better we help others.'

'So it's a kind of philosophy, then.'

'Yes, I suppose so.'

'Okay....So who teaches you?'

'I have a mentor, or rather I had a mentor, but, well, something happened quite recently which changed that.'

'Why, what happened?'

'There's a place which we call the white house, which is the centre of everything. You might call it a coven, in fact it's *the* coven, but anyway I was invited there and I met the head of our order, and my next meeting with my mentor was my last. I think my going to the white house was like a rite of passage, and I'll never see my mentor again.'

'Right....I'm sorry, but I've got a lot of questions which aren't ordering themselves very well.'

'It's okay, this is all new to me, too, I never told anyone before, apart from my family.'

'So your parents know, then?'

'Yes, they know.'

'And are they cool about it?'

'They got used to the idea.'

'Yeah, I imagine they would...'

'What do you mean?'

'Well, they're great people, don't get me wrong, but they're not exactly what one might call mainstream, are they?'

'They're very special people.'

'Seems to me like you're all special people, but, okay, so back to my original question, what was Ash Spears talking about?'

'That was something which I did, which was really silly, but....The thing is, something else we can learn is a kind of mind control. That is controlling the thoughts and actions of others, which also has its' roots in healing, and well, late one evening when he was living in the village church, I went there and sort of talked him into playing his guitar really loudly, which woke the village up. It was a stupid thing and I wish I hadn't done it now, but there it is, it was just some mischief, you know?'

'Mind control....Right, so is that a kind of hypnosis or what?'

'Kind of, yes, but it's okay, I mean I haven't used it in any bad way since, and don't intend to. So there, now you know, so you can make whatever you want of it, and as I say you're the only person I've told, so it's a big leap of faith, you know? I mean I'm not ashamed of any of it, and it's just a name, you know, but people make associations, which aren't usually good associations.'

Quentin took a moment and drunk his beer, which was not his first of the evening and would not be his last. The young woman who now sat opposite him in a bistro had had such a profound effect upon him since they had quite by chance sat opposite one another on a train, that he was in truth having trouble keeping track of his feelings. Quite apart from the young woman herself, she was sister to a famous musician, and now there was this, which had been the most profound revelation of all. Quentin was a quite well – travelled, well - educated and well - read young man, which had imbued in him a broad and liberal outlook on the world, but he had never so far as he knew encountered a witch before, and now he had apparently and quite inadvertently fallen in love with one, so some ordering of thoughts was necessary. For Rosemary this was also a moment of significance, as had been the moment for Sophia when she had first told Damien that she was a witch, and she waited now for any reaction, and when none was immediately forthcoming she felt the need to press for one.

'Well, say something then.'

'Okay, well the first thing to say is that whatever you are or do is fine by me, you know, and of course I won't betray the confidence. I mean it's you I want to be with, and now I know more about you, which is a good thing, isn't it?'

'Well, I'm glad you know, and I understand that it isn't every day you meet a witch, but we're still okay, are we?'

'Sure….I mean of course we're okay, it's no big deal, really, and I want to know more about it, but….So if the witch of Middlewapping isn't you, then who is she?'

'That I can't tell you, and I hope you understand that there are certain things which I can't do, and revealing the identity of others of the sisterhood is one of them. It's a part of what you might call our code, so you know, that's the way it is.'

'Okay….Okay, if you say so.'

Quentin looked away and smiled to himself.

'What…?'

'Well, you know, I always thought you were special, and now I know why, or part of why, anyway. I need another beer, you…?'

'No thanks, I'll have a fruit juice though.'

Quentin stood up and went in search of beer, leaving Rosie to contemplate the events of the last few minutes, and how they might affect the rest of the evening, and indeed the foreseeable future of the affairs of her young heart. She had told him, and he had not laughed or reacted in any adverse way to the telling, so with something like relief she concluded that her faith in him had been vindicated, thus far at least.

Our story has for now in fact run somewhat ahead of itself, and before we return to events which would occur later in this week, the author begs leave to return briefly to Monday, and to a moment of the quite late afternoon when Emily Cleves received a telephone call on her mobile telephone. Emily by now knew that Daphne had died, having 'phoned the hospital during the morning. She had been as good as certain that this would be the case, but still she felt the loss of her friend, and went about her daily tasks of milking her goats and processing her cheeses with an underlying sense of sadness, and the village would mourn the loss of she who was almost the last of its' elders. When the call came she was in her kitchen, making coffee for herself and beginning preparation of the evening meal, and she quickly washed her hands before taking the call.

'Hello….?'

'Good afternoon, am I talking to Miss Emily Cleves?'

'Yes, this is she.'

'This is Adrian Metcalf from Falbridge and Swan, solicitors.'

'Oh yes….?'

Emily knew of the small firm of solicitors, but only by dint of having walked past their quite modest offices in the town on many occasions, and she had not the least idea why they should be 'phoning her.

'Yes, well, as I'm sure you are already aware, a certain Missus Daphne Pouffe unfortunately passed away early this morning.'

'Yes, I am aware of that.'

'Right, good, well I am 'phoning to tell you that you have been named as joint executor of her last will and testament.'

'What….? I mean, are you sure?'

'Quite sure, my clients' wishes were very specific.'

'Oh, right…So who else has been named?'

'Only yourself and our firm, and I'll be dealing with all legal matters pertaining to the death, probate and so on, with your joint involvement and approval where necessary, of course.'

'I see….well….I must say that this is most unexpected.'

'Are you in any way related to the deceased?'

'No…No, not at all, we're, that is to say we were friends, but nothing more.'

'I see, well anyway, would it be possible for you to call in and see me at your earliest convenience.'

'Yes, of course, ummm, I can come tomorrow morning, say at eleven o'clock?'

'That would be fine, and you know where we are?'

'Yes, I know…Are you absolutely certain there's no mistake?'

'None whatsoever…. So, until tomorrow, then….'

'Yes, until tomorrow.'

The call was ended, Emily put down her telephone and sat down once again at the upstairs dining table, and looked for a moment at the half – prepared vegetables as if they might help her to process that which had just happened. Daphne had left no living relatives that Emily was aware of, and she supposed that she had wanted somebody aside from the solicitors to oversee the passing on of her estate, but why not ask Meadow, or even Percival? Well, perhaps not Percival, but why only her? She had never been executor to a will before, and didn't know exactly what it would entail, but doubtless the solicitor would tell her everything in the morning, and she would have time to do the milking before she left. In truth she had done most of her crying the day before, before she had even known that Daphne had actually died, but now tears welled up in her eyes once more, and she was sure that it wasn't only the onions.

At the Manor House, on the evening of this Monday, Michael was in search of his sister, whom he had not seen since receiving the electronic mail from Patricia Wagstaff. He had missed her yesterday, or else she had been occupied with her portrait, and he had been in town during this day. Indeed on occasion during Pandora's tenure during the painting of their fathers' portrait he had looked for her in vain, albeit quite late in the evening, and he had wondered at this. This evening, however, his coded knock on her bedroom door had been answered.

'Come in, Mike.'

He found her in her bathrobe and carpet - slippers, with her hair wrapped in a towel having just had her evening shower.

'Hi, sis, you okay?'

'Fine, thank you.'

'How's the portrait coming along?'

'Well, I think, although we're still in the early stages, of course.'

'So have you seen it?'

'No, and I've decided not to until it's finished.'

'You looked at father's most days, didn't you?'

'It's different when it's you, somehow. I don't want to look at myself half – done, it would be like watching oneself being formed, or created, which one is in a way, of course, and I find the idea of that creepy, for reasons that I can't really explain, but there it is. What's that?'

Michael was carrying a clear plastic wallet, in which was contained a single sheet of A4 paper.

'It's a transcript of the first of the sheets of paper which Keith found at Orchard House, and it makes fascinating reading, I think.'

He handed her the sheet of paper, she sat on her bed and read the document with care, whilst he sat at her dressing table and turned the chair to face her.

'Good lord...It does, doesn't it? How many more of these are there?'

'Four, I believe.'

'May 1663....Well, the house is at least that old then. I wonder who they were, and how Jane is related to William. She could be his sister, I suppose, and Rosalind could be his wife.'

'That's rather what I thought, and if that's so then she could be aunt to John and Margaret. I'm hoping all will be revealed in the following letters, assuming that's what they are.'

'Yes, I'm sure, and the sickness which she refers to must be the Black Death, I presume.'

'Yes, I imagine so.'

'This must have been amazingly well preserved for her to have got so much of the script...It is a she, isn't it?'

'Yes, her name's Patricia.'

'Well, well done Patricia...I'd love to see the rest as soon as you have them.'

'Of course....'

'Has Elin seen this?'

'I emailed it to her.'

'So you two aren't seeing each other at the moment then?'

'We're hoping she can come over at the weekend, but she's working fourteen hour days at the moment, they've got some tricky land – deals going on, apparently.'

'Right, oh well, as long as restoration work is progressing okay on the house.'

'I'm due to go over on Wednesday, meantime I'm looking to see what else is available to buy.'

'I thought Orchard House was taking all of your money.'

'It is, but I'm just looking around, you know, to see if I can make any reasonably quick money elsewhere, courtesy of my dear bankers, who seem ever keen to lend me money these days. I'll need income when the renovation's finished.'

'Of course, living there was never a part of the game - plan, was it?'

'No, but then nor was Elin, so there it is.'

'That's true….So have you shown the letter to mater and pater?'

'Yes, they think it's fascinating as well, of course, although they still assume I'll be selling Orchard House eventually, so it doesn't seem quite so significant to them. Anyway whist we're discussing matters financial, I was wondering how Rebecca's getting on these days, as regards finding herself alternative accommodation. I mean I'm not trying to kick her out, but she's had a while now to get back on her feet, as it were, and the arrangement was never meant to be indefinite, was it?'

'No, of course not, and I don't know how she's doing, Mike, because we still aren't seeing each other.'

'Right…Well that's a pity, I mean I don't know what you've fallen out over, but can't you make it up with her?'

'I don't know, Mike, it's what one might call complicated, but if you say so then I'll go and see her, I suppose. You're right, of course, it's time she moved on, I'll deal with it.'

'Thanks….Try to forgive her for any past transgressions, as it were, whatever they may be. After all it wouldn't be the first time, would it?'

'No, I'll sort it, Mike.'

'Jolly good. Well I'll leave you in peace, then.'

'Okay, and thanks for showing me the letter.'

Michael took leave of his sister, who sat where he had sat and brushed out her still wet hair.

('So, you would have me forgive her past transgressions, even if those include having your child?')

Victoria had known that it would come to this eventually, but had been putting off the moment for as long as she could, but now it came to it, and she would have to go to the village. She must confront Rebecca, and somehow they must find a way through this, otherwise it really would be over between them. Their love for one another had so far overcome everything, and survived many trials, but this was different, and this may prove to be the hardest thing of all.

Our tale now moves on to Tuesday morning, and Emily is in town, and walking toward the solicitors' office. Today she had put on a little makeup, and was feeling quite smartly dressed in skirt, blouse, jacket and moderate heels; suitable attire, she thought, for undertaking important official business, although she was still far from certain as to what that business would entail. Last evening she and Will had at some length discussed the matter of her being executor to Daphne's will, Will having been quite matter of fact about it, asking why she was so surprised, given that Emily had probably in the end been Daphne's closest friend in life. Nevertheless they had drunk a bottle of wine and eaten in the downstairs dining room, the occasion seeming to call for it, and Emily had needed alcohol.

In any case, she now walked through the double glass doors of the offices of Falbridge and Swan, and into the small reception room, which smelt of Jasmine, and where the young lady receptionist asked her to sign in and take seat for a moment, having issued her with a plastic, clip – on identity tag. Less than five minutes later, a quite smartly dressed upper middle – aged man emerged from one of the offices, who smiled pleasantly at her and introduced himself as Adrian Metcalf. She was ushered into the quite small but quite well appointed office, and invited to sit in the chair opposite his whilst he sorted papers on his desk and attended to a boiling kettle, which was situated on a small table in the corner of the room.

'Can I offer you tea, or coffee?'

'Coffee, please, thank you, just black, no sugar.'

He made coffee for them both, then sat down at the desk and picked up an official – looking document.

'Right, well here's the will, which seems to be quite straight – forward. There are certain and various monies and investments which will be used to cover our fees, funeral costs and the tax bill, after which, the sum of ten thousand pounds is bequeathed to a certain Meadow Maynard. Do you know her?'

'Yes, I know Meadow.'

'Good, well I'll need her address. All residual funds are to then be divided equally between two named charities, both concerned with animal welfare.'

'I see…'

'And that's it, really. I'll deal with transferring the house into your name, which should also be quite straight forward, so with any luck it should only take a matter of weeks.'

Emily had heard the words, but they didn't seem to belong anywhere, and certainly not in the real world.

'I'm sorry….What house?'

Adrian Metcalf glanced at her briefly before consulting the document again, whilst Emily's heart was deciding whether to beat or not.

'The property at….Number Six, The Green, Middlewapping... Nice village, I've drunk in the Dog and Bottle once or twice.'

'I'm sorry, I don't quite understand…'

'Ah, you didn't know then, that she was going to leave you her house?'

The words were going in somewhere, but there was a delay in their being processed, but she had to say something.

'I….No, I had no idea.'

'I see, well lucky you then, period houses in that kind of location are very much sought after…The house comes to you complete with contents, and otherwise she has left you her motor vehicle. Are you feeling alright?'

Emily was not quite sure what she was doing, let alone how she was feeling, but she must have been staring blankly at the paperweight on the desk, which she noticed was a souvenir from St Ives, in Cornwall. Sometimes small thoughts are needed to pave the way for bigger thoughts, and this was still work in progress, and she now realized that her eyes had gone misty again.

'I'm…I'm sorry, yes, I'm fine, I think.'

Adrian Metcalf opened a drawer in his desk, and handed Emily a box of tissues.

'I find these come in handy for grieving relatives and so on, but you say that you weren't related to the deceased?'

'No, and look, I'm sorry, this is just all a bit of a shock, that's all.'

'So it would seem…It's all here in black and white, though. Perhaps you need some time to take everything in, yes?'

'Number Ten…'

'I'm sorry?'

'Number Ten, The Green; that's Meadow's address, I'm sorry, I don't know the post – code.'

Adrian Metcalf made a note on a notepad.

'Right, well, I'll get the ball rolling then, but we need to discuss the funeral arrangements and so on as soon as possible. She's to be buried in St Stephen's churchyard. Isn't there a small church in Middlewapping, I'm surprised she's not being buried there.'

'What…? Oh, it's been deconsecrated, there's a rock – star living there now, well sometimes anyway.'

'Is there? Well there's a sign of the times, then.'

Adrian Metcalf smiled, and Emily did her best.

'Yes…Well look, I mean what happens now, I mean I've never done anything like this before.'

'Well, I can deal with the funeral directors if you like, of course, but we have to think about a gravestone, and what kind of coffin you would like to use. I'll give you the contact details, so that you can pay them a visit, always assuming that you want to have any involvement. You don't actually have to do anything if you'd rather not, since that's what I'm being paid for, but the less I do the less you pay, and most people like to have a say in the matter.'

'Yes, of course…I'll go and see them then, tomorrow, I suppose.'

'Jolly good. Well, here's your copy of the will, and here's a leaflet from the funeral people to be going on with, and I was also instructed to give you this in the event of my client's death.'

Emily took the document and leaflet, which were placed within a plastic folder, and also a white, sealed envelope with nothing but Emily's name written upon it.

'So what's this?'

'I believe it's some sort of letter to you. I was instructed to give it to you unopened. If it has any bearing on the will then you will have to declare it to me, but I doubt if that will be the case.'

'I see, yes, of course. So, I mean, where is she now; Daphne, I mean.'

'She's at the mortuary, pending the post – mortem report, and then pending her burial, the former I imagine will be quite without controversy. All being well we should be able to organize the burial in a week or so, so can I leave you to inform people when the time comes?'

'Yes….Yes, I can do that.'

'Of course whether to want to have a wake or anything is entirely up to you, but anyway there it is. As I say, I'll start the legal processes and get in touch with the Probate people, and we can keep in touch from there.'

Emily was there in body, but by now her mind was quite elsewhere, and Adrian Metcalf had to prompt any further response.

'Well, there it is then, unless there's anything else for now?'

'Sorry…? Oh, right, of course, I'll….We'll talk soon then.'

Emily left the office and then the building, having handed her plastic name – tag back to the receptionist. Once outside the building she 'phoned Will, whom she knew would probably not answer. Will kept his mobile telephone well away from working areas, but now he would 'phone her back during his lunch break.

She walked, without really knowing where she was going, being rather too preoccupied with directing her thoughts rather than her physical self, but she knew that she didn't want to go home yet; going home would be an ordinary thing to do, and this was too extraordinary a day. She found herself in the old town, and made for Dawson's Coffee House, where she ordered coffee and sat alone in an alcove, placing the document and still unopened envelope in front of her on the grimy, dark - wood table. Daphne hadn't said anything. Emily tried to recall recent conversations which they had had, and there had been references at various times to Daphne regarding her as a daughter, and that she knew she was leaving the house in good hands, and so on, but there had never been any mention of her inheriting anything, never mind her house. So now she turned her attention to the letter. Perhaps she had better open it this evening, when Will was there, but that was silly, wasn't it, it was only Daphne, after all. Still it took another moment and more of the excellent coffee before she picked up the envelope and tore the seal. Inside was a single sheet of hand – written script, in Daphne's unmistakable hand, and here was that which she had written.

'My dear Emily

You will no doubt be surprised to learn that you are now the owner of number six. I have had many happy years there, and many happy years with my beloved husband, and by the time you read this we will be together again.

I know, my dear Emily, that you and William will take good care of my home, which you must do with what you will, but it gives me joy to think of you of all people being there, even if it is only for a short time, and that the house will in any event be helpful to you in the future.

So, take care of yourself and of each other, and try not to be sad, for I am with my God now, and the greatest mystery of life will be revealed to me, as it will to us all in the end.

But first you have your life to lead, and may it be a happy one, and may you be blessed.

I leave you with my love,

Daphne.'

More tears, now, but at least this was confirmation of something so unbelievable, written in the hand of the person who had just changed Emily's life, in a way, so perhaps now she could begin to believe. She must have sat in her quiet alcove listening to or at least hearing the quiet jazz music for an hour or more, time passed without her having knowledge of it, as can happen when a person is deep in thought. People came and went in the establishment; people having ordinary days, meeting friends or taking a break from their working day, but only once during this time were her thoughts disturbed, when the proprietor, Isaac Dawson, appeared at the end of her alcove, bearing a jug of coffee.

'Sister looks as though she needs more coffee?'

'What…? Oh, yes, that would be nice, thank you.'

Emily reached for her purse, but Isaac Dawson raised his hand briefly.

'This one's on the house. Something bad may have happened in the sisters' life, maybe coffee will start things getting better, you feel me?'

Isaac poured the coffee and Emily smiled. She was glad that she had come here; this was really the only place in town where important thoughts could be had.

'Thank you, and it isn't all bad news.'

'Then I'm glad for the sister.'

'My name's Emily.'

Isaac smiled now.

'Nice name…'

The reverie of the girl with the nice name was only finally and in due course interrupted by the sound of her telephone ringing.

'Yeah, hi, you called me?'

So here was Will, at last.

'Yes…'

'So how did it go at the solicitors'?'

'She left me a house, Will, I mean, what do you mean she left me a house?'

'Hang on, slow down, it's you who's saying she left me a house. What are you talking about?'

'I'm being rhetorical. I think I'm kind of talking to myself, or something.'

'Em, you're not making any sense. Talk to me.'

'She left me the house, Will.'

'Yeah, you said that before, but what house are you talking about?'

'Number six. She left it to me, with all the contents.'

A moment of silence followed, before;

'Are you sure?'

'Right now I'm not sure I'm on the right planet, but yes, I've got the Will in front of me, and she wrote me a letter. I mean I keep expecting to wake up, but so far I don't think I'm asleep. She left ten grand to Meadow and the rest after probate and so on goes to animal charities, but the house comes to me. I mean what do we do with a house, Will?'

'Jesus…Well, from a detached perspective, one either lives in houses, rents them out or sells them, I guess. Where are you?'

'I'm in Dawson's.'

'Yeah, that's a good place to be...This is insane, Em.'

'I know....'

'I mean she had to leave it to somebody, I suppose, and I suppose you can't leave bits of houses to people...What does the letter say?'

'Read it later...I mean I've got to do things, Will, like organize gravestones and inscriptions, and I've got to choose a coffin, for god's sake. I mean I don't have to, but I should, don't you think?'

'Of course, but that's okay, we can do that together. I'll take some time off.'

'Bless you...This changes things, Will.'

'Yes, I guess it does...'

'I mean I don't want to live in the house. I want us to stay where we are, and anyway I can't be away from the goats or anything, and anyway I wouldn't want to be. But we have a house now, or will have soon, at least, and it's a bloody big house, so you know, I can't really get my head around everything yet, but it's a big part of our future, Will, one way or another.'

'Of course...So when do you get the keys, and such?'

'I don't know, soon, I suppose, but I suppose there must be legal matters to deal with and what not, and Christ I've just had another thought, I'm going to have to go inside the house, aren't I?'

'Well you can't really own a house without going inside it, so yeah, you'll have to do that.'

'I mean I'll have to go through all of her things, and give stuff away to charity and so on, and then there's the well.'

'You can't give that away to charity.'

'No, but it's all so significant, isn't it?'

'Yeah, there's stuff to think about, that's for sure, but we'll do it, Em.'

'I know....Oh god Will, I just...I don't know, one minute I think I'm getting straight, and then it all goes weird again., but you'll be there, won't you?'

'Of course....This is good news, Em, I mean no one wanted the old girl to die, but stuff happens, you know?'

'Anyway, the first thing we have to do is get the funeral organized. She's being buried in St Stephens, by the way.'

'That's a nice graveyard, as graveyards go. That's where she went to church, isn't it, since the village church was sold off?'

'Yes, I think so. I suppose I'll have to meet the vicar and everything. I keep meeting vicars at the moment.'

'That's the thing about vicars, once you meet one you meet them all over the place. It'll be okay, Em, and once the funeral's done you'll own the biggest house in the village.'

'Yes....'

'Which is weird....'

'Yes it is, isn't it, and I really want to see you now.'

'When are you going home?'

'I don't know, I'm sort of stuck here at the moment.'

'What do you mean?'

'I mean I don't seem able to stand up at present, but soon, I suppose. I don't want to leave Monty on his own for too long.'

'Yeah, well, I'll be home at the usual time.'

'Okay...Well you'd better get on.'

'Yep, I've got pipes to lay, I'll see you later.'

'Yes, see you...I love you Will.'

'I love you too.'

The call ended, and Emily felt better. That which had seemed unreal to her before felt more real now, now that she had told Will. Eventually she stood up, thanked Isaac for the coffee, and walked out into the cool, spring day; a smartly dressed young woman who had clearly been crying, but now, for the first time, she began to smile through her tears.

This chapter of our story now finds its' way back to its' beginning, and to Wednesday, and to a certain bistro in the town. The remainder of this evening passed without further incident or revelation, Rosie managing to convince Quentin that there was nothing else significant about her that he should know, at which he quietly expressed some relief. Their conversation had revolved mainly about the matter of her being a witch, but she was also keen to know as much of Quentin's life history as she could, and so the primary subject was by degrees absorbed into the greater whole, and by the evenings' end it was clear to both that he could and would in time accept this unusual aspect of her persona, and that it at least would have no effect upon their seeing one another again. In truth she had not expected that it would, and thus had she been emboldened to tell him in the first place, but having done so she was pleased that she had, and was quietly relieved at the mildness of his reaction.

They left the bistro at a little before eleven o'clock, this being necessary in order for her to catch the last bus home, and by the time they reached the bus stop a light spring rain had begun to fall. They stood for a moment in the bus shelter, which they shared with several other people who were heading out into suburbia and beyond. They moved slightly away from the crowd, which was of mixed constituency and included an elderly couple, and group of clearly quite drunken youths of mixed gender, and two nurses returning home after their shift at the hospital, and here they stood for a moment in close and intimate conversation.

'Well, thanks for a lovely evening.'

'The pleasure was all mine, I'm sure. So will I see you at the weekend?'

'Sure, if you want.'

'Of course I want....I'll 'phone you.'

'Okay...We're not far from your flat here, are we?'

'No, the flat's not much but the location's good, at least.'

'Right....Well here's the bus, I'll see you then.'

One final kiss, the duration of which allowed her just enough time to be the last person to catch the omnibus, which as far as she was concerned was in one respect fortunate, but was in a way and to a greater extent unfortunate, and she found herself dealing with a strong sense of disappointment as she took her seat next to a man wearing a suit and tie; she had school in the morning and had to get home tonight, but there were taxis, after all, and her mother had given her sufficient cash to cover any eventuality. Quentin had paid for the evening, and she had kept the cash in case, which would not now be needed. In this context it would here be worth recounting a conversation which Rosemary had had with her mother during her preparations to depart earlier in the evening, which had gone as follows;

'I might be late home, mum, so don't worry, you know?'

'Do you have enough money for a cab?'

'I think so…'

'Well take this in case, and don't tell your father.'

'Okay, thanks...Don't tell him about what, the cash or getting home late?'

'Either, and do be careful, won't you?'

'Of course, I told you not to worry, didn't I?'

And now here she was on a bus, with her sense of disappointment and ten pounds in her jacket pocket, which had come to represent more than its' monetary value. Whatever extraordinary powers she may possess to control the thoughts and actions of others, she had not used them tonight, and more subtle and gentle means of influence had on this occasion let her down.

Quentin put up his collar and wrapped his Tweed jacket around him against the rain as he walked the short distance home. So, the girl with whom he was emotionally engaged was a witch, however this might impact upon their future together, and this was a thought which would see him awake into the early hours of the morning, but it was not the only thought which would do so. Something else had occurred to him on the walk home; something which she had said, not during their long conversations at the bistro, but a seemingly throw – away remark which she had made at the bus – stop, regarding the close proximity of his flat. Why had she asked that? Perhaps it was after all a careless remark, but he felt that he knew Rosie well enough by now to know that she was a more careful person than that, and by the time he finally fell into slumber, he was quite sure that the idiot male had missed his cue. Perhaps his preoccupation with the revelations of the evening had dulled his awareness of other matters, and even so important a matter, but his last waking thought was to curse himself for his ineptitude, and for the lost opportunity to finally bring his desires beyond the fantasy of them.

As Rosie lay her head on her pillow at the end of this day, and despite any disappointment that she may be feeling, her last thought would be a happy one. For regardless of that which had happened, or rather had not happened on this occasion, there would be other occasions, of course. She was in love, and she was it seemed in love with a gentleman, who would not it seemed presume upon a young lady's favours, even when they might have been offered to him. She had told him that she was a witch, and that was a good thing, and a witch and a gentleman would in the end she was sure be a fine combination indeed.

Chapter 14

COMPLEX SEXUALITY

It was somewhat to the frustration and bewilderment of William Tucker that in the days immediately following Daphne's death, Emily Cleves would not go to the village, and this despite having learned that she was de facto and would soon be legally and beyond dispute the owner of the largest house therein. To Will it seemed as though owning the house might be incentive to at least see the property, perhaps through different eyes, whereas for Emily this was in truth a disincentive. Her rationale, which Will in fact saw as being far from rational, was that she was still getting used to the idea of her so unexpected inheritance, and was as yet unprepared to move on to the actuality of it. It may be all very well in theory to of a sudden be a young lady of property, although this was a hard enough thing to come to terms with, but the practice of it was apparently a quite different matter. Thus was her reluctance to even go near the house not only despite her ownership thereof, but because of it.

Aside from the idea of seeing the house itself, therefore, Will tried various other means of gentle persuasion.

'You should at least go and tell Meadow that she's been given ten thousand quid, don't you think?'

'I'm not telling her that.'

'You're joint executor to the will, Em, it's part of your job, isn't it?'

'Yes, well it could be, but it would feel like I was giving her the money, like, here's ten thousand pounds, oh and by the way I got the house. It wouldn't seem fair, I mean Meadow was friends with Daphne, too.'

'You didn't write the will, Em.'

'No, I know, but I'll let the solicitor tell her.'

'Won't she be wanting some cheese for the weekend anyway?'

'She'll 'phone if she does.'

'So supposing she 'phones, would you tell her then?'

'I don't know. Look, stop bugging me, okay? I want you to be there when I, you know, see the house for the first time. We'll go on Saturday morning, and you can tell her.'

Thus it was that on Saturday morning Will walked alone to the village, carrying cheese, it having been agreed that he would 'phone Emily once he had spoken to Meadow, and she would join him then. This made no sense to Will whatsoever, but there it was, and now he walked alone into the delicatessen, where Meadow was pleased to see him.

'Hi Will, haven't seen you here for a while.'

'No, well, Em usually, you know....But anyway she hoped you might be needing some cheese.'

'Of course, I took it as read that she'd be bringing some this morning, some of my regular Saturday customers would be lost without it. So is Emily okay?'

'Yeah...Yes she's fine, just had a couple of things to, you know...'

'I see.'

'So it's like, bad news about Daphne, then.'

'Awful news, Will. I went to visit her in hospital, and by that time she was already passed away, it all happened so quickly. I still can't really believe it, you know?'

'No, it's a shocker, for sure....'

Something was off about this. Emily always brought the cheese, and Will was here for a reason, and had something to say.

'Right, well then....'

'Sure, best be off then...'

'Right you are...Will, is everything okay?'

'What...? Yeah, it's all good...'

'But....?'

'Well, the thing is, Em was wondering whether you'd heard anything from Daphne's brief, that kind of thing.'

'Daphne's brief…?'

'Yeah, like following her untimely demise, Daphne's, that is.'

'No, I haven't, why do you ask, or rather why does Emily ask?'

'It's just that Em's joint executor to Daphne's will.'

'Is she, well that's not really surprising, I suppose, they were close weren't they?'

'Yeah, and anyway, she, that is Daphne…And I mean I know it shouldn't be me telling you this, and it's really none of my business, right, but she left you some money, or whatever.'

'Did she…?'

'Yeah, and between you and me, Em's a bit embarrassed about telling you.'

'Why, for heaven's sake?'

'Thing is, I think she left you ten thousand quid….'

'Ten thousand pounds…? Are you sure?'

'I've seen the will.'

'I see…Well I'm delighted, of course, and completely surprised, but I still don't see why Emily should be embarrassed to tell me this.'

'That's not the bit she's embarrassed about.'

'So, what then..?'

'She left Emily the house.'

Meadow took a moment, and Will waited for any reaction, and now Meadow began to understand, and she laughed, gently.

'That's absolutely wonderful news, Will, in fact I'm far happier about that than I am about the ten thousand pounds… Good for her, and for you, of course, that's just, well, wonderful. I'm really glad for you both.'

'That's good then, thanks, and a bit of a relief, if I'm honest.'

'So if I've got this right, Emily's embarrassed to have got the house and not me, do I have that right?'

'That about sums it up….'

'Oh Will, for heaven's sake, when would I ever have expected to get Daphne's house? And what would I have done with it anyway? Emily was much closer to Daphne than me. Anyway, since you've been brave enough to come and tell me this, let me tell you something in return. Daphne discussed the matter with me a few weeks ago, when she first became aware that she was ill.'

'She did?'

'She did, so I already knew, you see, what Daphne intended to do with the house in the event of her death. I confess that she didn't mention anything about leaving me anything, not specifically anyway, so I'm very pleased about that, or as pleased as I can be, anyway.'

'Yeah, like I said to Em, nobody wanted her to die, right?'

'Of course not, Emily less than anybody, I'm sure, but…. Honestly, this is so typical of Emily, isn't it? She gets wonderful news like this and the first thing she does is to think about everybody else, and how they're going to react.'

'It was only you, really, and well, you know Em….'

'Indeed I do, so you can go back and tell her that everything's fine, and that nobody's going to be anything but delighted by her good fortune, okay? Not even me.'

'Sure…She'll be pleased to hear that. She's coming to the village a bit later, actually. I think I've persuaded her that she at least ought to look at the place, you know? Try to at least start to come to terms with everything. It's not just you, you see, she's having difficulty getting her head around any of it, to be honest.'

'Poor lamb….'

'The thing is, I'm trying to make her see the positive side of owning a bloody big house...'

'Yes, well life and people aren't always as simple as that, are they? It will have been a profound shock to her, losing her friend, quite without anything else, and to be given a house isn't the sort of thing that happens every day, is it?'

'Nope…'

'So when does she get the keys?'

'We don't know yet, soon, I expect.'

'And no news yet as to when the funeral will be?'

'Not yet, I think it's still all about post – mortems and death certificates, you know?'

'Well, no doubt we'll be told when the time comes. In the meantime I'm sure you'll look after Emily admirably.'

'Well, one does one's best.'

'One does indeed.'

'Right, well, I'll be off then.'

'Of course, off you go.'

'And we won't say anything about this conversation, shall we?'

'I'll just tell her that you told me, that's all, and you can tell her that I'm quite alright about everything, that should cover it.'

'Okay, cool…See you then.'

'See you, Will.'

Will left, the wind – chimes sounded relieved, and Meadow smiled to herself as she put the cheese on display. She had truly expected nothing from Daphne, and also felt a slight sense of unease at profiting from the death of others, but the money would help to see Rosie through university, so it would be put to good use. That which was making her smile, however, was the young man who had just left, and his laudable if awkward attempts at diplomacy on behalf of his beloved, who was clearly struggling to come to terms with so sudden and extreme change in her fortune. Bad things had happened in the village; Percival's house had been broken into, with who knew what further implication for the future, and Daphne had died so unexpectedly, but she was sure that Emily would soon enough come to terms with her inheritance, and that this would in the end be a happy and positive thing for her. She could not yet know how this would manifest itself, or how it would soon have so direct an effect upon her own family, but for now she could allow herself a moment to be pleased for Emily, her good young friend and maker of fine cheeses.

On Wednesday of this week, Michael Tillington had visited the property which was now called Orchard House, a property which was already his beyond dispute or question. Here, he and Keith had discussed progress thus far, and the immediate future of the renovation project, which would include electrical and plumbing contractors to carry out the first fixing of cables and pipes. Michael expressed his pleasure at the speed of progress thus far, and once all practical and financial matters had been dealt with, and employer and contractor were alone and drinking tea together, Michael showed Keith copy of the first of the old letters which had been found there.

'So,' Keith had said 'at least we've got a minimum age for the place, which sort of fits with the construction. I wonder who Jane was, and how she relates to what's his name…William.'

'We don't know yet, but I'm hoping all will be revealed in subsequent letters, of course.'

'Sure…Well keep me posted.'

'Of course...'

'So are we to see the lady Elin here in the near future?'

'She's not the Lady Elin yet, Keith.'

'I know, but the name kind of fits.'

'Yes, it does, doesn't it? Anyway her current work – load dictates that she can't get away from Canterbury at the moment, which is rather to her frustration, but she's working behind the scenes, looking at bathroom furniture and so on. It's a bit early for those sort of details, though.'

'Bring it on, there's no harm in having it here, we're not short of storage space, after all.'

'That's true...She keeps changing her mind at the moment, so I'm leaving those kind of decisions to her.'

'Yes, well that's probably wise...'

'So what news from the village..?'

'Not much, aside from Percival's place being turned over.'

'Really...?'

'You didn't know?'

'No...Not much news reaches the Manor at the moment. So was anything stolen?'

'Apparently not, it was more of an entering and breaking operation, damage for the sake of it, you know?'

'Oh my word...I've not been to the house, and despite his giving Rose away at our wedding I've never got to know Percival well off the cricket pitch, but I'm sorry to hear the news, of course.'

'Yes, well, the guy's made some enemies along the way, but he's a stoic, you know, and the insurance will cover most of the damage, I'm sure.'

And so it was that news of the break - in would later in the evening of this day be relayed to Victoria, but prior to this, Michael had spoken to Elin, who was indeed feeling frustrated, and in more regards than one.

'We've taken on more work, Michael, which must be completed quickly, so I'm going to be working at the weekend.'

'Oh dear, that's a pity. So shall I come to you?'

'I'll be working long days and perhaps evenings, so let's see, but I expect to be more free next week. I very much want to see you, Michael, and our house, of course.'

'Yes, well it's going along very well, so have no fear on that score.'

'And there have been no more letters?'

'No, not yet...'

'Michael, I would very much like to have sex with you.'

Michael had known Elin intimately for some time now, but in certain regards she still had the ability to surprise him.

'Yes, well I'd like you to have sex with me too.'

'Have you ever had sex over the telephone?'

'What…? I don't quite see how that would work.'

'I have never done it this way either, but it must be simple, I would think. I intend to give pleasure to myself tonight, as I daresay will you, unless you have already done so, so it would be a good thing if we did so together, don't you agree?'

For a moment Michael was tempted to laugh. Perhaps this was a nervous reaction, but in the event he resisted the temptation. Sex with Elin was never after all anything but a serious matter, and he had no wish to offend, although why she should assume that he was intending to masturbate was for the moment beyond him.

'If for example I were to tell you that I have not dressed yet after my shower, and that I am lying naked on my bed, would that be a stimulating thought for you?'

Whatever intentions he may have had for the evening, be they of a sexual nature or otherwise, Michael found himself of a sudden warming to the idea. Against his better judgment it may be, but whether it be against his better instincts was a different matter.

'Yes, it seems that it would.'

'Good, so are you touching yourself, as I am?'

'Well, I suppose one could…'

'Stop being so English, Michael. You may now tell me what you would like to do to me, and what you would like me to do to you, with no restriction in either regard.'

Michael considered that in such situations as this, alcohol would be a useful thing with which to free up the thought processes and reduce inhibition, but since none was immediately available he would have to make the best of it. The remainder of the conversation was interspersed with moments of silence, and by expressions of arousal by the female party to the dialogue, until she had apparently found satisfaction. In this regard she had been only just behind Michael, and she was keen to know how the male party had fared in their long – distance intimacy.

'Have you also reached climax?'

'Well yes, as a matter of fact.'

'There, well that is done then, so I'll go now. I'll call you tomorrow evening, whenever I get home.'

'Oh right…Okay…'

'I have very much enjoyed our conversation, goodnight, Michael.'

'Goodnight, Elin.'

The call was ended, and Michael had scarce enough time to gather himself and to bring his thoughts back into line before there was a knock on his bedroom door, and the caller was his sister. Her timing was thus unfortunate, but it could so easily have been more so.

'Hello….?'

'What do you mean, '*hello*', it's me, Mike.'

'Oh right, of course, come in Vics.'

Victoria entered the bedroom and sat on Michael's bed, wearing bathrobe and carpet slippers, and apparently ready to retire for the night.

'Just thought I'd touch base, see how things were progressing with the house and so on….Are you okay, you seem distracted.'

'No…No, I'm fine, I've just been on the 'phone with Elin, that's all.'

'Nothing bad, I hope?'

'No, nothing bad at all, actually… Anyway you asked about the house, and all's well there.'

'Good, that's alright then.'

'Yes…You're welcome to come over with me anytime you're free.'

'Thanks, I'll bear it in mind, although currently I'm either working or being painted during daylight hours.'

'Yes, of course....'

There followed a short dialogue, at the end of which Victoria stood up to leave, and Michael had an afterthought.

'By the way, Keith told me that Percival's cottage has been ransacked.'

'What...? By whom and for what reason..?'

'Person or persons unknown, I believe, and the reason seems to be wanton vandalism, since nothing was apparently taken.'

'My god, that's awful...I'll go and see him when I....When I go and see Rebecca, which will have to be at the weekend now. Well, goodnight, Mike.'

'Goodnight.'

Different thoughts occupied the minds of brother and sister after her departure. Michael decided upon a late – evening shower, and Victoria now had another legitimate reason for going to the village, and she had put everything off for too long.

Emily did not in fact go to the village on this Saturday. When Will 'phoned her from a bench beside the village Green, just after his meeting with Meadow, she had told him to come home, and Will knew better than to argue. Emily may be mild and at times sweet of constitution, but she had an underlying determination, which Will sometimes called stubbornness, and although finding her way to her newly acquired property was in all usual regards an easy thing, emotionally she would find her way there in her own time, and Will knew this, and so he went home.

In the afternoon he had cleaned out Blossom's enclosure, which was nowadays not such an easy thing, there now being eight robust and deceptively quick piglets running about the place and getting under his feet. Mother and offspring were thriving, and by now the piglets were eating solid food, and eating voraciously, and growing at that which Will considered to be a quite alarming rate.

In the evening they had retired to the downstairs dining room and drunk two bottles of red wine with pasta and salad, which Will had prepared, and any reference to the house was studiously avoided throughout. Emily had been wearing high heels and her shortest dress, and though a young man may nevertheless not make any assumptions of a sexual nature, when it came to bedtime, and Will had made ready to take the dishes upstairs, Emily had stopped him from doing so.

'Let's do that in the morning.'

They kissed, and she had turned from him. He unzipped and removed her dress, and she carefully cleared space and lay the top of herself face down over the table.

'Don't do it yet.'

She was wearing a thong, which provided no impedance to that which she wished him to do, and only thereafter did he make love to her whist she remained where she was, and cursed him between her expressions of sexual ecstasy. The complexity of Emily's sexuality was something with which Will was familiar, which is to say that he was aware of its' complexity, but it remained an ever unpredictable and mercurial thing, which could at times only find safe and wholesome fulfillment within a loving and caring relationship. When considering the matter In more sober, rational moments, Will would rationalize that abuse or punishment are not really either when the abused or punished is the instigator thereof, and thus did he convince himself that all was well, and so could he also fulfill his own far less complex masculine sexuality with a clear conscience, otherwise he would never find it in him to in any way hurt or harm his beloved. Still, it was done now, for now anyway, and in due course they fell peacefully asleep together, and the next thing that Will was aware of was a voice in his ear.

'Will, are you awake?'

'What…? What time is it?'

'Early, it's not light yet.'

'Right, in that case no, I'm not.'

'Oh, that's a pity.'

'So what's happening?'

'I want to go and see the house.'

'What, now…? It's dark, Em.'

'It'll be light soon, and there'll be nobody about.'

'Nobody sane, anyway….'

'So, will you come?'

'Yeah, sure, if you want, but let's go quick before the sensible part of my brain kicks in...'

They dressed quickly and left the house, Monty giving them a *'what's going on?'* kind of look from his basket in the kitchen, but they left him to his slumber. They made their way by torchlight, and by the time they reached the village the first rays of the morning sun had begun to lighten the eastern sky, and the village Green was wet with dew as they approached and then stood in front of the red – brick house. Nobody spoke, so Will spoke.

'Well, there it is then…'

Still silence, until;

'This house is ours, isn't it?'

'Yes, well it's yours, anyway.'

'It's ours, Will, otherwise I don't want it.'

'Okay, it's ours. So, shall we go inside?'

'We haven't got a key.'

'We know where she kept it, though.'

'We can't do that, it's not our house yet.'

'It's as good as ours. She wouldn't mind, Em. She's dead, you know?'

'Don't say it like that, you make it sound horrible.'

'I don't really know how else to put it. Come on, may as well, since we find ourselves here at so ungodly an hour.'

'Are there ungodly hours on Sunday?'

'I don't know, but it feels like there are.'

Will opened the small picket gate which led into the side garden, and retrieved a small plastic bag from a gap in the stonework just inside the well, in which he knew there would be a key. He then walked to the side door, put the key in the lock and turned it, Emily following close behind him. There was by now barely enough light by which to see their way, but there was enough, and both now stood in that which had been Daphne's kitchen. The kitchen was large enough to allow for a small wooden table and four chairs, and Formica work – surfaces ran along two of the walls, between a gas oven and large, white ceramic sink. For no particular reason, Will turned on one of the taps.

'It's what you might call old – fashioned, isn't it? I think the plumbing came with the house.'

'Shhhh, don't talk so loudly. I don't like this, Will, it's a bit spooky, isn't it?'

'It's okay, if we come across the old girl I'll keep her talking whilst you make good your escape.'

'What would you say to her?'

'I'd tell her she's no business being here amongst the living.'

'Will, don't joke about it.'

Two doors led off the kitchen, one of which gave access to that which Daphne had called her 'pantry', which was in fact a room only a little smaller than the kitchen. Here Daphne had kept her washing machine, tumble – dryer and refrigerator, the room also serving as a larder, but there were currently only tins and other non – perishable foodstuffs; no fruit or vegetables in the racks which were intended for them. Emily opened the refrigerator, which was empty apart from some preserves, and some of her cheese. Another door led out from the pantry.

'What's through here?' said Will.

'I don't know, I've never been out there.'

'Will turned the key and they went outside, finding themselves in a fairly wide alleyway which ran the width of the house, in which Daphne had kept her dustbin and other items to be stored outside. Running along the outer edge of the alleyway was a high, brick wall, beyond which was a courtyard, which had in all likelihood formerly been stabling for horses, but now served as a back – yard for the Dog and Bottle public house, in which crates and empty beer – barrels were stored. The property thus had no rear garden.

'I don't get this,' said Will, the Foxes next door have a back garden, don't they?'

'I think so, yes.'

They went back inside and Will locked the door. She took his hand, and they made their way through the other door and out of the kitchen.

'This is what she used to call her living room.' said Emily, who was still talking in hushed and respectful tones.

'Well she's certainly got no business being in here then, seeing as how she's….'

'Yes alright Will…'

'Christ, there can't be a single item of furniture newer than about 1950, apart from the turntable.'

Will opened a cupboard next to the record player, pride of place amongst a quite impressive collection of classical music being the entire collection of '*Dead Man's Wealth'* albums.

'Look at this, even her taste in music was retro, bless her.'

'DMW aren't so retro anymore, Will. Meadow and I used to laugh about her having those. She used to play them when she thought nobody could hear her.'

Beyond the quite large lounge, the only other room on the ground floor was Daphne's study, where, when the muse was upon her, she would retreat to write her poetry. Everything was neatly stacked, her latest, hand – written poems resting at the centre of her leather – inlaid desk.

'She knew she wasn't coming back, didn't she?' said Emily.

'What do you mean?'

'No food in the larder, nothing in the fridge, and everything left neat and tidy. Imagine walking out of the house that you loved for the last time, knowing it would be the last time.'

'Yeah...Let's not dwell on that thought, shall we? Let's go upstairs.'

'I don't know, Will...I've never been up there before.'

'We didn't own it before. Come on, Em, we may as well since we're here.'

In common with many of the houses around the Green, the stairs leading to the first floor were an open, timber staircase, at the top of which and to one side was the master – bedroom, which took up the entirety of one side of the house. The front window offered views over the village Green, and the back looked out over the courtyard, which owing to a complex arrangement of boundaries allowed the Fox residence at number five to have a small rear garden.

'So that's how it works then.' said Will.

To the other side of the stairway was a quite short, quite narrow passageway, off which was the bathroom, in which were a large, free - standing enamel bath which had seen better years, and a high – level water – closet and sink which must have dated from a similar era.

'Christ, you don't see many bathrooms like this anymore.'

Across the corridor was that which in Estate Agent parlance would doubtless be called the third bedroom, and which Daphne had used as a storage room, and at the end of the corridor was another bedroom containing two single beds, which had the appearance of not having been used for a long time.

'Well,' said Will 'it looks as though you'll soon be the proud owner of a three bedroom period house, retaining many original features.'

All of the rooms had dark – beamed walls and ceilings, and fairly uneven, carpeted floors which creaked as they were walked upon, the carpets being of the old – fashioned patterned variety, and being various in nature.

'You mean *we'll* be the proud owners of it. You think we should sell it, don't you?'

'I don't know, Em, it's not even ours to sell yet, but whichever way we go we'll have to upgrade the kitchen and bathroom, and probably put a toilet and shower downstairs, people expect that these days. Whatever we end up doing the furniture will have to go, and the carpets, and the place needs a repaint.'

'We can't afford to do all of that.'

'We'll be able to borrow the money against the property easily enough, the banks will be falling over themselves to lend us whatever we want, so whether we rent it or sell it it's the same deal, the money'll come back.'

They returned briefly to the main bedroom. On the bedside table was a jewelry box, and the draws contained more jewelry, much of which was costume, but there were quite a few rings, earrings and brooches which Emily assumed contained genuine precious stones, and there was in any case a lot of gold and silver.

'You know,' said Will 'we should take some of this home with us, in case the place gets burgled. It's an empty house, you know…'

'That's theft, isn't it, until we officially get the keys?'

'Probably, technically, but who's going to know, or press charges? This stuff's yours now, and anyway the police have got better things to do. She clearly wanted you to have this, Em, and she wouldn't have wanted to see it stolen, would she?'

Even Emily could see the logic in this, so both now filled their jacket – pockets with that which appeared to be the most valuable items. Aside from these, there was apparently nothing in the house of any particular value to an opportunistic, would – be thief.

'Okay, it's done,' said Emily 'Let's go, shall we?'

'It's a great house, Em.'

'I know, and I'm a lucky person, I've just never had this kind of luck before, that's all.'

'Except when you met me, of course...'

'That was a different kind of luck.'

'Bad luck, you mean…'

'Silly boy…Anyway it wasn't luck, I had to work for that.'

This was better; the first positive statement from the girl, a corner had been turned somewhere in the depths of Emily's psyche, and the boy found himself wondering whether their unusual sexual encounter of the previous evening had had any bearing on this. He didn't think about it that hard, however, since from wherever it had come and for whatever reason, a process of acceptance had it seemed begun.

They made their way from the house the same way that they had entered, Will now keeping the key in his pocket. They had both made the assumption that nobody would be abroad at this hour, and that their progress home would go as unnoticed as had their arrival, but in this they were mistaken; a man was walking his dog along the road at the top end of the Green, and now he stopped and awaited their approach.

'Okay, I've got a dog to walk, what's your excuse for being up and around here at this time of day, especially since you don't even live here anymore?'

'Hi Percival.' Said Will

'Hello uncle Percival.' Said Emily

'We were just….Of course you wouldn't know, would you? I guess you know that Daphne died, right?'

'Yeah, I heard…Which makes it even more mysterious that you two have just come from her house.'

'Yes, well that's the bit you don't know. Daphne left number six to Emily, so we were just casing the joint, you know?'

'What…? Emily now owns the big house?'

'Well, as soon as all the legalities have been taken care of.'

'Christ, that's news to hear so early in the morning. Well done, I mean I'm completely thrilled for you guys, as I'm sure you must be.'

'Em's having some trouble coming to terms with it, but I think we're getting somewhere with that now.'

'Yes, and *'Em's'* here, so when you've quite finished discussing my current emotional condition I'd like to join in the conversation. So where are you off to, anyway, uncle Percival?'

'I was heading for the estate lands, I take Lulu there sometimes by way of a change.'

'I haven't seen you since the break – in,' said Emily 'I'm really sorry to hear about that.'

'Yeah, well I didn't like the furniture much anyway, and the place needed a repaint.'

'Nor have I seen you since you lost one girlfriend and then very quickly gained another, the first having conveniently left home, so it's Louise again now, is it?'

'She's gone back to sort some stuff out, but she'll be moving back to the village soon, assuming she finds work more locally.'

'And back into the cottage, may we assume?'

'Yeah, you may assume that.'

'Well then we're all hearing good news this morning, aren't we?'

Having negotiated an enthusiastic greeting from Lulu, who was on her lead, Emily hugged Percival.

'I don't know, I can't keep up with your love – life.'

'In that regard I'm probably not that far ahead of you, you always said I was complicated, and I think you might be onto something.'

She let him go, and they smiled for one another.

'Since we're all up, why don't you come back for coffee?' said Will.

'Yes,' said Emily 'then we can all catch up with everything.'

'Sure..' said Percival 'Tell you what, I'll take Lulu for a brisk walk and meet you in half an hour. I'll come to your place the back way.'

'Sounds like a plan.'

'And, you know, congratulations, Em, you're a lady of property now.'

'I didn't do anything to earn it.'

Percival exchanged looks with Will.

'You see what I'm up against? You're not the only one who's complicated around here.'

'Ummm, excuse me…?' Said Emily 'What did I just say about not talking about me?'

The three friends parted, and it was a happy parting, and all looked forward to their imminent reunion, which would in the event be a long one, for they did indeed have much to talk about.

On this Sunday, Victoria had spent long hours posing for her portrait, and it was not until the light was fading that Pandora announced that this would be enough for the day. Hitherto during the painting of the portrait, interaction between artist and subject had been entirely businesslike, and as had become routine, Victoria changed out of the blue dress that she kept in the temporary studio into more practical attire, and left without further ado. She went to see Henry and Abigail, but thereafter put on a light overcoat and left quickly, making her way through the estate lands in the direction of the village. It was all but dark by the time she reached the village Green, and a light was on at number seven. Rebecca was at home, but for now she skirted the Green and made her way down the lane, and knocked on the door of the cottage, where Percival was glad to greet his unexpected caller.

'Hi, Percival...'

'Well hello…Come in, you're just in time for coffee.'

Victoria smiled; at Percival's house one was always just in time for coffee, as both knew full - well.

'Unless you would prefer alcohol..?'

'Coffee's fine, thanks. I heard about the break – in, they didn't leave very much undamaged, did they?'

'All they needed was a wood – chipper and they could have finished the job. I'm sorry I can't offer you a comfortable chair.'

They sat opposite one another at the dining table, as they always did, and as did everyone who visited the cottage. He poured coffee and they lit cigarettes.

'I've never sat in a comfortable chair here.'

'No, well I've always thought comfortable chairs were overrated. So, how's life treating you?'

'About as usual, aside from my currently having my portrait painted.'

'By the lady Pandora, I assume?'

'Yes, head and torso only, and fully dressed.'

'Naturally…And how's my Godson?'

'He's well, thank you. You really should come and see him, you know?'

'Yes, well I've been a bit busy lately, what with having place trashed and all. I came back from the Maldives to this, only it was worse than this.'

'That must have been horrible.'

'On the positive side I also came back with a new lady – friend. Louise has gone home to get herself organized, but she'll be moving in quite soon, I would think.'

'So it was the Maldives, then, and Louise went with you?'

'Yeah, we went together in the end.'

'I wondered if you would. So, congratulations then, I suppose. I never thought Sally was right for you anyway.'

'Yeah, people have said that, although come to think of it it's only been women who have said that.'

'Women know about these things.'

'Well, it must be true, then.'

'So who did this, Percival?'

'Don't know, but the smart money has to be on my friends from the west – country.'

'So are you in danger?'

'I don't know that, either, but one hopes for the best,'

'Well, be careful, I've told you before that I would hate for my son to lose his Godfather.'

'And as I've said before, I'll try not to let that happen.'

Enough had been said. Victoria had reassured herself that Percival was okay, for now at least, and she had set her mind on other matters. It was Percival, however, who decided on a change of subject.

'I saw Will and Emily this morning.'

'There's somewhere else that I really should go. So how are they?'

'They're fine. It was a good thing that you did, selling them the land, it's really worked out well for them.'

'Yes, so it seems, and I'm glad, of course.'

For a moment Percival considered imparting the news of Emily's good fortune, but he quickly thought better of it. There was time enough for that news to break, and better it not be he who broke it, and in any case the house was not quite hers yet.

'Listen, Percival, I really can't stay. I came to see if you were okay, but I have to go and see Rebecca, and it's something that I want to get over with.'

'Sure…'

'When was the last time you saw her?'

'Last weekend; we had a meeting after this had happened, when we moved most of my goods and chattels to the municipal tip.'

'How did she seem?'

'Worried, I think, after what happened here, but determined not to let whoever did this rule her life. I may have been a warning shot across the bows, you know, but we're none of us going to give in to terrorism.'

'I see...Well, she's going to have to move out anyway. Michael wants the house back.'

'Of course, he's been good about it, hasn't he?'

'Yes he has.'

'Where will she go, do you think?'

'I don't know, and I don't care, really. She can rent somewhere like everyone else has to.'

'That was said with feeling. Are you sure you don't want a drink before you see her?'

'Don't tempt me...But no, thank you, I should do this with a clear head.'

She stood up to leave.

'I'm glad you're okay, Percival. I'm worried for you as well, you know?'

'Seems like a lot of people are worried for me...'

'Of course they are, and don't tell me that you're not worried yourself, I know you better than that.'

'I won't let them kill me, Victoria, I'm just beginning to realize that I've got too much to lose, now.'

'This is all her fault, isn't it?'

'What's all her fault?'

'The people who broke in here and did this; it all goes back to Rebecca in the end, doesn't it?'

'If you go back far enough, but we've all made decisions along the way. I have to take my share of the blame, and things are as they are, you know? There's no point now in looking back and wondering what might have been, we're none of us going that way.'

'Well, if you say so. Nathaniel's also fine, by the way.'

'I assumed you'd tell me if he was otherwise.'

She left, and despite or perhaps because of everything she wanted to hug him, but they had never had that kind of a relationship. She walked up the lane and across the Green in darkness, but there was enough moonlight by which to see her way without using the torch which she had brought with her. The cloud which currently hung over her was metaphoric rather than actual in nature.

Victoria stood for a moment at the door of number seven before she reached for the door – knocker. She had tried to prepare herself for this moment, for days or perhaps weeks, but there are times when no amount of preparation will see to it. Having knocked she then waited whilst Rebecca checked who was calling, and unbolted and unlocked the door.

'Hello….'

'Hi; it's funny, I thought you might call 'round this evening.'

'Well, here I am, so do I get to come in?'

Rebecca made way, Victoria entered and Rebecca locked the door behind her.

Florence was asleep in her crib, and the place had not much changed since Victoria had last been here.

'I've come to tell you that you have to move out. Michael wants his house back.'

'Of course….I've made other plans.'

'Well then, shall we say by next weekend?'

'We'll be gone by mid – week.'

'Very well then...'

'So is that all that you came to say…?'

'Yes, I think it is.'

And it was. Victoria had quite made up her mind that she no longer cared. That since she could not control the actions of others, she would not be affected by them, but this was a meeting which both had known must happen, and reality is seldom as simple as that.

'So after all that we've been through and been to each other, does it come down to this?'

'It wasn't I who made it come down to this.'

'Can there be no forgiveness?'

'I can't....I can't love you any more, Rebecca, can't you see that? How can I live with Michael knowing that which I know? I wish to god you'd never told me.'

'You kept asking me, Vics. I just wanted us to be honest with each other, that's all. I thought you'd understand, eventually.'

'Understand...? Understand how you used your devilry to so abuse my brother?'

'Not how, perhaps, but why...Christ I could have used anybody, but I so wanted it to be Michael, because then she would be a part of you. You remember when we discovered that you and I are distantly related? How we laughed about that? Well now everything comes together again in Florence. I wanted her blood to be our blood, Florence is us Vics, she's a part of you and me, she's the great joining together of our history. Of course I shouldn't have done what I did, and I'll say sorry a thousand times if you want, but one thing I'll never do is regret it. If you don't love me anymore then at least try to love her, in a way she's a part of your future just as she's a part of mine.'

Victoria had prepared herself as best she could, but she had not prepared herself for this; sometimes no amount of preparation is enough. Both were still standing, there had not even been time enough for any of the niceties or conventions of two people meeting, and now Victoria walked to the window which looked out over the moonlit village Green, where the curtains had not been fully closed. She closed her eyes, as if in doing so she could better clear her thoughts, and order her soul, which felt now as though it had been rent asunder.

'I didn't say that...'

'What didn't you say?'

'I didn't say that I don't love you, I said that I can't love you, and that is something which I want you to understand.'

'I do, Vics…I do so understand how you feel, and I know I'm asking more of you now than I've ever asked of you before, but that's just us, you know? I told you because….Well, because of all the reasons I've spoken of, but at least I've been honest.'

'What do you mean?'

'I mean you still haven't told me who Henry's father is, and this is me, you know? The woman who loves you more than anyone else could ever love you, and yet you keep me out, so now who's hurting who?'

'That's different, they were…It was nothing to me…'

'They…? Who are '*they*', Vics? You never told me what happened.'

'I didn't…This isn't why I came here.'

'No, I know, you came here to tell me to leave the house, and I will, but don't blame me for everything. You walk out of my life and leave me to all of the crap that I'm in, and all of the people who hate me, and want me dead, and of course I've done bad things, and I've told you everything. All the people that I've killed, and how I burned the witches, and damned them to hell for wanting to hurt you and to hurt your child, and Michael's child, or Percival's child, whose ever the hell child it is. I'm a black witch, Vics, because that's what I've become, because that's what people have made me, and I'll go on killing if I have to, until all of this is over. Until the last of the witches who have sworn vengeance against your family are dead, and until all of them leave me in peace, and leave you in peace, and Florence is a part of all of that, because I've made her a part of it, and for that I make no apology. Percival has tried to help me, and Percival saved my life, and for that his house has been ransacked, and I can't let them kill him, so yes, I'll do whatever needs to be done, when I should just take my child and go, and never come back, but I won't do that because of all the love that I have for you, and for Percival. So go, if you want. Go back to your Manor House, and be thankful for your life, and be thankful that nobody took your life away from you when you were sixteen. Be thankful that nobody has killed your mother, and that you don't carry the hatred that I've carried for so long.'

This was nothing that Victoria did not already know. She had searched her soul, and thought about all that had happened since she had tried to kill herself, because she had lost Rebecca, and in all that had happened since Rebecca had come back to her and saved her life, and since their meeting in the old ruined folly. Then there had been the letters which Rebecca had tried to burn, and since then she had sworn that she would stand by Rebecca, no matter what she had done, and now, as she looked out over the village Green, she was quite lost.

'So what should I do, Bex?'

'I can't tell you that.'

'Can I hold her for a moment?'

Rebecca took Florence gently from her drawer, and gently she gave her to Victoria, which was for the first time. The infant stretched her limbs, but did not awaken.

'She really is beautiful, isn't she?'

The child awoke, and for a moment her eyes met Victoria's, and she smiled, or so it seemed to Victoria; such innocence born of such corruption, which did nothing to clarify Victoria's feelings. She placed her carefully back in her sleeping place and the child fell back into contented slumber.

'I'm glad she's a girl.'

Victoria walked to the door, unlocked and opened it.

'You'll tell me where you are, won't you?'

'Of course...'

For the briefest moment their eyes met, but the moment was only brief; neither was strong enough yet to swim against the rising tide of confused emotion which now threatened to carry them both away. Victoria turned and walked across the gravel track to the village Green. Rebecca watched her for a moment before closing the door, being sure to lock and bolt it for the night.

Pandora was sat quietly, reading, when somebody knocked on the door of her temporary accommodation. She had had long evenings alone during the painting of his Lordship, so this time she had brought books, and had settled to an hour or so of reading before retiring for the night, and she had not expected visitors.

'Come in.'

Victoria entered, carrying a bottle of red wine. She had left only a matter of hours before, but she looked different this evening.

'I was wondering….'

'I'll get glasses.'

They sat and talked as they had the last time; Pandora opened windows and rolled a marijuana cigarette, which was her second of the evening, and in due course Victoria fetched more wine. Whatever had occurred since the light had faded earlier in the day, it had it seemed had a profound effect upon the person whose image had begun to emerge on canvass in the temporary studio, although nothing was said of it. In due course Victoria stood up.

'Well, I suppose I should be going.'

'If you want….'

Pandora now stood up, and they came together, and held hands as they walked to the bedroom. They undressed and got into bed, and the subject wrapped her body about the artist, as though it had become a quite natural thing to do.

'I just didn't want to be alone.'

Which would be all of the explanation which would be given, and none other was asked for.

'Sure…Whatever….'

Victoria was asleep in seconds, and Pandora lay awake for a few moments, wondering what might have caused so sudden and profound a change in the behavior and attitude of this clearly complex woman. The relationship between painter and subject was for the most part a simple one; she painted, she got paid and that was an end to it, and she had slept with only two of her subjects before, both of them male, and both times only once, but this was different. Tomorrow Victoria was working, so Pandora would work on the background, if she woke up with a clear enough head to paint at all. She might allow herself a day off, and perhaps visit the town, but in any case soon enough her subject would put on the blue dress and sit before her again, and she would paint her differently the next time.

Chapter 15

Empty Rooms

It would be a matter of some ten days after receiving response to his brief message to Madeline Young that Peter Shortbody would come to a decision as to whether he would contact her again, if even then it could accurately be called a decision. The next time that they would communicate, assuming that they did so, would be by telephone, as she had opened the way for him to so communicate, and speaking to somebody was a different and in a way a far more personal thing than was writing carefully scripted words on a computer screen. Initially he had decided to wait for a day or two before deciding what to do, which he deemed to be a kind of decision, albeit that the decision was not particularly decisive, but this became more than a day or two, and thereafter time drifted through a week and more. In his conscious mind he allowed himself to be distracted from the thought of her, perhaps in the hope that the thought of her would find its' own natural end, and he could forget the matter entirely. His subconscious mind, however, was having none of it, and knew full well that something must be done if he were to have peace, and finally lay the matter to rest. Thus it was that when these two parts of him finally met it was not a harmonious meeting, but rather his wishing very much to 'phone her found itself in conflict with the fact that he thought he had better not, and indeed had more or less decided not to. When it comes to matters of the heart, however, what is best done is not always done, and a persons' emotions can add a third and more fluid and unpredictable element to any given internal conflict.

Thus it was that it was not in the end a rational or well – considered thing which early one evening saw him revisit her electronic mail, write her number on a piece of paper, and pick up his telephone. He dialed the number, and with not a little anticipation awaited a response. He heard the dial – tone six times, and decided that he would wait until ten before abandoning the idea, perhaps forever. Yes, that would be the thing, count to ten and then forget the whole probably ill – conceived business, and forget Madeline Young, hard though this would apparently be. Then on the ninth tone his call was answered.

'Hello…?'

By now he had more or less assumed that she would not answer, and had so resigned himself, and he was in truth taken somewhat aback by the sound of her voice, and this despite the fact that he had 'phoned her. He briefly chastised himself for his stupidity, perhaps for 'phoning her at all, but also now for his lack of preparedness for her response, but now he had to say something. Either that or he could replace the receiver; even now it was not too late, and even now the whole thing hung for the briefest time in the balance, but then he heard himself speak, so that was that.

'Oh, hello, is this Madeline?'

'It is…'

'Yes, hello, this is Peter Shortbody, you may recall that we were recently in correspondence, so I th….'

'Peter Shortbody, well I never…Yours is a voice I never thought I'd hear again. You took your time 'phoning, didn't you?'

Which he had, of course, for which he had reasons which he could not explain to her, since he could scarce explain them to himself.

'Yes, for which I apologize.'

'Oh please don't apologize, I know how life can get… so how are you? I mean that's a stupid question really, isn't it, after so long, but anyway, how are you, and what have you been doing for the last, what must it be, forty years?'

'Well, I've been an accountant, for one thing, retired now.'

'Yes, well it figures that you would have been a bean – counter, you were always good at numbers, weren't you?'

'Yes, I suppose so….'

'Okay, so what else…Are you married?'

'No, actually….'

'So no kids then..?'

'Two, actually, identical twin girls, two years old, nearly three.'

'Christ, you left that a bit late, didn't you?'

'Yes, well it was sort of an accident, one might say.'

'I see, so are you with the mother of said children?'

'Well, in a manner of speaking, you might say, although we've never lived together. We live five houses from each other in a small village, so we sort of share the children, as it were.'

'Well that's not conventional, but then you were never that, were you? So, which village…?'

'Middlewapping…It's j…'

'I know Middlewapping, I mean apart from knowing about the meteorite, of course, but I've driven past many times and stopped once to look at your famous rock. So you live there…It's such a lovely village, in fact it's about the most beautiful English village I can think of, you did well to end up there.'

'You will have seen my house, then, which is beside the village Green. So what about you..?'

'I'm rather more conventional, I'm afraid. Married too young, divorced with two grown up children, a boy and a girl, in fact I'm just about to become a grandmother for the first time. I live in Crowhurst, which isn't a million miles from you, is it?'

'No, it isn't…'

'Career – wise I've been working as ground – staff at the London airports for various airline companies, and I was an air stewardess for a few years, but I'm back on the ground now and responsible for a couple of hundred people.'

'That sounds rather glamorous, I mean being an air stewardess, you must have seen a lot of the world.'

'I've seen a lot of airports and hotels, anyway, and mostly it was short – haul, although I was long – haul for a while once the children had fled the nest. So, what are your children called?'

'Bronwyn, who's the oldest by a few minutes, and the youngest is Elizabeth.'

'So what's the Welsh connection, or did you just like the name?'

'No, she…Alice is Welsh, in fact, that's the children's mother.'

'Mine are Charles and Olivia, Charlie and Oli….Oh bugger, look I have to go, I've got a girlfriend coming 'round for drinks, and she's just arrived. So, what say you we meet up sometime? I can give you all the dirt on some of our erstwhile fellow students.'

'Are you still in touch with them?'

'A couple of them, and I hear news of some of the others on the grapevine.'

'Well, yes, I suppose we could….'

'I would be great to see you….How about Friday evening, let's meet in town, we're about equidistant and we can get cabs home. Do you know the Saddlers' Arms?'

'Yes, at least I know where it is.'

'Shall we say seven o'clock, the foods not bad there, so let's eat, shall we?'

'Yes, of course…'

'Good, that's done then, and now I really have to go. I'll see you on Friday, and thanks for calling, Peter. And by the way please call me Maddie, I've never really been Madeline.'

The line went dead, and Peter Shortbody was left with impressions, and an agreed rendezvous. Her voice was older, of course, but it was still her voice, and she was more confident and outgoing than he had remembered her to be, which he supposed had come with age and experience. She had in fact rather dominated the conversation, and their meeting had been on her instigation, and not quite what he had been expecting, but then again, what had he really been expecting? So, she was divorced, and presumably lived alone, whereas he had perhaps assumed that she would be happily married, not that this made any difference, of course, but of course it made a difference. Hitherto, until his dream, he had assumed that Alice would be the only significant woman in his life, and although a perhaps once - only meeting in a public house was not a matter of great significance, he was meeting another woman in a public house, and it was something about which he would not tell Alice, which in fact leant the matter a certain significance, did it not?

Peter Shortbody went to his kitchen, where Tizer was awaiting his evening repast with some impatience. He set the electric kettle to boil for his nightcap, fed his cat, and sat at his kitchen table. His conscious and subconscious self, which had been at loggerheads until perhaps half an hour ago, had now at last reached harmonious consensus, the consensus being that he was pleased indeed to have made the call to the woman who was still Maddie, and had never really been Madeline.

On the morning after he had said goodnight to his sister, and had had the unusual conversation with Elin, Michael Tillington awoke early, and in need of tea. He put on his dressing gown, went to the kitchen and returned with his beverage before turning on his computer to check his electronic mail. There were the usual news bulletins, and mail from Estate Agents containing information regarding properties for sale, and one email which immediately caught his attention, and this email he opened first.

'Dear Michael

Here's the next letter. I'm quite pleased with my efforts this time, and I think we have most of it, although as you will see, and as I daresay will be the case with all of the letters, some of it was once again beyond me to salvage, especially in this case the second paragraph. Anyway it remains interesting, don't you think? You know my charges, now, so I'll bill you at the end, and start on the next letter as soon as I have time.

Best regards,

Pat Wagstaff'

At the foot of the email was another attachment, which as before Michael downloaded and printed without first reading it. He settled at his desk, and now read the latest transcript.

'9th June 1665

My dearest William

It is now one week and better since (dear) John and Margaret arrived here, and I dare now to believe that since they have not fallen ill with the sickness, they must surely now be past the danger of it, and that we may all of us after all be safe here in our sanctuary.

It is a fine thing indeed, is it not, that you in (your generosity) had (I assume Orchard house?) *built, else we would still all of us be residing in..............and where (would any of us now) find refuge at such an accursed time?*

I scarce can (imagine the) suffering that others now endure beyond our confined borders, and beggars enough have knocked upon our gate, which is kept ever locked, but we dare not open....... for the poor wretches. The world outside seems to me to be in such stark contrast to........lives within our bounds, where the days are sunny and the garden is in such glorious bloom, and the birds sing so sweetly. Even............is our first summer here, Katherine has such fine hands when it comes to the growing of herbs and vegetables that we should have provision enough to see us through, should this, God forbid, turn into a long isolation.

I pray daily, my dear William, that you are in good health, and each day we all hope for news of you, or far better still that you come yourself, which would be to our greatest relief.

Your ever loving and obedient sister,

Jane'

So, as all who had read the first letter had speculated, Jane was indeed sister to William, which made the two children, John and Margaret, who had sought sanctuary with her, her nephew and niece. Perhaps more interesting to Michael, however, was the revelation that the letters were being written in the first summer after the house had been built, so he now knew to within a year the date of its' construction, which would be either 1664 or 1665. He had by now checked the with the Land Registry Office, but no house bearing the name of Orchard House could be found which had been built any time in the county in the 17th century, but now he could narrow the date down, he would try again. And now a new player had entered the arena; who was Katherine? A maidservant, perhaps, but the reference to her had sounded more intimate and personal than that, so perhaps a daughter?

Michael forwarded the email to Elin, and all that he supposed he could otherwise do was to wait until the next letter was painstakingly read and transcribed by Patricia Wagstaff, and he received the next email from her. Tomorrow morning he would visit the house, he had a particular meeting to attend there, but he had little planned for this day, he would perhaps go through the accounts to date for the house renovation, and perhaps go to town later. For now though, he finished his tea, and made ready for the new day.

During the course of this week, two different removal companies would be employed to remove the contents of two properties beside the village Green. The circumstances surrounding these contracts were somewhat different, but the intention of those paying for them was in essence the same, which was in order that the respective properties would thereafter be placed on the open rental market as unfurnished accommodation.

The first of these, of which we will hear of first, was the property belonging to a certain Sally Parsons, which was number three. Sally had caught an early evening flight from Oslo to London the previous day, and had come with sufficient provision to see her through two days, and two as good as empty suitcases. Her arrival went unnoted, save any who may have noticed that lights were on at the house during this evening, but nobody thought this sufficiently unusual to call upon her to check that all was well, so Sally was left in peace. Having eaten a light repast, she went about the business of filling her suitcases with such items of clothing, jewelry and so on as she wished to take with her to her new life in Scandinavia, two suitcases being scarce sufficient to see to this, but it would have to do, as she had no intention of returning here in the foreseeable future. The remainder of her worldly goods, from her china and cutlery to her cross – trainer, would be removed to a rented storage unit, there to stay until such time as she may need them again. Sally had always held deep affection for her house, and despite the excitement and novelty of her new life, the process of ordering and emptying the place where she had lived for most of adult life was a sad and poignant one. Here had she and Percival been together the first time, and here had she waited so long and bitter a time for their reunion, which had in the end when it had come been only a brief thing, and she still at times wondered how and why that end had come to be. She had had such plans, to give up the convention of her working life for something far less certain, and yet for herself, or for him, or for both of them she would have lived with the uncertainty. And then almost from nowhere had come the position in Scandinavia, which she and Polly had between them persuaded her that she should take; that she should leave, and break her own heart once again, before Percival broke it for her a second time.

She slept alone this night amongst all of her so familiar things, and yet already she felt like a stranger, revisiting an old place or an old life in which she no longer felt welcome, or comfortable, and it was a strange feeling indeed. So much had happened here, happy things and sad things, good times and bad times, but that was what it felt like now; like sleeping in a place of old memories, as though she were not really here, but was only a ghost of herself, and of how she had been. This was no longer her life, or her future, and all of this had happened in such a short span of time.

In the morning she awoke early and began to sort through the contents of cupboards and drawers, allocating everything therein to either be disposed of or stored, and by the time the removals lorry arrived in the early afternoon she was as good as ready, and she watched now as the stuff of her former life was carried out and placed in the huge vehicle, which for the time that it was there blocked the lane beside the village Green completely. By early evening it was done, and all that remained to be done tomorrow morning was to hand her keys to the letting – agent, who would arrange for commercial cleaners to make the house ready for occupancy, and to place number three, The Green on the rental market. She had already informed the gas and electricity companies, and would pay her final closing bills on line, and that would be that. Tonight she would sleep at Polly and George's house. George had a friend who had garaging space for her Mini Cooper, so she would hand him the keys and he would collect the car in due course, and tomorrow afternoon she would catch her flight back to Oslo, and her smart and well – equipped rented apartment. Polly had suggested a dinner party for a few intimate friends, by way of an informal farewell, and to offer best wishes for Sally's future, but Sally had rejected the idea. She wished for no ceremony, however informal, nor did she wish to endure the inevitable caustic remarks from Ray regarding the end of her relationship with Percival, or his equally inevitable attempts to say goodbye to her with more enthusiasm than she would wish. So instead, she and Polly would have a meal out, wherein no doubt the current state of Polly's marriage would be discussed, and analyzed, as would the likelihood of its' survival into the immediate future.

The taxi arrived at 7pm, and Sally made a final tour of her empty house, which symbolized well enough the life that she was leaving behind. She had been here a night and a day, and had scarce been inconspicuous, but she had neither seen nor spoken to anybody from the village, and most notably Percival had not been to see her. She could hardly have expected him to, since this time it was she who was leaving him, was it not, and perhaps he had after all been unaware of her presence from the cottage. Yes, she would try as best she could to convince herself that this was the case, but anyway, he had not come.

She carried her two suitcases and shoulder – bag out of the front door, and closed it behind her. The taxi – driver put her cases in the trunk and took up his place behind the steering wheel, and asked his fare where she was going. This was an easy thing to answer from an immediate and geographical perspective, but in the deeper and more metaphorical sense of her life, it was a very good question, and one which she would not at that time have been able to answer.

The second property on the Green to be made empty of furnishings and other contents this week was a somewhat simpler if in a way a no less emotive affair, and this was number seven. Michael Tillington met the representative of the house clearance company on site, all contents were to be removed and either sold on by the company or disposed of, since Michael Tillington had no use for any of it, such as it in any case was. The house had had a quite chequered recent history, from the time that Nathaniel, Rose's father, had sometimes lived here, until the time that he had died here, and then Rose herself had resided here with Will and Emily, before Rebecca had returned and been allowed refuge here with her daughter for a short time. Michael hoped that Rebecca would find other suitable accommodation, and felt somewhat uncomfortable about evicting her and her infant, but the situation could not be allowed to continue indefinitely, and for whatever reason Victoria and Rebecca were not close, currently, and indeed had scarce seen one another of late, which made the matter easier for him. Despite owning the property, Michael had only been here on a few occasions, but it was here that he had declared his love for Rose, and this had been her house. It was here that she had had her portrait painted, and had thus immortalized her beauty for all to see and admire, even long after all who had known her would have passed away. So the day was not without its' poignancy for the Lord in waiting. He had Elin now, of course, and his love for Rose had for the most part become a memory, but it was still only for the most part, and for the short time that he was here, the old house threatened to pull him back into his still recent past, and he was glad and somewhat relieved when at the end of this day he was able to close and lock the door on that part of his life, which would he hoped be once and for all. Tomorrow he would 'phone the cleaning company, and shortly thereafter the letting agents, so that finally he could receive income from the property, which in his current financial circumstances would be all to the good. So practical matters could be seen to, but it was not practical matters which occupied his thoughts as he turned from the house and began the short walk back to the place which was presently still his home, and he did not look back; it would be better that way.

'So, what do you write on a gravestone, for heaven's sake?'

'I don't know, how about something like *'I told you I was feeling a bit off – colour.''*

'Will, please be serious.'

It is late morning, and Will and Emily are in the Land – Rover on their way to the funeral directors, Emily having already seen to the milking of her goats and Will having taken the day off work. Daphne's post – mortem report had been signed off, her cause of death having been ascertained and agreed without controversy, and Probate was now in progress, whereby Daphne's financial affairs would be subject to scrutiny. Nothing however now stood in the way of the burial, and the date had been set for next Sunday. Sooner than she had expected, therefore, Emily had to make decisions as to the finer details of the laying to rest of Daphne, and to this end she and Will were making the short journey to *'Roberts and Maybridge, Funeral Directors'*, who were located some two miles out of town.

'And I mean how much should I spend on the coffin, and what not? All the funereal costs are being paid for out of her estate, of course, but I don't know….'

'Yeah, it's a bad case of the funereals…So her estate is being divided between animal charities, right, once everyone's paid off?'

'Yes…'

'Well I would keep the costs down then, the less we spend on the funereals, the more money's left for the animals. Might save a couple of extra squirrels…'

'I can't be seen to be being too cheap about it though, can I?'

'So we avoid chipboard, but anything wood's okay. I mean Daphne was quite big on conservation, right, so we can't use Mahogany or whatever, think of the rainforests, she wouldn't have wanted that.'

'No, I suppose not...And what sort of gravestone should we use?'

'I would avoid anything black and shiny, bit of good old Surrey granite would do it, keep it natural. We'll just have to see what's available. I suppose we could always have an angel.'

'I'm not having an angel.'

'Unless they're doing a special offer on angels, two angels for the price of one kind of deal....Reginald would be impressed.'

'So what would we do with the second angel?'

'I don't know, it might look quite nice in the bathroom.'

'God, Will...I don't know, it's all so macabre, don't you think?'

'We've been ceremoniously burying our dead for thousands of years, it's just what we do. You can stick me in an urn when I go.'

'Will, don't talk like that.'

'Just saying....So we need to let people know, I guess.'

'I've told Meadow, so that's as good as telling everybody. She's going to put the word out in the village, and I don't know of anybody else that we should tell.'

'No, she didn't have many close friends, did she? I suppose they must all be dead.'

'Can't you find another word for that?'

'What, *'dead'*?

'It's not a nice word, is it?'

'It describes the condition admirably if you ask me. Anyway, here we are....'

'Oh bloody hell, here we go then. I'm going to need a drink after this.'

'I think a pub lunch is called for.'

It was only somewhat less than two hours later by the time they emerged once again from the funeral parlour into the bright, spring day. A headstone had been selected, and the simple inscription would be carved, and the stone delivered to the Church on the day before the funeral. Emily had earlier this day spoken to the Reverend Mark Inman, Vicar of St Stephens, who would organize the digging of the grave prior to the day.

'Christ, those places are depressing…'

'Yeah, imagine doing that for a living. Still, it's done now, Em. I think that's about everything, isn't it?'

'I think so….I mean I don't think I've forgotten anything vital.'

'You know in some cultures they leave their dead on the mountaintop for the vultures. That sounds like a much better idea, at least someone gets some benefit from it.'

'There aren't many mountains around here, or vultures for that matter.'

'Well, blackbirds then. It's the same principal only it might take a bit longer.'

'Come on, take me to the pub.'

'Which pub..?'

'Any pub...'

'Have you considered mummification as an alternative?'

'William, shut up…'

They left the premises of the undertakers, and had not driven far before coming across a public house, which although not particularly prepossessing in appearance would suit their present purposes well enough. Will parked the Land Rover and they entered the establishment, which was called 'The Weybridge Inn', and took seats by the window. Will fetched ale for himself and Vodka and Tonic for Emily, and both decided upon todays' special which was written on the chalk - board, and which was Shepherds' Pie. Emily still seemed deep in thought, so Will decided to make conversation.

'So, who do you think will come to the funeral, then?'

'What…? Oh I don't know…Meadow and Keith for sure, and Meadow's dad, probably, and Ron and Barbara I would think.'

'I hope Reginald comes, he always brings something different to the party. He might even bring his new lady - friend, whatever she's called.'

'Gwendolyn, who nobody's met yet...'

'Yeah, it's about time he came out with her. Peter, do you think?'

'I don't know…'

'No, you never know with Peter. I think Sands should come though, if only to see what she missed.'

'Will, that really isn't funny.'

'You spoken to the chaste one lately..?'

'Not for about a week, she's still heavily into her research, I think.'

'That can't have much longer to run, can it?'

'I think she'll be back at uni soon.'

'Hmmm…'

'*'Hmmm*' what..?'

'Not much time left for you to get her set up then.'

'I've more or less given up with that, after my last attempt backfired so spectacularly.'

'Yeah, that didn't work out, did it…'

'Mat wanted me and Sands didn't want Duncan, so that was all the wrong way 'round.'

The Shepherd's Pie was delivered to the table, which both would agree was no better than mediocre, but it served its' purpose, as had the alcohol, and arrangements for the funeral had in any case been taken care of, which was somewhat to the relief of Emily.

The intent of Sharon Tate had been moving forward toward its' end. She had been to the village on occasion and had established her presence there, and had spoken at some length to Keith, who was partner to Meadow, she who had killed

Eve on the steps of the Manor House. She had then written her article, and had sent it to various editors, and as she had hoped, it had been published. So the village would know of her now, and she would be known as Georgina Hamilton, freelance journalist, and in this persona could she now move freely in the village. But then, something far more mundane had entered the arena of her life; she had been offered work as a dancer in a theatrical production, which would see her move to the north of England for the duration of the show, and thus had her plans been delayed. She travelled light nowadays through life, and she gave up her rented room and headed north, where she had lived until the show had run its' preordained course. She knew well enough where Rebecca lived, and as best she could she had tried to become familiar with her movements, and she had followed her once to her studio. And then had come the offer of work, which in the context of her ordinary life she could not turn down; she had to eat, and pay rent, and so only thereafter could she return. On her return, however, she found Rebecca gone, and the house where she had been was empty, and awaiting a new tenant. She was by now on quite familiar terms with Nigel Hollyman, the landlord of the Dog and Bottle public house, but neither he nor anyone that he had spoken to knew where she had gone. Certainly she had not gone to live at the Manor House, but this was an unexpected turn, and one which Sharon had not anticipated. For now, therefore, she withdrew, and found accommodation in the town, and from there she would decide how best to proceed.

Upon a certain evening, which was the day following her departure from Michael's house, Rebecca looked around her new living quarters, and tried to do an assessment of how life would be here. She had running water and a large sink, and a kettle with which she could make sufficient warm water for bathing Florence. She herself could wash in cold water. She had a small electric heater, and spring was now well advanced anyway, so soon she would be in less need of heating and would be able to leave the door open more often. Living in an enclosed place with clay – dust was not conducive to a healthy environment for herself or her beloved infant, but she would do her best to minimize the problem, and this would perhaps not be for long. She had bought a single futon, a duvet cover and pillow, which would serve her well enough for her sleeping place, and a single – ring gas burner on which she could cook their food. She had internet connection, and could set up a makeshift office in one corner of the room. She was certain that to live in the studio was in contravention of her lease, but the owners or people from the leasing company seldom came here, and she could she was sure bluff her way through, otherwise she would use her learned skills to convince anyone interested that all was well, and that this was not her permanent residence; she only slept here on occasion when she was working late, or needed to rest during the working day.

Rebecca's ceramic work continued to be in demand, and she had sufficient work ahead of her, and orders enough for several weeks. Her main dilemma was nowadays whether she should make plates, bowls and smaller items which she could make quickly and sold for a small profit, or whether she should devote her time to larger and more prestigious and luxurious or collectable items, which were much slower in the production, but would sell for a deal more, and upon which she could continue to build her reputation as a unique craftsperson. But still, she could get by, and could provide for herself and Florence, provided that she was careful.

Rebecca's last place of residence had been a place or relative luxury for her, with hot running water and central heating, but she had known her tenure at the house would be a limited one; it had been good of Michael to provide temporary refuge for her and his daughter, and she could ask no more of him. By comparison to that, this would be a harder place to live, but Rebecca was no stranger to hardship, and she had lived years of her life in worse conditions than this. She had promised Victoria that she would tell her where she was living, so she would say that she had found somewhere in town, and if Victoria wished to see her again then they could meet somewhere, even if she was no longer welcome at the Manor House. She would perhaps tell Percival where she was, and make certain that they were always in any case in telephonic communication, and she would go and see him sometimes. He was perhaps in danger now, and she could not lose contact with him, but being here had one great advantage for her, which was that nobody knew where she was. If the witches or the people from the west – country came looking for her in the village, she would be gone, and safety for her and Florence must for now remain her only priority. Eve had found her, and had come here once, but Eve was dead now, so that danger at least was over. And then there were Keith and particularly Meadow, whose part in the killing of Eve and thus the safety of the Tillington children had been so important, but their part was over, at least for now, and of that she was glad. She was by now quite certain that not all of the witches from Farthing's Well had been killed, but here was a place where she could wait, and think, and decide how best she might face them, if or rather now when they returned to seek their vengeance against her. Of the woman who called herself Georgina Hamilton she had heard no more news, but she remained convinced that this would not be her real name, and so all that she could do now was to wait, and to work, and to be careful.

She had taken nothing from Michael's house, so for now Florence had nothing in which to sleep, but she would manage somehow. She looked now at her sleeping infant; this was no way to start a life, and they would need to move on before winter came, but Rebecca held fast to the belief that life would get better one day, for both of them, and she felt as good as certain that by next winter all the troubles of her life would be over, one way or the other

Chapter 16

Summer Pathways

Lord Tillington was seated at his desk in his study under the grand staircase, where ostensibly he was assessing his financial situation, and going over accounts relating to the Manor House. Since the dissolution of his businesses, he had money variously and for the most part carefully invested, although some funds had been channeled into more risky but potentially more profitable ventures, some of which were accruing dividends, and some which were not. He took comfort from the fact that he would at least leave his estate in a healthy financial position for Michael and Victoria, who as far as possible would share the estate equally after his death. The Manor would go to Michael, as had always been the tradition, but he trusted his son and his love for his sister sufficiently to be certain that he would see her well provided for, and both owned houses in the village now, something which had come about by such different ways. In any case as he knew well enough, to own the Manor House was a mixed blessing, it being at once an asset and a liability. One could not easily sell it, even if one wished so to do, so its' value was always somewhat theoretical, and to maintain such a large and ancient property was inevitably a burden upon ones' immediately available finances, and would continue to be so. It was likely, therefore, that purely in terms of their inheritance, and leaving the Manor House aside, Victoria would in fact be the more wealthy of his two children as a result of his eventual demise. Decisions would have to be made in due course as to which aspects of said maintenance would be carried out during his lifetime, and which he would leave to Michael, but these were decisions for another day, and he had no intention of dying in the near future. Indeed aside from having invested the capital gained from the selling of the assets of his former companies, thus seeing to his family's longer – term financial wellbeing, his own state of health had in general and undoubtedly improved since he had been forced to retire from business. He did not have the energy or the passion for life that he once had, which he supposed was only to be expected; it is after all the lot of all people who live to a good age to become less than they were, and a person will reach a time of life where they begin to sense the end, but his particular end was, he hoped, still some distance away.

Nevertheless, in the mind of his Lordship, the future of the Manor now belonged to Michael, and Michael had now begun to find his own way to financial independence from anything which he might inherit, which could only be a good thing.

And now of course there was Nathaniel. It had taken Michael's second and ill – advised marriage to Rose, the beautiful prostitute, to provide him with his son and heir, but now the Lordship would continue for two generations at least, regardless of whether Michael ever remarried, and whether there was issue from the marriage. Nathaniel had very nearly not survived his birth, and remained the sole heir, but this was not for the first time. Lord Michael knew of other occasions during his lineage where there had been only one surviving son to carry on the Lordship, so the link had been tenuous over the past centuries, but his line had nonetheless thus far survived plague, pestilence and war, and thus had allowed him to sit where he now sat, and to speculate upon the future of his own and sole surviving son. And in this regard had Lord Michael indeed lately begun to speculate. Michael scarce ever spoke of Elin unless prompted to do so, and even when prompted would offer only vague and insubstantial comment, which led Lord Michael and more particularly his wife, Lady Beatrice, to believe that the relationship was of a more serious nature than he was admitting to. He seemed also to be showing an uncommon interest in his latest venture, so perhaps there was more to the matter of Orchard House than met the eye, the eye perhaps not being permitted to see all that was going on in the heart and mind of his only son. But still, all would doubtless be made clear in due time, and he would not press his son on the matter, for now there was Nathaniel in any case, who would perhaps one day sit where he now sat, and ostensibly go over the Manor House accounts, whilst his mind might drift to other more esoteric matters.

Victoria had ever and anon and for different reasons been a source of vexation for her father. He could not be certain, and he would not spy on his daughter, but he had become convinced that she had on occasion, and who knew on how many occasions, slept with the artist Pandora during the time that his portrait was being painted. Whether this was the result or cause of her apparently falling out with Rebecca he could not know, and perhaps Rebecca had nothing to do with it, but anyway, he was as sure as he could reasonably be that this was the case. There was nothing to be done about this, of course, even should he have wished to do anything about it, but in any case Pandora was back now, so who knew what might go on between them, and who indeed cared, since in truth he did not. All that mattered was Victoria's emotional wellbeing, and now that Rebecca had left the village, and left Michael's house, perhaps Pandora might as it were step in to fill the emotional void, and this may be all to the good. Rebecca had a daughter now, of apparently unknown parentage on the male side, at least Victoria did not know, or did not say that she knew, so both women who had been so much to each other had children of illegitimate origin, and neither had made public pronouncement regarding the paternal side of the genetic makeup of their respective children. But still, little Henry was a hale and hearty child, and at least Nathaniel had been born within legitimate marriage, so although all was not as he would have it be, Lord Tillington was one who would nowadays count his blessings, and let all else be as it may. He had lived his life as best he could, and it was for his children now to make what they could of the world, which was nowadays such a different and in many ways a more complex and difficult place.

His reverie was interrupted by his dear wife, who perhaps suffered more than he as a result of the vagaries of the lives of their children, but who for the most part managed to come to terms therewith, for in the end what choice did one have? Parents may assume control of and have influence over their children's lives during their formative years, but control and influence take many forms, and in this regard are by no means a one – sided affair.

'Michael, I'm sending Molly into town, is there anything you need?'

'No, my dear, I don't believe there is.'

'Very well then...'

So there it was then, a definitive conclusion to his thought processes, and Lord Tillington left himself with the supposition that the person did not exist who had everything that they wanted, but to be able to say that one has everything that one needs is something, is it not, and that which it is not is something which should be taken for granted.

During the course of his having renovated and subsequently sold various properties, Michael Tillington, son to the current Lord, had for the most part employed the services of a local landscape gardener, with whom he had developed an adequate working relationship, to bring the gardens of said properties to an at least acceptable condition for re - sale. Mostly this had been a matter of erecting new boundary fences, clearing overgrown borders, or laying new lawns; simple, budget – conscious projects requiring little by way of imagination or creative input by either party. When it came to the matter of Orchard House, however, which it now did, it was a different matter altogether, since this would one day soon be the garden where he and Elin, and Nathaniel, of course, would pass their summer days; that which was created now would have influence upon their lives for years to come. Here was a quite large plot of land surrounding a period property, which was in need of a complete re – design, by somebody who would have sympathy with the type of house, and for the style of garden which Michael had envisaged. This was not to say that he had any specific or particular vision in mind, but he had imagination enough to realize that the general ambience and choice of materials and ultimately plants would be important.

There was little doubt in Michael's mind that the actual building and planting of the garden would be carried out by the small team of craftsmen already on site, with Damien taking the lead – role, since this was his particular field of expertise. Firstly, however, the garden must be conceptualized and drawn; that which would in due time be created in three dimensions must begin in one dimension, and to this end he and Elin had both spent time on line visiting various websites, with a view to selecting a designer whom both thought would be the best. This process had been carried out entirely at a distance, he at the Manor House and she in Canterbury, and in this way would they arrive at a short – list, from which a final decision would be made, and it was not in the end an easy process. They, or rather as it was likely to be Michael, were of course not limited to meeting only one landscape architect, but they and particularly Michael were having uncharacteristic difficulty making any kind of decision. The designers, who whilst being for the most part male were of either gender, ranged from those who had not long been established, to others who had national and in some cases international reputation, but all had on display an impressive array of drawings, and in truth none stood out as being a natural choice. As was perhaps predictable, however, given her forthright opinions on almost all matters, and Michael's more pragmatic approach to life, coupled with his wish to please his lady, it was to be Elin who would make the final choice. This was by her own admission more a matter of emotional response to a particular designer, or rather their website, rather than anything more tangible, but in any case so it was that on the day following receipt of the second letter written by the sister to his ancient forbear, Michael, was to meet the person who would likely be responsible for creating the garden in which he, his betrothed and his son would one day spend their time.

She, for it was a she, was one of the less well established designers, who had only plied her business for a matter of some three years, but her curriculum vitae was nonetheless impressive, and the text which accompanied her displayed works was energetic, and spoke of somebody who would have sympathy with the job to be done. The young lady's name was Fifi Fielding, which rather made Michael smile to himself as he drove to the place which would one day be his home, but a name, after all, was only a name, and if she could create for him and his beloved a beautiful garden, he cared not all what she might be called.

'29th June 1665

My Dear William

It is now near (one month since) the arrival of John and Margaret, and since we have heard news of you. My hope is ever that you are doing as we are, and staying within the bounds (of) (...........?) (and not) travelling abroad (for fear of the sickness,) but this is (now becoming) a faint hope, which grows more faint (with each) passing day.

We dine now on simple fare, and eat only one wholesome meal each day, such as (the garden) can provide, and even this meal I fear I must forgo (in due course?), in order that your dear children may take sufficient nourishment in the weeks to come, if weeks they must be. I do this with glad and willing heart, for the sake of dear Margaret, and so that your line may continue through John, which (must ever) take precedence over all else.

John would have me send out for word of you and Rosalind, and would ride himself, but this I have quite forbidden, as you (have instructed.)

Margaret asks ever when she (and her brother will) be going home, and this is a vexatious thing for me, and indeed near breaks my heart. My greatest solace now are the gardens, the pathways of which I walk daily, and daily I give thanks that you did (take such care) with their concept (and construction?), the roses give such beautiful perfume and colour as gladden my heart even at these dark times, and my heart is now verily in need of gladness.

I remain your loving sister,

Jane.'

Fifi Fielding, as it transpired, was as energetic and forthright in person as was indicated by her website text. She stood, Michael assumed, somewhere around five and a half feet tall in her sensible shoes; she was exceptionally pale of complexion, and carried a head of luxuriant red hair, which was loosely tied up behind her. Otherwise she wore jeans and a loose – fitting blouse and jacket, which did little to disguise the fact that aside from her beautiful hair, her most immediately noticeable physical characteristic was something which was immediately noticed by Michael, and by all of the men there present. She had an easy smile, and she carried with her a clip – board and a businesslike manner as she walked from her pick – up truck, across that which would one day be a garden toward the front door of Orchard House, where Michael was waiting for her. Michael assumed that she was somewhere in her mid to late twenties.

'Hello…'

'Fifi Fielding, I presume.'

'Yes…'

Two words only had she spoken, but something else now became apparent which had not been so before, which was that Fifi Fielding was Scottish.

'Michael Tillington, I'm pleased to meet you.'

She extended her hand, which he took, and they shook hands, briefly.

'You're not *Lord* Michael Tillington, are you?'

'No, at least not yet, you've probably heard of my father. We share the same Christian name, which can at times cause confusion.'

'Well yes, that is I know of your father…..And I know Middlewapping Manor, of course.'

'Where I currently reside, but this is one day to be my home, I hope, and as you can see, the garden needs some attention.'

'Well, that's why I'm here, and my god what a beautiful house, and the gardens must once have been beautiful, too.'

'Yes, I suppose so…'

'You can still see outlines of the paths, and so on, and where we're standing would once have been a terrace…Is that a working well?'

'No, it's filled in now.'

'Then I'll incorporate it into the design. So, do I have a working brief, I mean is there anything in particular that you want or don't want from the garden?'

'Well no, not really, apart from the usual, I suppose, seating areas and so forth.'

'Of course….A house like this will need a kitchen – garden for herbs and so on, but do you think you'll be growing vegetables?'

'Yes, I would think so, although I never have, but yes, I think we should include a vegetable garden somewhere.'

'Well you're not short of space, that's for sure, and you're okay with mowing lawns? I'm just trying to get an idea of how much maintenance you envisage doing, that kind of thing.'

'Oh yes, I mean I imagine that eventually we'll employ a part – time gardener, so within reason maintenance won't be a problem.'

'I see, well good then... The boundary walls are superb, those that I've seen anyway, so you'll be keeping those, I assume?'

'We'll need to do some repairs in places of course, but essentially they'll stay as are.'

'Good, then I'll ignore them in terms of the design, and I'll try to keep as many of the mature trees and shrubs as possible, and we'll re – use the flagstones wherever we find them, that'll save money and help give the garden what we designers call instant antiquity.'

'Well, that sounds marvelous then, so how do we proceed?'

'I do a site – survey, then produce some outline sketches before we move to the final design. I'll be here for an hour or so I would think, and I'm sure I'll have more questions before I leave.'

'Right, well I'll be here...Can I offer you tea?'

'That would be lovely, thank you.'

'And I mean, do you need anyone to help with the survey, hold the other end of the tape or whatever?'

'Och no, I'll be fine, I work better alone, and I can be thinking whilst I'm measuring. If anything else occurs during the walk – around I'll let you know'

'Right, fine then, I'll make the tea and let you get on.'

Parting smiles and Fifi Fielding got on, whilst Michael fired up the small generator in order to set the electric kettle to boil. The electrical contractors were due to start work in a few days, and he hoped that soon thereafter the house would be safely connected to the mains supply of electricity, but for now the generator continued to serve its' purpose.

Inside, the three workmen were about their business, Keith having been the only one close enough to have overheard the conversation between client and designer, and he now rejoined Damien and Will, who had only briefly observed the meeting from a distance.

'She'll likely be your designer then, Damien.'

'She's a bonny lass by all appearances, is she not?'

'You could say that.'

'I think it's wrong,' said Will 'to so objectify the female form.'

'She can make it subjective any time she wants.' Said Damien 'Anyway how do you know what it is to which we refer?'

'I'm taking a wild guess…'

'She's Scottish, too.' said Keith. 'Even speaks the language.'

'I suppose she could hardly be very much else looking like that.'

'So she may not be a pretentious ponce after all.' Said Will 'Isn't that how you generally describe landscape designers?'

'Probably, something like that, and the jury's still out in that regard, but the signs are encouraging, I grant you.'

'I suppose if she gets annoyingly pretentious you can always admire her physical characteristics, like her auburn hair, for example.'

'Ay, there's that…'

In the event Fifi Fielding stayed for as good as two hours, during which time Michael discussed finer points of the building work with Keith, and by which time it was lunch – break for the workmen. Now that the warmer weather had come they invariably took their lunch outside on the old terrace, where Jane and Katherine had sat so often and taken their tea on warm afternoons, during the only summer in which they had lived at Glebe House, for aside from the plague times, there had been happy days as well. From somewhere a fifth mug was produced, and Fifi drank her second cup of tea in the company of others, to whom she was now introduced by Michael, who increasingly nowadays found himself in no hurry to return home, since this had already begun to feel like home.

'Everyone, this is Fifi. Fifi, this is Keith, Damien and Will. Keith's in charge of the overall contract, but Damien will likely be the prime mover in building whatever we eventually agree on as a garden design.'

'I'm pleased to meet everyone, I'm sure.'

'Likewise…' said Damien.

'Oh, a fellow Scot….'

'Edinburgh, I presume?'

'Born and raised….West coast?'

'About as far west as it gets without crossing the water…So how did *'Fifi'* come about, were you born with it?'

'That's a very personal question.' Said Keith

'I'm Scottish, I'm allowed to ask.'

'It's okay, you're not the first, and no, I was born Fiona, but Fifi sort of stuck.'

'Fair enough…'

'Anyway, Damien, I look forward to working with you.'

'Likewise, I'm sure.'

'So any first impressions…?' Said Michael

'Lots, but I think this has to be an old English garden in the classical style, lots of roses and so on. What about car – parking?'

'There'll be a double garage eventually, where we've parked.'

'I'll allow for that then, otherwise I think I have all I need, at least for sketch - designs.'

'Well, you can always 'phone me.'

'Indeed…'

'I see you drive a pick – up,' said Keith 'does that mean you get your hands dirty sometimes?'

'Quite often, actually, and it's handy, you know, for moving plants around and so on.'

'Sure...'

In due time Fifi Fielding took her leave, and so shortly thereafter did Michael Tillington. Later he would 'phone Elin, who would wish to know his first impressions of their landscape designer, of whom he would give good initial report. Only on returning home would he receive transcript of the third letter written by Jane Tillington to her brother. There was little new that could be learned from the letter, but it was a matter of some coincidence that the garden which had occupied his own thoughts during this day, had also been so much in the thoughts of the woman called Jane, whoever she had been. She had lived in such a different world, and had seen such adversity, but Michael perhaps for the first time began to sense a connection between them, and it was of all things a garden which had begun to forge this connection, regardless of how they and their respective lives were otherwise so different. He had now an image in his mind of a woman walking the grounds of Orchard House on sunny, summer days, in all of her period finery, for she would have been a well - educated and well – to – do woman to have lived in such a house, and her brother, William, who was also her benefactor, would likely have been a man of some wealth and position in seventeenth century society. His frustration at not knowing who she or they had been continued, but there were still two letters to be read and transcribed, and perhaps in the end he would have more idea of them. At least this remained his hope.

Pandora Winterton had time to think. During most week days, Victoria was not available to sit for her portrait, and whilst Pandora could work on the background of the painting, this by no means kept her occupied for the whole day. Otherwise she might take the bus to town, where she had found a coffee shop which sold the most excellent coffee, and where she could smoke her hand – rolled cigarettes outside in the narrow, cobbled lane. The proprietor, whose name was Isaac, referred to her as 'sister', which she found rather endearing, and here she could happily while away some time watching the world go by and letting her thoughts wander where they would, and in large part they would wander to the subject of her latest painting.

She and Victoria Tillington had slept together on occasion whilst she had been painting Victoria's father, and this had been about the business of fulfilling physical and sexual desire, and had in a sense been a matter of opportunism and convenience for both of them. Pandora had been there, they had been drunk enough, so where was the harm in it? The last time, however, had been different. This time, aside from Pandora being mildly intoxicated with marijuana, they had been quite sober, and Victoria had come to her seeking comfort and, well, what? Pandora had loved before, but had never been in love by her definition or understanding of the words. Neither did she regard herself as being essentially homosexual, the great majority of her brief sexual encounters having been with men, which was a different thing, and which fulfilled a quite different need in her. With men, everything from a first look or a first conversation culminated in an end, and the end was really the point of it, and once done both parties had either walked away as good as immediately, or fallen asleep and walked away the next morning, and neither had ever needed or asked for anything else from the other. She had also on occasion shared a bed with female friends simply by virtue of the fact that both had needed somewhere to sleep, but Victoria had her own bed, and had nevertheless come to her, and they could scarce be said to be friends, or lovers, so what were they, and what had happened? Had they crossed a line somewhere without Pandora being aware of it; had she been taken or was she being taken somewhere which she had not taken account of, and was she more to Victoria than she had hitherto assumed? In the morning Pandora had awoken to find

Victoria dressed, and after the briefest farewell she had left to prepare herself for work and for her journey to London, and she had not seen her since. Pandora had risen, showered and then stood before her easel, where she had mixed the lightest blue. She had painted Rose against a dark background, her pale body and the white shroud which partly enwrapped her being in sharp and radiant contrast with the darkness; it had been painting for the nighttime, with all of nights' mystery, but now she painted a blue painting, of a young woman in a blue dress, who would have a different kind of radiance.

It would likely be the weekend before Victoria would sit for her again, so she may not see her until then, unless she made another unscheduled and unexpected appearance in Pandora's temporary living quarters. This was in a sense a strange way to carry on. The Manor House went about its' daily business apparently quite oblivious of Pandora's presence, but this suited her well enough, and she would enjoy her second and once again temporary tenure here, and whilst she waited for her subject to be available she would make the best of her time, and paint only for a few hours a day. The painting was going well enough, and that which currently occupied her thoughts was not the painting itself, but the subject thereof, and more specifically how they actually felt about one another. For the most part her craft was a simple matter; she painted her subject, was paid, and aside from any occasional and temporary dalliance that was an end to it, but her relationship to her latest subject was far more complicated, and had just become more so, not by virtue of the fact that they had had sex, but by virtue of the fact that they had not.

Our story now moves forward to Friday evening, and into a certain omnibus, wherein is seated Peter Shortbody. The bus route was not unfamiliar to him, and he had passed the Saddler's Arms on several occasions, but had never stopped here. He was uncertain, therefore, which bus – stop would be the best at which to alight, so thought it prudent to pass the establishment before standing up to indicate to the driver that he wished to get off. A light shower of rain was falling, which, by the time the bus reached the stop, which as it turned out was some considerable distance beyond the public house, had turned into a deluge. Peter had been uncertain what to wear to such a meeting. He had dropped the twins at Alice's house, telling her only that he would be out for the evening, a statement which had provoked no more than a passing if somewhat questioning look from the children's mother, since for Peter to be going out anywhere of an evening was a fairly uncommon occurrence. No further explanation was asked for, however, and none given. He then returned home and gave consideration to his attire, in the end concluding that a suit would be far too formal, so perhaps casual trousers and a jacket and tie would be best, and in the end he forwent the wearing of a tie. Peter considered that he had a quite good head of hair for a man of his age, which he took uncommon care with the combing of before he left his house by the Green, but in any event by the time he had walked to and had entered the establishment which was the Saddler's Arms, he was soaked to the skin, and any care taken with his appearance had become largely academic.

He saw her immediately; she was sitting alone, and thus, since Peter was more or less exactly on time, she must have arrived early on her journey in the other direction to his. He approached the table, and she looked up at him and smiled. She looked older, of course, than the last time he had seen her, but the smile was the same, as were her eyes, which although no longer bearing sparkly makeup, but rather more sophisticated and subtle mascara and eye - liner, were unmistakably the eyes of Maddie Young.

'Hello….'

'Oh my god, look at you, you're soaking wet!'

'Yes, that would be the rain.'

'Well, Peter Shortbody as ever was…..Unmistakable even when saturated…It's very good to see you, Peter.'

She stood up and despite his somewhat wet condition gave him a hug, which he returned, and which was more physical contact than they had ever had during their years at school together.

'It's good to see you too.'

'Can I get you a drink?'

'It's quite alright, I can manage. May I refresh your glass?'

'It's okay, I've just got here myself.'

'Very well then...'

He went to the bar of the establishment, which was moderately patronized, and ordered a pint of ale. Peter did not habitually drink alcohol, and thought it a quite strange thing that the imbibing of a liquid could alter ones' consciousness and perception of the world, but tonight he would make an exception. Aside from his believing that occasion called for it, he was still feeling somewhat nervous and indeed not a little guilty at this which was after all a secret meeting with another woman, however innocent the meeting might be, so mild intoxication might be helpful in this regard. He had not come here with any intent other than to meet and talk with an old friend, if such she could be called, and there need of course to be nothing physical about the matter. But then she had hugged him, which had immediately added a physical dimension, and had thus changed everything. A hug, however, was only a hug, and people hugged each other all the time with very little reason or provocation, so a hug was quite acceptable, was it not?

He returned to the table and sat opposite her, where she was still smiling and observing him in some detail, as women will do. The world, Peter had long ago concluded, was full of women observing things. Indeed he had mused on occasion that if men such as he could see the world through a woman's eyes, they might give better account of themselves and of their appearance, and might even find the whole matter somewhat intimidating, so things were probably best left as they were. It was also the case that in the general run of things, Peter took account not so much of that which could be observed, but rather that which could not be observed, since it was not there, but in any case he must not let his thoughts become distracted from this moment, for at this moment the woman who had been observing him, and who was by all outward appearances very much here, was now speaking to him.

'I told Fliss that I was meeting you. Do you remember Felicity Bird, she's one of the girls I keep in touch with. She was quite amazed, actually.'

Felicity Bird; a quite tall and rather well – covered girl who giggled a lot; yes he remembered her.

'Yes, I remember Felicity...'

'She's skinny as a rake now, you'd hardly recognize her. You, on the other hand, have hardly changed at all, really. You always looked years older than you were, and now you look years younger than you are.'

'Even when soaking wet...'

'Even then...So this is where you say;' *you haven't changed either, you still look eighteen...'*

'Oh dear, I seem to have missed my cue.'

She laughed, and they shared a moment of light humour.

'So, who else are you still in touch with?'

'Sheila Stevenson I see quite regularly, the three of us meet up a few times a year in various combinations, and I've been on holiday with Fliss a couple of times since the divorce.'

'So is she divorced as well?'

'Yep, we're all three of us single now, although Sheila never married. Otherwise I hear from Fiona Graham occasionally, who's not divorced, and I exchange Christmas cards with Jen Parkinson and Maurine Martin.'

All names which Peter now endeavored to put faces and personalities to. He particularly remembered Sheila Stevenson, who by repute wore her school skirts particularly short, and if the rumours and claims put about by the boys in the sixth form could be believed, was active in a sexual nature behind the boiler - room, and even in the boiler – room during inclement or cold weather. He was somewhat surprised therefore to learn that she had not married; perhaps her reputation had gone before her and proved an impediment to her success in the matter of longer term relationships, or perhaps she had found another boiler room somewhere. The others he remembered less well, but he remembered them nonetheless, and all contrived to form an overall impression in his mind of his last years at school, or at least the female element thereof.

'So what happened, if I may ask…I mean why did you divorce?'

'Well, you know, it's familiar story, David and I were married at twenty, by which time I was pregnant with Olivia, and Charlie turned up two years later, so we never really had a chance to live, you know? After that it was just a slow drift apart, and we divorced by mutual consent when we were both thirty. It wasn't a good ten years, really, but we took joint responsibility for the kids, and we're still in touch, but rarely see one another. Charlie's married now and Cynthia, his much younger wife, is expecting their first child, but Oli hasn't found love yet, which is a mystery to everyone because she's a lovely girl. The children both stayed in the county, and I now live in a small terraced house in darkest Crowhurst, with a few years to go on the mortgage and two weeks away in the sun a couple of times a year, and that about sums me up, really.'

'You wrote a novel…'

'Well yes, there's that, but it will probably be the one and only.

So what about you? I have to say that there was a lot of speculation amongst us sixth – form girls as to how you'd turn out.'

'Really…? Why….?'

'Well you know, there were the cool guys on one side, or the guys that thought they were cool, anyway, who would have been all over us girls given the chance, then there were the nerds on the other, but you never really fitted in anywhere.'

'More *'nerd'* than cool, I daresay.'

'Oh I don't know, you just never gave anybody a chance. You were hopelessly shy, for one thing, and always kept yourself to yourself, but nobody thought you were a nerd….You were just always an enigma, but there were a couple of us girls who would have fallen for your charms had you allowed us to.'

'I see…Well I must say I'm surprised to hear that.'

'Yes, I daresay you are…Anyway, shall we eat? I'll give you the dirt on a few people over dinner, that's if you've dried out enough to think about food?'

'Yes, I think so…'

'And I want to know all about how you became a father at, what, fifty six years old? I've been told to report back with as much information as possible, otherwise the others will never forgive me. Anyway, I'm interested, and I'm also interested as to why you contacted me…'

They ate, respectively lasagna and a baked potato with cheese and salad, and they talked as they ate. Peter bought another round of drinks, and would consume three pints of ale during the evening, which was more alcohol than he had drunk in a long count of years. He told her about Alice and the twins, and of their domestic circumstances, and something about life in the village, whist she regaled him with more detail about her life, and the lives of her children. Despite retaining her good looks into later adulthood, Maddie Young had apparently not formed any further romantic attachment since the ending of her marriage, but she had in fact visited much of the world during her years as an air stewardess.

When it became time to leave, she ordered two taxis via her mobile telephone, which arrived only a few minutes later. Outside the evening was now dry, and it was time for their farewell.

'You still haven't told me, you know?'

'What about...?'

'Why it was that after all this time you decided to look me up. Still, that can wait 'til next time.'

'Yes....Next time.'

'That is of course if you want to meet again?'

'Oh, yes, absolutely...'

'Good, well goodnight then, Peter.'

'She reached up and kissed him gently on the mouth, as if it were a quite natural thing to do.'

''Phone me, okay?'

'Yes...Yes, I'll do that...'

'I'll have to thank you properly one day for helping me with my maths homework.'

'Oh, it was nothing.'

'I know, and I could have managed quite well on my own, you know?'

A final smile and she turned and got into her taxi.

On the ride home, Peter tried to order his thoughts as to how the evening had gone, which was difficult in view of the fact that he had drunk three pints of ale, and his thought processes, which could be wayward enough at the best of times, refused to be brought to heel. In his perception she had changed now, from an eighteen year old schoolgirl to a woman in her maturity, which was something, at least, but beyond that he was in murky waters. She had been flirting with him, of that there was no doubt, and the revelation that she had not really needed help with her mathematics homework had come of something of a surprise to him, to say the least of it, and now she wanted to see him again. And then there was Alice, of course, whom he had assumed would be the only significant woman in the rest of his life, but after this evening even that assumption was no longer set in stone, but rather had now been shaken to its' foundation. It had only been one meeting, so he must not allow himself to be carried away by unnecessary flights of fancy. A dream was only a dream, after all, and a kiss was only a kiss, but things which were only something were something, nonetheless.

Sharon had now only one means by which she could discover where the witch Rebecca was living. She could have asked people in the village, of course, but to do so without arousing suspicion or drawing unwanted attention to herself would have been difficult, and so to this end she went to the courtyard in which was Rebecca's studio, where having established that Rebecca was there, she waited in a nearby café; from here she had a view of the only way in or out of the courtyard, and she would follow her when she left. She watched as the other artisans departed at the end of their days' work, but Rebecca did not leave. Afternoon turned into evening, the café closed for business, and still she had no sign of her. She moved into the courtyard, and under cover of darkness she waited, and watched. Once, Rebecca left the studio to put her rubbish out into the communal bin, and now she was but a few paces away, but Rebecca returned to the studio and closed the door. Still, with the patience of the hunter, Sharon waited, and now the only sound from within were the brief crying of a baby, and then, quite late in the evening, all lights within the studio were extinguished, and all was quiet. She moved silently to the door, and listened intently, but there was no sound. So, this was where she now slept; this was better, she was isolated here and quite alone. In the village she had protection, but here she would be beyond help. There was no coven nearby; no sign of any other witches that Sharon had seen during her time in the village, so perhaps after all Rebecca and the other witch had acted alone when they had burned Farthing's Well, and murdered her friends. Anyway it mattered not; it was the witch Rebecca whom she sought, she who Sharon had saved from the flames, but now she had her, and she would return here soon, once she had made herself ready. She left as quietly as she had come, and walked through the darkness of the by now near empty streets of the old town; the huntress had cornered her prey, and now it was just a matter of time.

Chapter 17

TEARS AND LAUGHTER

The day of Daphne's funeral dawned bright and clear, with a light breeze blowing from the west. Modestly cut black dresses and dark suits were taken from dark wardrobes and put out to air, telephone calls were made to finalize arrangements, and to organize the transportation of people from the village to the church, and everyone from within the small community of Middlewapping who was to attend made themselves ready, and spoke to one another in hushed and respectful tones.

In the morning Emily milked her goats and processed her cheese, whilst Will washed the Land Rover. The funeral service was scheduled for two o'clock, and having carried out her morning duties, Emily 'phoned Roberts and Maybridge, the funeral directors, and then the Reverend Mark Inman, to ensure that all final arrangements were made, and that all would go to plan.

In contrast to St Peter's Church, which was large and austere, and situated in the town, St Stephen's Church was a small church in a deeply rural location, which had its' foundations in the fifteenth century, the present church having been built some two hundred years later. Here it was that Daphne had attended morning service each Sunday, since her church in Middlewapping had been bought by a rock star and was no longer a holy place, and here would she be laid to rest.

Keith and Meadow would naturally attend, although Meadow on the whole did not do well at funerals. Basil had been persuaded to go, and would take Emma, whose sister, Sandra, would also be there. Rosemary had 'phoned Quentin, who had worked late on the previous night; they had planned to meet on this day, but she had told him that he really did not need to come. Quentin, however, had insisted that he would be there, based on the principle that he would sooner be with her at a funeral than not be with her at all, and anyway it would serve as a further opportunity to him to meet people from her village, and Rosie had been glad of his coming. Then, in the late morning, Meadow had received a telephone call which gave her day an almost entirely new perspective, and the telephone call was from Tara.

'Hi mum, guess what....We've just landed at Heathrow.'

'What...?'

'I know, it's unbelievable, really, but Ash insisted that we fly back, so here we are, and I had no reception so couldn't let you know; it was all very last – minute as you may imagine, but anyway we've got a few days between gigs so here we are. Samantha's here, and so's Evie, who's going to visit friends, so there'll be three of us at the funeral.'

'Oh my stars...Ash insisted? I mean I know he and Daphne were friends, and more unlikely friends I can hardly imagine, but, well, I mean I'm absolutely delighted, of course, but I can.... So when will you get here, the wedding's at two....I mean the funeral's at two...'

'Calm down, mum...We're just waiting for luggage, Sam's bought some stuff over, but we should be able to get there in time, although we may have to go straight to the church. We can shower and change here, I've brought the only black thing I've got, which is a bit short to be honest, but it'll have to do.'

'Yes, of course, whatever, but....I still really can't believe this...'

'Centre yourself, mother, like you're always telling us to do, this isn't like you. Anyway, listen, is anything happening afterwards?'

'Well no, Emily tried I think, but the village hall was already booked, and anyway it's a deathly place, if you'll excuse the expression, and nowhere else half suitable was available at short notice. There's really nowhere in the village big enough for a reception, or wake, or whatever one calls it.'

'Right, well look, Ash thinks we should have a sort of get – together on the village Green, and I think it's a great idea. The weather looked okay flying in, although I haven't been outside yet.'

'It's a beautiful day, but what sort of get – together, there'll be no food or drink.'

'Couldn't you send someone to the supermarket, or wholesaler or whatever, pick up some wine and whatever else? Ash'll pay for everything, but we won't have any time to get anything organized between now and getting there.'

'Well yes, I suppose we could….'

'Brilliant…I'll leave it with you then. Gotta go, see you at the church…Oh fuck, hang on, which church is it?'

'St Stephen's Church, just outside Brookfield...'

'Okay, we'll find it, see you later, love you….'

'Love you too, honey…'

The call ended, just as Keith, Basil and Emma entered the bus, to find Meadow in thoughtful pose and expression.

'Who was that?'

'That was your eldest daughter, she's just landed at Heathrow.'

'What…?'

'That's what I said. It was Ash's idea to come, apparently. She, Ash and Samantha are going to meet us at the church.'

'Bloody hell…I mean it's great news, but why didn't she tell us she was coming?'

'She couldn't, apparently, but I mean imagine dropping everything in the middle of a world – tour just to come to Daphne's funeral.'

'Guy was always well grounded…I mean we all knew that he and Daphne got along well, but it obviously went deeper than we thought.'

'Apparently so….and by the way Tara thinks we should organize an event afterwards on the Green, and I said we would.'

'What kind of an event?'

'I don't know, just people getting together and, well, having an event, you know?'

'Yeah, well it's a good idea, actually. I don't know why none of us thought of it, but we'll need booze and so on.'

'I know…Someone will have to go and buy wine and soft drinks, and some kind of finger – food.'

'I'll do it,' said Basil 'I am willing to forgo the pleasure of attending the funeral for the good of the community at large. Emma and I will sally forth to the supermarket, and have everything set up by the time you get back.'

'Everyone's car will be at the church.'

'Then I will employ the services of a Hackney – Carriage. How many people do you reckon will be there?'

'I've no idea, but we ought to allow for thirty or forty, I suppose, I mean it'll have to be a kind of free – for – all, not just for people who went to the funeral. Ash says he'll pay for everything.'

'Then let's call it fifty. I'll get four cases of wine, two white, one red and one pink, and loads of orange juice, fizzy water and so on.'

'You'll have to buy things that people can walk about eating, and not everyone's vegetarian, don't forget.'

'Pork pies, that's the answer….Some of those cool mushroom things coated in breadcrumbs, that kind of thing.'

'Are you sure you're up for this, basil?'

'Mum, I'm seventeen, you know…I know how to shop. Why only the other day I bought myself a bar of chocolate without assistance from others.'

'It's okay, we can handle it.' Said Emma

'Yes, well you'll need to be the sensible one, Emma.'

'Thanks for the vote of confidence…' Said Basil

'What do you think, Keith?'

'Sure, go for it you two. How are we going to pay for it?'

'I'll use my debit – card.' Said Emma

'Well that's settled then.' Said Keith

'I'll 'phone Emily, tell her what's happening.'

'Better 'phone a few other people as well.'

'Yes, of course….'

And thus was it decided, and without further ado Basil and Emma made ready to depart, whilst Meadow retired to the bedroom and began to prepare herself for the funeral. To find herself so unexpectedly happy on such a day gave Meadow pause for thought, and to chastise herself. Her friend Daphne was dead, she who had bequeathed ten thousand pounds to her, and she was just about to attend her funeral, so she had no business feeling this good. This was a day for sadness, but Tara was coming home, maybe for a few days, so how could she be anything other than happy? Keith entered the room, to find his beloved dressed only in the briefest and sheerest of underpants.

'I'm confused, Keith….'

'Yeah, me too, now….Until now I was thinking about funerals…'

'I mean I can't make myself feel unhappy anymore.'

'That's a drag…'

She came and put her arms around him, he touched her breast.

'Down boy, we've got a funeral to go to, remember, and our daughter's coming home.'

'Yeah, there's that, and all of that happens later, but there's also you dressed like that, which is my more immediate consideration.'

'I'm hardly dressed…'

'My point exactly…'

'These are the only pair of black knickers I could lay my hands on, and one always wears black to funerals.'

'Maybe we should go to more funerals…And one would quite like to lay ones' hands on them as well, if one might make so bold.'

'One may not, but one seems to be in any case, which is very forward of you, if I might say so.'

'Anyway what's Tara coming home got to do with anything? She wouldn't mind, our daughter knows about sex, she even sings songs about it.'

She smiled.

'You make me laugh at the funeral and I'll kill you, you know that, don't you?'

'I wouldn't know how…'

'And would you please remove your hand from my breast… Christ, Keith, say something depressing, for heaven's sake.'

'I'm just about to remove my hand from your breast, I find that thought depressing.'

'Well, don't then.'

'You just told me to.'

'So now who's confused…? Try again.'

'Ummm…. I can't think of anything.'

She laughed, and they laughed together as she let him go and walked away barefoot across the ruffled sheets of the futon in which they slept each night.

'Do you really think Bas'll be okay handling the catering?'

'Of course, takes after his dad, does Basil.'

'You're rubbish at shopping…'

'I've got you, he's got Emma, it's the same kind of deal.'

'Well, if you say so….Oh god this is hopeless, how can I be unhappy when I've got so much to be happy about?'

'Yeah, it's a dilemma, I grant you, still, we must do our best, in the end it's all we can do, really.'

On the day before the funeral, Louise had arrived by taxi at the cottage down the lane in the late afternoon, carrying a suitcase and two overcoats. Percival had offered to hire a car or borrow Will's Land Rover to help her move out of her rented room in her shared house, but she had said that she could manage, and so she had managed. She placed her belongings on the lounge floor, said hello to Lulu, and then turned her attention to Percival, who had just walked in from the kitchen.

'Well, there it is then.'

'There's what?'

'The sum total of my worldly possessions. Not much to show for forty two years, is it?'

'Build on that…'

'I am now officially homeless, so if you tell me you've just married the woman next door then I'm buggered.'

'There isn't a woman next door.'

'Phew, lucky me then….'

'I just made lentil hot – pot.'

'So is this the beginning of our domestic bliss?'

'Yeah, I guess….I mean I think it can loosely be described as hot – pot, I put onions, herbs and tomatoes and stuff in, it, and it looks a bit like soup, but I'm not really sure what the difference is.'

'Didn't you follow the recipe?'

'Recipes are for wimps. I've got good bread to eat with it.'

'Well that might rescue us then, but what I need most right now is a shower and sex, and not necessarily in that order, so you can have me as I am or clean.'

'What about the hot – pot?'

'You really know how to turn a girls' head, don't you, but I won't take much wooing at the moment, so you can forget about the domestic bliss idea for now and come here.'

They moved to each other, she put her arms around his shoulders and he held her to him.

'Hello, new man in my life.'

'Hi…'

'This is us, you know? The new beginning of us…'

'I know.'

'And that's my bum you've got your hands on.'

'It's all part of the wooing process.'

'I see, well, it seems to be working, so I'm going to get cleaned up, then let's get dirty.'

'Don't you want to unpack first?'

'Later, sweetheart…'

Later, they were sitting opposite one another at the dining table, having just eaten something like lentil hot – pot, accompanied by red wine and good bread, the hot – pot having in their collective opinion tasted delicious, despite any difficulty in its' culinary categorization. Louise had still not unpacked her suitcase, and was wearing Percival's dressing gown, which was far too big for her and she had had to turn the sleeves up, but when it comes to dressing gowns such things do not really matter. She had secured a position with her company in Brighton, to whence she would commute daily for the time being, pending any transfer nearer to home. This was not an easy commute, there being no direct rail – link from Queenswood Station, and nor was it cheap, particularly in relation to the wage which she would earn out of London, so the situation was not ideal, but she liked Brighton and would live with the circumstances for now.

'God, I'm bushed….I think this is where we cuddle up on the sofa and watch television, isn't it, basking in the afterglow of our new – found love?'

'Yeah, pity we don't have a sofa, or a television for that matter.'

'So what happened to domestic bliss?'

'It's on hold pending the buying of furniture.'

'We need to work on that. Let's go to one of those terrible out – of – town furniture warehouses tomorrow, shall we?'

'Actually I can't tomorrow, well maybe in the morning, but I've got a funeral to go to in the afternoon.'

'Who died?'

'Daphne, the woman who lived in the big brick house...She was a nice old dear, wrote terrible poetry.'

'Yes, I know Daphne, I mean not well, but...Christ, what did she die of?'

'Cancer, I believe, she'd been ill for a while but in the end it was very sudden.'

'Bloody hell....So the first time I arrive here the house has been virtually destroyed, and this time I have to go to a funeral. A girl could get quite put off the idea...So now I have to go to town in the morning and buy a black frock.'

'You don't have to come.'

'Of course I'll come, it'll be a good chance for me to meet everybody again anyway, but I haven't forgotten that you promised me a beach soon, and I don't mean Brighton.'

'I'll work on that, too.'

'Well then, in the absence of any soft – furnishings around here I suppose we might as well go back to bed.'

Which they did, and they fell asleep in each other's arms on the first night of their new lives together, which notwithstanding any initial setbacks, both considered was a fine thing indeed.

Those from the village who had assembled at the church had done so by virtue of having been driven there by Will, Damien and Keith, who had driven Daphne's 2CV, Damien and Will having made two trips in their respective Land Rovers in order to ferry the mourners. This may not have been the most comfortable or appropriate means of transport, particularly since Damien had no permanent seats in the rear of his vehicle, and people sat on sand or cement bags which were temporarily covered in old blankets, but nobody complained, and all arrived at the church looking reasonably well turned out. Here were Keith, Meadow and Rosemary, who had come with Quentin,

Sandra Fox, Peter Shortbody, Alice having stayed at home with the twins, and who would join the party on the Green later, Constance and Alfred, Meadow's father, Reginald, who had bought Gwendolyn, Percival and Louise, who had yesterday taken up residence at the cottage down the lane, Ron and Barbara, Damien and Sophia, and Will and Emily. Otherwise in the small congregation were some of those who had attended the church during Daphne's time there, and had thus come to know her. The short service began in the church, and as yet there was no sign of Tara, but she had shortly before let Meadow know that they were well on their way, and she and Keith sat at the back of the church to await their arrival. Two hymns, prayers and a short sermon by the Reverend Mark saw the service finished, and mid – way through the final hymn, Tara stood in the arched doorway and signaled to her mother, who with Keith went quietly out from the dark, cool church and into the fine afternoon sunshine. Mother and daughter hugged, and all said their greetings.

'Christ I'm sorry, we were ages at the airport and had to wait for a taxi.'

'It's okay, my love, you're here now, and she's not buried yet. Hello Ash, it's really good to see you…'

'Yeah, like you too, man.'

'And it's good of you to come so far, actually.'

'Had to do it, you know?'

'Yes, of course…We may as well stay outside now…Keith, I think you may be needed.'

A few minutes later the coffin was carried out of the church, Keith, Damien, Will, Ron, Peter and Percival being the six bearers, and all now processed through the old graveyard to the place which had been made ready, at the edge of the graveyard beside the ancient flint wall which marked its' boundary. Meadow and Tara hung back, and Tara walked beside her mother, and they spoke quietly together with bowed heads.

'Are you okay, mum?'

'Yes, I think so....I see what you mean about the dress, it is a bit short isn't it?'

'It was the best I could do, it was either this or pink sequins, you know?'

They laughed quietly in their intimacy.

'Don't get me going, for heaven's sake...It's so good to see you, my love.'

'You too...'

'So how's America?'

'Well, musically it's going fine, and we're well received everywhere, but I wouldn't rush back there. I fell in love with the Far East, that's the trouble, and there are loads of places there I want to go back to, just to go there, you know?'

'Of course, and I'm sure you will...'

'I think I'll plan a trip when this is all over. Anyway we've only got a few more gigs in the States, then we start the European part of the tour, which is much shorter but more frantic, we've got loads of gigs in quick succession, but I'll try to fly home sometimes between shows, whenever we have breaks, you know?'

'Of course, and it'll be nice to have you nearer home, anyway.'

'Everyone's feeling homesick now, to be honest, and it's starting to tell. I mean we all get along fine, even Ash and Al, but people are starting to get a bit tetchy. It's tiring, you know, and Ash, Al and Rick in particular are starting to feel it, I think. To maintain the level of performance takes its' toll on everyone, and the joy and adventure of foreign travel are starting to wear a bit thin, you might say, and the original band members have been around this block a few times anyway.'

'Yes, of course they have...'

'Samantha's a rock, and she holds Ash together, and as long as Ash is together then the rest sort of follow. The longer you spend with him the more you realize what a special person he is, and as soon as you told me that Daphne had died, he wanted to be here for this, which really surprised me.'

'I think it surprised all of us. Oh, I think we're here…'

The coffin was laid beside the rectangular hole which had been dug for it, and made ready to be lowered, whilst the small assembly took their places around it at a respectful distance. The Reverend Mark said a few words, and then offered that anyone else who wished to speak could now do so. All was quiet for a moment, and then Ashley spoke.

'Yeah, I'd like to say something….'

All eyes turned briefly to him before heads were bowed respectfully again.

'Like, Daphne was a good person, you know. She understood the music.'

That was all, apparently, but it was enough, and those who were going to weep now did so, including Emily, Meadow and Tarragon, but Ash had in fact not quite finished. He took a somewhat crumpled sheet of paper from his jacket pocket, and held it up briefly.

'This is like, a list of songs which Daphne once gave me. She called it our greatest hits, and anyway they were her favourite DMW songs, I guess. So I'm going to talk to the record company and have them release the songs as an album, which we've never done before. All profits will be sent to whatever charities Daphne left money to. May she rest in peace, or whatever…. Lady had a good spirit.'

Through her tears, Meadow gave Tara an enquiring look, which only received a shrug of the shoulders in response; Tara had no idea that he was going to do this. There was now another brief silence, but now Emily spoke.

'Ummm, Daphne asked that a poem be read out at her funeral. She wrote it just before…Anyway….'

She held the paper and was about to read, but then;

'I'm sorry, I can't….'

She gave the paper to Will, who had not read the poem before; he cleared his throat.

'Oh death, that I do now embrace, as thou….'

Will did his best, but in the tense and emotionally charged atmosphere the desire to laugh was almost beyond him to control. He cleared his throat once more, and tried again.

'Sorry…*Oh death….Oh death that I do now embrace, as thou embraceth me, whither….whither thou leadest….whither thou leadest, there also shall I be. For life and death are but the same…'*

In the end it was hopeless, and whether it was the poem or Will's attempt to read it aloud, amongst those who knew him, and had known Daphne's poetry, a state of something like collective hysteria now set in, and certain of the congregation collapsed in uncontrolled laughter, and some withdrew to a safer distance. Those not from the village wondered what was going on, and The Reverend Mark, who in all of his years of leading funeral services had never witnessed anything like this, decided that the matter was best brought to a close. He began to speak the standard text, which was the cue for the coffin to be lowered into the ground, and so it was. By the final *'amen'* the good people of Middlewapping were in no state to remain, and all hope of solemnity was a distant memory, so they left, and collectively made for the car park.

'Christ, I'm sorry Em, I just couldn't hold it together.'

'What am I going to do with the poem now, nobody even heard it.'

'I'll photocopy it and hand it out, and I'll come back here alone when she's all done and say sorry.'

'Yes, I think you'd better.'

'You couldn't do it either, I wasn't expecting that, you know?'

'I know….Anyway we'd better start getting people in cars. I'll stay here and go on the last trip.'

On the way home, Will had Percival beside him and Louise, Sandra and Barbara in the back.

'Well, I really fucked that up…'

The statement was spoken to all present, but it had been addressed to Percival.

'Don't beat yourself up, it wasn't only you, and nobody could have done it.'

'Still, I feel like an idiot now.'

'It's okay, Will, it was Daphne, you know? This was personal, and everyone knew Daphne, and how bad her poetry was. I think even she knew how bad her poetry was, she would have been okay about it. I mean we collectively bury our dead, but it's only ritual, and what matters is how we each feel about the person. Daphne's dead, and everyone's sorry that Daphne's dead, and everybody knows that everyone's sorry she's dead, and she knew you and Em, which is why she left you the house.'

'Yeah, it wasn't a great way to say thanks, was it, laughing at her…'

'Nobody was laughing at Daphne, that's my point.'

'I'll still be in the doghouse about it, I expect.'

'Em'll come 'round, it's just funerals, you know…Everyone's wired – up, and in years to come we won't remember the day as being a sad day.'

'Yeah, we'll remember how everyone pissed themselves laughing.'

'Which is better, don't you think? It could have been her master – stroke.'

'What, you think she set us up?'

'Could be, there was more to Daphne than just Daphne, you know?'

Keith, Meadow and Emily were amongst those left in the car – park awaiting the return of the vehicles, and now these three came together.

'Well, that went off okay.' Said Keith

'What, you mean apart from everyone laughing?' Said Emily

'Oh come on, Em, that was just some bullshit, everyone was crying as well, you know? Will did his best, Christ, I couldn't have put two words of it together.'

'Keith's right, Emily' said Meadow 'you mustn't blame Will, he was in an impossible situation.'

'Which I put him in…'

'You're not to blame either. I mean I'm always sad when people who I love die, but Keith'll tell you that I always laugh at funerals, I just can't help myself.'

'It was a fit of collective hysteria waiting to happen,' said Keith 'it means nothing, forget it.'

'I'll try…So anyway, we're all meeting on the Green now, yes?'

'Yes,' said Meadow 'I should have gone with the first convoy, make sure that out dear son hasn't messed up the catering arrangements.'

'Have faith,' said Keith 'it'll be fine.'

Nobody from the Manor House would attend Daphne's funeral. Lady Beatrice had met Daphne once, on the occasion of Daphne having told her that Victoria was dangerously ill having tried to commit suicide, but otherwise there had been no contact between them. Emily had telephoned Victoria out of courtesy to tell her the news, and flowers would be sent, but this was all that would be done. In any case, for Victoria this was a 'blue dress day', and she would sit two or three times which amounted to several hours of the day whilst her portrait was being painted. In the warm light of day, nothing was said about their last night spent together, and certainly Pandora would not be the one to raise the matter. She was, after all, ostensibly there in her paid professional capacity as an artist, and upon this did she now concentrate all of her energy and emotion; if Victoria raised the matter, or if she turned up unexpectedly again, then words would be spoken, but for now Pandora let the matter be.

Michael had had more indirect contact with Daphne than the rest of his family, by dint of having seen her on cricket days during the last summer, but it would not be expected that he would attend. In any event but he had other things on his mind, for on this day Elin had travelled from Canterbury, and they would go together to Orchard House. This would in fact be the first time they would be alone there, and it is here that we now join them.

Some parts of the upper storey were still missing floorboards, but they had access to all rooms, and Elin inspected each one carefully, gaining imagined impressions of how each would look in the end. Michael ran the generator for tea, over which detailed discussions were held regarding certain aspects of the renovation, and certain decisions were made which could be relayed to Keith that week. This done, Elin's thoughts turned somewhat uncharacteristically to more esoteric matters.

'I wonder where she sat, and in which room…'

'Who..?'

'Jane, whoever she had been. I wonder where she wrote the letters. I try hard to imagine her.'

'Yes…'

'I so much love your English history. I very much hope that the last letters reveal who she was.'

'So do I...Just a surname would help, then perhaps we could try to trace her.'

'I also love this house, Michael, and I believe that we will be very happy here. Do your parents suspect that you and I will live here?'

'I don't know, probably, not much gets past the old man to be honest. I suppose we should tell them sometime, officially announce our engagement and so on. There doesn't seem much point in not telling them, does there?'

'Very well then, we will tell them soon, and I will inform my parents also, but we must tell them together.'

'Yes, of course...Well, we'll tell them, then, when the moment feels right.'

'Yes, when the moment feels right.'

Catering arrangements had in fact been quite adequately seen to by Basil and Emma, and by the time the last of those who had attended the funeral had been delivered to the village Green, the space nearest to Daphne's previous residence was a mass of people, who were variously standing or sitting in small groups amongst cardboard crates of wine, orange juice and other beverages which could be drunk from paper cups, and upturned cardboard boxes, upon which was food which could be eaten without the aid of any implement. Basil had gone so far as to bring his mobile telephone and some small speakers, through which was playing some gentle and ambient background music. Meadow was amongst the last to arrive, and having kicked off her funeral shoes she sought out her son, who was at the time filling a large paper plate with sausage rolls.

'You've done well, sweetheart.'

'Yeah, well, there was nothing to it, really, and Emma was there to make sure there weren't any glaring omissions or excesses. I may have overdone the custard – tarts, but deep down that was probably to make sure there'd be some left over. I went for mid – range kind of wines which shouldn't be offensive to even the most discerning pallet.'

Meadow smiled at her only son.

'I'm sure all will be fine.'

'So how was the funeral, anyway? I hear Will made fools of everyone.'

'It really wasn't his fault, but yes, we did all rather contrive to mess things up.'

'Yeah, well, to read one of Daphne's poems aloud without laughing would be bad enough at the best of times, but under those circumstances it would be nigh – on impossible I would think.'

'Anyway, that's over now, and I'm sure a lot of us will go back to pay our respects when she's properly buried and all's quiet.'

'I daresay she was given a good Christian send – off by the heathens.'

'She had a lot of friends there, that's the most important thing. Anyway have you got the receipt for the food and drink, and you must let me know how much the taxi was, I'll catch Ash later.'

'Sure…Here….'

Basil handed her a till receipt, upon which had been scribbled an account of all expenses incurred.

'So anyway, this part of the day seems to be going well, everyone seems to be having a fine old time.'

'Yes, they do….'

'You've gone thoughtful, mother.'

'What…? Oh well, I was just thinking about what Ash did. Has anyone told you what he did?'

Meadow had been present when Daphne had given Ash the piece of paper upon which the song titles were written, but she had not thought of it since, for why should she? Ash was as she recalled quite damning of the idea of a *'greatest hits'* album at the time, but he had kept the piece of paper nonetheless.

'You mean releasing the album? Guy's something else, isn't he?'

'Yes, he is….I really can't think of a better legacy for Daphne, or anything that she would have wanted more. So are you okay then?'

'Yeah, I'm cool. I'll keep an eye on things, make sure we don't run out of cheese – fingers, you go circulate, you're good at that.'

She smiled again and departed, and next came upon Reginald, who was standing to the edge of the congregation with Gwendolyn; both of them were drinking orange juice.

'Hi, Reginald...'

'Hello...'

'I'm sorry we didn't have a chance to talk at the funeral. Well, aren't you going to introduce me, then?'

'Yes, this is Gwendolyn, who once cleaned my house, but doesn't anymore.'

'Hello Gwendolyn, I'm pleased to meet you at last, I'm Meadow, I run the delicatessen.'

The two women smiled, and gently and briefly held hands.

'Hello, Reginald has told me a great deal about you, and about everybody, actually. It's good to put some faces to names.'

'Yes, I'm sure, and I'm sorry it has to be under these circumstances, of course, but I'm sure we're all glad to welcome you into our small community. We're an eclectic bunch, but harmless enough, on the whole.'

'Yes,' said Reginald 'apart from the people who have unfortunately killed other people.'

Meadow laughed gently, if a little awkwardly, since she herself and quite unbeknownst to Reginald could be counted in that particular number.

'Well, we can't all be perfect all the time, can we? Come on, let me introduce you to some people.'

'So am I forgiven, then?'

Will and Emily had found each other, and Will was keen to know where he now stood after the poetry reading.

'I suppose so, seeing as how we're at a funeral, or wake, or whatever this is.'

'If we hadn't been at a funeral I wouldn't have done anything to be forgiven for.'

'Well, I forgive you anyway, since everyone else seems to have done. In fact you seem to have become a bit of a celebrity.'

'The man who dared to laugh….I'll go down in folk legend.'

'I wouldn't go that far, and don't sound so proud of yourself or I'll unforgive you.'

'The unforgiven man who dared to laugh…Yeah, that has a certain ring to it. Hey, Em, that's our house there.'

'Don't….I mean this is bloody surreal enough as it is.'

'What is?'

'People having a jolly time outside the house of the person who just died….I mean it's like she's going to walk out of the front door at any moment, or something. It's creeping me out, to be honest. And then there's Sally's house all closed up, and number seven…'

'Rebecca's gone now, and we were okay living there, Em, those are good memories.'

'Yes, except when I killed someone, and that was the reason that Daphne and I got close, and how it came to be that we got the house. It's all just too weird, and I can't stop thinking about Rose, you know, and how beautiful and tragic she was. There are too many ghosts…Too many people have died here, Will.'

'That's just life, you know….I mean…Okay it's death, but like Daphne said in the poem, *'life and death are but the same…"*

'Shut up, and stop being so insensitive, it isn't like you.'

'I'm sorry, but you know, life's good, Em, and everything's okay, you know?'

'I know, but….I don't want it, Will.'

'What don't you want?'

'I don't want the house. I mean, sell it, or whatever, but I don't want to go in there anymore. It's a house for dead people, full of dead people's furniture, and, well, I just don't want it, I've made up my mind.'

'Okay….I mean, sure, Em, whatever….We'll put it on the market immediately if that's what you want.'

'Yes, that's what I want.'

'We'll work on it this week.'

'Promise…?'

'Promise...'

'What are you two talking so earnestly about?'

This was Percival, who with Louise had now approached them.

'We were just talking about the house.' Said Will

'You don't have a key with you, do you, I could do with a pee, as I'm sure could some other people. It's a pity the pub's not open Sunday afternoons.'

'No, sorry...'

'You can't go peeing in her house.' Said Emily

'Why not..?'

'I don't know, it seems disrespectful, why don't you ask Sandra, I'm sure she'll open the house for you.'

'Sure, okay…Although I don't know her that well.'

'I'll ask her then.'

Emily took her temporary leave.

'She okay….?' Said Percival

'She's not taking the whole thing very well, to be honest…'

'No, well, of all of us she was probably the closest to Daphne, but she got a house out of the deal, so it's not all bad news.'

'Sure….I suppose not…'

'Who's that guy over there?'

This was Keith, who was addressing Meadow. Such a private gathering in such a public place was bound to attract the attention of people passing by, and Keith, together with Ron, had taken it upon himself to act as bouncer, and to politely ask anyone not invited to leave. The problem was that nobody had actually been invited, and this was after all a public open space, and there were people from the estate who could legitimately claim friendship to those present, so categorization was at times an imprecise thing.

'That's Barrington, he lives in Percival's house. Haven't you seen him before?'

'Thought I recognized him…So he's cool then, is he?'

'Yes, he's cool. Keith, where's Rosie?'

'No idea, haven't seen her for a bit.'

'No, nor have I, and I didn't see her leave…'

Barrington was amongst those who had not attended the funeral, but thought it appropriate to join the congregation nonetheless. Barrington had had no further contact with Miranda Spool. He had 'phoned her on three occasions, but there had been no reply, and she had not returned his calls. He had thus concluded that their relationship was over, and was recovering himself well enough after the fact.; the young woman who had been so significant in the way his life had gone since their brief and unusual encounter at university would no longer be a part of that life, so there it was, and there was nothing more to be done. Barrington was in fact and in any case at this moment feeling somewhat distracted by a quite different encounter which had just occurred. A certain young lady had passed him by and smiled, and a brief conversation had ensued.

'Hi…'

'Hello, I'm Barrington.'

'Yes, I know.'

'We've lived a few doors from each other for a while, now, and we've never really met, have we?'

'No, and that's a pity, don't you think?'

'Yes, it is…'

At that moment their conversation was interrupted.

'Sands, any chance you could let people in to use the loo…? Percival was asking.'

'Sure, okay Em.'

Sandra walked away, but she did not quite walk away, and in the brief delay Barrington was emboldened to speak.

'So, uuum, let's have coffee together sometime, shall we?'

'Yes, I'd like that.'

And now she was gone, and Barrington was feeling distracted. There are moments and encounters in people's lives when it is not so much that which is said, but how it is said, and Barrington was left with the distinct impression that he had just shared such a moment with Sandra Fox. He knew little about her, other than that she was at university but was currently living at her parents' house, and that she had recently been quite seriously ill. She seemed well enough now, however, in fact she appeared quite radiant in her young and undoubted beauty. He did not speak to her again on this day, but determined to put that to rights as soon as may be, and decided that for now another cup of wine would be in order.

Also amongst those who had not been expected to attend the religious aspects of the day, and who in any case would not have understood them, were Bronwyn and Elizabeth, who had been brought by Alice, and who worked their young charm on those assembled on the Green. They were dressed in matching yellow summer frocks and white shoes, and each made the most of such an unusual gathering of people, Bronwyn interacting noisily with all whom she met, whilst Elizabeth rather observed the congregation in her detached and thoughtful way, wondering perhaps why these people were here, who had not been here before.

'I hate wearing black, especially on such a lovely day, I think I'll go home and change.'

'Sure, okay.'

Rosemary had used this occasion to introduce her beaux to such people as she thought appropriate, and thus had Quentin become acquainted with certain people whom Rosie had talked about with him. She had by now spent a little time with her sister, Tarragon, with whom she had promised to speak further later, and who had now rejoined Ashley and Samantha, who were presently sitting on the grass with Basil and Emma.

'So, are you coming, then?'

'Yes, of course.'

They walked together to the main road, and from thence down the lane to the bus, or in fact on this occasion straight to the trailer, where Rosemary slept. They stepped inside, where they kissed, and where between them they gently and without need of words removed her dress. Quentin had by now filled his paper cup three times with wine, and even Rosie had done so twice, and so it was that they came to make love for the first time, and it was for both of them the fulfillment of their desire for each other which had thus far stayed in harbour, but which now found its' way out into the wide and indefinite ocean.

Ashley Spears, once and now once again internationally successful composer and performer of rock music, who had also composed a classical symphony, sat now on the village Green beside which stood the ancient church that he had on a whim one day bought for cash. We have before in the pages of these books learned something of his chequered history; how he was born of sometimes wealthy but always bohemian parents, and how he had begun his musical career in the humblest of circumstances, in a bed – sit in London, with nothing but an acoustic guitar and a cast – iron belief in himself and the songs that he had by then begun to write. How he had survived the more destructive elements of his nature, and particularly his once legendary drug – abuse, which was perhaps a matter of luck, strength of constitution and medical intervention, but survive he had, and the creative energy which had been the other side of the same life –force which stirred within him had seen to his rise to fame and fortune, neither of which had been his primary motivation. And with his success had come the success of others who had swum in his slipstream, the latest of whom sat now beside him on the warm grass of this early summer afternoon; Tarragon, who was known to the world as Tara, and who in common with others who were close to him did not truly understand why such a person as he would travel a goodly distance around the world, to mourn the death or celebrate the life of someone such as Daphne had been. But come he had, and he sat now in characteristically modest repose, amongst people who had by degrees come to see him as one of their own, and it was perhaps this which brought him here; a deeply held need for companionship and equality amongst people, where he had for so much of his life been the leader of others, and still for now remained so. Samantha had alone amongst them known of his intent to dedicate an album of some of his best songs to Daphne, and to her chosen causes, and even he had allowed her to choose the songs, and there could perhaps be no greater gift or mark of respect that he could have bestowed upon her than this.

Besides Tarragon, Basil, her brother, and Emma, his young lady – friend and Samantha, who was herself an internationally respected musician, formed the most part of this close circle of people who sat on the ancient village Green, and spoke of any matter which came to their collective mind, or perhaps did not speak at all, but merely took enjoyment from each – others company, as people who love or respect one another will do.

The sky was darkening, and the light westerly breeze had brought an evening chill to the air, by the time the last of the people who were for the most part still dressed in black left the village Green. There had been enough wine, and sufficient food, and all who thought or spoke of it agreed that Basil and Emma had done their job well. For the young gentleman named Quentin this had been a significant day, for not only had his love for the young witch called Rosemary moved on to a new and different place, but he had met and been introduced to certain of the people who were a part of the community in which she had always lived. It had not escaped Meadow's attention that Rosie had changed her clothing, and so must have gone home to do so, or that Quentin had doubtless gone with her, and Tarragon had also witnessed their return, and they had a look about them which was not hard to interpret, particularly for one who knew Rosie so well as did her sister. Reginald had brought Gwendolyn out into the small community for the first time, and Louise had re – met certain of them, and was glad to have done so.

Three houses around the village Green now stood empty, including the big brick house where the bodies of the two young people had been found, who had reached their tragic end so long ago, and in which Daphne had lived so much of her life. All were history, now, and Daphne had been laid to her final rest, so that was done, and as they went the separate ways, all who had gathered to this end would agree that it had in the end been a good day, and Daphne, they were sure, would have been glad of that.

Chapter 18

The Importance of Having Friends

Our story now briefly moves forward to Monday evening, when we find Victoria Tillington in her bedroom, having retired early for the night to read, and to write emails to friends. This latter activity was in one sense a positive thing, but it was at times such as this that Victoria was wont to realize how few friends she actually had. Victoria had been raised and had spent her formative years in the rarified environs of the aristocracy, where she had met sons and daughters to Lords and Ladies, Earls and Viscounts and so on, more than one of whom had made romantic advances toward her, but none of whom had in the longer run found their way into her young soul to a sufficient extent to warrant more than the exchange of Christmas cards, or very occasional correspondence. Her contemporaries in her exclusive, fee – paying school were for the far greater part a product of the upper echelons of British and foreign society, and whilst such privilege could be seen as such, it had not prepared her well for the wider and more diverse world of university, or work, which saw to the inevitable downgrading of the financial and social circumstances of the people around her. Thus had she at a deep and conspicuous level been set apart from people whom she encountered in her daily life, a schism had been created which would endure, and which she would carry with her for the whole of her life. She had not asked for this and nor did she want it, but it was a part of her nonetheless. There were those in the village whom she could nowadays call her friends, despite her first attempt to integrate into their number having ended in near disaster. There were Will and Emily, and Keith and Meadow, and Percival, of course, whom she saw as more than a friend, and who cared not at all about their so contrasting backgrounds, so the schism was not so marked here, for which she was glad. The schism was there, nonetheless, and even the ignoring of it merely in a certain sense reinforced or at least reaffirmed its' existence. There was Jessica, of course, with whom she was in quite regular contact, and with whom she could say that she nowadays shared deep friendship, particularly since Ginny had apparently gone into self – imposed exile from the gang of four, but Jessica's domestic and emotional circumstances were so very different to her own, and otherwise there were few people whom she could truly call her friends. The truth of the matter was that her current estrangement from Rebecca, regardless of the reason for it, left such a yawning chasm in her emotional life that no amount of friendship could compensate for it, and although she was aware of the adage that one should not count ones' friends, there are times when a person cannot help but do so, or at least be aware of the lack of them.

And now had come Pandora, for whom her feelings were unclear, and undefined, and who would in any case be gone once the painting was finished, so she must not allow herself to be in love with her. For the sake of discretion and propriety if nothing else, that relationship must from now onwards be only that of painter and subject, of this she had quite made up her mind.

Such were Victoria's musings, which were now interrupted by a familiar knock on her bedroom door; this was quite late for Michael to visit her, but she found herself being glad of the interruption to her present thoughts, which were in danger of becoming bad thoughts, and she had not so much as begun writing her first email.

'Come in, Mike.'

So here was her dear brother, who had always added warmth to her life, which had at times had seemed to her to be cold, and empty. She wrapped her bathrobe around her and sat down on her bed; he would sit at her dressing table, as he always did.

'Hi, not interrupting anything, am I?'

'No....No, not at all...'

This Monday was in fact a public holiday, and whilst this need have no effect upon private building contracts, Keith, Damien and Will had decided between themselves not to work, and the delicatessen would be closed for business. Ash and Samantha had made no sleeping arrangements for the night of the funeral, and sleeping on the church floor without so much as a sleeping bag was nowadays a step too far into discomfort for Samantha, so they had planned to find a hotel in the town. In the event, however, the village rallied to find them a bed for the night. Daphne's house stood empty, of course, but until probate had run its' course it remained a part of her estate, and so was not yet officially to be slept in. Nevertheless spare bedrooms existed in abundance around the Green, and Damien and Sophia offered theirs, as did Sandra, but in the event they would sleep in 'Maisy's room' at number two, under the care of Barrington. In fact this care would consist only of making coffee, since all had eaten, and Ash and Samantha were on American time, and had brought with them a deeply felt tiredness from the tour, which saw them retire to bed quite early. Breakfast would by prior arrangement be taken by all at the bus, so throughout their short stay only washing facilities and a bed were needed. Nevertheless Barrington was pleased to offer such hospitality as was asked for, and was certain that his sister May would be impressed at his having two such famous musicians sleep in her occasional bedroom.

In the morning, which was Monday morning, Meadow was about early making a mild vegetable curry, Dahl and rice, which would be shared by any and all who turned up hungry, whilst Basil and Emma set about making a bonfire beside the trailer of the used paper cups, cardboard boxes and so on which were residue from the previous afternoon and evening. Thus did they conclude their considerable part in the festivities, and the remaining few bottles of wine and soft drinks, and any food which had not been consumed would be theirs to keep, Ash having reimbursed Emma in full and in cash for the purchase thereof.

Thus during the course of the morning, and indeed the afternoon, did various people visit the bus, and stay for as long as it was their will, and amongst the first to arrive were in fact Ashley and Samantha, who had slept well, and awoken early and hungry. Tarragon was already abroad by now, and it was a pleasant thing indeed for these three to have time together in such an ambient and cordial environment, away from the constant and heavy demands of a world tour, and Keith and Meadow were pleased to have their company. Once breakfast had been taken, they as a group sat beside the remains of the fire, on such makeshift seats as were available, and Meadow had something to say.

'It was a fine thing that you did, Ash, to give away the proceeds of your album, and even to agree to having the album made at all, actually.'

'Yeah, well, it seemed fitting you know? Lady had a good heart, and it's not like any of us need the money. Her poetry was something else…Guy who tried to recite the poem, what's his name again?'

'Will, and I'm afraid we all made rather a mess of that.'

'No man, it was cool. Funerals are like, dire, you know, and laughter's a good way through. Lady wouldn't have minded.'

'No, I suppose not.'

'So like, what happens to her house now?'

'She left it to Emily, although Emily doesn't want it, apparently. That is to say she doesn't want to live in it, she and Will have a lovely place on their land, anyway, but I think it goes beyond that. I spoke to Will briefly yesterday and I think selling it looks most likely.'

'Is that so....' Said Tarragon

'Yes, why, sweetheart...?'

'Well, I'm thinking on my feet here, but why don't I buy it? I've been looking for somewhere to put some money, anyway, and a house seems like a sound investment.'

'There's none sounder.' Said Keith

'Are you serious, my love?' Said Meadow

'Sure, I mean right now I can't think of anywhere I'd rather live than the village, and I could always rent it out anyway, or sell it on if I change my mind, so, you know, sure. Next time you see Em find out if she's serious, and if so let's get a valuation. I'd pay the asking price.'

'Okay, I'll be sure to do that.'

'Sounds like a plan,' said Keith 'it's about time somebody in my family bought a house, or did something sensible with money, at least.'

'Oh come on dad, you and mum couldn't live anywhere but the bus, it just wouldn't be right, and I sort of feel as though I'll be betraying a family principal, or something. I thought ownership was theft.'

'Only when I'm having a bad day...You want the house, you buy it with my blessing.'

'Okay, well, we'll see.'

'Sure, whatever....So, how's the tour going, Ash?'

'Yeah, it's cool, you know. I mean we're well received everywhere, which is amazing, really, but it's harder this time around. The accommodation's better than it was in the early days, you dig, but touring with a rock band's a younger mans' game. I mean back in the day we kept it going with amphetamine and just about everything else, then at the end we just kind of collapsed for a month.'

'Not all of us took drugs, honey.' Said Samantha

'No, sure, but you know what I mean…And this is a long tour, you know. I'll be glad to get America done, Europe always felt more like home, at least, but this is the last time around the houses, for me anyway.'

'I think you said that last time.' said Samantha, who smiled and took her beloved's hand.

'This time I mean it, it feels too much like work, and I've had it with the adulation. I was never in it for that anyway, but I don't want to work anymore is the thing, not in that way, anyway. I've been lucky, you know, but I don't want to ride the luck anymore, after this I'm done, so I live with the thought that each place we play will be for the last time. The band's been great, better than ever, and Aiko's brought something new to the party and so has Evie this time, and I wouldn't have missed it, you know, on the whole it's been a great vibe, and we're playing some great music, so it's a good place to end.'

'You know,' said Meadow 'that I've always wondered how you do it, I mean both of you.'

'Do what?' Said Tarragon

'Stand up and sing in front of tens of thousands of people, I mean neither of you are exactly natural extroverts, are you?'

'It's just the music, that's the reason.' Said Ash

'Yes, I mean there's that, of course,' said Tarragon 'but walking out on a huge stage, with all of the noise, and lights, and all of those people, it's like nothing else, and nothing I can describe, but it carries you along, somehow.'

'So what next, Ash, if this really is the end of your singing career?' Said Meadow

'Well, for a start there's your daughter, and we need to start work on the third 'Tara' album.'

Here mother and daughter exchanged looks.

'So has Tara brought something new to the party as well?'

'Can't imagine doing it without her any more, and she's even starting to sing like she can these days, so yeah, but she needs to go solo now, and I feel like being a backing musician, so it all kind of fits.'

Now there were smiles all 'round, and Tara looked suitably demure. About where they now sat saw the beginning of Tarragon's musical career, when Ash had first heard her sing, and she and Ash had come a long way since then, to their considerable mutual benefit.

'I've been lucky too, Ash….So very lucky, in fact.'

'No, that's all bullshit,' said Keith 'you write good songs Ash, and you're a great front – man, otherwise you'd never have made it this far, and I need hardly say that in my opinion my daughter has the best female singing voice on the planet.'

'It's practice and experience, man, like everything else. It wasn't like this when we first started out, back then it was about all of us just trying to hold it all together, hence all the drugs. I nearly died of it, couple of times, and Mickey didn't make it through.'

'Do you still miss him?' Said Meadow

'Not musically, any more, Aiko's a better base – guitarist now than Mickey ever was, but sure, I miss the guy, he was one of the best people I ever met, and he was my lucky break, you know? Without Mickey I would never have made it, and without Sam here to keep us all together when it mattered we'd have imploded a lot sooner than we did, so, you know, lucky, yes?'

'Well, we all need somebody.' Said Keith

'Seems that way…'

'You're even getting on with Al these days,' said Samantha 'which was never a given when this all started.'

'Sure…Still, Al's the reason we re - formed at all, end of the day this was all his idea, so I owe him for that if nothing else, and he's still the same ego – maniac as ever, but he's a good guitar player so we let him off, and Rick's still the best drummer on the circuit as far as I'm concerned, so it all fits, somehow.'

Candid and open discussion of the band, the music or his feelings toward them in a public forum was not usually Ash's way, and Samantha perhaps for the first time realized just how significant these people had become in Ash's life, and why he had travelled so far to attend the funeral of one of their number. It also perhaps explained why he had taken Tarragon so firmly under his musical wing, and dedicated so much time and energy to bringing out her latent abilities. She had a fine and quite unusual and distinctive voice, but there were other voices, and better trained and stronger voices at that, but for Ash it had always been Tara, and there were better guitarists on the circuit than Keith, but it was Keith who had played on Ash's symphony. Ash had made a lot of friends on the musical circuit over the years, but such friendships tended to be fragile and insubstantial, and Ash she knew was at heart a simple man, who took as much pleasure from quiet, simple things as he did from performing before his adoring audiences, so perhaps after all it was no wonder that he sought refuge here from time to time, amongst these fine and more ordinary people. Despite his wealth, which even before the latest world tours had not been insubstantial, he had been content to sleep on the stone floor of an old church. Ash employed a cleaner twice a week to take care of his domestic needs when he was at home, and he had a washing machine, but Samantha had more than once found him washing his clothes in the kitchen sink, such as were his clothes, and he washed up their dishes after every meal, foregoing the use of his electric dish – washer, and cooked about as much as did she. He had begun his independent life in a bed – sitting room in a less than salubrious terraced house, and had learned to live a life of modest self – sufficiency, and this way of life had it seemed never entirely left him.

'Anyway this whole animal thing has got me thinking, animals are cool, you dig, I'm thinking about getting a dog when the tour's over.'

'Was I to be consulted regarding this?' Said Samantha

'I mentioned it before…'

'Yes, you did.'

'Have to be a big dog, like some mutt or whatever from a rescue home.'

'Dogs need to be walked.'

'I'm cool with walking.'

And so did the day continue, in mostly idle and inconsequential conversation, and at various times did various other people from the village arrive and pass time at the bus, and introductions were made between those who had not met before. Perhaps the most notable and noticeable absentees from this ongoing soiree were Will and Emily, who had awoken to find that some of their goats, who were, as they had long since discovered, about the animal kingdom's most persistent and capable escapologists, had gained their liberty from their main enclosure, and were working on the secondary defenses which surrounded the vegetable garden. Their day was thus spent in returning said goats to their rightful place, and taking measures to further ensure that this would not happen again. For Barrington in particular this day was a further if somewhat belated integration into the village community, but perhaps most significantly for him, Sandra Fox made a quite fleeting appearance, she seeing this as a further opportunity to build bridges into friendships with people whom she had previously largely ignored, and she and Barrington had a brief and private conversation as she was leaving, of which he was the instigator.

'So, further to our conversation yesterday, how about we meet for a drink sometime?'

'Yes, why not, I'm home most evenings but weekends are best, I suppose.'

'Should we say Friday, then?'

'Yes, perhaps we should.'

'I'll call for you, shall I?'

'Yes, do that, any time after seven would be fine with me.'

So that was done, and the day in general was seen by all as a happy event, and a fitting tribute to the lady in whose honour and memory the previous and this day had been organized. Ashley and Samantha left for their own home in the afternoon, where Evelyn was to join them, and Tarragon stayed for a further two nights, much to the pleasure of her family. Rosemary had no school the next day, and the two sisters briefly made their own private arrangements to go to town.

'I need more stage clothes.'

'Right, we leave after breakfast.'

'I should spend some time with mum and dad.'

'So we shop, do lunch and be back early afternoon.'

'Okay, deal…'

'So what brings you here at this hour, Michael?'

'Oh, nothing in particular, other than to see how my sister is faring with life in general.'

'Well that's good of you, and I'm okay, thank you. So has Elin returned to Canterbury?'

'Yes, she left early this morning. She's having to work the bank holiday, of course, being snowed – under with work as usual. She works very long hours, which means a lot of overtime pay, but what they expect from her is unreasonable, in my opinion.'

'I didn't even know she'd stayed the night.'

'We got home late last evening, and she left before you were awake.'

'So are you still sleeping apart, officially I mean?'

'Yes, officially, which is ridiculous really, isn't it?'

'Yes, it is, rather. You're going to have to tell them soon, you know…'

'About our marriage plans, you mean?'

'Yes, of course, I mean it must be bloody obvious to everyone that you're having a relationship with her, and questions are being asked, you know?'

'Yes, I suppose….To be honest one is rather enjoying the subterfuge of it, and Elin certainly is, but anyway we've decided to announce our engagement, when the time is right.'

'Well good for you then. So is everything going okay at Orchard House?'

'Yes, we spent a very pleasant couple of hours there yesterday, and the work's going well enough, although it's certain to cost more than I'd anticipated, and god knows how much the garden's going to add to it all.'

'Well, you of all people should be aware of cost overruns.'

'Yes, and this time there's the Elin factor…Everything's going to have to be to the highest specification, if you know what I mean, I'm not going to be able to get away with anything, and I hadn't reckoned on having the garden designed and properly constructed, but she insisted upon that.'

'Oh dear….So the woman's touch is proving rather expensive, then.'

'You could say that…I'm going to have to turn some money over soon, or I'll have to go cap – in – hand to the bank, which I'll probably have to do anyway. I mean it should all work out in the end, but Elin won't be contributing her part until she sells the flat, of course, which leaves a bit of a gap in the cash flow, you might say.'

'Still, you wouldn't be without her now, would you?'

'Oh lord no, of course not, and I couldn't conceive of selling the place now, it's funny how things change, isn't it?'

'Yes, it is….'

'Anyway I've met the landscape designer, she goes by the name of Fifi, would you believe.'

'Oh lord, well that inspires confidence...'

'Actually I quite took to her, she's Scottish, actually, so the garden will be an entirely Scottish affair, assuming that we approve the plans and so forth.'

'Well, good luck with that...No more letters yet then, from our mysterious Jane?'

'No, and there're only two more to go, so she'd better start giving us more information soon. So, any news of Rebecca since she left the house..?'

'No, I've not heard from her, despite my asking her to tell me where she was going to live.'

'She's okay though, do you think?'

'How the hell would I know, like I said, I haven't heard from her.'

'Sorry....'

'No....No, I'm sorry, I didn't mean to snap....Christ, I don't know what's the matter with me at the moment...What's the matter with me, Mike?

'I don't know, but that question needs tobacco at least, don't you think, and I thought you said you were okay.'

'I've changed my mind, I think.'

They both stood up and went to the window, she pulled up the sash and they leaned out into the mild, breezy evening, where a half – moon shone through light, scudding clouds. They lit cigarettes, and she said nothing, so Michael prompted.

'So, what's going on, Vics?'

'I'm just....I don't know, I just nowadays catch myself sometimes, thinking things that I shouldn't be thinking, and doing things that don't seem quite rational, afterwards.'

'What kind of things?'

'Well for example the other day I went for a drive, you know, and ended up at Watersmeet Cove.'

'Good grief, that's a long drive, isn't that where we went once with Mater and Pater?'

'Yes, and I swam out, you know, well beyond the headland, and without being too dramatic I got really cold, the waves got up and I nearly didn't make it back to the beach. It was stupid, really, but I just felt at the time that I really needed to do it, if you can understand that, it's like I was deliberately putting myself in danger, or something.'

'Right….Well that *was* rather stupid. I mean aside from anything else, as I recall the currents there are strong and unpredictable, it isn't called *'Watersmeet'* for nothing, you could have been swept out to sea. So what else have you done?'

'Nothing….Well, nothing else like that, anyway.'

'So what have you done which is like something else?'

'I just…Nothing, really...'

'Come on, Vics, this is me, you know? You can tell me anything.'

'Can I….?

She could not, or would not. If there was to be any reconciliation between her and Rebecca, then Rebecca would have to tell him herself, and what happened thereafter would depend upon his reaction, and as for Nathaniel not being his child, or in all likelihood not being his child, she wondered if she would ever under any circumstances be able to tell him, and she thought probably not. There were too many secrets hidden within the recent past, quite apart from much older secrets which only she knew.

'You don't have to, of course.'

There were other things, however, which she saw no harm in telling him; it might help to mitigate the confusion, so start from there.

'Well, you know I'm having my portrait painted…'

'Yes, of course….Don't tell me, you're not half - naked as well, are you?'

She laughed briefly as she exhaled her cigarette smoke; that was funny.

'No, I'm quite well covered.'

'Thank goodness for that, you might have had trouble getting that past the big bedroom, we had enough trouble with Rose if you recall.'

'I do recall, and it's nothing like that…It's not the portrait itself, although I haven't seen it yet, but the thing is, I've been sleeping with the artist.'

'Oh Christ….Was that a good idea?'

'It seemed so at the time, but then I was rather drunk, the first time, anyway. It started when she was painting father, actually.'

'I see….Well, I suppose there's no harm in it, as far as it goes.'

'Yes, well there's the thing, I'm not sure how far it does go.'

'What do you mean?'

'I mean I think I may be falling in love with her, in a way. At least….I went there the other evening, to her bed, I mean, just because I wanted someone to be there, you know, so what does that say about me, and what must she make of it all?'

'I really can't say.'

'I'm daughter to nobility, Mike, and yet sometimes I just do things which aren't appropriate, and I'm not going to talk about how Henry was conceived, but well, it was hardly what one might call conventional, and then there's Henry himself. I mean I have feelings, you know, and I can be in love with a bloody painter, and I can deal with that, I think, but how can I have those kind of feelings, when…When I don't seem to have other kinds of feelings.'

'What are you talking about? What other kinds of feelings?'

'I'm talking about Henry. I mean I quite enjoy being with him, I suppose, for the short time that I see him every day, but I only go and see him because he's there, and he's often asleep anyway, and sometimes I almost forget to go and see him at all, and that isn't right, is it? Aren't I supposed to feel something, like an overwhelming sense of love, or whatever mothers feel?'

'Christ, I don't know, Vics, not everyone has strong maternal instincts, I suppose, I mean Mater was never exactly an earth – mother, was she? Perhaps because we never had much by way of parental love we don't know how to give it, it can work like that, I think.'

'Well maybe that's it then, I don't know.'

'We had nanny, after all, and Abi does such a good job with Henry and Nathaniel that one in any case one feels as good as redundant in that regard, and Elin wants nothing to do with children, she's made that abundantly clear, so there's no connection there. My love for Elin and my love for Nathaniel are completely estranged, and always will be, I suppose. She and I are together despite Nathaniel, and certainly not because of him, so you know, I wouldn't be overly concerned about it.'

'Well perhaps not, but Nathaniel's not her child, is he, and I see Rebecca with Florence, and Florence sleeps in a drawer, for heaven's sake, and Rebecca has no money, really, and she manages to be a devoted mother and still work obsessively, and one can feel the love between them, the air's thick with it, and it's something which I've never felt, and I very much doubt if I ever will.'

They lit more cigarettes, and were silent for a moment. The lights in the few village houses which they could see from their vantage point were being extinguished, and the traffic on the main road was now only occasional passing cars; the evening was drawing to a close, and giving way to night.

'You don't think I did wrong, do you, evicting her from the house?'

'No, I don't, she had to go, Mike.'

'Yes I suppose….So you're not going to tell me what's gone so badly wrong between you, then? I mean this isn't just a lovers' tiff, is it, because somebody forgot to water the Geraniums.'

'No, there's more to it than Geraniums, and I really can't tell you, Mike. I want to, in a way, although in another way I absolutely don't, so please don't ask.'

'I wouldn't, except I'm fairly sure it would be good for you to tell me, or to tell someone, anyway. If you're not yourself then there's a reason for that, and I'm also fairly sure that it's all connected to Rebecca, which leads me to think that it has to do with Florence, or whoever is father to Florence. Am I warm…?'

'Stop it, please…'

'Okay, so I'm warm, then, and if it's to do with Florence's father, how bad can it be? I mean why would I care who Florence's father is?'

'I can't, Mike….'

'Thing is, Vics, if by your own admission you're beginning to lose the plot, and it has something to do with this, then I think you should tell me. We nearly lost you once before, and I don't want that to happen again, in fact I won't see it happen again. I mean I'm sure whatever it is isn't worth killing yourself for, but that's not the point, if you're breaking up because of it then it could have an indirect effect, as it were.'

'You're worried that I might be going mad again….'

'You raised the subject, and I think you should deal with it whilst you can still rationalize, that's all. Tell you what, I'll tell you about something that happened in my life recently which I'm not particularly proud of, if you tell me what's going on, do we have a deal?'

'I don't know, but I need a drink, anyway. Let's go to the steps.'

'You're not properly dressed.'

'It won't be the first time, will it, and they'll be asleep by now.'

They put out their cigarettes on the outside of the wall, left the window open and made their way through the house via the drawing room, where they picked up two glasses and a bottle of high – grade Irish Whisky, which they took to the grand front door, and so out into the balmy late spring night. He was right, of course; she couldn't hold it inside her forever, and if secrets were to be told, this was the only place to tell them. Even now she still wasn't sure that she would tell him; she could make up some lesser reason, but they were here now, so she would see. She sat down on her step and he sat beside her, and they lit cigarettes.

'Right, you first....'

On Tuesday morning, Tarragon awoke to the sound of someone knocking on her bedroom door. She glanced at her watch, which lay on the table beside her, and saw that it was a little after nine o'clock. She then further ascertained her location, which changed these days with such frequency that on most mornings she took a moment to be certain, but this was not a hotel room in Boston, or San Francisco, but the somewhat less salubrious but so much more comforting surroundings of her own room, in the bosom of her own family. The knock came again, this time with quietly spoken accompaniment.

'Tara, it's me...'

'Oh, come in...'

She sat up and pulled the bedcovers over and around her, and a fully dressed Rosemary entered and sat on the edge of her bed. Tara yawned, wiped the sleep from her eyes with the back of her hand, and awaited a reason.

'So what's going on?'

'I've got a bit of a problem.'

The voice was still quiet, and now had a conspiratorial edge.

'What sort of problem?'

'We overslept...'

'Who overslept?'

'Quentin and me....He was going to leave early, but now it's too late, and I've got to try to smuggle him out somehow.'

'Christ...He stayed the night...? Well obviously, but just give me a minute, okay?'

'Okay....So what should I do, do you think?'

'Just...Hang on, I'm thinking....He can go out the back way, through the woods, can't he?'

'Yes, but I have to get him out of the door without anyone seeing. I need you to create a momentary distraction, that's all.'

'Alright, just let me get dressed, get him ready to go in five minutes.'

'He's ready to go now.'

'Well bugger off then, and give me five minutes anyway.'

Ten minutes later, both girls were in the kitchen of the bus eating a light breakfast, Quentin having by now made his escape undetected, and less than an hour thereafter the two sisters were in a cab on their way to town. As a concession to her relative fame and fortune, Tara preferred nowadays to avoid public transport, and she often, as today, wore lightly – tinted sunglasses when walking busy streets, and wore her hair loosely tied at the back to further avoid recognition. They had, as before, decided on a strategy of targeting certain upmarket dress emporiums before making for the old town for coffee, but in the event, since the bus stopped quite close to the old town anyway, Rosemary suggested a diversion.

'We could try that little place down Chantry Lane, you know, what's it called...'

'What, *'Lolita's'*, that's where the prostitutes buy their clothes, isn't it?'

'Probably, but you're not exactly trying to look like Mother Theresa, are you? Come on, let's try it, it'll be a lot cheaper, anyway.'

'Well, okay, if you're sure...'

'You're looking great on the monitor screens, by the way, and you've lost more weight. You need shoes?'

'No, I've got about four pairs now that I can stand up in for a couple of hours, so mostly I wear those.'

'Lolita's' would in the end provide all that was needed, which would consist of six dresses of various designs and colours, none of which had required very much by way of material in their manufacture, and as before Tara was not entirely convinced by that which had for the most part been Rosemary's choice, a fact that she made clear as they were walking the short distance to the coffee house.

'I'm going to look even more like a tart than before, at least up 'til now I haven't exposed by midriff to the world, or so much of my back for that matter.'

'It's a good stage image, you're looking good, you've got a fantastic figure these days, and you need to show it off, sex it up you know?'

'Well, I can't *'sex it up'* much more than this without wearing nothing at all.'

'That wouldn't be sexy.'

'I mean I get that this works with DMW, but *'Tara's'* not really like this, she's more kind of wholesome and homespun.'

'You mean like the album covers?'

'Exactly….Tara sings intelligent, cerebral songs. There's a lot of soul – searching going on.'

'Like *'Turn me Over'*, you mean? That's about the most sexually provocative song ever written for a woman, or sung by one for that matter.'

'Okay, point taken, but you know what I mean, this would be the wrong image for her.'

'Well, when you start performing solo you can change your image, then, anyway this way you can be sexy *and* intelligent, and you talk about her as if she isn't you.'

'Yes, well of course she's me, but I have to sort of turn into her on stage, especially when I'm singing her songs, which is a hard thing to explain, but there it is.'

'Yeah, I get that, I think. So what do the others make of your stage image, anyway?'

'What do you think, especially the older men, and Aiko's all for me looking like a lap – dancer, so for now I'll run with it. It's only a stage image anyway, I mean I live life in a state of complete celibacy, which is more than you're doing these days, it seems. Anyway, here we are.'

They entered Dawson's Coffee House, and Isaac Dawson was behind his counter, as always, and as always gentle jazz music created the unique ambience for which the establishment was renowned. Isaac by now knew well enough who Tara was, despite her attempts at anonymity, but he would say nothing.

'Two coffees, please, unless you've started branching out into other forms of hot beverage?'

'Last I saw, hell hadn't frozen over yet, if the sister sees that happen she'll be sure to tell me, yes?'

'You'll be the first to know.'

They exchanged smiles, and the two coffees were taken to an alcove, where the two girls took opposing seats, and Tarragon was the first to speak.

'So, how's it going with Quentin, anyway? I mean other than the fact that your relationship has clearly moved on since we last spoke, in one respect at least.'

'Yes, it has, although only just since, actually, and are you being a disapproving elder sister?'

'No…No, not at all, I think I'm just still bloody tired, or something….So, give me the overview.'

'Well, he's still working awful shifts, nights and so on, which rather gets in the way of our seeing each other, so there's that, but he has to work somewhere, and he's luckier than most, I suppose. At least he hasn't got vast debts hanging over his head from uni, his inheritance took care of that, but he really wants to find some proper work, you know?'

'Like digging around for fossils and such, you mean?'

'That kind of thing....There's a project coming up in Java this summer which he'd love to get involved in, but there'll be a lot of people trying to jump on that, and there'll be no money in it, just flights and living expenses if he's lucky, but he'll go if he's invited.'

'I imagine it's a fairly closed community, paleoanthropology or whatever it is.'

'Just a bit, and it's like a lot of things, it's not always what you know...And you know, they all sound like a bunch of ego – maniacs, the people at the top, anyway, they all think that their theory of the origins and lineage of humankind is the right and only one.'

'Sure...So other than that?'

'What do you mean?'

'Well, I don't know...'

'Do you mean am I head over heels in love and is he the only man I'll ever have feelings for, that kind of thing?'

'That'll do for a start.'

'I don't know, I mean yes, I think so, to the former, anyway...'

'And how does he feel?'

'The same, I suppose, I mean I wasn't expecting the third – degree, and we still haven't known each other that long, you know?'

'No, of course, I'm sorry. I suppose I'm just concerned for my younger sister, that's all, and I'm sure he's a really sound guy and everything, but I've never seen you like this before.'

'I've never been like this before, and it feels good, Tara, it really does.'

'Well all's fine then, but just for god's sake don't get pregnant, okay?'

'I won't, and I'm still not convinced that you approve.... What's the problem, is it that he's older than me?'

'No, I mean it's not *his* age that concerns me so much.'

'So you think I'm too young, is that it, to have these kind of feelings for somebody?'

'I didn't say that, either.'

'So what is it then?'

'It's just that....Okay, here's the thing, you'll be leaving home soon and going to uni, and that's just such a whole new experience, and god knows where you'll be living, and you'll be meeting new people and so on.'

'And you don't think our relationship could survive, that, is this what you're saying?'

'No, I don't mean that....I think what I mean is that university is so important, and it's better not to have distractions, or anything that's going to pull you back.'

'Says she who gave it up....'

'I gave it up for a reason, Rosie, and you're much cleverer than me, and who knows what you might achieve academically. And I know there's more to life than that, but it's important that women like you make the best of themselves, you know?'

'God, you sound like you should be my mother....'

'Mum never went to uni, so she couldn't really understand, and I know that she and dad have always drummed into us the importance of education, but you know what she's like, Rosie, she's a great and talented woman, and I love her to bits, but she's off with the fairies, and dad doesn't really care what happens as long as everyone's happy.'

Rosemary took a moment, and both drank their coffee.

'Well well, so now who's being different, you've never spoken like this before, not to me, anyway.'

'I know, and I'm probably speaking out of turn, and it doesn't really have anything to do with Quentin, and I know he's a clever man and will probably go far himself. Look, just forget it, okay?'

'No, I won't do that...I've just...I mean I always thought it was you and mum, you know? I've always felt excluded from that.'

'It's because she doesn't understand you, Rosie, and that says something given that she's about the most perceptive and empathetic person in the universe, but I can understand that lack of understanding. Anyway it's no secret that you're dad's favourite, and I'm absolutely fine with that, but I mean hitherto you've always been a closed book, and it's not everyone's daughter becomes a witch, is it? And your mentor, whatever she's called, is bound to have other influence on you, and that must have been hard for mum sometimes.'

'Do you think so?'

'Yes, I do.'

'Shit....You know, I never thought of it like that. I don't have a mentor anymore anyway, and as for the whole witch thing, that for me has always been about helping me focus on the rest of my life, it was never going to be my life.'

'No, well, I'm sure on the whole it's been a positive thing, and we all need something to help us focus. I mean I never knew what focus was until I started getting up on stage and singing to thousands of people, but I had to learn that one fairly quickly.'

'Is it getting easier?'

'You mean is it getting less bloody terrifying...? Yes, I suppose it is, the balancing factor being that it's also very exciting, if you can get over the fear...I mean it's not just me, you know, we all have our coping strategies, you might say.'

'Like what?'

'Well, Aiko usually has a day of fasting and meditation between gigs, and she never takes any stimulants, she won't even drink coffee. Rick's back on the speed now, when he can get it, which he usually can, and Ash is taking more cocaine these days and there's usually weed about, somehow. I mean it isn't like it was in the early days of the band, compared to that they're as pure as the driven snow, but it's started again, you know?'

'Yes but how? I mean who supplies it all?'

'There are ways...One of the road - crew, Ray, seems to have made that his responsibility.'

'So what about Samantha..?'

'Samantha copes anyway, she's a classical pianist who plays rock music, I don't actually think she knows what stage – fright is, bless her, and Al gets by on his ego. Of all of us he's the most natural performer, he thrives on the attention, I think, but he's not singing, you know, which is different. Guitar playing is much more external, singing has to come from inside you.'

'Yes, I can see that, not that I've ever done either...'

'Well anyway, it's my chosen path into big life, and it's my job to deal with it, and I wouldn't have missed it for anything. I've cast my die, now, and for better or worse I'm a professional singer, which is probably all that I'll ever be.'

'Like the album title.'

'Like the album title.'

'I didn't know it meant that...Was the title your idea?'

'Yep, all mine.'

'I never thought it was a negative thing.'

'Well, it isn't really, and like I said, I've been very lucky.'

'So are you doing drugs?'

Tarragon smiled.

'Well, you know me, moderation in all things.'

'So you are, then.'

'Sometimes...Sometimes it helps, gets you through the time – zones and all, and it takes the edge off.'

'Be careful, Tara.'

'I will...Anyway, I wish you well with your beaux, I really do, but all I'm saying is don't lose sight of your own big life, little sister. You're a one – off, Rosie, you're clever and you're beautiful, and all I want as your big sister is for you to make the best of it, okay?'

'Well, I'll try...'

'And by the way, don't ever expect dad to think that Quentin's good enough for you, because nobody ever will be.'

'I'll bear that in mind.'

'Sorry, this was meant to be a shopping trip, I didn't intend it to get heavy.'

'No, it's okay….We've just never spoken quite like this before, have we?'

'I suppose not, and I also suppose that we should be getting back, otherwise mother will start to see this as a highjack situation.'

'Okay, but just one more question….Are you really going to buy Daphne's house?'

'Probably, if Emily wants to sell it, although I've never actually been inside the place, but mum says it's as you'd expect, all oak beams and whitewashed walls.'

'So would you live in it?'

'Yes, I think so. I'd have to clear out most of the old furniture I daresay, but otherwise I don't see why not. I've enjoyed visiting all the fantastic cities that we've been playing, at least what I've seen of them, and I'll be going back to some of them, but I'm still a simple country girl at heart.'

'Is that all you'll ever be as well?'

'Possibly, but that remains to be seen, doesn't it, like everything else...'

'Yes, I suppose so…'

They smiled for one another, and it was a smile of understanding. These two had grown up together, and knew one another as well as two people may, but in their years of separation since Tara had left for university, they had both grown further and in important ways. They were neither of them the mainstay of the others' life, and Tarragon would be gone again soon, but such love which exists at the periphery of people's lives can be important love, nonetheless, and reaffirmation is sometimes needed, and this was something which both understood well enough, although these things are seldom spoken of.

'Okay, here's the thing....You know I went to Oslo with Elin recently?'

'Yes...'

'Well, on the short flight back, we...well, we made love in the toilet, if that's what you could call it. The making love part, I mean, not the toilet, it was definitely a toilet.'

Victoria smiled into the darkness.

'Well, I don't see so much wrong with that.'

'It's a bit sordid, don't you think?'

'Do I take it that this was not your idea?'

'I was quite happy watching the in – flight entertainment....I mean I'm not saying that I didn't enjoy the experience, in a sordid sort of way.'

'Well, *'go Elin'* is about all I can think to say about that. It's not that uncommon, you know, I believe they used to call it the *'mile – high'* club, or something.'

'I see...Well I don't think that's the kind of club I much care to belong to.'

'Well, you're in it now, my dear Michael....'

'Yes, well there it is, now it's your turn.'

Victoria lit a cigarette and refilled her lead – crystal glass with a more generous measure than would normally have been the case, from which she now drank. Now would be the moment, if she were to tell him. She loved her brother, and because of this she had not wished him to know that which Rebecca had done, and yet more or less equally she had known that she should tell him, because she loved him. This had always been her dilemma, which had stood at times in perfect balance, but perhaps now, with Rebecca gone and her dear brother beside her, it was time, and there would, she knew, never be a better time than this, or a better place.

'Okay....Okay, you're right, Mike, it is about Florence, and about her father.'

'Yes, I thought so....'

'And we do both know him….'

'Yes, well….?'

Another drink, which as good as drained her glass, and she took a long draw on her cigarette, and then took her brothers' hand.

'The fact of the matter is, it's you, Mike.'

At first there was no reaction; just the sighing of the wind through the old oak trees, which had always been there, ever since they had been children. The trees were older now, but they had always looked the same, and sounded the same on nights such as this. Then Michael laughed.

'Don't be bloody ridiculous, do you really imagine that I would have slept with Rebecca? Whatever she's told you, Vics, it isn't true.'

'I know…I know you would never have knowingly slept with her, but she's a witch, Mike, and witches like Rebecca can do things, you know?'

'What on earth are you talking about?'

'She slept with you, once, but let's stop calling it that. She once had sex with you, and then she made you forget. She bewitched you, and became pregnant with your child, and that child is Florence.'

Silence again for a moment. The whole notion was utterly absurd; this was a pack of lies, perpetrated to do harm to Victoria, and to him, and his sister surely did not believe it? But for a moment, let this play through.

'And when, pray, was this act supposed to have taken place? I can't even recall a time when she and I have even been alone together in the same room, or the same house, for that matter.'

'That's just it, Mike, you weren't supposed to recall it. Think back to a time about nine months before Florence was born. Did anything happen that struck you as being odd, or unusual?'

At first there was nothing, but then the seed of a thought split open gently, and something like a memory began to grow in his mind. There had been the time when he had been alone in the house, and had inexplicably fallen asleep, and woken up knowing that something had happened; a feeling in his loins which was familiar; a dull ache which he could not account for, since there was no evidence for it. He had even searched the house afterwards, but nobody was there, and he had felt rather stupid for so doing, and had thought nothing more of it, until now. But surely this was not possible, was it?

'My god….'

'I'm so sorry, Mike.'

'How long….How long have you known this?'

'Not long…I made her tell me, and now I wish that I never had, and I've wanted so much to tell you, but, well, I didn't know how, and I even thought that perhaps I would never tell you. She expects nothing from you, Mike, and she told me not to tell you. She wanted….She wanted her child to have your blood…Our blood, that was her reason, and her only reason, and that's the reason that I can no longer see her. I've forgiven her for so much, but for doing this to you I can't forgive her.'

Utter dismissal had turned to disbelief, and then to doubt, and now, as the memory of that strange day became clearer, even the doubt had lost much of its' substance. Of course, it explained everything, and that which Victoria was telling him was true, he knew and understood that now, and it was knowledge and understanding which must be processed, somehow.

'So what you're telling me is that I'm father to Rebecca's child….I have a daughter, called Florence.'

'Yes Mike, you do, but please, you must never tell her that I told you, or even that you know.'

'Yes….I mean, no, if you say not….Well, here's a rum do, then.'

Whether it was the utter relief at having told him, or his initial and so characteristic reaction to such news, or the sudden and quite profound intoxication she was not sure, but whatever it was, Victoria laughed.

'Well, I'm glad you think it's funny....'

Which only served to make the situation worse, and now she leaned over and buried her head in his cardigan just below his shoulder, to try to stifle or at least to quiet her laughter. He put his arm around her and held her to him, and it was perhaps half a minute before she had recovered herself sufficiently to emerge once more into the free night air, and to speak, and even then her words were faltering.

'Only you....'

'Only me, what...?'

'Of all the men on God's earth, only you, my dear, idiot brother, could have full and productive sex with a woman without realizing it.'

Which rather set her off again, but this time her composure was a little quicker in returning.

'I'm sorry....'

She sat up, he released her and she wiped her eyes on the sleeve of her bathrobe.

'It's okay....I mean I suppose it is quite funny, when one thinks about it. At least I suppose one has to see the funny side of it.'

'So, I mean...Aren't you in the least bit angry?'

'Hmmm....? Angry...? Well yes, I suppose so, although one has not fully ordered ones' thoughts quite yet. I wonder if I enjoyed it...?'

What was it with men? He had been abused, taken against his will, and a woman had taken his issue into her without his consent, and his first coherent thought was whether or not he had enjoyed the experience. Percival had reacted in similar vein, although he had remembered, because the witch Rebecca had allowed him to, but neither had been anything like angry. This, she supposed, was the female equivalent of date – rape, or similar, and if a woman had been so taken against her will, having been rendered effectively unconscious, or at least helpless, then anger would certainly be high on the list of things which she would feel, but it wasn't the same, and that, she supposed, was the point. But even so, there was a child, so what of that? Of a sudden her brother had discovered that he was father to a daughter, and to the daughter of her once lover and best friend, and should there not be some adverse reaction to that, at least? Still, he had by his own admission not yet *'ordered his thoughts'* as he had put it, so perhaps after all there would be a delayed reaction. For now, however, she could but answer his question.

'I suppose you must have done.'

'Yes, otherwise one would hardly have....This is all rather like the punishment without the sin, don't you think? I mean the worst of it is that I've seen her, Florence, I mean, and I had no idea...It's all just so damnably odd, and now I've evicted my own daughter and her mother from my house, so that takes some thinking about...'

'I don't think you can see it quite like that, Mike.'

'No, perhaps not, but I'm not quite sure how I should see it, to be honest, but anyway, for your part, and as far as you and I are concerned, I'm glad you told me, Vics, and I understand how difficult this must have been for you.'

'Oh Michael, how the hell are you always so understanding about everything?'

'I mean...Another odd thing is that I never thought of myself as having any feelings of that nature towards Rebecca.'

'You mean sexual feelings?'

'Yes...'

'I think perhaps she made you have those. I've thought about this a lot, of course, and I think she used your most base, male instincts and manipulated them to her own ends.'

'Yes, I suppose at that level all women are attractive, all attractive women, at least.'

Thoughts and impressions now came to Michael as fast or faster than he could process them, and something now came to the fore which gave him further pause for thought.

'Christ, what the heck am I going to tell Elin? I mean, my having one legitimate child is okay, but this is something which she would scarce understand. She doesn't believe in witches or witchcraft any more than I would have done, before.....Well, before everything...'

'Do you have to tell her, Mike? Let me say again that Rebecca will make no claim on you, in this at least I think I believe her, and you could always deny it in any case, so if I were you I might feel inclined to keep the knowledge between the three of us.'

'I don't know, Vics, I'll have to think long and hard about everything. Sleep on it for a bit, you know?'

'Yes, of course....God I feel awful about all of this, I really do.'

'Why should you feel awful about anything?'

'She's my friend, Mike, or was, anyway....'

'You're not responsible for the actions of others, Vics.'

'Any more than are you, Michael, and that is something which you must never forget. This is none of your doing.'

'No, oddly enough I suppose it isn't.'

It was late, the night air had become chilly, and the Tawny Owls were calling to one another from the ancient oak trees by the time brother and sister went inside, and to their respective sleeping places. Even so it would take Michael Tillington a while before he fell asleep, but instead he fell to wondering about this new and strange revelation. Victoria's last thought before she fell into slumber was a good thought; this at least was one less secret for her to hold, and though it may in a way have been the least of them, it was at least something, was it not, and it had been well told. It was also that case that she felt the better for the telling of it, when this had never been a given.

Chapter 19

WOMAN IN A BLUE DRESS

Late upon the morning after Tarragon and Rosemary had been to town, Emily Cleves was going about her business on the smallholding. She was at this moment carefully removing her latest batch of cheeses from their molds, when from outside the door of her 'cheese room' into which he was not permitted, Monty made her aware that someone had just entered the land through the kissing gate. This he did by first taking up an alert position, ears and nose working, growling gently to himself, and then leaving his position to further investigate who the caller might be. Emily left the carefully temperature – controlled environment and walked out into warmer air of the spring morning, the caller by now being halfway to the house, and Monty having already introduced himself.

'Hi, Emily….'

'Oh, hi Tara, what brings you to the heart of my humble enterprise?'

'Well apart from the fact that I haven't been here for a long time, and my god you've been busy, the place looks fantastic!'

'Well, we're a bit of a shambles, but try keeping anything tidy with goats around.'

'Yes, I'm sure.'

'Anyway, coffee…?'

'If I'm not disturbing you..?'

'Not at all, early mornings are always busiest, and I've already done the milking, which is the important thing.'

'Fine then, coffee would be great.'

They went indoors, and Emily set the kettle to boil.

'Sorry we didn't see you at the party on the Green, or wake or whatever it was.'

'Yes, I was really cross about that, but the goats got out, somehow, and we had to reinforce the defenses.'

'Oh well…Anyway it was a good day, despite the reason for it.'

'Yes, I'm sure.'

Emily poured coffee and sat opposite her unexpected guest at the kitchen table. These two had known each other for many years, but had during those years spent very little time alone together.

'So it must be strange for you to be back here, away from all the bright lights and what not.'

'Strange but good, actually, I needed to get away from all of that for a while, although it's only a short while. I mean I love it, don't get me wrong, but it's hard to sustain it, sometimes, and this is a long tour.'

'Sure…Still, you have a more glamorous lifestyle than me, that's for sure.'

'Glamour can be overrated, believe me, and this place looks idyllic, at least from an outside perspective.'

'Yes, well, if you'd told me a couple of years ago that I'd be doing this I probably wouldn't have believed you, but here I am, and I do enjoy it on the whole, although the goats are a bit of a tie to say the least. We can't go away anywhere, really, that's the problem, so you and I currently have very contrasting lifestyles, you might say.'

'That's true…You want to get away and I want to come home. So anyway, I hear that you've inherited Daphne's house.'

'Yes, I have, and I didn't see that one coming. I think I'm still recovering from the shock, to be honest.'

'So, what do you think you'll do with it?'

'I'm going to sell it. I'm going to set the wheels in motion as soon as it's officially mine. I would never live there, and well, a large lump of money will be handy, we'll be able to make some improvements to this place, for a start.'

'Sure...Thing is Em, mum told me that you might be selling it, and that's the other reason I came, actually.'

'Oh yes...?'

'Yes, the point being that I might be interested in buying it.'

'Oh, I see.'

'I mean I've not so much as been inside the place, but I assume it's got two legs and two arms, so, yes, in principal I'm interested.'

'Well, that would be perfect. I mean I haven't officially got the keys, yet, and I don't know if I'm supposed to. I'm executor to the will, but I'm also a beneficiary, so it's complicated, I think.'

'Right, well that's the other thing, I'm leaving tomorrow, staying over at Ash's place, then we catch an early flight the next morning to Washington, or is it Philadelphia first...Anyway I mean I can give power of attorney for dad to buy on my behalf, that much I can do before I go, but I'd like to look at it before I leave, if possible.'

'Yes, of course...Well let's go today then, shall we?'

'What about keys?'

'I have keys, unofficially.'

'Oh, well let's do it, then. I think how we should proceed is that you have a valuation and structural survey done, and assuming that's all okay I can pay the asking price.'

'And assuming that you like the place...'

'Yes, assuming that, and I can pay by bank – transfer, so you'd get your money quickly once contracts had been exchanged.'

'Okay, well look, give me an hour or so to finish off here, then I'll call 'round for you, shall I?'

'Yes okay, I'll wait at home for you.'

They drank their coffee and engaged for a few moments in lighter conversation, but shortly thereafter Tarragon left, the meeting in the end having been quite brief and to the point, and she left Emily with the sense that here indeed would be the perfect solution, and she liked the idea of selling Daphne's house to somebody whom they both knew. Daphne would have been pleased about that, she was sure, and the fact that it would be Tarragon gave the matter an even better feeling; Daphne had been close to Meadow, and Tara was Meadow's daughter, so it was rather akin to keeping the property in the family.

So they met as appointed, Emily having under the circumstances overcome her desire not to go inside the house which would soon be hers, and aside from wanting to keep hardly any of the furniture, Tara liked the property well enough, and after less than an hour in the house the deal was struck, in principal, and in due course Tara would buy Emily's house, once it was her house to sell.

The next morning, Tarragon went with Keith to a solicitor in the town, and a document was swiftly drawn up and signed, giving Keith power over his daughter's affairs in regard to buying number six, The Green, and later that day Tarragon left on the first stage of her journey back to America, and back to her other life, where she would become *'Tara'* once again. She had come home ostensibly to accompany Ash, who had wished to pay his last respects to a friend, but she had gone back to her work as a singer with new stage clothes and potentially at least with a new house, which was more than she had expected, and this, so far as she was concerned, was all to the good.

During the course of this week, two emails were sent which have a bearing on our story. The first of these was sent by Patricia Wagstaff to Michael Tillington, which after the preambles read as follows, by way of an attachment as had become usual;

'14th July 1665

My dear William

We (are now in the) sixth week of our siege, and our circumstances become worse with each passing day. We are all of us hungry, save for the few hours which follow the one wholesome daily repast which we still allow ourselves. Even do our supplies of flour grow small, and I thank God that we received delivery just prior all of this, else I know not what we would by now do, but (what is worse?) than this is the torment of uncertainty which haunts our days, and seems to be in the very air that we now (breath.

As you know, we have from) the upper floor a view of the cart – track which passes close to our gate, whereupon in the first days and weeks poor wretches, either alone (or in whole families, could) be seen travelling with their worldly goods, (each no doubt) seeking safe refuge from the sickness. Would that I could have helped them, but I dare not, the safety of your children must come above all things, and we scarce have enough food for our own needs. Now in any case no one passes, the world beyond our boundaries has (quite stopped, it seems, and no news reaches) us.

I live in fear also that we will at any time be set upon by those desperate for nourishment, but so far the locked gates have been deterrent enough, and we have kept (such food as we have, but) soon even this will be gone, and we needs must leave here, whatever will be our fate.

In large part our long days pass now in sullen silence, and a black mood is upon us all. John (does his best to) lighten the spirit of little Margaret, as do we all, but on some days near despair comes upon me, such is our parlous condition of mind and body.

Thus have I made a (decision), which is that at the months' end will I ride forth for news, and perchance will we all go, for we cannot stay here beyond then, we will have nothing left to eat, and we must take such chance as we may.

Our (prayers are) with you as ever, dear brother, though even prayer seems now to be a forlorn hope. To look upon you again would be my dearest wish, though in truth near all hope of this is now gone.

Your loving sister,

Jane.'

Michael had, during the course of his reading the series of transcripts, become ever more sympathetic to the plight of Jane and her brother's children, who had clearly and increasingly suffered during their self – imposed isolation. It was also the case, however, that he had become increasingly frustrated by the fact that he still had no idea who Jane was, who her brother was or where he had lived. There was now but one more letter to be transcribed, and he hoped that this final letter would throw some light into the darkness which hitherto surrounded the matter. He had looked once again to try to find any house with the name 'Orchard House' which had been built in the county in or around the year 1665, but had had no success. He had pondered the notion that perhaps William, the brother, had been living in the house, and had received the letters from Jane, who had been elsewhere, but he still thought it more likely that Jane had written the letters at Orchard House but had never sent them. Why this should be he could only speculate, and why the letters should have been subsequently concealed within the house was for now beyond him, and for these reasons he awaited the final letter in a state of hope and anticipation, faint though that hope had now become.

In any case during this time Michael had certain other distractions. In the first place there was the ongoing work to the house itself, which now that electrical and plumbing contractors were on site was moving forward apace, and from now onwards the contract would require more money on a weekly basis, and would require his presence more often. So there was that, but in quieter and more contemplative moments his thoughts turned to Rebecca and her child, which if she and Victoria were to be believed was also his child. He believed Victoria, of course, for why should she invent such a thing, and the more he contemplated the events of that strange afternoon, when he had awoken from his strange sleep, the more convinced he became that this so improbable thing was in all probability true, and that this was when it had happened. So then, assuming that this was a given, there was the matter of how he felt about it to be brought to order, and what, if anything, he should do about it. Morally, Rebecca had been wrong, of that at least there was no doubt in his mind, and particularly in view of the apparent fact that it had not merely been him that she had wanted, but that she had quite consciously intended to become pregnant as a consequence of their so unequal intercourse. In this, of course, had she succeeded, and given the quite narrow window of opportunity during a woman's monthly cycle, the whole thing must have been quite carefully planned, and her timing had it seemed been perfect. Beyond that, however, he entered murky waters, and there was no precedent to be referred to, since to the best of his knowledge no such thing had happened before, or at least nothing had been written down that he had ever heard of. To have been first seduced by her, when under normal circumstances he would never have allowed such a thing to happen, and then to have been made to forget that the seduction had ever occurred was something almost unbelievable, but it was something which he must believe in order to make any kind of further headway with any of it. So then, the rational part of his brain told him that what she had done had been wrong, but there were also his emotions to contend with, and in this regard he came to realize during his consideration that something was missing, and a thought which intertwined amongst all of his other thoughts and impressions would reveal itself sometimes, and make the absence of this element still more apparent. For if Rebecca had, as Victoria had said, exploited his most base, male instincts to have her way with him, then another base male instinct seemed to follow naturally thereafter; he had a child, and a daughter at that, and she was likely to be his only daughter, and however she had been conceived this fact remained. Victoria was angry with Rebecca, to the extent that they were apparently no longer in communication. This was not the first time, and Michael knew well enough that their relationship had always been of an intense and fragile nature, but this time Victoria's anger ran deep on his behalf. But still, something was missing, and he even tried, but try as he may, Michael could feel no anger.

Of the second electronic mail to be sent and received on this day we will hear at the close of this chapter, but for now we rejoin the life of a certain Peter Shortbody, who as we rejoin him is at home and receiving a telephone call. It is the mid - evening of the day, and Peter is alone.

'Hello….'

'Hello Peter, it's Maddie.'

'Oh, hello…'

'You were going to call me?'

'Yes, I was….'

He was, in fact, but in fact he had not. Since their meeting in the Saddler's Arms, Peter had been fighting with a dilemma, there being two elements hereto, which were he supposed in fact in the end one and the same thing. On the one hand, he very much wanted to see her again, of that there was no doubt, but on the other hand his wanting to see her went so against the grain in terms of how he had seen the rest of his life proceeding, that had even now not ordered his thoughts in regard to her. This was a similar dilemma to that which had faced him before he had contacted her the first time, but now, because her circumstances were as they were, and because she had reacted as she had, the dilemma went deeper, and he was not at all certain how deeply into the dilemma it was wise for him to go. Wisdom, however, was an unlikely bedfellow for the feelings which had become aroused within his soul, and he had now to make a choice, and this was his problem.

'Well, never mind…The thing is, you've been invited to a dinner party on Friday.'

'A dinner party..?'

'Yes, you know, when by prior arrangement a group of people sit around a table and have dinner?'

'Yes, I know what they are…'

'Good, well anyway it's at Felicity's house in Broadacre, to be held in honour of her birthday, and Sheila's coming with her new man - friend, and there'll be two gay couples coming who are sort of friends of Sheila, and whom I've not met, two boys and two girls.'

'Right…'

'Sooo, would you like to come…? Fliss and Sheila are dead keen to meet you again, as I knew they would be.'

'Well yes, I'd like to meet them, too.'

'Are you sure, Peter?'

'I'm sorry…?

'You don't sound overly enthusiastic about the whole thing, that's all. I mean if you'd rather not come just say so, I won't be offended, and I can go on my own, lord knows it wouldn't be the first time, but I'd prefer to have an escort and I thought of you. It's only a dinner party, you know?'

'Yes, of course…'

So now it came to it; the dilemma stood before him seeking immediate resolution, and for a moment the balance was perfect. At the end, however, wisdom took second place.

'Of course, and I'd be delighted to come.'

'Excellent…I don't suppose you have a pen handy, do you?'

'No, actually...'

'No, I thought not, you never did, as I recall. I'll email you the address. You know Broadacre, I suppose?'

'I know of it.'

'Then you'll know that it's quite a way and in the middle of nowhere, so you're welcome to the spare room at my place if that would be easier for you. I'm halfway there for you at least, or rather halfway back, and it'll save on taxi fares.'

'Oh, right…Yes, well that sounds sensible.'

'Good…Until Friday, then, eight for eight thirty's the general idea.'

'Right, I'll see you there, then.'

'Looking forward to it already…Bye then, Peter.'

'Goodbye…'

The line went dead, and Peter replaced the telephone receiver. It was only a dinner party. It was only a dinner party, and Alice was often off doing things without him, quite aside from her trips abroad, so why should he not foster a new social network? The fact that Peter Shortbody had never in his life fostered anything like a social network was something best not thought about, and anyway he supposed it was never too late to start. What had she meant, though, about his never having a pen to hand? As memory served it was oft times the case that he went about his school and into classrooms without a writing implement about his person, and relied at such times on one of the girls to provide, who had such things as well stocked pencil – cases, but for her to have remembered such detail after so long surprised him. On the other hand, as regards how the girls who were contemporary with him during his school years were concerned, he was beginning to get used to surprises. Felicity Bird and Sheila Stevenson; more names from his past, frozen in his memory as young women, and both wished to meet him again, so there was something to think about.

Peter had been about to take a bath and begin to make ready to retire for the night, but now and instead he made for the drinks – cabinet, and poured himself a glass of dry Sherry. For the most part he kept such a bottle for special occasions, and now he felt that the occasion called for it, and his mind was in any case certainly calling for it. Something was happening in his life that he could not foresee the end of, and it occurred to Peter on occasion that it would be a far better thing to know the end of things, so that one could properly manage the preambles, and this was such an occasion. But still, this was not to be, and he would get where he was going in the usual linear and uncertain fashion, and things would unfold as they would. For the moment in any case Tizer was asleep on the settee, as was his wont in the evenings, Bronwyn and Elizabeth were with their mother, and Peter was alone, as Peter had been for so much of his life, so perhaps after all it was time for that to change.

For Barrington Thomas the week moved forward exceeding slow. In the normal run of things, in his awaking, going to work and spending his evenings at home, cooking his evening meal and then reading or watching the television, the days passed in quite anonymous and smooth transition, and the weekends arrived when they would. This week, however, all of his significant thoughts were focused on the end thereof, and the time between any given time and then seemed long indeed, and each day seemed to him to stretch beyond its' natural span. Such was his distraction that he found it hard to settle to his usual evening routine, and so, once he had showered and eaten, he took to walking out in the by now quite long and pleasant early summer evenings. He would walk perhaps to the lake, where he would pass half an hour or so sitting on one of the rough – hewn seats, watching the ducks or the kingfishers going about their business, or he might take to the heathland which lay beyond the woods, returning home in the dusky twilight. He had a certain sense that his tenure in the village had of late reached a state of maturity, whereby he could now consider himself an established part of the small community in which he lived, and this thought gave him contentment, which helped to mitigate at least in part the sense of anticipation with which he awoke and fell asleep each of these days. Friday would come, eventually, but it was a long time in the coming.

The one notable event which did occur happened one evening, when, as he entered his cottage after his walk his telephone was ringing, and he quickly closed the door and covered the short distance to the small table upon which the telephone resided, and picked up the receiver.

'Hello...'

'Hi Bats, it's me.'

He had not heard from his sister May for better than two weeks, she having been away and working on location in Scotland and elsewhere, and such was her frenetic life that he would wait for her to have the time to contact him.

'Oh, hi Maisy, how are things?'

'Oh you know, it's the usual madness, but okay, generally.'

'So where are you calling from?'

'Portugal, actually, we're here for a couple more days to wrap up some final shots, then home, so I thought I'd seek refuge at yours for the weekend.'

'Oh, right, fine...So when might you be arriving?'

'If all goes to plan, sometime on Friday evening, though god knows what time.'

'Right...Thing is, I won't be at home, so you'll have to let yourself in.'

'Oh, okay...Going anywhere special?'

'I don't know. That is I don't know where, but I'm going out with the girl who lives three doors down.'

'Who she...?'

'Her name's Sandra, she's a research scientist, well, that is to say she's still at university, but she's on secondment at the moment, doing some manner of research, I believe.'

'How old...?'

'I've no idea...Well I suppose she's in her early twenties.'

'So what else can you tell me about her?'

'Well, she's presently living in the parental home whilst she does her research, although her parents are seldom there as I understand it, she's been quite seriously ill recently, she's got a younger sister called Emma, and that's about the sum total of my knowledge of her.'

'Seriously ill with what..?'

'I don't know, nobody I've spoken to seems to be quite sure.'

'She's okay now, though?'

'Fit as a fiddle, by the look of things.'

'So is this a date?'

'Yes, I suppose so. Someone died in the village, the old lady who lived in the big brick house, and we got talking, briefly.'

'What...? You pulled at a funeral?'

'Like I say, we got talking, and actually it was at the wake, afterwards, which was more of an informal get – together on the village Green, but anyway the day after the funeral we spoke again, and agreed to go out.'

'So this is your first date?'

'Yes, if you could call it that.'

'What would you call it, then?'

'Well, I suppose it is a date, now you come to think of it.'

'It's how you think of it that matters, and her, of course, but well done that man...So are you sure it's okay for me to come, I don't want to cramp your style or anything.'

'It's just a drink, Maisy, or probably a meal, actually, but no, come, by all means.'

'So you don't know where you're going yet then?'

'Look, we're just having a drink, okay, which might involve pub – food, but beyond that nothing's been arranged.'

'Okay, fair enough...So you've not heard from the naked one, then?'

'No, I've quite given up on that.'

'Good for you...So anything else happening..?'

'Well, I had a couple of house guests on the night of the funeral.'

'Who..?'

'Ashley Spears and Samantha Rodrigues, as it happens.'

'What, they slept in my room?'

'Yes, they flew over from America for the funeral and needed a bed for the night, so I offered my place.'

'Blimey, my brother and two world – famous rock musicians sleeping under one roof, who'd have thought that... So what are they like?'

'Very polite, actually, I mean Ash Spears in particular is the product of a different age, but I liked them both.'

'You must tell me all, brother, sounds like you've been busy since we last spoke. Anyway I'd better go, we'll catch up on Saturday morning, I expect, I'll probably get to your place, shower and crash, I badly need sleep.'

'Will you need food?'

'If I do I'll forage whatever's in the fridge, or open a tin of something, don't make anything, and don't forget to wash behind your ears.'

'What...?'

'For the date...Wear a decent shirt and some aftershave, that kind of thing.'

'Maisy....'

'Okay, I'm gone, see you at the weekend.'

So that was done, and Barrington now had still more reason to look beyond the working week to the weekend; May was coming, and to that he always looked forward. He had during his still young life led the life of a sexually promiscuous drug addict, both activities having cost him money which in the end he did not have, and otherwise he had been a celibate monk, and retrospectively, and particularly in the light of recent knowledge, his relationship with Miranda Spool could scarce be described as conventional, so perhaps he would be more lucky this time. It was only a date, but upon such matters a young man cannot at times help but speculate. This was Wednesday, so only two more days and nights of anticipation lay ahead of him. He took off his light summer jacket and set the kettle to boil for his nightcap, and waited.

During this week Victoria was working at the gallery, and would not as a matter of course have gone to see her painter on returning home from London, but she had not seen her now for two days, and to ignore her completely seemed to her to be inappropriate. In any case she detected in herself a reluctance to do so, which was ridiculous, and must be overcome; this was her home, after all, and the artist had been commissioned to paint her portrait, and there need from now on be nothing more to it than that. The painting was in any case almost complete, and she was not required to sit any more, and Pandora would soon be leaving. Thus it was that of an evening, which was Wednesday evening, she knocked on the door of the extension, and from a distance there came an immediate response.

'Come in…'

Victoria entered, as Pandora came in from the door which led out to the driveway. She was dressed as usual in jeans and a casual smock, and was holding a glass of red wine, which Victoria noted, and which Pandora noted the noting of.

'I don't usually drink when I'm painting, but I was in town today so I bought a couple of bottles. Shall I get another glass?'

Better not, this would only be a short visit.

'No, thanks…'

'Okay, I don't much like drinking alone though.'

'Well, just one glass then.'

It need only be one glass, after all, and Victoria had not drunk alcohol all week, and the desire to do so was of a sudden quite strong. Pandora went to the kitchen, Victoria walked through the living room, which always nowadays smelled of oil paints and turpentine, and went outside to the terrace and sat on one of the seats which overlooked the new driveway. It was a pleasant evening with only a slight breeze, and the light was fading with the setting sun. Pandora returned with a second glass, which she half - filled and put on the table, after which she picked up a half – smoked marijuana cigarette from the ashtray, which having smoked from she passed to Victoria.

'No, thank you…'

'Oh come on, I don't bite for heaven's sake.'

'What do you mean?'

'Nothing….'

Victoria took the cigarette and drank from her glass, and the world around her changed slightly as her nervous system reacted to the different external influences. They should talk now about the portrait, a safe, common subject, and which although nearly complete was in truth not yet to the artists' satisfaction. Victoria's state of being had changed so much at various times during the painting of her, that Pandora had not yet she thought captured that which she called her subjects' essence. In this respect Victoria had been a moving target, and although the painting would be good enough, she was sure, it was not yet right from the artists' perspective. For a moment, however, neither spoke, but rather let the moment speak for itself. The moment, however, was not speaking loudly enough.

'You meant something.'

Pandora looked at Victoria, who was looking outwards and was it seemed avoiding eye contact. So, she wished to engage then, having been given the opportunity not to do so, but rather to ignore Pandora's somewhat spontaneous and less than thoughtful remark. So what were they today, artist and subject, passionate lovers, or intimate friends?

'Well, you've hardly spoken to me since our last night together, and whatever that was about is fine by me, and need not be spoken of, if you'd rather not, but it was hardly my doing, was it?'

Another escape lane, which would perhaps have been used had Victoria not just so altered her state of mind.

'That was....I don't know, I'm sorry, that should not have happened.'

'It's fine, really, we all need people for different reasons at different times.'

Victoria turned now in the half – light, her expression now and once again as Pandora had not seen her before, somewhere between love and hatred, or beseeching and defiant. It had only been there for an instant, but Pandora had seen it, and captured it in her memory. Many of her subjects merely looked at her, their expression neutral and unchanging, but Victoria had always been different. So, here perhaps was Victoria, then, and here perhaps at last was the essence of her, so perhaps the painting was not so finished after all, and perhaps here was a way to finish it.

Victoria all but drained her glass, which Pandora re – filled, and she passed the cigarette again; sometimes barriers must be broken down, and expression at times needs encouragement.

'Nevertheless I should not have...I've just...I've had some things to deal with lately, which I can't tell you about, but which have been, well, difficult for me.'

'I see....As far as I'm allowed to see anyway, and as I say, it doesn't matter.'

'It won't happen again.'

'Fair enough...I'll be leaving in a few days anyway.'

'I think that would be for the best.'

'If you say so, you're the one paying the bill, after all.'

'What's that supposed to mean?'

'Whatever you think it means.'

'I didn't pay for….For what happened.'

'Which particular part of *'what happened"*..? Would that be me fucking you or being there when you needed a shoulder to sleep on?'

'I didn't come here to be insulted.'

'So who's insulting who?'

'I…I don't understand what point you're trying to make.'

'My point is that you're paying me to paint your portrait, and it's going to be a bloody good portrait, but in whatever happens other than that we're equal, and I don't appreciate being dismissed…'

'I wasn't dismissing you.'

'Well you weren't expressing yourself very well, then, because that's what it sounded like. Anyway aside from this being your house so you can do as you please, what did you come here for?'

'I don't know, but whatever it was I think I'd better leave, don't you?'

'As you wish…'

But she did not leave, and neither did Pandora encourage her to do so. Instead she took a cigarette from her pack and lit it, whilst Pandora rolled a cigarette and did likewise. That done, Pandora laughed as she exhaled.

'Well that was interesting…Where the hell did all of that come from?'

'I don't know.'

The moment had run its' course, and the next moment was a more gentle affair during which neither spoke, and then Pandora spoke.

'Woman in a blue dress…'

'What…?'

'I have an anthology of paintings on my website, and with your permission I'd like to include yours, and if so I've just decided that that is what I'd like to call it, so as to retain your anonymity. Anyway I think it's a good title for a painting.'

'I don't think I object to that.'

'Thank you.'

'You're welcome.'

A nightjar called from somewhere quite close by; one of the denizens of the night which had as a species survived the coming of people, and whose ancestors had been here long before the houses and the roads. Victoria was less used than Pandora to smoking dope, and for a moment her mind had wandered where it may, and once again it was Pandora who broke the silence, and brought her thoughts back into focus.

'God, this place…'

'What about this place?'

'There's so much history here, isn't there? I mean I know I've mostly been in the new part, and you've grown up with it, and my house is old, but a Manor House is something different. So much has happened here, and so much goes on happening, does it not?'

'In which respect..?'

'I don't know, but I painted Rose, remember? She and I were alone together for a long time, and I heard a lot of things that she wasn't saying.'

'What about..?'

'About her life, and about you, and your brother. I wouldn't expect you to tell me, and I'm not going to ask, but things aren't as they seem, are they? History rubs off, and you are a part of it, whether you want to be or not. It's in your blood, and that makes you different.'

'Different from what..?'

'From things that you wouldn't understand, any more than I could ever understand how it is to born into all of this, and I daresay they would have had you marry some nobleman or other, just to keep the old blood lines going, and they would have had Michael make a better marriage, and sire legitimate children.'

'Michael has a legitimate child.'

'If you say so, and forgive me if I'm speaking out of line, but I'll be leaving here soon, so it won't matter. My small part in it all will be over.'

She was saying things which rather surprised Victoria, and which were, as she herself had said, somewhat inappropriate, but she supposed that this rather depended on how their relationship might be defined, and this was something which for Victoria defied definition. How much did Pandora know, and how much of that which she said was guesswork, or speculation? She had known Rose well, of course, so what had Rose told her during their long sessions together in the village, and how much did she know of Percival? In any case she decided to say nothing; she could after all scarce defend Rose's fidelity if it came to it, so she said nothing, but she must say something.

'So, how soon are you expecting to leave?'

So there it was, then. There had been no denial or defense, which as far as Pandora was concerned was tacit admission that Nathaniel was not her brothers' child, and perhaps it was this which was causing her distraction. History it seemed was indeed still in the making.

'I'll finish the painting tomorrow, I would think, or the next day, and anyway I'll be gone by the weekend. So this could be our last evening together, and I'd just like to say that, well, it's been an experience. I mean the way I painted Rose, that's something which I've not done before, and then there's you, of course....The woman in a blue dress. I actually think that you might be my finest ever painting.'

'Well, I'm glad you think so. So when can I see it?'

'When it's done....I'll let you know.'

'So, would this be a good night to say goodbye, then, do you think?'

'If you would like to...'

'Would you, taking equality as a given, of course?'

They stood up and went to one another, and the night was theirs to do with as they would.

'Megan

You should know that I have found her. She has left the village, but I have discovered her whereabouts, and she is quite alone, and it will be easy for me now, I think. The child I will leave where she will be found, and may she never know who her mother was. I still so much regret your decision to break our bonds of sisterhood, which were our lives for so long, and to walk away from so much history and suffering is something which I cannot do. I do this for Fiona, and for Corrine, who burned, and were not buried as they should have been, in the way of the sisterhood. I do it for Eve, and for Edith, the first of us, and for all of us who have lived and died since the first curse was put upon the murderer of Jane Mary. She stands now between me and our final aim, but this must wait. She is strong, I know that, but she will not be expecting me, and so, my dear Megan, if this is the last you hear of me, and if you are to be the last of us, think well of me. I will take some time now to prepare myself, and then it will be done, one way or the other.

Sharon.'

Chapter 20

UPON A CERTAIN EVENING, AND THE FOLLOWING MORNING

'Broadacre' was in fact in a sense anonymous, unless one knew where one was going, and had prior knowledge of its' whereabouts. It was in any case nothing more than a small hamlet of a dozen or so houses, separated by a matter of two or three miles in either direction from the next and nearest settlement. It was the kind of place which one might pass through on the road to nowhere in particular, and which slowed vehicular traffic on the 'B' road upon which it was located due to the number of cars parked on either side of the highway, since none of the houses had driveways or garages. There was no road - sign indicating ones' arrival at or departure from the place, and no remaining evidence of old farm buildings or the like, which might once have been here, and might have given the place its' name or seen to its' founding, and it seemed to Peter Shortbody to have no particular reason for being where it was. It could, he pondered as he approached the end of his bus journey, equally well have been moved to anywhere along the road to a more convenient location, nearer to shops, amenities and so on, and nobody who chose to dwell here would have been any the worse for it. The landscape surrounding the hamlet was of flat, pastoral and otherwise agricultural land, broken only by the occasional coppice of oak or hazel, and the somewhat nondescript houses which were its' constituent were for the most part semi – detached, having been built, he assumed, sometime during the last century. In any event it was here that sometime in her more recent life, a girl whose parents had named Felicity, and whom Peter had for a time encountered during their teenaged years, had decided to make her home, and so for the first time in his life he had reason to stop at this small conurbation, since here it was that had he been invited to spend the evening.

Felicity Bird, Sheila Stevenson and her latest man – friend, four others of homosexual persuasion, and of course Maddie Young; an eclectic mix of people with whom Peter was to share his evening repast, but as he alighted from the omnibus, which would be the last to pass this way before the morning, it was the latter of these to whom his thoughts turned. The girl in his dream had become manifest in her womanhood, and significant in his life, and he was about to meet her again in this most unlikely of circumstances.

For Barrington Thomas the appointed hour finally arrived, as will all appointed hours, however slow they may be in the coming, and upon this hour he closed the front door of number two, The Green, behind him. He walked past number three, the house which belonged to a certain Sally Parsons and which currently stood empty, thence past the Dog and Bottle public house, and so to his destination, the front door of number five, which was the residence of the Fox family, and at about the time that Peter Shortbody had located the house within the small hamlet in which he would pass his evening, Barrington sounded the door knocker. Barrington had during his recent life lost his faith in his former god, and had been infatuated with a young woman who as it had turned out was not deserving of his infatuation, if such things can be said to be deserved, and from whom he had by now severed all emotional ties. He had been a Catholic monk, with all that this had implied, had slept with more prostitutes than he could remember, and had fought with an addiction to opiates which had seen his life fall to near ruination. He could therefore be said to have experienced certain quite uncommon extremes of life and emotion, and yet as he waited by the door he felt a nervousness quite disproportionate to that which he was about to do, which was to go on a date with a young woman. Apparently, he briefly mused to himself, people lose no sensitivity to the lesser things in life, regardless of how extreme their lives may have otherwise been. His muse was short – lived, however, and within less than a minute the door was opened, and before him stood Sandra Fox. She was attired in a modestly cut dress of a light grey colour and low – heeled shoes, and wore subtle makeup on her undoubtedly lovely face; moderation in all things, appropriate perhaps to a first date with a gentleman admirer, and she smiled for him.

'Hi….'

'Hello…'

'So, where are we going, then?'

'I've no idea, actually. I don't get out very much, I thought I'd leave the venue to you.'

'Let's head to town then, shall we? I'll call for a cab to pick us up on the road.'

'Sure; good idea….'

She retired briefly indoors and collected her jacket, which she put on whilst closing the door behind her, and simultaneously tapping a key on her mobile telephone which would put her in touch with a local taxi – company. She ordered a cab for the village Green, and they walked together the short distance to the road.

'Are you hungry?'

'I could eat, certainly.'

'Well I know some places, let's see where we can get a table, if not we'll find a pub.'

'Okay....'

Within a minute a taxi pulled up beside them, and Barrington and Sandra were on their way, to wherever they might be going.

The departure of the two near – neighbours went largely unobserved, save by a certain Isabella Baxter, who had happened to be looking out of her bedroom window at the time. Isabella had, by her own and by any outward and objective observation and analysis, been doing okay. By slow degrees, with the passing of time and the distraction of more ordinary life, she was leaving the trauma of her having been raped behind. It was there, still, but now it formed a lesser part of her, and as far as such things can ever be forgotten or absorbed into the wholeness of a person, this process was happening. She currently had in any case her final, advanced school examinations to consider, and to work upon, and whilst neither she nor her tutors expected that she would do anything other than excel in all subjects, this was at least a further distraction for her. And then, two days ago, something had happened which had halted her still sometimes finely balanced emotional recovery in its' tracks, and of all places it had happened the last time she had gone to her chess club. The evening itself had been unexceptional, save that none of her more regular and challenging opponents had been in attendance, so she had won two quite easy games and had caught an early bus home. Whilst she was there, however, the club secretary had approached her with news which he had thought would be good news for her, and indeed it should have been good news, but it was news which on the bus journey home had brought her disgust and anger at that which had happened to her back into sharp focus. Apparently, the last informal international chess contest had been considered by all to have been such a success that the event was to be repeated during the summer, and this time seven countries were to be represented, and the contest was to take place over a ten day period. Players from the nations of Britain, France, Italy and Germany were once again to be there, but now Denmark, Norway and Sweden would send players, and the event would be hosted in the city of Copenhagen. Furthermore, her chess club had been asked by the events' organizers to again provide two of the eight British players, the numbers by country having been reduced by two to partially compensate for the greater number of participating countries, and she and Richard Templeton would be the obvious choice, being the two highest ranking players at the club.

This was indeed an accolade, and this time she had been selected on her own merit, rather than by default, as had happened the first time. She had thanked the secretary, walked out into the still quite warm evening, and felt once again the cold chill of fear with which she had fought for so long. She could not go, of course, this she knew well enough. It was one thing to function in the familiar and usual surroundings of her home, her school and her club, but to take her current state of mind and being back into anything like similar circumstances to Dusseldorf, to be amongst strangers and to stay in a foreign hotel would be beyond her, and this she understood with little need for further thought or consideration. There was otherwise no reason for her not to go. Her examinations would be over by then, and whichever university she would attend would not yet require her presence, and in all other regards the opportunity of gaining further international experience against players who would be at least her equal, was something which under different circumstances she would not for a moment have refused, quite apart from the fact that she had never been to Copenhagen, and would have very much liked to have done so. But the circumstances were not different, they were as they were, and earlier this evening, having given herself sufficient time to be quite certain, she had 'phoned the secretary and thanked him for his consideration, but informed him that for personal reasons she would be unable to go. He had accepted her refusal, of course, if only reluctantly, and she had ended the call with a sense of relief, but also with a feeling of sickness in the pit of her stomach; Barnabas Overton, Neil Finley, Paul Stewart and Edward Fullerton, four names which were indelibly etched into her psyche, and who knew if any of them might even also be selected to compete in the contest. She had won a victory against them, and had exposed their horrible deeds to the world, or at least to those closest to them, but however that might be they were ever and anon in her thoughts, and still they held her life in check. Thus it was that as she looked from her bedroom window out onto the village Green, and watched distractedly as Barrington and Sandra caught their taxi, her hatred for her attackers found new voice in the ever complex chorus of her young soul.

'Hello….Felicity, isn't it, if I have the right house?'

'My god, Peter Shortbody, it really is you, isn't it?'

'I believe so, the last time I checked.'

'Maddie said you had hardly changed, and she was right… Come in, for heaven's sake, it really is good to see you.'

'You too, I'm sure.'

The hostess for the evening stood aside, allowing her latest and last guest into her house, and Peter crossed the threshold. In contrast to himself, apparently, Felicity Bird had changed a good deal since his last memory of her, and he would have passed her in the street without recognition. The most notable change was that at some juncture during her life she had shed the last of her adolescent body – fat, and her facial features had changed accordingly. He was shown into a narrow hallway, where the next person whom he encountered had apparently left the assembled throng to come and greet him, and who by contrast to his hostess merely looked like an older and slightly more rounded version of her former self. Sheila Stevenson had always had a reputation amongst the boys at school for wearing her upper clothing more tightly about her than was strictly necessary; she could comfortably have gone a size up with her school blouse or pullover, but in any case thus, by accident or design, and all of the boys had assumed the latter, did she show off her undoubted feminine attributes to their full advantage, and some things apparently did not change with age or the passing of time, save that she was no longer restricted to wearing anything like a school uniform.

'Well my god, hello Peter, it's been a long time, hasn't it?'

Such a voice could, Peter imagined, melt ice from a considerable distance, and she lowered her head whilst keeping him in her gaze and smiling her most coquettish smile, before making her final approach and kissing him gently and for a longer than necessary time on the corner of his mouth.

'Hello Sheila, yes it has, hasn't it?'

'Anyway,' said Felicity, 'come through and meet everyone else, we can catch up on old times later.'

'I look forward to that.' Said Sheila, who was still melting ice as she exchanged knowing looks with Felicity, although quite what they knew was beyond Peter, since he had not to the best of his memory had any encounter with either woman which could have been considered even flirtatious; Sheila had always reserved her most provocative self for the boys who had been in a more advanced or pronounced state of masculinity than had he, and now Felicity briefly looked somewhat embarrassed or impatient with the behavior of her friend.

The everyone else to whom Felicity had referred were already seated at table by the time Peter entered the quite small dining room. Maddie Young was the only other person present whom Peter knew, and she was seated at a place from whence it would have been hard for her to extricate herself, so she merely smiled at him across the assembly, and he returned her smile; they were pleased to see one another.

'Right, well, have a seat, Peter,' said Felicity 'and help yourself to wine, unless you'd prefer something else?'

'Wine's fine, thank you.'

'Somebody do the introductions, I'll get the first course.'

Peter took his place at table, which was not a large table, and there were nine people sat around it in quite close proximity to one another. Sheila took her place beside him, and throughout the meal there was perhaps unavoidable physical contact between them both above and under the table, although Peter was quite sure that the lady was doing nothing to try to avoid this, particularly as the evening proceeded. For now in any case she took it upon herself to introduce him to the others. Beside Peter at the furthest head of the table from the kitchen door sat Roderick, who Peter supposed must be Sheila's latest conquest, so why he had been placed between them was a mystery to him, but there it was. Roderick was child psychologist. Opposite Peter sat Maddie, and next to her were Mark and David, who were respectively a camp and un – camp gay couple, David, Peter surmised, being some two decades or more the elder of his partner. David and Mark were in the antiques business, specializing in furniture. Next to Sheila sat Ingrid and Caroline, respectively a civil servant and an interior designer, who were of similar and indeterminate age, but were by some measure the youngest females present. In any other context or situation Peter would not have assumed either to be homosexual, and nor would he here, aside perhaps from the fact that they were both wearing trousers, and sensible shirts for that matter, which he thought was not the usual feminine dress – code for dinner parties, and he also noted that neither wore any makeup, and both had short and fairly severe hairstyles. He then found himself briefly considering the nature of lesbian sexuality; was the idea of it to look more like a man, and was this an attractive thing to other lesbians, or was he missing the point of it? In any case this particular train of thought was interrupted as Felicity now took her place at the other head of the table. Here was not the classic boy – girl – boy - girl seating arrangement which he believed was often the thing at such gatherings, but perhaps given the varying sexuality of the assembly such things did not apply, or so Peter mused to himself as Sheila finished the introductions. He also wondered briefly how such a various and eclectic representation of humanity had ended up around a dinner table together, but this was never explained to him, and nor did he ever ask.

'Everyone, this is Peter, who we three girls were at school with together.'

'So,' said David 'quite a reunion then.'

'Indeed it is.' Said Sheila

Felicity had reentered the room bearing a large serving plate and salad dish, so food was now on the agenda, which Peter was pleased about as he was by now feeling rather hungry.

'Peter, I hope you don't mind going veggie for the evening, there are more vegetarians than omnivores here so it seemed the obvious thing…'

'No, not at all...'

It would also transpire during conversation that two of the party had a gluten allergy, and two others were lactose intolerant, and Ingrid was unable to eat either, and Peter briefly took to wondering what else was left which could be eaten. Stuffed mushrooms, however, seemed to be acceptable to all, and thus was the first course served, and so did Peter Shortbody's evening begin.

The first establishment which Barrington and Sandra came across which had a free table on this weekend evening, where it seemed that most of the town and its' environs had gone out for dinner, was a Mexican restaurant which neither had been to before, but which offered a quite intimately situated table in the quite noisy environment. Latin American music formed the backdrop to a generally energetic ambience, created by busy staff and a mostly quite young clientele; not perhaps ideal conditions for two people to become better acquainted, but on the other hand any awkwardness which might have existed between them was absorbed and distracted by the general melee, and they ordered bottled beer and tacos to start their evening. They touched bottles, and Sandra began that which would prove to be an enlightening conversation for both parties, which began at their shared place of abode.

'So, how do you like living in our village?'

'Very much, actually, I mean the people who I've met or had dealings with have all been good people, I'm very happy living there. How about you..?'

'Yes, well I've lived there most of my life so I don't know what it's like to live anywhere else, really, apart from at uni, which is completely different, of course, but it's a nice enough place to come home to, I suppose.'

'Have you had many dealings with my landlord, Percival?'

'Not many, really, I mean I've talked to him a few times over the years, but otherwise not. He's something of a maverick, I believe, made his money in the city and now, well I'm not sure what he does. I believe he writes, or something.'

'Yes, I've not met him often myself...Your parents don't seem to be home very much, as far as I can tell.'

'Mum and dad work abroad, mostly, and even if they're not working they tend to stay away. They take six – month contracts on places on mainland Europe, that kind of thing. It's the way they've always been since my sister and I have been able to look after ourselves.'

'Your sister isn't that old though, is she?'

'Emma's seventeen, and can fend for herself okay. Mostly she lives with Keith and Meadow, anyway, or rather with their son, Basil, and that suits her well enough. Apart from Emma and I we've never been what you might call a close family.'

'You're close to your sister, though?'

'We're nothing like each other, but yes, we do okay, as sisters do, you know? So what about before Middlewapping?, People say you were a monk, but I've never been sure about that.'

'It's true, actually, I was in semi – closed order for a while, in Wales of all places.'

'So what happened?'

'Put in a nutshell I lost my faith. I was born and raised a catholic, you see, and was destined for Priesthood, which is what my parents wanted for me. I even took a degree in theology to pave the way, so to speak, and I was all set to go, take my holy orders and so on.'

'Christ, if you'll excuse the expression, so what happened to change the course of your life so radically?'

'I met someone….I mean in retrospect she was not the whole cause of it, and it's all quite complex, in a way, but well, let's say that part of it all was that I was put off the idea of celibacy for life. I now see celibacy as a kind of perversion, and a denial of ones' natural self, so I sort of went the other way for a while. I went to Thailand, became addicted to heroin, ran out of money and was all set for a monumental crash, but I pulled out at the last minute, thanks mainly to my sister.'

'Your sister…?'

'My younger sister, May; she rejected our inherited religious doctrine early in life and remains a staunch atheist. She came to Thailand to rescue me, otherwise I actually believe I might be dead by now.'

'Good grief….So hang on, what was the order of things, were you a monk before the drugs or afterwards?'

'No, the drugs came first, and, well, I was so dysfunctional when I got home that I did what a lot of off – the – rails young men do in Thailand, actually, the difference is that they become Buddhist and I stayed with Catholicism. I decided to give God one more chance, so I became a monk, but in the end God and I weren't right for each other so we parted company once and for all, and more or less that's when I came to live in the village, seeking a quiet refuge and a life more ordinary, I suppose.'

'It must have been hard, losing your faith.'

'It left a gap I must confess, but in the end giving up god was a lot easier than giving up heroin. Heroin puts your head in a place that it's hard to come back from, so I put myself away from the world in a place where there would be no temptation.'

'And that worked, I take it.'

'Yes, I'm free of it now, though you never really lose it, or the memory of it, and since I left the order I suppose I've been looking for something to fill the spiritual void.'

'So have you found it yet?'

'It's still work in progress, you might say.'

'And there was I thinking that you were a fairly normal person, if you see what I mean…'

'Well, I suppose you could say that I am, now. I mean I work for the local Parks Department and go to the pub about twice a week, but it's a life which suits me, for now.'

'Yes, I can see how that might work, after what you've been through…So, what about the girl or woman who kind of sent you off the rails in the first place, where is she in all of this?'

'She's gone, I don't see her anymore.'

He could perhaps have elaborated upon this, but preferred not to, and the statement was made in such a way as to discourage further enquiry, or so he hoped, but any case just then a waitress came to their table and thus in a sense to his rescue. Hitherto they had not thought much about food, and they quickly ordered from the menu, and agreed to share various dishes, and they ordered more beer. He had said his part, for now, and aside from brushing over his near obsession with Miranda Spool, he had been honest with her, for what else could he have been? The interruption in any event gave them pause for thought, and time for Sandra to realign her thoughts regarding her companion for the evening, and now it was her turn to give some account of her recent life; foundations were being laid upon which the new relationship could be built, if both wished to do so.

'So, what about you..?'

'What about me?'

'Whatever you like, it's all new to me.'

The main course at the dining table of Felicity Bird was to be gluten – free pasta, mixed with various vegetables and fresh herbs tossed in olive and truffle oil, served with gluten – free bread and the remains of the salad. The conversation had thus far been dominated by the four former classmates, who each recounted incidents and events from their school days, and recalled the names and characteristics of their various fellow students and their teachers. For Peter's benefit, more substance was added to the post – school lives of Fiona Graham, Jen Parkinson and Maurine Martin, of whom Peter by now had better recall, and now into the frame came some of the boys, who in truth he had scarce thought about since his last day at school. Among these were Neil Woodhouse, who had been known to all as *'Woody'*. and Neil Tyson, who as memory served had been the most sexually mature and active of his peers, and who made no secret of this fact, and also here were Paul Weaver, Kenneth Hogan and Mark Harman; names and people who were now made to stand out against the backdrop of his early and not entirely happy academic years. Sheila Stevenson was the most vocal in this regard, and Peter momentarily wondered how well she had come to know the young men in question. In any case, continuity and further substance to her recall was provided by Maddie and Felicity where required, and it was Sheila who first brought Peter into the historical picture.

'Of course, you were always the enigma, Peter.'

'Yes, so I've been told, although I still find this hard to believe.'

'Well yes, you would. I don't think you had any idea what was going on, but certain of us girls were quite taken with you, actually.'

This statement came with a knowing look which was directed across the table in the direction of Maddie, and Peter in any case assumed that it was not Sheila who had been taken with him, since if she had been taken with people she had tended to allow them to take her behind the boiler – room, and he had not received such invitation.

'Yes, well we live and learn, I suppose.'

'Indeed we do, and it's never too late to make up for missed opportunities, you know.'

With this she pushed her thigh against his with more force than had hitherto been the case, the hemline of her anyway quite short dress having by now ridden some way up her leg, and Peter wondered at this quite open and obvious flirtation with her partner seated on the other side of him, but Roderick for the moment seemed quite oblivious to or ignorant of the goings – on, and it was in any case he who now took the conversation in a new direction.

'So, Peter, Sheila tells me that you've been an accountant all of your working life, now retired.'

'Then Sheila was correct in her summary.'

'I always thought accountants were by reputation supposed to be boring people, but you seem to be anything but, if I might say so.'

Peter could not recall his having done or indeed said anything particularly interesting during the course of the evening, and he wondered momentarily what might have been said about him before his arrival, but he let this speculation go unresolved.

'I can't say that I've ever really thought about it.'

For reasons best known to them, this statement caused mild amusement among the three women who had known him at school, and Peter surmised that sufficient alcohol had by now been consumed to make laughter an easy thing, requiring little provocation.

'So what do you think about then, when you're not creating balance – sheets?'

The question was too big. How by the stars was one to answer such an enquiry when a thousand thoughts came and went through the course of an ordinary day, never mind extraordinary days? There was no place from which to start, and of a sudden Peter became lost in the question, and in the memories of the people who sat around him, and impressions of how they now were, and for a moment he wondered what on earth he was doing here. In truth he had never been comfortable in social situations, and of a sudden he felt a strong urge to stand up and leave. He did neither, however, and neither did he say anything, and just then he glanced up at Maddie, who was smiling her understanding across the table. So that was it, then. There was Sheila with all of her ridiculous flirtation, and Roderick with his ridiculous questions, and Felicity with her gluten – free bread, and then there was Maddie, and of all of them it was Maddie who understood him, and had pretended not to understand her mathematics homework, and had walked part of the way home with him. She was the reason for his having come here, to this place of ritual eating and casual and pointless conversation, and he found himself wishing very much now that they could be alone together.

'Well, I'm sure raising two small children must occupy a good deal of ones' thoughts, at least I remember how it was when my two were small.'

Maddie to the rescue, then, and Peter was off the hook.

'Yes,' said Felicity 'tell us about, what are they called… Bronwyn and Elizabeth, isn't it?'

'Yes…' said Peter, finally 'well they do rather, I suppose, occupy ones' thoughts, that is.'

'Bronwyn's an unusual name, how did that come to be?'

'Their mother is Welsh, she named the firstborn, I named the second.'

'I expect they're very pretty children…Identical twin girls, I daresay you'll have some fun with them when they get older. Right, are we all done, I'll fetch the dessert.'

'Well, my life to date hasn't been anywhere near as interesting as yours.'

'Not to you, perhaps, and anyway a bit less interest isn't always a bad thing. Try me anyway.'

'Well, I'm mid – way through university, on loan to a scientific institute which will help with my thesis, and help pay the tuition fees. I'm basically working on chemical elements and their practical application in potential new products, which isn't exactly the stuff of riveting conversation, but I'm interested in that kind of thing; breaking things down to their smallest component parts. I could tell you what this table is made of, if you really want to know…'

'Some other time, perhaps, but it's testament to your ability that they want someone as young as you doing their research, isn't it?'

'Well, I work cheap, but yes, I suppose so.'

Barrington smiled as he drank from his beer bottle.

'What's funny?'

'Nothing's funny, but I was just comparing our academic lives. Yours is all about cold, hard facts and the quest for scientific knowledge, mine was all about faith and matters spiritual, and nothing to do with science or knowledge whatsoever, really. Couldn't really be more contrasting, could they?'

'No, I suppose not, can't prove the existence of god, right?'

'If we could it would cease to be faith and would become science, which would sort of defeat the object of it, I suppose.'

'Yes, I suppose so, but deep science has its' mysteries as well. The more we discover, and the more we prove, the more we realize how little we actually know, and there are so many things we can't explain yet. We're really only scratching the surface, fumbling about trying to make sense of things.'

'Give me an example of that.'

'Well, I suppose the most obvious one is the beginning of everything, you know?'

'The '*big bang*' theory...'

'I mean we reckon that theoretically we know what happened in the first few nanoseconds of the universes' existence, and can try to calculate how much of each element was created, and theoretically we think we can now measure the rate of expansion of the universe, and so on, but we're no closer to explaining how or why it happened.',

'*Created*' being the operative word, I suppose.'

'Exactly...Everything had to come from somewhere, and in this respect we're no closer to the answer than religion, so, you know, we may be closer together than you think. Things which are perceived wisdom or known facts one day are debunked the next, and the next '*known facts*' take their place.'

'Scientific truth being a transient and flexible beast, in fact...'

'Exactly, which is okay so long as ideas and theories don't become dogma, then we get stuck, and nothing moves forward. And then of course there's the other big one, how life began on a lifeless planet. All the evidence says that this happened, and of course it must have happened, and we can theorize as to how this could have been, but nobody's ever witnessed it happening, of course, and the chances of it happening are vanishingly small, theoretically speaking. Experiments have been carried out on a small scale to try to replicate conditions on a young earth, but nothing's happened so far.'

'Hard to replicate something which took billions of years to happen, I suppose.'

'Exactly, and then millions of years of only single – celled organisms busily replicating themselves, until one day and somehow life becomes more complex, and the cells begin cooperating and specializing, and from there all things are possible.'

'The beginning of evolution...'

'Which hasn't stopped since, and during what is generally known as the *'Cambrian explosion'* things really get going, but even that's measured over millions of years. The timescales are hard to imagine, and by now virtually all things which have existed have become extinct, what we see today is far less than one percent of all species which have lived, and eventually there's you and I in all of our massive complexity and intellect, sitting here and talking about it, but how it all began is still only theory.'

'As opposed to god the creator of all things...You can see why people believed that, and still believe it, of course, and why they still default to it. Just call it a mystery, believe in ancient scripture and a divine creator and have done with it.'

'Even ancient scriptures are open to interpretation though, are they not?'

'Oh absolutely, and we, or rather they now, aren't without religious dogma, and we only see what we're allowed to see.'

'I've heard it said that science and religion are like two people climbing different sides of the same mountain, and if they ever met at the top neither would have the answers to the big questions.'

'Best to keep climbing hopefully, then...'

Both smiled now, and the food was delivered to the table, which gave further pause to the conversation, but Barrington was keen to learn more about this clearly intelligent and thoughtful young woman.

'Okay, so that's your academic life to date, so what about the rest of it?'

'Which particular part of the rest of it..?'

'How about the romantic aspects of your life...?'

'Well, romantically my life thus far can best be described as a blank page, at least in terms of anyone who has ever reciprocated, as you might say.'

'I'm surprised to hear that...'

'Well, that's how it is.'

'So you've never been in love?'

'I don't know, what's love, but no, you could say not...Next question?'

'Well, if it isn't getting too personal, and please tell me if it is, you were quite ill lately, and nobody I ask seems to know why.'

Sandra ordered two more beers from a passing waitress, and tried briefly to order her thoughts. He was right, she did not have to answer the question, and for a moment she fought an inner battle as to whether she should. They hardly knew one another, after all, but her instincts were telling her that here was a person of integrity, who as far as she knew had been honest with her regarding the most intimate aspects of his life, so what was to be lost by the telling? The evening was going well, and she liked him, and if they were to move beyond tonight then she would have to tell him sooner or later, and he may be no priest, but confessions do not always need a priest.

'Some people know...They're just being kind.'

'Sorry, I don't understand....Look, you really don't have to tell me.'

'It's okay...It's just not the easiest thing for me to talk about, but putting it simply, well, I tried to kill myself.'

This took a moment. Here was a beautiful and intelligent young woman, who had never been in love, so that wasn't the reason, so what on earth had been the reason, and what on earth could he say now?

'I see...Well, I'm sorry, of course.'

'It wasn't quite that simple...'

'Life seldom is in my experience.'

'No, well the thing is, at certain times during my life I've struggled, you know, and I've been on prescribed medication, and I was having a bad day, and over – medicated, you might say. Then I got drunk, and everything went into free – fall, and so I took more pills. I can't say that I set out to consciously commit suicide, because I didn't, but things sort of built on themselves, and my little sister found me the next morning, otherwise...Well, let's just say that we both seem to have cheated death, don't we?'

'Yes, it does seem so...'

'I'm okay now though, mostly, anyway.'

She smiled, which was when as far as Barrington was concerned she looked her most beautiful, and if anybody could empathize with the state of being which could push a person to such extremes it was he. There were times in Thailand when it would have been an easy thing for him to have taken the easy way out of his life. For a moment he was lost for words, and she spoke first.

'So there, now you know, and you must make of it what you will.'

'I make nothing of it, other than to be well, sorry....And just to say that, you know, I understand how life can get like that.'

'It's the blank sheet of paper, you know. Sometimes life can seem empty of everything, and that isn't a good feeling.'

'No, it isn't...It seems that we both have a void to fill.'

'Yes I suppose so...Still, we're both still here, so that must be something to celebrate, mustn't it?'

'I'll drink to that...'

By now they had eaten as much of the food as they had appetite for, and within the hour they had drunk another beer and shared the bill, and were in a taxi on their way back to the village. Barrington's thoughts on the journey home were focused on how he should end the evening. Should he walk her to her door, in the hope that he might kiss her goodnight, or merely say thanks for her company and leave her to go her own way? How had their relationship changed since they had met earlier in the evening; were they friends now, or were they beyond that, the point being that he did not wish to assume anything, and did not wish to push his attentions upon her, so better perhaps to be patient, in the hope that they might see each other again, and see how things might go from there. The unseen ties which bind people to one another were newly formed between them, and could easily be broken. The vixen, meanwhile, was keeping her thoughts to herself.

The remainder of the evening around the dining table went on somewhat as had its' beginning, save that at some juncture and much to his relief, Peter ceased to be the centre of attention, his novelty amongst those who aside from Roderick for the most part knew one another quite well having apparently worn off. Therefore although he was still keen to leave, the urgency to do so had diminished, and he was able to relax somewhat, at least in so far as Peter Shortbody ever relaxed in such surroundings. As the evening went on, Mark became increasingly vocal and emotional in direct relation to the amount of alcohol which he consumed, with David providing occasional reassurance that his life was not in fact so bleak or terrible as he seemed to think.

Ingrid was clearly the most politically minded of the assembly, sounding forth regarding the perceived shortcomings of the present government and people in general, particularly men, her intolerance for certain foodstuffs clearly extending into the wider world. The oppression of women was high on her agenda, which apparently included the need or expectation of society, and for society Peter read men, for women to dress in sexually provocative manner, although the young lady did not seem to Peter to be particularly oppressed, and Sheila, who was by some margin the most sexually provocatively dressed among them did not seem to him to be particularly oppressed either. Quite the contrary, in fact, and indeed it seemed to Peter that if any of the party were oppressed then it was Caroline, Ingrid's partner, who was mild and unassuming by nature and spoke very little, and when she did speak she was rather put down by Ingrid, and told that her opinions were either wrong or insufficient. Perhaps then there were different kinds of oppression, some being more acceptable than others, but in any case he let the matter go in the interests of not drawing further attention to himself, or involving himself in subjects where others, and particularly female others, clearly knew or perceived better than he. Meanwhile Felicity fulfilled her role as hostess well enough, and Sheila, who apparently had no interest in politics or the world at large whatsoever, concentrated her attentions on Peter, sometimes leaning into him to share intimacies, or to make further enquiries as to his life, which by the close of the evening he had begun to find somewhat irksome. Maddie clearly knew her friend well, and made it known to Peter by non – verbal means that she understood his discomfort. He in turn and by similar means asked her when it would be polite for them to depart, by which time he had begun to find the house, the conversation and the ambient background music rather depressing, and apparently at some point just before midnight they had reached this significant social juncture. By now cheese and crackers had been served, and somewhat to Peter's surprise Ingrid ate both, despite the fact that he was quite sure that the crackers must contain wheat, and last time that he had checked cheese was a form of processed milk, so perhaps the lady suffered only from selective intolerance of such things, which he mused must be a lesser form of the condition. In any case quite shortly after coffee and mint – thins had been served, Maddie excused herself and returned a few minutes later. She spoke a few quiet words with Felicity, then announced to all and sundry and particularly to Peter that she had ordered a taxi, and within another fifteen minutes and having said goodbye to all assembled, Peter found himself once again in the small hallway with his three former classmates. Each in turn hugged one another goodbye and promised further meetings in the near future, Maddie left the house to secure the taxi whilst Peter bid his hostess farewell.

'Goodnight, Peter, it really has been good to see you again. I hope we weren't too much of a trial for you.'

'Not at all, thank you for a pleasant evening, the food was excellent.'

'Well, I hope to see you again soon.'

They kissed cheeks and exchanged smiles, she returned to her guests, and Sheila was now all that stood between Peter and his final escape. Sheila was by now clearly quite intoxicated, and this time as she put her arms around him the kiss was full on the lips, hers opening slightly to invite his entry, which he declined.

'Goodnight, Peter, don't be a stranger…'

Which Peter considered to be an odd and unreasonable instruction, since no matter how many people he met he was bound to be a stranger to most people, but by now he had backed a sufficient distance toward the door, she released him, and having picked up his small overnight bag, he was free. Only later did he discover that she had quietly slipped a small card into his jacket pocket, upon which was printed her telephone number, but for now he joined Maddie at the taxi, and they were on their way, leaving the small hamlet of Broadacre behind them.

'Well done, you made it through.'

'It was interesting to meet them both again.'

'Yes, I'm sure it was...'

She smiled again in the darkness, and turned to look out of the window.

The next morning Peter awoke with a slight headache, and a sense that his life had changed during its' most recent day. He sat up in bed, and looked down at the figure who slept contentedly beside him. He drank from the glass of water which had been placed on his bedside table, and relived his last waking hour. Peter had come carrying in his overnight bag clean socks, underpants and casual shirt, and a pair of pyjamas, and it was whilst wearing the latter that he had encountered Maddie outside the bathroom, who was attired in her nightdress. He had come from the spare bedroom, which had been made up in anticipation of his coming, but now Madeline Young had something to say.

'Look, Peter, I'm not expecting any kind of grand passion, I think we're both a little past that, but since we're here together it's a shame to sleep alone, don't you think?'

These were not the passionate and imploring words which she had spoken to him in his dream, and the lady who stood before him no longer wore sparkly eye makeup, but they were words, nonetheless, and they were real words, and they begged a response. So don't think, Peter, for once in your life be spontaneous.

'Yes, I suppose it is.'

'I mean if you'd rather not, then that's fine, I understand.'

She understood, and the understanding between them which had in so short a time come to be was enough, and they took one another's hand and walked together to her bed, she wearing her nightdress and he wearing his pyjamas. They held each other, she quickly fell asleep, and Peter's last waking memory was of a feeling of gentle and contented love, the like of which he did not believe that he had ever felt before. This had not been the way that he had expected this day to end, and he wondered to what extent this was true from her perspective, but like so much of that which had happened in regard to Madeline Young, upon this Peter Shortbody could for now only speculate.

Only a little later the same morning, May awoke in the bedroom of her brothers' house which they called her bedroom, feeling sleepy but refreshed, and in need of coffee and a pee, and not necessarily in that order. She kept some clothes here, and now she threw on a T shirt which was long enough to be decent enough if she encountered her brother, and in her semi – sleep state she covered the short distance to the bathroom and opened the already semi – open door. Before her, at the sink and facing away from her, stood the figure of a young woman, and she was naked. In the second or so that it took May to register the strangeness of this encounter, and to convince herself that she was not in fact still asleep and dreaming, the young woman had turned around, wrapped a hand towel about her waist and put her arm across her chest to further cover her modesty. May took one step back and averted her eyes, although in truth her surprise still rather had the better of her. At least by now though, she was almost fully awake.

'Christ, I'm so sorry, Barrington didn't…I mean I had no idea there was anybody else here.'

'Nor did I….'

'Right, well, so you must be…'

'I'm Sandra.'

'Sandra…Yes, of course.'

'And you are…?'

'I'm May…Maisy, Barrington's brother, I mean Barrington's sister. So he didn't tell you I was here, then…'

'No, he didn't.'

By now there was little point in further averting her gaze, so May locked on to the light blue eyes, and instinctively concluded that in all regards, and she had by now seen most of the regards, here was the most attractive young woman that she had seen in a long time.

'Well anyway, I just wanted to, you know, use the bathroom, so I'll just wait 'til you've done, then.'

'Okay, well I won't be a moment.'

'No rush, I'll go and make some coffee, would you like some?'

'Sure, why not, when I've got some clothes on...'

'Yes, of course. I'll see you in a bit, then.'

May continued on to the stairs, which she descended in search of coffee. So, her brother had scored, then, and by all appearances it was a high score, and as she reached the kitchen and set the kettle to boil, she mused that it was a noteworthy thing that Barrington's lady – friends had a habit of presenting themselves naked to the world. In this instance, however, she was certain that it had not been intentional, which made definitive distinction between the two situations, and, she assumed, between the two women. Anyway, well done, brother, you appear to have done rather well for yourself. Maisy smiled inwardly, which made it to her outward self as she found the cups, which this morning would be three cups.

Before we conclude the events of this morning for Barrington and Peter, we will hear of a matter of significance which occurred on the same morning, not so far away from the village, in Middlewapping Manor. At least the matter was of significance to the daughter of the household, who was shortly to see her portrait for the first time. She and the painter, Pandora, had spent the last two nights together, and during the previous evening Pandora had declared the painting finished. Victoria had been keen for a first viewing, but Pandora had persuaded her to wait for the better light of the morning, when the painting would look at its' best. On such mornings it was the habit of Victoria to rise early, to return for a short while to her bedroom, and to use her more usual bathroom, so as not to arouse the suspicion of her parents regarding her nocturnal activities. She was her own woman, of course, but under her parents' roof she thought it better and anyway easier to avoid confrontation regarding that which may seem to them to be unseemly or inappropriate behavior. Her covert love affair and the situation which allowed for it were, however, about to end; Pandora was leaving her temporary accommodation and returning to her home in Sussex, and the unveiling of the portrait would in a way symbolize the end of their secret liaison.

So it was that on this morning Victoria dressed and returned to the new extension, where Pandora had made coffee, and had made the painting ready for inspection. During the night they had been lovers, but now they resumed their other role, as painter and subject, which was a quite different thing.

'So are you ready?

'Yes, I suppose so. I'm a bit nervous though, which is silly, isn't it?'

'Well anyway, here you are.'

Without further ceremony, Pandora removed the paint – stained bed sheet which covered her work, and Victoria looked at the image of herself for the first time. Pandora, as was her wont, turned away and made herself busy whilst Victoria stared at herself, and it was fully a minute before either spoke.

'Well, what do you think?'

Still silence for a moment longer, before;

'It's....Beautiful....As a painting, I mean. Really quite beautiful, and it's me, isn't it?'

'Whatever you are, Victoria, but I think I've got you.'

'Yes, I think you have. I look kind of skinny and messed up.'

'Still beautiful, though.'

'Well, if you say so...'

'I do. Do you want your family to see it today, or shall I have it framed first? They always look better framed.'

'No...No, frame it first.'

'Sure...I'll use the same frame as for your father, and the canvass is the same size, of course, so you should look well together.'

'It'll be the first time...I'll be the first woman to hang in the grand dining room.'

'Then you'll outshine them all.'

'Yes, I believe I will. Thank you, Pandora.'

'Thanks for the opportunity.'

'I'll have father transfer the rest of the money today.'

'Well, whenever. I'll have it sent to you, I expect, it should take about two weeks for the framing.'

'You could deliver it yourself.'

'I think better not, don't you? I don't really want to come back here again, if you understand.'

'No, well perhaps best not, then.'

'If I come back the magic might be gone, and I want to remember us as we are now.'

'Of course...Well then, I'll let you get packed. Is somebody coming for you?'

'Yes, now I have your approval I'll let them know I'm ready to go, they should be here in about an hour.'

'Very well then....I'll come and say goodbye.'

'If you wish...'

'Right, I'll see you, then.'

'Sure....'

They smiled, and Victoria left, and she would not return, as Pandora had known that she would not. Pandora packed her few belongings and prepared the painting for transportation, after which she rolled a cigarette and looked for the last time around the place which had been her temporary home, and it had been a good home, for the most part. She would not come back here, but the woman in a blue dress would soon make her final journey, to the place from whence she would never leave, and here she would be long after painter and subject were dead, who had been lovers, for a short while.

'I'll make breakfast for everyone.'

Shortly after May's encounter with Sandra, a fully clothed manifestation of the woman came downstairs with her brother, who would more usually have made the introductions, but this had now become somewhat academic.

'I understand you two have met one another.'

'Yes, we met briefly, thank you, brother.'

It was now that May made her offer to cook, having already made coffee for them all.

'I'll help.' Said Barrington

'Okay, but stay away from the eggs, you're crap at making eggs.'

'I think I'll just go home and take a quick shower and change,' said Sandra 'I feel a bit dressed up for breakfast, I'll only be a few minutes.'

She left, and brother and sister were alone.

'Christ almighty, Batty, you didn't tell me she looked like that.'

'Well, no, I suppose I didn't.'

'You suppose right, and she's some kind of scientific genius, is she?'

'She's very clever, yes.'

'Well be nice to this one, she looks like a hell of a catch.'

'I'm always nice to people.'

'I know you are, but you know what I mean. You didn't tell her I was here.'

'No, sorry, that sort of slipped my mind, I was rather preoccupied last night.'

'Yes, well spare me the details. You're on mushrooms and tomatoes.'

Last night had not gone at all as Barrington might have expected. They had alighted from the taxi, and he had made his offer.

'I'll walk you to your door.'

'How about coffee at yours...?'

So they had gone to number two, and once inside she had looked around at a place where she had never been with her quick, female eyes, before turning to him. The vixen had made up her mind, and they kissed without further ado, and she spoke quietly into his ear.

'This is a nice house. Do you want to show me upstairs?'

So for now all thoughts of coffee were banished in favour of more immediate and stronger and more base desires, and they had gone together to his bedroom, where the young man had discovered that the young lady had been less conservative in her choice of underwear than in her outer clothing. She wore the same stockings and thong that she had worn on the night that she had almost died, when the medics had attended to her, and now she was every young mans' fantasy, and she was feeling very far from dead.

The thoughts which for the most part and not for the first time came to occupy the mind of Peter Shortbody on his bus journey home, centered about the ever thought – provoking subjects of love and infidelity. She had awoken shortly after him, and the morning had passed in quite ordinary fashion; he and Maddie had breakfasted on toast and Marmalade, and had discussed events and people from the previous evening, recounting conversations and in particular in this regard the behavior of their once again mutual friend, Sheila, and the extent to which and manner in which she had wished to renew her acquaintance with Peter; light and convivial conversation, with almost no reference to themselves or their relationship, where it was or where it might be going. That which had happened between them had done so quite naturally, as though it was merely an inevitable extension of their friendship and of their respect for one another. She had demanded nothing of him other than that he be with her whilst she slept, and he had demanded no more of her, and when it had been time to go they had kissed goodbye, and agreed to meet again soon, and that had been an end to the matter.

So then, all was well and good, except that it was not, because in the mind of Peter Shortbody the night had aroused more uncertainty in his already uncertain mind, and raised more questions than it had answered, chief amongst them being whether even now he had been unfaithful to Alice. He had in the literal sense slept with another woman, but in the sense that this was generally taken to mean he had not. He could after all equally well in theory have shared a bed with another man, which would not have been regarded as an infidelity, unless perhaps he had been homosexual or bisexual, which he was not, as it happened, and in any case this would not have been comparing like with like, so to speak, so even here was a certain uncertainty.

And then there was the question of love, and who he loved, and in what way he loved them. He loved Alice, of course, in a way. She was mother to his children, and with her he shared his life, when it was convenient for them both that he do so, but

Maddie Young had by degrees stirred something within his soul that was quite different, which was a different kind of love, he supposed. He also supposed that the next, natural thing would be to invite Maddie to his house, and introduce her to his daughters, but equally well he knew that as things stood this could not be done, so here was another perspective on the matter.

In any case by now the bus had arrived at the bus depot in town, from whence he would catch another bus in order to complete his journey home. He would however stop somewhere first for a cup of coffee, in order to perhaps better define or settle his thoughts. One thing however was at least and by degrees becoming clear to him, which was that if this state of affairs was to continue then sooner or later he must tell Alice about Madeline, the woman that he had slept with, in a way, although in a way he had not, but in any case he loved her, and was perhaps in love with her, so here was a different kind of infidelity, was it not? It was a kind of infidelity of the soul, which he supposed was just as significant, and perhaps more so. He found himself walking towards the old town, so he would go to Dawson's, and considered that all of this might take two cups of coffee, at least.

Sandra walked the short distance home, let herself in, undressed and stood for longer than was usual in the shower, letting the hot water flow over her head and down her body. It had hurt, at first, but then everything had been alright, and much more than alright, actually. The once would – be celibate priest who would not be a priest had taken her maidenhead, and she smiled to herself at that particular thought, and how life could go on in the most unexpected of ways. Finally, she turned off the shower, and stood for a moment with her hands resting against the tiled wall. They had just met, of course, and their journey together had just begun, however long that journey might be, but perhaps, just perhaps, here was a person who could begin to fill the void with which she had lived and fought for so long, and perhaps even she could do so for him. Sandra Fox did not often weep. The morbidity and darkness of spirit which she carried with her through life like a curse would not often allow her emotions the latitude to be either sad or happy, but now as she stood there in her wetness she found that she had tears in her eyes, and they felt like good tears, for any relief from the blackness and blankness of emotional neutrality felt like a good thing. But inside, and it was quite deep inside, the vixen was smiling to herself, and her sometimes so troubled soul was speaking gently to her through her tears, and they were words of comfort, and hope. It was a strange sound, and one that she had not heard for the longest time, but it was a good sound. So, breakfast, then, and beyond that who knew, but she was alive, and from there all things were possible, were they not, even for such as her. The world was hers now, and the world seemed for once and for now like a good place in which to be.

Chapter 21

LOOKING SIGNIFICANT

Michael Tillington, first and only in line to the Tillington Lordship, awoke on this Sunday morning with a sense that today would be a day of significance in his life. Elin was coming to the Manor, having caught a quite early train from Canterbury, which in itself gave the day importance, and further she had secured a day off work tomorrow, when they would go to Orchard House together and meet with Keith, to discuss any and all matters regarding the continuation of the restoration work to their future home. Today, however, was for the Manor House, and the family would eat Sunday luncheon together, and he and Elin had decided that this would be the perfect opportunity for them to announce to his mother and father their engagement to be married. His sister, of course, already knew of the engagement. Significant enough a day, then, but Michael could not have known at this quite early hour how much more significant the day would shortly become. He put on his dressing gown and slippers and went to the kitchen to make coffee, before returning to his bedroom and switching on his laptop computer. He opened his electronic mail, and discarded to 'trash' all of the promotional and other unwanted mail, which left two emails which looked to be of interest, and shortly thereafter did his day and the time to be spent with his parents take on a whole new meaning.

Megan Thomas had made her way to the north of the country. She had found work and accommodation, and had made the first tentative contact with her brother, who worked and lived here with his wife and two children, none of whom Megan had met. She had not seen her brother for many years, and his first reaction to her telephonic contact had not been a positive one, and they were still yet to meet, but she lived in hope that they could in time be reconciled. She had had no word from Sharon since the email which she had written regarding her intent to confront the witch Rebecca, and she worried now for her friend. And then by chance it came to be that on this Sunday morning, as she was scrolling through news items on her laptop, she came upon a small and seemingly insignificant article, at least it would seem insignificant to most people, but the article would change Megan's day completely, and might indeed change her life.

Michael opened the first of the two emails, which had been sent last evening by Fifi Fielding, and which read as follows;

'Dear Mr Tillington

Please find attached an outline plan of my initial proposals for the garden at Orchard House. This is merely intended to show the positions of the various features and pathways, which are of course subject to your approval in principal before we move on to a final design, planting scheme and so on. Of course this is only a photograph, and the pencil is to give you an idea of scale. Perhaps you could let me have your impressions, any major changes that you would like me to make, or any additions which you may have thought about since our last meeting. I would of course be happy to meet you again to discuss my ideas before we move to the final design stage.

Best regards
Fifi Fielding.'

Michael opened the attachment, whilst thinking it an amusing thing that he had quite unconsciously read her words spoken in her soft, lilting, Scottish accent. Before him were the grounds of Orchard House seen from above, as he had not seen them before, which gave the house itself a new sense of proportion and perspective, and she had placed a pencil on the drawing to give him a better idea of the actual scale of the design. There also in outline were curved pathways leading from the proposed terrace to a Gazebo, other seating areas, a rectangular vegetable garden which would be enclosed by low brick walls, informally shaped lawns, a formal, hexagonal herbarium and other, lesser features, all of which seemed to Michael to give a balanced and pleasing impression. He would discuss the drawing with Elin over the next days, and would take a printed copy of the proposals with them tomorrow, which could be shown to Damien, but his first impressions were that their designer knew her business, and that the result in the end would be a beautifully landscaped garden. There would be considerable financial implications, of course, so much would depend upon the final cost of renovating the house, but the advantage of employing Damien and the small team of established builders to construct the garden was that if necessary he could have the work done piecemeal, and over a period of time. To renovate and furnish the house was an essential, whereas he considered the landscaping of the gardens to be something of a luxury, to be afforded as they could. These, however were thoughts and considerations for the future, and he would reply to the email in positive manner in due course.

The second and last remaining email was from Patricia Wagstaff, and this he had deliberately left until last. This would likely be the final letter that Jane had written to her brother, William, which would either give further clues as to her identity, or, as he expected, would be as frustrating and in a sense disappointing as her previous letters had proved to be. In any case it was with some anticipation that he opened the mail, and read the following;

'Dear Michael

Well, here is the last letter, which I read with some disbelief, but the transcript is genuine, I assure you! I will say no more and let you read the letter for yourself, but would welcome the opportunity to discuss the letters with you sometime, and particularly this letter, which I think you will find interesting to say the least. I am still in something of a state of shock, and on a practical level this one gave me more problems than usual, as drops of liquid fell on the manuscript before the ink was dry. I do believe we may have 17th century tear – stains.

Over to you and best regards,

Pat Wagstaff.'

Michael once again opened the attachment, and as was his habit by now he printed the transcript before reading it. Whilst the printer was doing its' work he opened his bedroom window and lit a cigarette, before picking up the sheet of A4 paper and taking it to the window, and this time he read the following;

'27th July 1665

My dearest and most beloved brother

Today your (trusted) servant, Mark, has come with the gravest of all news, and……so confirmed our worst fears, that you and your (dear wife) are both passed away from the sickness, as are so many other poor souls. I have broken these tidings to John and Margaret, and John has (taken) the news like……young man that he has become, but dear Margaret is as yet beyond consolation……for me the most dreadful of days.

We have since Mark's (departure made) our own preparations to leave, since he has brought news that the Manor House stands now empty, and we must make all haste to return there, and I do not know when next I shall return to Glebe House, the house where I have hitherto been so content. In…….writing this letter will my last task here, though now I am sure that you will not read the letters which I have (been writing) to you, but this has been and remains at least some comfort to me. My first (thought) has been to burn the letters, but I now think that I will conceal them about the house, that perhaps one day they will be found……..this small part of our great history will be known to any who may follow hereafter.

We are all so hungry now, hunger has (become a part of) our way of life ……..with it daily, but John and Margaret remain in good health, and soon our ordeal at least will be over, and thanks to you, dear brother, me thinks that we have suffered less than most. My one and (avowed intent) is now that the name of Tillington shall continue……that your dear son John will be the sixth Lord to bear that name, when the (horror of this) most accursed plague is over. To this end and with heavy heart do I return now to our ancestral home, and may God have mercy upon us all.

Your ever loving sister
Jane.'

Michael was for the most part of calm and stoic nature, not given to extremes of emotional condition or expression, but having read the transcript for a second time he was still having difficulty in processing the words and finding a reaction thereto. He held the letter down for a moment and looked out over the grounds of the Manor House, the better perhaps to order his thoughts, and to begin to believe that that which was all but unbelievable; to convince himself that what he was reading really was the truth of it, at last, and what truth it was.

'My god….'

Her name had been Jane, and since her brother was William Tillington, she must have been Jane Tillington, and if her brothers' son was to be the sixth Lord Tillington then William must have been the fifth Lord. Michael was uncertain of the nomenclature and order of all of the Lords who had preceded his father, but he had heard these names before, and what else could the letter mean? And there had been a Manor House, and there was only one Manor House which had been the ancestral home of the line of Tillington, and he was standing in it, and had been born in it, and one day he would be Lord of the Manor, as William had been, and as his son John had been. These were his ancestors, his bloodline, and he was related in direct ascendancy to them all. And little wonder that he had been unable to find a house called *'Orchard House'* which had been built in the county at that time, because the house had not been called Orchard House, not then; then it had been called Glebe House, the house that he had purchased for so reasonable a price. William had built the house for Jane, his sister, and so had she and William's children, John and Margaret survived the Black Death, else there would have been no offspring born to John, and he, Michael Tillington, would not have been born, and would not be now looking out over the grounds of the Manor as William must have done through this very window, and as Jane had done. Almost she had burned the letters, and then he would never have known, but she had not, and Damien had found them below the floorboards where she had hidden them in a leather wallet, the last person to have touched them for three hundred years and more. Had she known that so far in the future her distant ascendant would be reading her words, what thoughts would she have had, and yet she had not known, of course, as she wept her tears for her dead brother, and she nor would she never know.

Michael, who was quite lost in his thoughts, now found himself wiping tears from his own eyes. Whether this was in sympathy with Jane, or merely due to the shock of this revelation he was uncertain, but his tears seemed to him to unite him over the centuries with his distant forebears, who had suffered as he could only imagine. He read the letter for a third time before somehow bringing his thoughts back to the present, and beginning his preparation for this important day, which had just become so much more important. He was due to meet Elin from her train in about an hour, and he would show her the letter on the way back, and now he and she would have not only their betrothal to announce over the luncheon table.

On this Sunday morning Isabella was in her bedroom, somewhat distractedly practicing mathematical equations in preparation for her forthcoming examinations, when she heard the doorbell ring. In truth she had little enthusiasm for the task in hand, finding it all rather easy, but she did not welcome the interruption to her morning when Benjamin, her brother, knocked on her bedroom door; her parents having both gone out for the morning. She stayed lying on her bed, and Benjamin knew better than to enter uninvited.

'What…?'

'There's someone at the door.'

'Yes, I gathered that, who is it?'

'Some old guy, wants to talk to you.'

'Who…?'

'I don't know, some old geezer.'

'Didn't you ask him his name?'

'I skipped that part.'

'Idiot…Okay, tell him to give me a minute, and don't let him in.'

'I already did that, he's in the kitchen. Maybe I should go check he's not making off with the best silver.'

'Christ…Just give me minute.'

'Is that a different minute to the last minute, or is it the same minute twice?'

'Benjamin, fuck off and wait downstairs.'

'I'm fucking off even as we speak.'

Isabella, who was dressed in T shirt and knickers, put on jeans and slip – on shoes, checked her reflection in the mirror, and descended the stairs, having no idea who the caller might be. She entered the kitchen, and sitting at the kitchen table was somebody who she would never have expected to come here, and someone who was not as old as her brother had indicated. Benjamin had now taken on the role of protector to his sister, and waited for further developments, and particularly for his sister's reaction to the caller.

'Oh, hello…'

'Hello Isabella…'

'It's okay, Benjamin…This is okay.'

'I'll fuck further off then, shall I?'

'Yes, this is private.'

'If he acts suspicious or tries anything on I'll be in the next room, ready with the sharply – pointed stick.'

Benjamin departed, and Isabella sat down opposite Richard Templeton.

'That's quite a brother you've got there.'

'He has his moments. Look, can I offer you coffee or something?'

'It's okay, I won't keep you for long, and first let me say that I'm sorry to have interrupted your morning.'

'Well, whatever…But how did you know where I live…?'

'I took the considerable liberty of asking our club secretary, who would not normally have divulged such information, but it's me, you know, and I didn't know when next you and I would be at the club together.'

'I see…I think…'

'Yes, well I'm here for a specific reason, of course. Our esteemed secretary has told me that you aren't coming to Copenhagen for the tournament.'

'Yes, that's right.'

'He also told me that it was for personal reasons, and your personal affairs are yours, of course, and none of my business, but if it has anything to do with what happened in Dusseldorf, then I'm here to try to change your mind.'

What….? If anybody else had had the audacity to come to her house and speak thus, Isabella would have asked them to leave in no uncertain terms, but here was Richard, her friend, mentor and sometimes protector, so she would hear him out, at least.

'Well, I'm not going.'

'Yes, I understand that, but I thought I'd make sure there's nothing I can do or rather say which might influence your decision. You have exceptional abilities, Isabella, and if I might make so bold I think you should make the best of them, and this is a good opportunity, which should not be wasted for no good reason.'

'I understand all of that, but…Well, it wasn't a decision which I made lightly.'

'So just tell me, is it anything to do with Dusseldorf? If you say no then I will leave without further ado.'

So, just one word then and he would be gone, it was that easy, but of course it was not that easy, and never had been, and Richard was one of the few friends she had in the world, so she owed him more than that, did she not?

'No….'

'Very well then...'

He stood up to leave, and it was almost too late.

'I mean, no….No, don't leave yet, it is to do with…With what happened.'

'And is that the only reason?'

'Yes, it's the only reason.'

Richard sat down again.

'Well then, how about if I take it upon myself to look after you? I don't know how much trust you have in me, but if I give you my word that nothing bad will happen to you then will you reconsider? I'd even be willing to share a room. I've shared hotel rooms with my daughter before, when she was about your age, so I understand well the sensibilities and etiquette of sharing with a young woman.'

It occurred now to Isabella that however well she knew him over the chessboard, she knew almost nothing of Richard Templeton's private life.

'You have a daughter?'

'And two sons…My wife by the way has given tacit approval of the idea, if it should come to it.'

'You've told your wife about me?'

'I consider you to be a friend, so yes, I have told her about you, and I have told her as much as you have told me about your ordeal, insofar as I considered that it might be pertinent to do so for reasons of this conversation. She has given her approval for you to speak to her, if you wish, as has my daughter, actually, should you wish to, as it were, be assured of my credentials.'

'No…I mean…I mean I trust you absolutely. In fact you are one of the very few people that I trust.'

'I consider that to be an honour.'

'But…I mean I can't go. That is to say I'll have to think about everything, you know?'

'That is all I'm asking, that you think about it.'

'But supposing any of them are there?'

'Yes, I've thought about that, and over this we can have no influence, of course, but I imagine that they would be thinking the same thing about you. From a male perspective, they would I'm sure be no more willing to meet you than you are to meet them, and what better way would there be to show them that they haven't won, and that despite their despicable actions you aren't afraid of them? You are the victim, after all, and they are the perpetrators. It is they who carry the guilt, and I am quite willing to face them with you, as far as that is a useful or reassuring thing.'

It had been quite settled in her mind. Her disappointment and frustration at not being able to go, and her hatred for them for making this so had put iron in her soul, but she had learned somehow to live with that, and she could not have faced any of them alone, but now there was this. Now there was Richard, who was a man, after all, and her simmering hatred for all men could not be let to burn inside her forever. Perhaps here could be an end to it, once and for all, if she was strong enough, and therein lay the question.

'My wife and daughter are angry on your behalf, Isabella. You carry the anger of all women who have been so abused, and they very much want you to go, as do I, although I confess that my motivation is less highly principled, since quite aside from any such deep moral considerations, I would miss you if you weren't there.'

He smiled now, and had said his piece, and now Isabella knew that it was up to her.

'I don't know...'

'Well, it's your decision, of course, but the reason I came today is because the club is under pressure to give names, and genders, actually, as much for the hotel booking as anything, and as things stand you won't be going, so you need do nothing, if your final decision is not to go, as it were.'

'How long have I got?'

'I said I'd let him know tomorrow.'

'So he knows that you've come here, then.'

'We talked about my doing so, hence his giving me your address, although let me assure you that he knows nothing of the reason for your reluctance to go, and nor will he. I said merely that I would look into the matter of your not going, that is all, to see if I could ascertain the reasons, with a view to perhaps changing your mind. He wants you to go, too, you see, and looking at the positives from your perspective, it's an all - expenses paid trip to Denmark with some good chess thrown in, so if you've got nothing better to do….'

So now it came to it, and for a moment conflicting thoughts and emotions vied for precedence in her mind, and Isabella paced the kitchen in characteristically nervous manner as she fought her inner battle with herself, and with her fear, but in the end the idea of beating them began to grow stronger within her, and began to override everything else. He was right, of course, this way she could win, and the victory would be final. So, let them be there, let them all be there, as of this moment she no longer cared.

'So we'd share a room…'

'If you want...'

Say it, Isabella, you know how much you want to say it, and Richard would be with you.

'Okay…Okay, I'll come, if we share a room.'

'Good for you, I'll let the club know, and now I'll leave you in peace.'

He stood up, and they both walked to the front door.

'And you know, thanks…'

'You're welcome. I'll see you at the club sometime soon.'

'Of course…'

'There's something else I've been thinking about.'

'What?'

'I've been playing through our most recent game in my head. I think you need to work on your bishops' game. You're good with your knights, but your bishops still need some work, especially your King's bishop.'

'I'll bear it in mind.'

They smiled goodbye, and she watched for a moment as he walked up the track beside the village Green, before closing the door, and encountering her brother in the hallway.

'What was he talking about?'

'What do you mean?'

'Victim…? Perpetrators…? What happened in Dusseldorf?'

'You were listening to my private conversation.'

'Not really, I just happened to be holding a glass against the wall so I put my ear to it.'

'Never mind, little brother, you don't want to know.'

'I do want to know, that's why I asked. You've been even more of a fruitcake than usual since you got back from Germany, and I thought there must be a reason for it.'

'There is a reason for it, and maybe one day I'll tell you, but not yet, okay, so please don't ask me, and don't say anything to mum and dad, will you?'

'Mum's the word, or not in this case.'

'I'll tell you when I'm ready, I promise.'

'Well okay, but if there's anything I can do, you know?'

'Thank you, but just continue to be your usual idiotic self, okay?'

'Shouldn't be a problem….'

She ascended the stairs and closed her bedroom door behind her. There would be no more studying of mathematics now; of a sudden her life had changed, she was going to Copenhagen, and she would play international chess again, and in a moment she would look up the best things to see and do in the city, but there was so much more to it than that. She sat down heavily on her bed, closed her eyes and thanked this day for being, and thanked the day that she had met Richard Templeton.

Sunday lunchtime had by tradition been one of the busiest times of the week at the Dog and Bottle public house. On weekend evenings, the good people of Middlewapping and its' environs would likely go in search of more exciting or stimulating surroundings in the town, but Sunday lunchtime was for comfort and quietude, a warm if somewhat smoky fire in the winter, and the picturesque backdrop of this unique seventeenth century village during warmer times. The establishment in any case continued to fare well enough, mainly by dint of the famous Middlewapping meteorite, which still brought a good deal of outside business, and the pub had maintained its' independent status; the worthy landlord Nigel Hollyman had always kept a good pint of 'Old Thumper', whilst his wife Susan saw to the provision of good and wholesome fare. In any event at this juncture in our story, spring had come to the village, and the day was warm enough to allow those who patronized the pub to sit around wooden tables at the front of the establishment, on the area of tarmacadam which overlooked the village Green, and today around one such table sat Keith, Meadow, Percival and Louise; two pints of ale, a vodka and tonic and an orange juice, and convivial conversation among good if somewhat unlikely friends, and as we join them Keith is speaking.

'So, how are you two dealing with life since the break in?'

'We've been buying furniture,' said Louise 'which badly needed to be replaced anyway, so it's given me the chance to influence things which needed to be influenced.'

'Are you casting dispersions on my choice of furnishings?' said Percival.

'You mean you chose all the crap that we threw away?'

'There was nothing wrong with it, although I have to confess that some of it had seen better days, and some of it was there when I moved in, actually, so I can't claim responsibility for that. I have a theory that whoever broke in and did this was just a regular burglar who didn't like the upholstery, and suffered from a spontaneous fit of furniture – rage, and just couldn't help but take a knife to the place.'

'Pity his rage didn't extend to curtains.'

'Curtain – rage is a much rarer and less well understood condition, and we're replacing those anyway.'

'They need replacing, my love, they're probably the worst curtains I've ever seen.'

'Well, if you put it like that….'

'Burglars don't usually leave death threats painted on the wall.' said Keith.

'Maybe they *really* didn't like the furniture.'

'Still no further word from the chicken – stranglers then, I take it...'

'No, nothing so far….'

'So what's you latest thinking on that?'

'I still think they're waiting for a reaction, which isn't going to happen.'

'Most people would react by moving to Inverness.'

'I won't bow to terrorism, you know that.'

'Sure…'

'Anyway, you're here.'

'So what's your take on all of this, Louise? I mean you move down from sleepy old London to this hotbed of rural whatever the fuck it is just to be with this guy. Ever wonder why?'

'Keith….' Said Meadow

'I'm taking tablets for it,' said Louise 'but they don't seem to be working.'

'Must be love then….'

'They say it's blind, don't they…?'

'So what's the latest on Daphne's place?' Said Percival

'Yeah, we've got some good news on that, probate's been passed so we're all good to go. The house is Emily's now, so the sale should go through quite quickly as these things go.'

'Probate was swift, wasn't it?'

'I think Daphne kept her affairs in good order, god rest her soul.'

'So what will Tara do with the place, will she live there?'

'We don't know, I mean for a while, probably, when the tour's finished, but I don't think she knows either, to be honest.

She's buying for the investment, mainly. She could end up renting it out if she decides to live elsewhere.'

'Hardly the rock – star lifestyle living here, is it?' Said Louise

'Yeah, thing is, though, I don't think she wants the rock – star lifestyle, last we heard, anyway.'

'She's done so well, hasn't she?'

'I try really hard not to be the proud father, but that isn't working, either, gets the better of me sometimes, you dig?'

'You should be proud of her, I mean she's on a world tour with Ash Spears, for heaven's sake, and I love her albums, she's got a great voice.'

'She sings well, for sure, and meeting Ash was just about the best break anyone could ever wish for.'

'So, when's the next album being released?'

'I don't know, I think they're all just full of the tour at the moment, and I think most of them will be glad when it's all over. Tara's getting us tickets for the O2 concert, the grand finale, you two should come with us.'

'I'd like that….'

Just then Ron arrived at the table, having walked down the track beside the Green.

'Hi everyone, I hoped you'd be here.'

'Hey Ron,' said Keith 'you staying for a beer?'

'Love to but I can't, we've got the aged mother in law for the day.'

'All the more reason to stay for a beer, I'd say.'

'I value my life too much….Anyway, sorry to interrupt but we need to talk about cricket.'

'Yeah, when's the first fixture?'

'Next Sunday against Ashbury, so we need team practice this week. Let's make it Tuesday evening if that's okay with everyone?'

'Okay by me….You up for it, Perc?'

'Sure, whenever…'

'Could you put the word about? I'll tell Don and Andy, and I'll see Nigel now, but could someone tell Will and Reginald?'

'Sure, leave it to me.' Said Keith

'And could someone let Mike Tillington know? You've got an in to the big house, right Percival?'

'Yeah, I'll do that one,' said Percival 'I should go to the Manor anyway, see how Victoria and Henry are getting on.'

'Thanks…Okay, better go, see you on Tuesday.'

Ron departed, and a thought occurred to Meadow.

'How is Victoria, Percival?'

'Okay, last time I saw her, or as okay as it gets, anyway, although I haven't seen her for a while.'

'Nor have I, she's not in the village much these days, and Rebecca's gone now…Any reason for that that you know of?'

'Nope, and I know better than to ask.'

'Anyway,' said Keith 'I guess Michael will be looking for new tenants for number seven, and Sally's place stands empty.'

'Actually it doesn't.' Said Meadow 'Or at least it won't for much longer. I met the new tenants in the week, they were moving some furniture in and should be moving in themselves any day now.'

'Who are they?' Said Louise

'They're brother and sister, about our age, I would say. You would say they had posh accents, Keith.'

'That's a bit odd, I mean the brother and sister combination.'

'Not like all the other normal people that live hereabouts…' Said Louise

'You haven't heard the best part,' said Meadow 'they go by the names of Theodor and Theodora.'

'What…?' Said Keith

'I kid you not.'

'Well,' said Percival 'they might bring something interesting to the party. You glean any other information about them?'

'Only that he likes soft cheese and she doesn't. They bought some of Emily's cheese, anyway.'

'Speak of the devil….' Said Keith

Will Tucker and Emily Cleves were walking hand in hand across the village Green, and the party awaited their arrival.

'Well hello you two,' said Meadow 'we don't often see you in the village together.'

'I milked early and escaped the compound for a few hours.' Said Emily

'I'll get the beers in.' Said Will

'It's okay, It's my shout,' said Keith 'you've earned your beer this week. Em, what's your poison?'

'Gin and Orange, please…'

Keith left the table, and the others moved along bench seats to allow for the newcomers. Emily sat opposite Percival, and Louise spoke.

'Keith tells us you're now the proud owner of the big brick house.'

'Yes, so I'm told, once everything's finalized, but it won't be for long, I hope. I'm really glad someone nice is buying it, though.'

She exchanged smiles with Meadow, and Percival now addressed Will.

'Ron was just here, we've got our first game next Sunday, practice Tuesday evening.'

'Who's the opposition?'

'Ashbury...'

'We beat them last season, didn't we?'

'I believe so, yes.'

Keith arrived with a tray of precariously balanced drinks, which he placed on the end of the table and began distributing.

'It's not about the winning, Will…'

'No, it's about beating the crap out of the opposition, right?'

'Exactly….'

'There,' said Louise 'and I thought cricket was a civilized game played by gentlemen.'

'It is,' said Keith 'it's about beating the crap out of the opposition in a civilized and gentlemanly manner.'

'I see….'

Keith resumed his position between Meadow and Emily.

'It may look like a gentle and refined game, but primal and base male instincts broil beneath the surface. Step out onto the pitch and it's the law of the jungle out there.'

'Well, you live and learn…'

'Don't get Keith going on cricket for heaven's sake,' said Meadow 'or we'll never hear the last of it.'

'I'll bear that in mind.'

'If we're looking for a change of subject,' said Percival 'did you ever see or hear again from that journalist woman?'

'What,' said Keith 'Jennifer, or whatever she was called?'

'She was called Georgina,' said Meadow 'and no, we never saw her again, did we Keith?'

'Nope…She wrote her article and disappeared, which I suppose is what journalists do.'

'It was a bit of an odd way to carry on though, wasn't it?'

'Yeah, it was a bit, especially since I chatted her up, and made out like I might have been willing to let her have her way with me in due course, if she played her cards right, you know?'

'You mean she didn't fall for your charms?' Said Louise 'What kind of foolish woman is this..?'

'You have to wonder…'

'You'd have run a mile.' Said Meadow

'True, but she didn't know that. Anyway aside from the fact that she clearly can't see an opportunity when it presents itself, I see no reason to think she had ulterior motives for being here, though, if she was who she says she was, or is, and there's no reason to think she isn't, if you see what I mean. Nothing untoward happened anyway, apart from the magazine article.'

'What magazine article?' Said Emily

'She wrote an article, talking about witches and so on, you know, *'the witch of Middlewapping'* and that kind of bullshit, and how this village is a bit weird, and such.'

'I wonder what ever gave her that idea.' Said Louise

'It isn't bullshit though, is it,' said Will 'since there is a witch living here, or was, anyway.'

'I've still got the article at home,' said Meadow 'I'll let you read it sometime, Em.'

'There was nothing to it, really,' said Keith 'and Rebecca didn't seem to think there was anything to it, or to her, and she should know, I suppose, being the main witch around here.'

Ron now passed the table again, going in the opposite direction to that which he had arrived.

'You still here, Ron..?' Said Percival

'I got talking to Nigel, and now I really am in trouble…If I don't get home ten minutes ago my balls are on the lunch menu.'

'I would go then if I were you,' said Meadow 'you know what Barbara's like when she's angry.'

'I know what she's like when she's not angry…Nigel thinks the surgeon should open the bowling with Don, but I'm not convinced.'

'Who's the surgeon?' Said Meadow

'Your dad...' Said Keith

Meadow laughed.

'I didn't know you called him that.'

'What's talked about amongst the team stays amongst the team,' said Keith 'it's on account of the precision of his bowling, as it happens.'

'Is the good doctor up for it this season?' Said Don

'As far as I know, yes...' Said Meadow

'I think Nigel's right.' Said Percival 'I also think Will should open the batting with Peter, what do you reckon, Keith?'

'Yeah, good idea, and we should move Nigel up the order, I'll bat six or seven.'

'That would never…Is this a wind – up?'

'No Don, of course not.' said Percival

'Never been more serious...' Said Keith

'I think what this is,' said Meadow 'is a conspiracy amongst your team mates to make you late for lunch.'

'Well fuck you very much…' said Ron, who now departed rather hurriedly to the sound of laughter around the table.

'You really shouldn't, you know.' Said Meadow

'He's alright,' said Keith 'it's just something to see a big guy like Don being kept in order by Barbara, who must be about half his size.'

'I don't think I've ever met Barbara.' Said Louise

'They're totally devoted,' said Keith 'despite the fact that she beats the crap out of him most days. Anyway, whose round is it?'

'I think it must be mine.' Said Percival

Convivial conversation between friends, and the beginning of the cricket season, with all that this implied for this small and tightly – knit community, united by past and sometimes traumatic or dangerous events, and a shared future, whatever that future may hold. For now, however, we will leave the friends to their Sunday lunchtime, and move our tale to a place not so far away, where a family is preparing itself for luncheon. Once upon a time and not so long ago, the social divisions which then existed would have set the Manor House and all who dwelt there apart from the village, but lines had been crossed now. He who is next in line to the Lordship will play cricket on the village Green, and there exist other, more significant connections, which for now remain a secret known only to the few. The few, however, are for now saying nothing, for there are some things which are best not spoken of, even between friends.

Michael had shown Elin the printout of the transcript of the last letter written by Jane Tillington to her brother on their drive back from the railway station. Elin had first expressed her disbelief, and then a few minutes later and having read the letter again, she had told Michael that she was uncommonly amazed and extraordinarily happy at the revelations which the letter had contained. Michael had long since noted regarding Elin that she was wont to tell him of her emotions at any given time, without necessarily going to the bother of otherwise expressing them. He mused at times that to call his still quite newly beloved undemonstrative would be to rather understate the matter, which was in stark contrast to Rose, who during their best times together would often seek to reassure, and to be reassured. Only once had he ever asked Elin whether she loved him, which had met with the rebuttal that of course she loved him, and why would he doubt it, or need to ask her? Michael supposed that as far as she was concerned, they were in love forever, and she had told him so, so why would she trouble to repeat herself? Even during their most passionate moments, she would rather tell him how he could better satisfy her and his desires, and so in any case he took her words in reaction to reading the letter as indication enough of her sincerity, and that she was genuinely moved on this occasion. She also told him in no uncertain terms that knowing that which they now knew, they must never under any circumstances sell Orchard House. Even when, at some time in the future, they would move into the Manor House, Orchard House would either be rented out, or kept for Nathaniel to move into when he was old enough to need or desire his independence, if such was the case, before he in turn took up his rightful place at Middlewapping Manor. Given her and her beloveds' present situation, nobody was more acutely aware than Elin of a sons' need to be independent from his father, and in any case Michael was quick to concur in all regards, and thus had an important life decision been made and agreed before they had so much as reached the Manor House.

Upon arrival, his mother and father in their turn and as they encountered her greeted Elin with customary warmth, and her Ladyship took Elin to one side for a few moments to ask after her parents, which gave Michael time to seek out his sister. He found her seated on the terrace to the back of the house, reading and enjoying the late morning sunshine.

'Oh, hi Mike, I thought I heard you arrive...'

'Hello Vics.'

'What's up, you're looking significant…'

'We're going to tell them today, over lunch.'

'Oh, right, well thanks for the forewarning, I'll try and look surprised, shall I?'

'Well, whatever, but I also wanted to show you this before they see it.'

He took an envelope from his inside jacket pocket and gave it to her. She removed the single sheet of paper, and he was silent whilst she read the words of his ancient forebear, who was also her ancient forebear.

'Christ….I mean, is this genuine?'

'I've no reason to think not.'

'No…No, of course, but….This is huge, Mike….So you just happened to buy the house that was built by William Tillington for his sister, Jane. I've got that right, haven't I?'

'Yes, you have.'

'And we're related to them…'

'There were no other '*Lord Tillingtons*', so yes…Father will no doubt know the order of lineage, but the names ring a bell even with me.'

'And the Manor House that she was returning to must have been here…'

'There can be no other interpretation, I don't think.'

'No…No, nor do I….Well bloody hell, I really don't know what to say, other than that it puts the whole thing in a quite new perspective, doesn't it?'

'Yes it does, and *'Bloody hell'* sums it up quite well, I think.'

'And it was called *'Glebe House'* when it was built.'

'Indeed it was, which explains why I couldn't find it, of course...'

'Of course…Well, thanks Mike, for giving me a preview, you know?'

'There's another thing you can try to look surprised about.'

'I don't think I'll need to try, I probably won't quite believe it even the second time around. Elin knows, I take it…'

'Yes, I've just told her. She was amazed too, in a Nordic kind of way.'

'I'll bet…Anyway here's company, you'll want this back, I think.'

She gave him the letter, which he placed back in its' envelope, and thence into his jacket pocket.

'Ah, there you are,' said Lady Beatrice, 'your father's hungry, so we're taking lunch early.'

'What, this early?' Said Victoria

'It's a conspiracy, he's been speaking to Susan, so we're about ready when you are. You know how your father is when it comes to roast beef.'

The young woman lay unconscious in the intensive care ward, where Sophie Summerfield had just come on duty, and was being debriefed on the new arrival.

'She came in last night, multiple injuries, crushed ribs and both legs and one arm broken. No significant head injuries but internally she's a mess, Doctor Ford's done his best with her, over three hours in surgery, but it's touch and go.'

'So who is she, and what happened?'

'No I.D., she got hit by a truck, apparently, which is about how I feel at the moment.'

'Was she drunk…?'

'Nope, blood's clean, not even a headache tablet. She seemed to be in the best of health until this.'

'Okay, so nothing to do, then...'

'I think all we can do now is pray for this one…We're just keeping her under and see what happens.'

'Okay, thanks…'

Sophie studied the clipboard at the bottom of the bed, to look at the injury report in more detail, and the constituent of the so far anonymous patients' intravenous drip. She then did a quick round of the other three beds, which were all occupied by cases with which she was already familiar. She had been out last night and was feeling somewhat jaded, and was in any case in need of a holiday from the relentless shiftwork which was the lot of intensive care nurses, and of the nurses in general. There had been too many cutbacks lately, people were leaving to find an easier way to make a living and weren't being replaced, and too much was being expected of those who were left. This was Sunday, and it would be a long day.

At that which all but one of the assembled party considered to be a quite ridiculously early time, the Tillington family and Elin Tomlinson were seated around the dining table in the grand dining room, and Susan had served their luncheon of roast beef and Yorkshire pudding, with roast potatoes, vegetables, and gravy. Michael and Elin were the last to be seated, and now Michael found himself in something of a dilemma. He had in a sense two announcements to make, and had already decided to show his parents the letter first, thereafter announcing his engagement to Elin, this seeming to him to be an appropriate order of things, but everything was happening too quickly. He had intended and expected to have at least a little time before the food had been served, and therein would he sound forth, so that everybody might enjoy their meal basking in their newfound knowledge, and discussing the finer points of everything. This window of opportunity, however, was now closed to him, and it seemed hardly fitting to speak of such weighty matters whilst he was passing somebody the Brussels Sprouts. It was perhaps quite appropriate to wait until after luncheon to announce the engagement, but to not tell them immediately about Orchard House would open him to the question as to why he had not spoken sooner of such an historically significant family matter. In the end, however, he decided to wait on both counts, and discussion over the meal revolved around the lesser subjects of Elin's family, Victoria's pending portrait, the present political and economic state of the country, and so on. Thereafter dessert was served, and it was not until apple pie and custard had been consumed, along with by this time red and then white wine, and the coffee tray had been put on the table, that the next most appropriate moment presented itself. At a certain juncture he had received an enquiring look from Victoria, to which he had responded with a slight shrug of his shoulders, and a look which said '*What chance does a chap have?*' and she had smiled back in sympathy and understanding. Now, however, his moment had come, and at the next lull in conversation, he began.

'Anyway everyone, I have something to show you all. I received another email last night from Patricia Wagstaff.'

He pulled the envelope once more from his jacket pocket, his jacket now being hung over the back of his chair, and without further words he passed the letter to his father across the table. Lord Tillington read the transcript with serious and studious expression, then he was clearly reading it again, before;

'Good Lord, but this really is quite extraordinary...Beatrice, look at this.'

Lady Beatrice read the words which had been written so many years ago.

'Oh my....But this means that...'

'That I have quite unwittingly bought Glebe House, which is a part of our family history.'

Lady Beatrice passed the letter across to Victoria, who read the letter again anyway, and Lord Michael was next to speak, whilst Elin looked on with interest at her future family, and at their reaction to this undoubtedly extraordinary revelation.

'Had this letter been a one – off, one would have been tempted to wonder as to its' authenticity, but in the context of the series of letters I suppose there can be no doubt, can there?'

'None whatsoever.' Said Michael

'I am aware of William, of course, and of Lord John, and after him came another Lord John.' He turned his gaze to the line of paintings which hung quite high up on the wall, and all eyes followed his. 'We're missing one, of course, but if you count four along, there's William, and next to him is John, and next to him is his son, the second Lord John, who was the seventh Lord Tillington.'

'Do you know them all, father?' Said Victoria

'Well, no, that is I can just about reel them all off in order, but I know less about some than others. I remember a little about this part of our heritage, mainly I think because this is the only other time apart from now that we have two successive Lords with the same name, so it sort of stuck, I suppose. At least we know now how William met his unfortunate end...Poor chap died of the plague in this very house.'

'That's a bit morbid, father.'

'Perhaps, but that makes it no less true, Victoria, but really, of all the houses that you could have bought, Michael....You seem to have hit a very large and significant nail right on the head, so to speak.'

'I can still scarce believe it myself, particularly since, well, since we may as well tell you now that Elin and I intend to live at Orchard House, as it now is, once the renovations are complete, of course.'

'Is that so…Well, I have to say that speculation has been rife between your mother and I as to when you two were going to shack – up together, so this at least comes as no great surprise.'

Elin laughed, gently; she had always liked Lord Tillington.

'Can you afford it, though, I mean it's quite clear that the house must stay in the family now, but weren't you relying on the proceeds of the sale to refloat the business?'

'Michael,' said Lady Beatrice 'this is hardly the time to be discussing such things.'

'Why not, there are no strangers here, and therefore no secrets, are there?'

'I will help in this respect,' said Elin 'I will sell my apartment when it is the right time to do so, from which there will be considerable profit.'

'Oh, right, jolly good then, that I suppose should see to any shortfall, but if things get tight you will tell me won't you, I'm sure if we dig deep enough into the family coffers we can come up with some money, provided that we keep all things equal between you and Victoria, of course.'

'Well, we've done the calculations as far as we can,' said Michael 'and we think we should be okay.'

'Yes, I'm sure you have, and by the sounds of it you'll have a very fine house to live in, so well done, you two. Your mother and I will have to come and see the place sometime, now that the house has taken on a whole new significance.'

'We're going down tomorrow, if you'd like to join us?'

'Yes, we would, I'm sure, would we not, my beloved?'

'Yes, of course….'

'In fact,' continued Michael 'there's something else that we have to tell you, which is sort of related to everything, in a way, which is that Elin and I are engaged, unofficially, at least, although I suppose this makes it official. No rings, yet, you know, but we intend to marry in due course, perhaps at the end of the summer or even sooner.'

'Oh, Michael,' said Lady Beatrice 'this is truly wonderful news.'

She stood up, as did he, and she walked around the table to hug her son, from whence to her future daughter in law, to whom she presented her cheek.

'Congratulations, my dear…'

'Thank you, Lady Beatrice.'

Elin now turned to his Lordship and kissed his cheek.

'Yes, well done…I would say I hope you know what you're taking on, becoming one of us lot, but since we've known you for so many years there's really no excuse, is there?'

Elin laughed again, Lord Tillington shook his sons' hand, and Victoria thought she may as well join in, so she also hugged her brother, and then her future sister in law, after which everyone resumed their seats.

'Well well,' said Lord Tillington 'this is a day, indeed. Does anyone have any more announcements to make, or are we all done?'

'I think that's it.' Said Michael

'So,' said Lady Beatrice 'what are your plans for the wedding?'

'I don't think we've thought that far ahead yet, mother.'

'No, of course, well we must have the reception here, of course, as is tradition, and it will be a church wedding, naturally, and then…'

'Mother,' said Victoria 'I'm sure Michael and Elin will let you know as soon as they've had time to consider such things.'

'Yes….Yes of course….Oh my word…'

'What is it, dearest…?'

'Of course, how stupid of me, in all of the excitement I'd quite forgotten...'

'What had you forgotten, my beloved?'

'We have a portrait of Jane Tillington.'

'Do we?'

'Yes, it's the quite small, oval painting that hangs in the second guest room. I hadn't thought much about it until now.'

'Are you quite sure it's her?'

'Yes, I'm quite certain. Unusually the painter has written the subject's name in small letters at the bottom of the painting, and the year that it was painted, which was 1674, as I recall.'

'Nearly ten years after she wrote her letters.' Said Victoria

'During which time I assume she would have been living here.' said Michael. 'I wonder what happened to Orchard House, or Glebe house as was.'

'I imagine it would have been sold at some point by one of my illustrious predecessors, some of whom would have needed the money, no doubt. They weren't all good businessmen, and if history is to be believed the family fortunes have dwindled at certain times over the centuries to as good as nothing, and worse than nothing on occasions, I daresay. Anyway now we know what the place was called I'll research it, see if I can dig anything up. It's not a complete history, of course, but one will do ones' best.'

And so it was done, and the house which was Glebe House would become once again a part of the Tillington legacy, and so would it remain. Michael would Marry Elin, and so would a small part of the Tillington family history be recorded for all who would come thereafter, and this day in the lives of the Tillington family would be remembered by all as a happy day. Little Nathaniel, who had slept throughout and in Abigail's caring hands, remained in blissful ignorance of events and discussions which would also in time shape his future, and of his past only one amongst them knew, and Victoria on this day merely smiled and kept her secrets, for history, after all, is only made one day at a time.

Sharon stole through the courtyard in the dead of night; aside from the now quite strong wind which blew through narrow places and sighed through the eaves of the old buildings, the only sound was that of the occasional car still passing in the middle distance through the town. She was aware of all peripheral noise, and by now she knew the courtyard well by sight even in the darkness, but her primary concentration was fully upon the door in front of which she now stood. The door was half - open, as it had been every night that she had been here; the evenings were warm, and the studio would be poorly ventilated; a slight smell of wet clay emanated from the studio, and a dim light shone from within; mother and baby would be sleeping. A moment longer to gather herself, and then she made her final approach, pushing the door gently as she made her entry. All was silent within. Before her, across the studio, was a quite ornate crib on a raised platform or table in which the child was sleeping, and on the stone floor in the far corner lay a sleeping adult form beneath a blanket; this would be easy. She felt the blade – handle in her pocket as she took a few paces into the room, and took in every detail of her surroundings; she felt the aura, something in the room was wrong, and everything was not as it seemed. For a moment she stood quite still, and listened; there was a presence, but she had felt it too late, and the next sound she heard was the sound of the door being closed behind her; the blanket had been a decoy, and she turned now to see a dark figure standing by the door, and the figure now spoke.

'Well, well, if it isn't the journalist. I have been waiting for you. You may fool others, but you do not fool me, and never have. You think that I don't see you, sneaking around in the darkness, but I have been watching you, as you have been watching me. You have been preparing yourself for this moment, but you have underestimated me, and that was your mistake, and now you have made your second mistake. You have come between a mother and her child, and that you should never have done.'

The voice...Do not let her speak again, but now Sharon found that her own words were like ash in her mouth, and of a sudden she was ravenously thirsty, but she must not let her take control.

'I have come....'

'I know why you have come, you who saved me from the fire, and perhaps your mistakes began there, at the place where the others perished in the flames. You defeated me then, for then you were stronger than I, and you should have let me die, but you did not, and now you come to kill me. Well, perhaps you will, let us see, but the weapon you carry will be of no use to you. Take the weapon out and drop it on the floor.'

She was right, of course. There was danger in her words, and she should not give up the one advantage that she still had, but there was also truth in the words which could not be denied. Knives were for killing ordinary people, but against a witch of this power they were useless; this would not be the way. She felt herself take the knife from her pocket, and after a moment of hesitation she heard the sound as it dropped onto the ancient flagstones.

'There, now we are equal, in all ways. I could have killed you as you entered the room, but I did not, so now each of us owes our life to the other. So, let us talk, for we are the same, you and I. We are both assassins, who would kill one another, but only I have killed before. I killed the people in the temple, and at Farthing's Well, and I have killed others. I killed the Mother, the head of our order, for reasons which you will know well enough, so I know how it is to kill, and you do not, and that is the difference between us.'

The words which spoke such reason struck like knife – blades into Sharon's soul; she was right in all that she said, and yet she must not believe her, or lose her own wits and independence of thought. The people in the temple, who were they? But she must not be distracted by such thoughts, this was Rebecca's ground, which she had prepared, and Sharon knew and understood now that she had walked willingly into a trap. She must buy time, and gather herself against this unexpected turn.

'So...What should we speak about?'

The figure approached her; the witch Rebecca, who had lived amongst the others in the village as though she had been one of them, but this she had never been, and could never be. A black witch she had become, long ago, and now Sharon saw her as the others could not, for here, perhaps, was the blackest witch of them all.

'Take my hands.'

Sharon took the hands which were proffered to her in the semi – darkness.

'Now, let us begin at the beginning. Let us go back to the death of a young woman, who was called Jane Mary, and to the first of your order, who swore vengeance on the house of Tillington.'

This was better, of course; to forget all thoughts of death, and of killing, and to feel instead the joining together with the kindred spirit who stood before her. Together they walked hand in hand, to a different time, and to an ancient and dark Manor House, where they heard the screams of anguish of a dying woman, who had died at the hands of a madman. Sharon's thoughts now moved out of time and space, and all that she could hear were the words which were being spoken to her. This was wrong. This was not how it should have been, but now the voice came again, and she was lost to it, and lost to the great history with which she had lived for so long.

'Do you hear her? She is my ancient forebear, and I am of her blood, just as Eve was the last of the line of Edith, and with her the curse died.

It was I who took the boy, Henry, to a safe place on the night that Eve died, and the curse which had been put open the house of Tillington died with her, and you know this, and there should have been an end to it. You have failed, and now you come here to seek my death, but even that would now be in vain. You are empty now, and devoid of meaning, and I could kill you now if I so wished, but I do not. You saved me from the fire, and gave me life, so I will not kill you, but you know what you must do. We are as we are, you and I, and our lives are cursed, and nothing now can change that, and we must all of us meet our fate. Consider our beginnings, and all the good that has been done by such as us. We should be angels, now, yet here we stand, and there is nothing more dark nor more powerful than a fallen angel. So go now, and be at peace, for we will not meet again. Go and do as you know you must, for your time has ended, as has the time of your order.'

From somewhere far away, Sharon heard the sound of the door opening, and all that she could now think of was to leave this place, and for all of this to be over, forever. She knew so much, and how this was Sharon did not know, but in the end there had been no anger, and no death, but only the softly spoken words of the black witch, with whom she felt such great kinship and understanding, and now she understood, and she knew well enough that which she must do, for there was now no other way.

When she had gone, Rebecca closed the door behind her and went to her child, and Florence scarce awoke as her mother took her in her arms, and spoke to her in soft and gentle tones.

'There, my beloved daughter. She is gone, now, and she will not return. You need have no fear, for I will let no harm come to you. The blood of Jane Mary flows in your veins, little one, and one day you will understand this. One day I will tell you how it all began, a young woman, who was a healer, and a cruel and insane Lord, who was the first of them, and now the blood of these two meet in you for the first time. For your father will one day be a Lord, and one day you will meet him, and he is a good man, so sleep well, little one, and grow strong, and we will grow strong together.'

She placed her child gently back in her crib, and walked out into the darkness of the cobbled courtyard. From not far away she heard the sound of raised voices, and soon thereafter a siren sounded. She bowed her head, briefly, walked back into the place which for now was their only home, and closed the door behind her.

Michael and Elin retired quite early at the end of this day, a guest room having been made up for her, although in fact they would sleep together in his bedroom.

Earlier in the evening, Michael had gone alone to the room which his mother had told him contained the portrait of Jane Tillington, and there he had found her. Jane had never married, or had children of her own, but she it was who had cared for and nourished he who would become the sixth Lord through the time of the great plague, and now Michael looked into the eyes of the woman who in her anguish and hunger had written the letters to her brother, and in a way and unbeknownst to her she had written them to Michael, otherwise he would never have known. She had sad eyes, in a way, and he wondered how her life had been, and for a moment he imagined her standing in this very room, as she must have done.

And now he drifted into sleep with his beloved, but Elin was not quite done with the day, and she spoke to him, her head resting upon his shoulder.

'I think today went well, do you not think so, Michael?'

'Yes, I rather think it did.'

'We must start to make our wedding plans soon.'

'Yes, we must. You'll have to deal with my mother in that respect. She'll want a big wedding.'

'I will also be pleased to have a big wedding, I only intend to marry once.'

'Well that's encouraging, anyway.'

She laughed, gently.

'I think I very much like Englishmen.'

'I'm glad to hear that, too. Are you happy, Elin?'

'Yes Michael, I am very happy.'

'And….'

'And what, Michael…?'

'Do you love me?'

'Yes, Michael, I love you very much.'

Michael Tillington had begun this day with a sense that this would be a day of significance in his life, and that it would be a good day. He still had not told her that he had a daughter; that a witch called Rebecca had borne his child, but that was for another day, and now, at this days' end and as he closed his eyes, the next Lord Tillington could scarce keep the smile from his face.

Megan read the news article again, perhaps in the hope that she could convince herself that she was entirely wrong. Despite the hour of the night there had been several eye – witnesses, a group of young people had been returning home from a party in the town centre, and had seen the young woman walk *'as if in trance'* directly into the path of a goods – lorry, the driver having had no chance to pull to a complete stop. One of the group was a local news reporter, who followed the ambulance to the hospital and somehow gleaned the information that the young woman, who was yet to be identified, had a clear blood test, and had not been under the influence of alcohol or drugs. She was alive but gravely injured, though there were no details given as to the nature of her injuries. Nobody could explain her behavior; perhaps she had been traumatized, or suicidal, or perhaps, as Megan could not help but speculate, there was another explanation. Sharon had not contacted her again, and now she was not answering her telephone or responding to emails that Megan had sent, asking her to just let her know that she was alright. Of course, she could be wrong. The young woman had been carrying no identification, and there was no further physical description, so perhaps her imagination was running away with her, or perhaps the young woman had even been the witch Rebecca, but the other explanation, which none would understand or believe, was that she, whoever she was, had been bewitched.

So now Megan had faced a dilemma; should she travel south, and if all else failed visit the hospital where the young woman lay unconscious and close to death? This she could do and be back the next day to resume her work as a hotel receptionist, the first employment that she had found, so this was possible, but her dilemma went much deeper than this. Her elder brother had as good as rejected her overtures of friendship and reconciliation. She had seen none of her siblings, all of whom were older than her, for many years, and since her last contact with any of them her sister had married and moved to New Zealand, and her youngest brother now lived in France, and she had no means of contacting them; Maurice, who was the eldest of them, was apparently acting as arbiter, and he would decide how and whether she would be allowed back into the family, so there would be no reunion unless he would have it so, and thus far he would not. Perhaps, then, she was deluding herself. She had given her entire adult life to the coven, and to learning her craft, and so had perhaps and forever lost the way back to an ordinary life, amongst ordinary people. She was the ritual, and the ritual was her, and perhaps after all for her there could be no other way. If the injured woman was indeed Sharon, then she would need her help, and if she were to die then Megan would be the last of them; the last who could avenge the death of Corinne and Fiona, and the burning of Farthing's Well. She was a witch, and she had always been the strongest of them, and if she returned to her former life then it would be forever, and there could be no more turning back.

Upon these things did Megan meditate until the small hours of the morning, and by the time she awoke from her short and troubled sleep she had made up her mind. She packed her bag, and in the cool, dim light of the early morning she made her quiet way through the town, on her way to the railway station. Those who passed her would know nothing of her, or the long and dark history of her sisterhood, which had begun with the cruel death of a young woman who had been called Jane Mary; they would never have known that she was a black witch, and a witch of great power, for such is the way of witches, and thus has it ever been.

End of Part XII

CPSIA information can be obtained
at www.ICGtesting.com
Printed in the USA
BVHW070816110319
542310BV00001B/23/P

9 781490 794068